The Pursuit of Pleasure

The Complete Collection

Natasha Allen

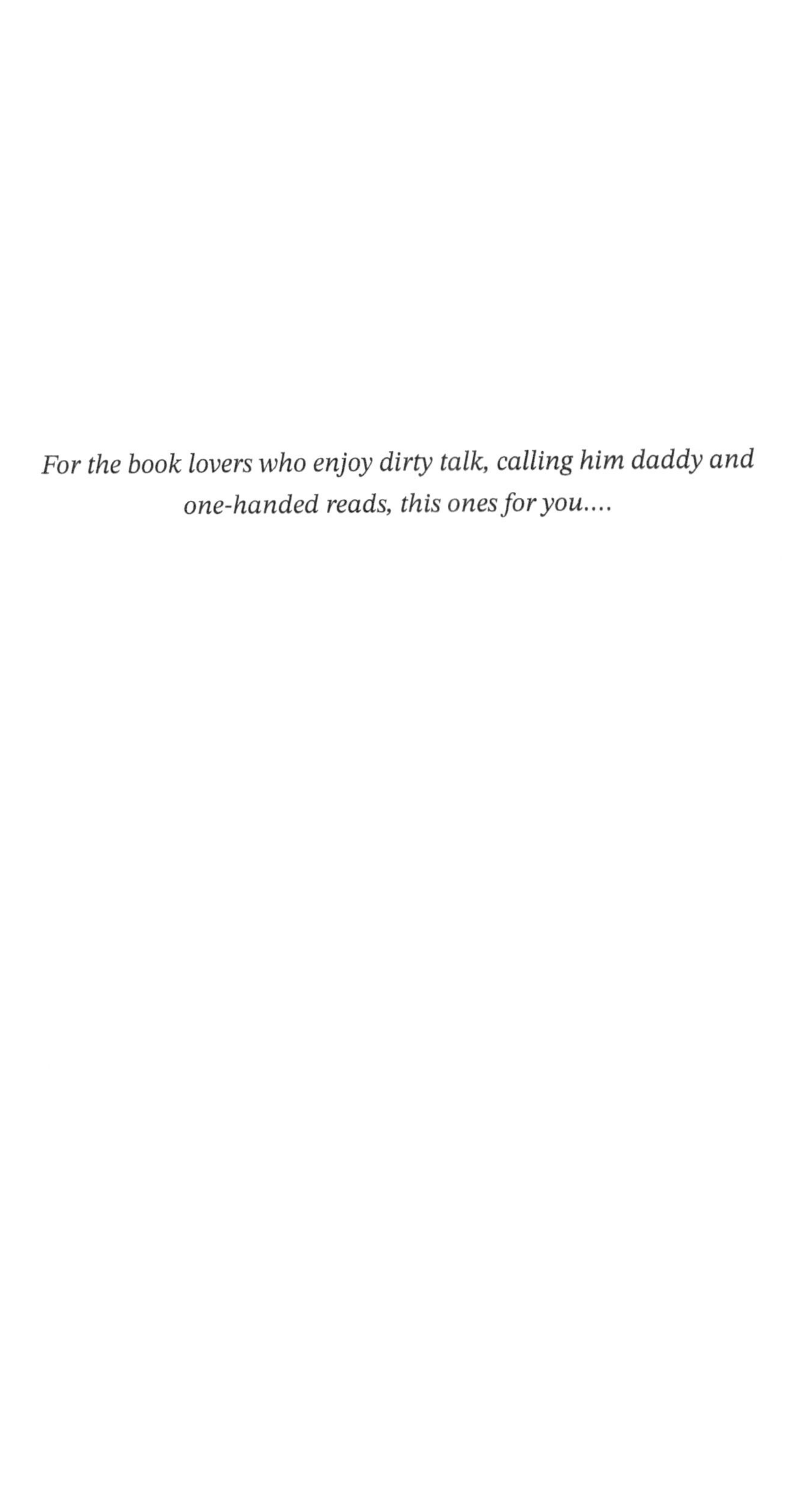

For the book lovers who enjoy dirty talk, calling him daddy and one-handed reads, this ones for you….

Trigger Warnings

This book contains some sexually explicit scenes, BDSM references including spanking, daddy kink, praise and degradation, mentions of unique sex toys, stalking, kidnapping, fire & arson, home invasion, sensitive and *possibly* offensive language, mature topics and is recommended for those aged 18 years and up.

The Perfect Stranger

Chapter One

Willow

My sweaty hands grip the phone a little tighter as I scroll to the bottom of the profile page. This is the second time I've attempted to create and upload my profile to this dating app. I know this is pretty much the only way for me to enter the world of dating, but Lord knows, it's bloody scary.

As a single mum of twin ten-year-old girls, living in a small suburban town, there isn't much time, space, or opportunity for me to get out and meet someone. My girls take up all my time and energy—and patience. The sound of a high-pitched squeal, then screaming coming from downstairs proves my point. I take a deep breath to calm myself before dealing with whatever drama awaits me. Not giving myself chance to chicken out, I take a deep breath, chewing my lip as I press submit, and upload my profile.

Willow, 35. Small business owner, WFH, Curvy, mum of two, enjoy reading, cooking, and creating. Looking to meet someone fun and see where it goes. Favourite colour is turquoise, least favourite are red flags.

There, it's done.

As the screaming downstairs continues, I don't have the time to second-guess myself. Instead, I shove my phone into my back pocket and head down to break up whatever argument the girls have gotten into. I love my daughters, but I'm not gonna lie, life is hard and fucking exhausting sometimes.

"Mum, Ayana stole my necklace and won't give it back."

I look over at Ayana and watch as she balls her fists before stomping her feet. The actions make me want to burst out laughing but I know there's no way it would help the tension brewing in the room.

"I didn't take *your* necklace. I took *mine* back. You took it from me last week," Ayana grumbles.

"No, I didn't."

"Yes, you did."

"No, I didn't!"

I zone out, counting to ten in my head before I interrupt their argument.

"Girls, that's enough. Mya, that's Ayana's necklace. Please, just give it back to her. I don't have time for this, and we need to get going or we'll be late for your ballet class. And I still need to do your hair." I do my best to hide the annoyance in my voice, as despite everything, I know it's not their fault I'm feeling so overwhelmed now.

I make my way into the living room and grab the wicker basket which contains everything I need. For once, Ayana and Mya make things easy for me. I get their hair in perfect buns and by some miracle and we manage to leave the house on time.

After the girls make their way to the studio, I head over to the canteen to get some work done. I'm so focussed on the task at hand that I don't even grimace at the watered-down coffee as I log into my emails on my iPad.

As a single mum with no family close by, it's difficult to find a job that makes the extra childcare costs manageable. All the well-paid ones were a long train commute away, which means more outgoings on train fares. It's a lose-lose situation. I had been working as a freelance proofreader, which allowed me to work from home, but the work wasn't guaranteed. When Covid hit, like so many others, I was desperate to find extra ways of earning money.

I tried all sorts of things from homemade candles to custom print t-shirts, mugs, and glasses which helped pay the bills, but it wasn't fulfilling. Then one day, after reading another spicy romance, I kept thinking about how the main female character complained about struggling to find sexy lingerie that would work on her body type. This was something that I absolutely resonated with, as my body is very different to my days in musical theatre—twins will do that to you.

For the next four days, I couldn't stop drawing and designing. It was like the floodgates opened and ideas poured out of me. What started as a simple idea, blossomed into a burning desire to create custom lingerie.

I dragged my old sewing machine out of the attic, downloaded a bunch of different patterns I found online, and started practising.

It took a while for me to get the hang of it, with more mistakes than successes, but eventually, I started producing pieces I was proud of and selling them.

Given that I was only doing custom orders, it meant that I could give myself the time to make each piece perfect.

And, after a year, I was able to solely focus on my Etsy shop. Things worked out well enough that I could financially support me and the girls. And knowing I am able to do that while doing something I love feels like I'm living my dreams.

Recently, I've even expanded into making custom sex toys like ball gags and harnesses, and after a very interesting craft course, I've added personalised dildos and plugs as well.

I have converted my shed into a workroom as there was no way I could continue making these on my kitchen table and risk one of my girls coming in as I took a blue dildo—complete with suction tentacles—out of its mould.

Focusing back on the task before me, I take another sip of the mediocre coffee as my eyes scroll down the orders I need to ship when notifications start pinging on nonstop on my phone.

It doesn't take me long to work out what's going on as I find numerous awkward, cringey, and downright inappropriate messages from the dating app. Rubbing my temple in hopeless frustration, I start to give up hope that this is the way for me to meet someone.

Chapter Two

Willow

I somehow manage to endure the Christmas madness, and for the first time in what feels like forever, my girls are with their dad, so I'm able to get a break. Well, a break from parenting, but that still leaves the housework and my actual work. But for a whole forty-eight hours, I only have to worry about feeding myself, and I don't plan on leaving my house or putting a bra on.

By the time I head in from the workshop where I've been making a start on some of the orders that came in over Christmas, my body feels stiff and achy, so I run myself the hottest bath, open a bottle of wine, light some candles, and set my Kindle next to the tub.

Steam swirls around the room and I swipe to the next page in the dark bully romance I'm deeply engrossed in when my phone vibrates. Thinking it's something to do with the girls, I set my Kindle to the side and reach over to grab it.

I don't even try to suppress the groan that rolls through me as I see it's another message from the dating app.

I've become really despondent with it over the last month, as I was bombarded with an endless sea of men that looked nowhere near the ages they claimed to be, unsolicited dick pics, and aggressors who got offended when I wasn't interested in them. Definitely not what my thirty-five-year-old single mum self needs.

I click on the message, readying myself for more disappointment, but my eyes do a double-take. It isn't just that the guy—Dominic, thirty-two from London—is attractive, it's that he's not sent anything inappropriate or rude. Even more shockingly, he's asking an actually interesting question. He's clearly taken note of the interests I've listed on my profile and gone from there.

Taboo romance in your top five and not even a second chance or arranged marriage? Now I need to know what your top ten are.

I quickly tap out a reply.

I'll do you a deal. I'll tell you my top ten and you reply with the first thing that comes into your head.

Sounds good. Hit me.

Dark Romance

Risky

Why choose

Greedy

Mafia

Guns

Bully

Discipline

Age gap

Fun

Billionaire

Fun gifts

Interracial

Desirable

BDSM

Intriguing

Workplace

HR nightmare

That made me laugh.

And number one, taboo

Yes

My eyes zone in on that one word. I can't deny the way my body burns as we go back and forth, and it isn't from the hot water of the bath.

I let myself melt into the bubbles and my smile widens as we continue to chat, comparing our favourite tropes and books.

By the time I'm in bed, I realise we've been messaging for almost two hours. I drift off to sleep with images of my favourite romance scenes running through my head. Instead of the usual Henry Cavill type main male character, it's the attractively cheeky grin of the profile picture I stared at all evening that takes the starring role.

Dominic and I messaged for a couple of days before we took things off the app and swapped numbers. His profile said he was a TV Executive for a production company, not that I fully understand what that job entails, and it turns out he lives near where I grew up.

As the days go on, our conversations drift from our favourite books to our own personal fantasies.

Another fantasy of mine is, I'm at a bar
having a drink and feel someone's eyes on
me. I try to work out who it is but can't tell
but I feel ghost-like touches across my skin
and every time I turn to look, there's no one
there. On my way to go get some fresh air, a
hand covers my mouth and I'm pulled into a
secluded spot. Instantly I know it's the guy
that's been watching me all night. He pins
me against the wall, my hands above me as
he reaches under my dress and rips my
underwear off before stuffing it in my mouth
to silence me, and so I can taste my own
arousal. Then he frees his hard cock before
slamming into me and fucking me
senseless. As my moans get louder, he
brings his hand around my throat and lightly
chokes me. It's rough, hard, primal. And
after we both come, he whispers my name
in my ear and that I should watch out as he
will be back again when I least expect it.

Mmm, I do like the sound of that. Do you
know what would make that even better?

No, but I'd like to know.

After you are left there, as the man's cum
slowly drips down your thighs, you receive a
text from an unknown number. It states that
you are to walk over to the bus stop that's
just down the road. As you're waiting there,
he wants you to run your fingers along your
pussy, collecting up the cum, tracing it
along your chest, across your lips, then
suck the remaining drops off your fingers.
As you do it, you know that he is watching
you, seeing you follow his orders and
marking yourself.

Fuck, that is so hot. And very dirty.

I am burning with desire as each interaction becomes more heated and detailed. Not only that, but the man has perfect grammar and punctuation, which only turns me on even more.

These fantasies are so hot. And I've noticed a bit of a theme in them. Can I ask you a question? And you don't have to answer them if you don't want to

Sure, now I'm intrigued. What you want to know?

Well, on more than one occasion in these scenes, you've described the guy as very dominant. So I was wondering, are you into that? Are you a dominant yourself?

I wait patiently as I see the typing bubbles pop up.

Yes. I am a dominant. I enjoy the thought of pinning you down, being at my mercy, on your knees waiting to service me. Offering yourself up for my pleasure. And given the way that you've reacted to my messages so far, I think you're a submissive. Am I right?

A buzz of giddiness runs through me and I take a second to think about how much I want to tell him. Obviously, I want to be truthful, but this feels like a big step.

I am a submissive. It's something I realised quite a while ago, but it took time until I started exploring and really giving in to that side of myself. But yeah, the things you have said are very much the kinds of things I enjoy, and have really turned me on.

Good, that's what I like to hear. I think we are going to have lots of fun. And when you're doing the tasks I set you, I want you to call me Daddy. Do you understand?

Yes, Daddy.

Good girl. Now I've got to head into a meeting. But later, I want you to tell me some of the favourite ways you're going to show me your submission. I want you to think of five things you would do that you think I'm going to enjoy, alright?

Yes, Daddy, I promise to follow your instructions.

As much as I am enjoying this game, these sensual exchanges of our fantasies that we keep having with one another, I know not to get carried away. Firstly, I am older than him and have the kids to consider. Secondly, he lives hours away, so meeting up for a casual drink is impossible. But I'm enjoying myself and like the way his messages perk up my day. Or distract me when I'm in a spiral or having mum guilt. Whenever we were going back and forth, he seems to bring back a piece of myself. Something that has been lost for a while. A sense of self.

His words turn me on. I reread his fantasies in bed and

reach for my preferred toys, picturing his hands running over my body and circling my clit.

After a couple of weeks, my head feels like it's all over the place. I have my normal life full of routine, school runs, work, cooking, and housework. Yet another part of me is getting lost in the what ifs and if onlys. My phone buzzes and I look down to see the familiar name and that ever-growing buzz picks up again.

> Next time Daddy gets his hands on you, he's going to have you kneeling in front of him. I will blindfold you and tell you to hold your tits, pushing your knees apart. You will not be permitted to speak whilst you're blindfolded. Daddy will walk around you so you will hear my movements, not knowing if or when I'm going to touch you, if it will be soft or hard, my hand or something else. As you kneel there, Daddy will tell you to open your mouth, and hold out your tongue. As you kneel, you'll feel Daddy's fingertips brushing against your body, not touching the same spot twice. Never lingering, making you jump as you feel my touch before it's taken away from you. The longer you're left there with your mouth open, the more spit runs down your tongue and drips onto your tits until you're a delicious mess.

You have this way of making me want to submit more than I've ever wanted to before. Other people would say it sounds disgusting, but for me, imagining you giving me those orders and seeing how much it turns you on will only make me crave it more.

What turns you on more? Knowing that I want you a dirty, needy mess or knowing that once I have you on your knees, you'll be desperate to want to stay there for me?

Both

That's just the answer I want to hear.

My hands are twitching to feel the sting as I mark your skin. My cock throbs, wanting to feel the hot, wet heat of your mouth and pussy.

We need to set a time. Close in on a date when you will give your body to me. I want to know if our chemistry will be as hot in person as it is in our messages.

I know we can't just pop to the pub, so I've come up with an idea. Want to know more?

I reply instantly.

Yes!

How about four weeks? Four weeks where we continue opening up. Being completely honest. You can keep asking anything you want to know about me. Get comfortable. And after the four weeks are up, we have a night fulfilling our fantasies. How about it?

We'd been tentatively talking about dates, and it had been a bit of a nightmare as between his holiday, his travel schedule with work and me not exactly having an abundance of free time, there was a part of me that started to wonder if we would ever meet up. Ever get together in person or would this just always continue being a sexting kinda virtual thing between us. My mouth is completely dry as I read and reread his message. My knee-jerk reaction is yes. *Hell yes!* I know that's my hormones talking rather than my head. I need to think this through, and I know the one person who will be able to help me do that. With a big smile, I dial my best friend's number and she answers on the second ring.

"Megan, are you sitting down? I need your advice. And maybe even a drink."

Chapter Three

Willow

 *few days later*

I'm tidying the mess in the kitchen after putting dinner in the slow cooker when my phone goes off.

I'm already laughing when I see Megan's name pop up and I know she's desperate for me to fill her in on the latest.

"Woman, you said you'd call me back after lunch. It's now two and I need to know what you and your dirty Dom were talking about last night." Her voice is breathless with excitement.

My cheeks heat at her choice of words when suddenly I realise something.

"How did you know I was messaging him last night?"

"Well, I kept seeing you were online and as you weren't chatting to me, I put two and two together."

The sigh she lets out is utterly comical.

"I could have been talking to my mum."

"Yeah, not past ten pm. Come on, now spill."

Laughing at how infectious her excitement is, I make myself a coffee and sit down on the sofa. Checking the clock, I see I have enough time to fill her in before needing to leave for the school run.

"Okay, so fill me in on everything that's going on."

"Alright," I say, taking a breath. "So Dominic is currently on a boys' skiing holiday in Austria. I've actually looked up the place he told me they are staying at and it looks beautiful. Although, I also looked up a thing called après-ski and that defiantly isn't my kinda thing. But I definitely think if it's a boys' trip then they will be enjoying that."

"Oh stop it, Willow. It's so much fun. I'm gonna drag you on a trip and we can party together."

"Mmm, yeah. We'll see. So yeah, he's currently on that holiday. Then when he gets back, he needs to head to Wales for work."

"Sounds like he's a busy man."

"Yeah, but I think he seems to have a good balance of work and fun. And like I always say, that's definitely an easier thing to do when you don't have kids. Anyway, so I wasn't really expecting to hear much from him with him being away, but he's asked me to send him a list of hotels that I'd be happy to stay in."

Megan's eyes go wide. "Now that's the kind of thing I like to hear. I like a man that backs his words up. And girl, you better pick the fanciest of hotels."

I laugh at her silly point.

"Well, I didn't look up places and then filter them by price tag. You know that's not how I work. But I did look through several and sent him the ones I liked. I like them all equally, so I told him he can pick from those that I sent."

"Nice. And has he picked one of those yet?"

"Yeah, he did. And then send me a copy of the booking confirmation. He also offered to book two rooms."

"Um, okay, why?"

"You're going to love this. He said he doesn't mind booking two because where we both have to travel a bit of a distance to get there, he didn't want me to feel pressured with anything. So he said if I change my mind or don't feel comfortable, we could just have a drink and then I could stay in my own room and there would be no issue."

The shriek from Megan makes me pull the phone away from my ear.

"Yes, yes, yes. Sounds like you've got yourself a good one there. I like this. I like this a lot. Now, I know you, and I doubt you're going to need that other room. But I am glad he thought ahead and didn't just make presumptions and has created a safe backup plan for you. Did he say anything else?"

I smile to myself, as I know she is going to enjoy this.

"Yes. He described what he would like to happen. Basically, gave me a breakdown of how he hopes our meet-up will go."

"Hurry up. Why are you taking so long to get to the juicy parts?"

Cackling, I put her out of her misery.

"Well, he said we'll have a drink in the bar first. Then, if and when I'm ready, we head to the room."

My fingers continuously tap along with excitement.

"Mmmm, yes, I'm liking this. Okay, so what else?"

I take a sip of my coffee even though it's still too hot. I need a second before delving into the juicy bits I know she's desperate for.

"Well, you know how we've been sharing fantasies?"

"Yes." The way she drags that word out has me biting my cheek nervously.

"So, over the last two weeks, things have got more detailed."

"Go on. You're killing me here." She sounds impatient.

I don't know how to say this, so I just blurt it out.

"He's a Dom."

"Yes, I know his name is Dom. Well, you always call him Dominic."

I laugh so hard that I spill some of my coffee on the sofa. Luckily, you can't see the drops against the dark forest-green fabric.

"No, no, no." I splutter between laughs. "He's a Dom. As in a dominant."

There is a silent pause for a second before loud screaming bursts through my ear, causing me to pull my phone away.

"You have got to be fucking kidding me!" Megan shouts jubilantly.

"Nope. I'm one hundred per cent serious."

I can still remember how my whole body hummed with excitement when that message came through.

"So, does that mean you're a submissive? Or want to be one?" she asks, her voice raising a few octaves with what sounds like excited curiosity.

My finger catches a drop of coffee that is running down the outside of the mug as I attempt to find the right words to articulate how I feel. I guess it also means finding the right words to express who I am. Or really who I've always been but have suppressed, and Dominic is allowing me to open up and embrace that side of myself.

"You know I've always loved reading romances and they've always been a form of escape for me. The more I read, the more I've gravitated towards books about kink and stuff. And as I read about characters being able to give up control, give up making decisions and worries and everything, it was as if a lightbulb went off in my head.

"I love my girls more than anything, and my business is doing better than I ever imagined it could, but there are so many moments I just wish everything wasn't always on me. I wouldn't have to think about what I need to do for dinner. Or how many loads of washing still need to be done. Sometimes it's just too much. Sometimes I wish I could just give all that pressure and responsibility up."

The tightness in my chest eases at my admission, like the biggest weight has been lifted. This is the first time I've openly talked about all this. Being a single mum is so over-whelming at times. So lonely.

"Did you only realise this when he told you he's a Dom, or have you felt like this for a while?" Megan asks, bringing me out of my thoughts.

"I realised about two years ago, but I never acted on it. I've never had the chance to. Not properly, at least."

"And now you have the perfect opportunity to explore and experiment with every dirty and kinky fantasy you've ever thought of." I can hear the smile on her face through the phone.

"I wouldn't say *every* fantasy. Remember, this would only be one night. How much do you think we'll be able to fit in?"

"Ha, if you're lucky there'll be at least seven inches of something he can fit in," Megan cackles.

"Meg, seriously, you're like a teenage boy sometimes."

"I know. But come on, you practically set that up for me. Anyway, I'm sure you won't have any problems getting what you want from him."

My body shudders as I wonder just how far I am willing to go with Dom.

Chapter Four

Willow

The radio is playing in the background as I'm working on an order. I'm so engrossed that I don't even hear my phone go off. It's only later when I check the time and see four messages from Dominic.

> How's your day going? I just finished a boring meeting and had another fantasy pop into my head.

> And it was about you being here at my work.

> I wanted to share it with you.

I swallow down my nerves before I open the final message, knowing he's going to have written his fantasy in delicious detail.

My boss has brought in his niece for a week's work experience. He's asked me to look after her as this is her first time venturing into the entertainment business.

I'm reluctant at first because I'm picturing some immature teen that I will need to babysit when I should be working. But as I wait for her in the greenroom, I'm blown away by the woman that walks in. She's not a teen. I'd take a guess at late twenties.

She has this aura around her, carrying herself as if she's a queen, instead of an intern.

As I introduce myself and give her a rundown on what I'll be showing her and the things I'm expecting her to do, she makes it clear this isn't where she wants to be. She doesn't give a fuck about the job.

She spends all week being disinterested when I try to make her do some work, rolling her eyes, and ignoring all my instructions.

On her last day, it's just me and her in the office because everyone else is at a big pitch. I ask her to do something, but she ignores me, focusing on her phone instead.

Something in me snaps. I walk up to her, snatch the phone, and throw it down on the desk. I stand over her and grab her hair while looking into her eyes, telling her that I'm going to teach her spoiled, bratty ass a lesson.

I pull her from her seat and bend her over, pushing her skirt up around her hips.

She wriggles in my hold, but the way she pushes her ass out, I know she wants what's coming.

I spank her once, listening as she moans softly.

Then I bring my palm down again and again until her body arches and her arousal glistens on her inner thighs.

Desperate to feel how wet she is, I slide my hand down to feel her pussy through her panties.

"You like that, don't you, you cocky little slut?"

"Yes, Dominic," she moans.

I pull her panties to the side, spreading her wide with my fingers before spitting, letting my saliva land right at her centre, and watch as it dribbles down between her lips. She moans my name as I shove my cock deep inside her. I fuck her rough while she tells me that nobody has ever fucked her like this before and that she likes that I'm taking control and teaching her a lesson because she's been a bad girl. She comes on my cock, her walls so tight I almost blow my load, but at the last minute, I pull out and push her to her knees so I can cum on her arrogant face.

When her uncle gets back to the office ten minutes later, she's barely had time to clean up while I've tucked my cock away and am focusing on work like nothing ever happened."

Jesus. My nipples are painfully hard, and my pussy is throbbing.

My eyes flick over to the locked cabinet that has some of the toys I've got ready to dispatch, and I'm utterly tempted to take one out and use it on myself. The way this man can tap into something deep within me is like nothing I have ever experienced before. I'm seriously contemplating doing it when another message comes through.

> Are you being a good girl right now? Or are
> you doing something you shouldn't?

My pulse spikes as my fingers race to reply.

> I'm not doing anything.

> But you want to, don't you? Are you
> thinking about it?

> Yes.

I'm panting now. Completely turned on by his words alone.

> Okay, as you're being honest with me, I
> want you to tell me something.

> Okay.

Are you alone?

Yes.

I watch impatiently as the bubbles appear, showing him typing. Eventually, his message comes through.

I want you to run your hands softly across your collarbone, just using the tips of your fingers. Then I want you to work your way down to your tits, grabbing them to pinch your nipples. Hard. And if you're sitting down, I want you to grind your pussy on the chair. Keep grinding and keep pinching your nipples. Even if you think it's too much, I want you to keep going.

I don't care that I am in the workshop, I do as he asks. My skin heats like it's on fire as my fingers move in the way he instructed. My breasts are heavy in my palm and as I pinch my nipples. Moaning out in pleasure, my back arching for more. A rush of pleasure soaks my panties as I rock back and forth on the stool. With my eyes closed, I let myself get lost in the sensation. I am on a knife's edge between pleasure and pain. And just as I'm getting to the point where I feel I can't take anymore, I get another message. I've left the screen unlocked so I can see his words without having to stop what I'm doing.

> Good girl. Keep going. Don't stop. Pinch
> down hard and don't let go. I want you
> grinding that pussy until you come.

Fuck. It's like a live wire is running through me. My moans get louder and I'm thankful the radio is on to hopefully muffle the sounds pouring out of my mouth. Although right now I couldn't care less if anyone hears me.

Another message appears.

> Now be my good girl and come. And when
> you do, I want you to shout, "Yes, Daddy."

Fuck. Fuck. Fuck.

"Yes, Daddy," I scream as an atomic bomb of pleasure detonates within me, turning the world around from black and white to vibrant technicolour. Chest heaving, my pussy aching to be filled, I slowly open my eyes, and with heavy limbs, I reach for my phone. He's already sent me another message while I was lost to my release.

> Did you do as I said? Were you my good
> girl?

> Yes

> Yes, what?

I momentarily pause. Then it hits me.

> Yes, Daddy.

That's my good girl.

Chapter Five

Willow

I don't know if I'm over-analysing every little detail simply because I've been single for so long, whether it's because Dominic is opening a side of myself that I have never embraced, or if it's because now that our night of fantasies is only days away, I'm beginning to doubt myself and what we have planned. Not that I don't want to go ahead with it. On the contrary. Every exchange I have with him excites me more and more. No, the doubts have to do with my self-confidence. Or rather lack of.

My body doesn't look how it used to. Obviously, having twins had a big impact. My hips are now wider, carrying more weight on them. I have boobs that show the toll of breastfeeding. Stretch marks decorate my arms, belly, and thighs. Those silver lines stand out brightly against my umber skin.

It has taken me years to accept this version of my body and I wouldn't say I'm at a stage yet where I am proudly showing it off. There are days I wish I could pull off certain styles of jeans or have a flat belly and no loose skin. And then there are others where I wish I had the confidence to wear what I want and not give a fuck what anyone thinks. But I have got to a point where I don't hate myself when I look in the mirror, and for me, that is progress. But I still haven't let someone else see me. Still haven't bared myself like that. And Dominic is still a stranger.

Yes, we've been texting for months, but we haven't spoken on the phone. Which was my doing as I've always been self-conscious of how my voice sounds on the phone or recorded and a part of me didn't want to ruin what I had already begun to picture in my head. But it wasn't just that. There's also a part of me that felt it made it more exciting, raising the suspense even more. So, I appreciated it when Dominic agreed that the first time we speak will be in person. The only images we have of one another are the ones from the dating site. That's the thing, I hate most about things online. If you meet someone in a pub or out somewhere, they can tell right away if they're physically drawn to you. Whereas this feels like going in with your eyes half closed. *How close is the real you to the best images you choose to upload of yourself?*

And what if, when you finally meet, the person is disappointed?

I'd told Megan all about my worries, and she spent almost an hour shouting at me to get those silly thoughts out of my head. Then went on to remind me that if at any point I change my mind, or my gut is telling me something is off, I should leave straight away. I couldn't help but laugh when she suggested I send her the pictures of him from the dating site along with his phone number, the booking confirmation, and hotel details. It's not because of the information, as I'd have given it to her anyway for my safety, but it's the fact she requested for me to put it together like one of those police files you see on crime shows. Ready for her to slam down on the table, ready and waiting, should anything go wrong. You know you have a true best friend when she's the first in line, ready to fight a war for you.

And speak of the devil. I pull off my gloves from cleaning and answer my phone.

"Meg, I was just thinking about you."

"Really? And what amazing things were you thinking?" she queries.

"Just how lucky I am to have you as my best friend. And should Dominic be anything other than he says he is, he better watch his back," I jest.

"Too damn right. He might want you to call him Daddy, but I'll be the one making him scream like a baby if he upsets or hurts my girl," she growls.

Only Megan could make me blush and my heart squeeze at the same time. When I told her about what he wanted me to call him, she couldn't stop cackling for a good five minutes. And has been sending me endless daddy memes ever since.

"Anyway, I was calling to see if you've got everything ready for the weekend?"

"Yes, I've got my wax booked in for tomorrow, nails on Thursday and my brother is picking up the girls after school on Friday so I can get the last of the orders I need to post out before the weekend."

I was so grateful when I'd asked him if the girls could go with him and his wife and their eighteen-month-old to the holiday park with them. He jokingly said he was agreeing to it for himself, as he knew how much the girls loved helping with the little one. I'm pretty sure if it was down to my girls, they'd bring my nephew back home with them. They love him so much. In their eyes, he is just a real-life doll for them to dote on and play with.

"Woohoo! I am so excited. Even though I know this is happening to you, I'm buzzing too. My girl is finally getting some."

"Yup. It's all really happening." My voice is filled with excitement.

"So, what are you gonna wear?"

"I decided on a black wrap dress with heels."

"Yeah, you already told me that. I meant what lingerie? I know you made yourself something sexy. Or grabbed something from your back-stock. So, what did you go with?"

Once again, I blush at how accurate she is. I've been debating for ages what to go with. I wanted something sexy, but comfortable at the same time. So in the end, I've gone with a black basque edged with red lace around the cups. The mesh panelling I used for the sides is thicker, so it smooths and supports me at the same time. I'm adding matching suspenders and belt to complete the look. I send her the picture I took of it the other day and wait to hear her opinion.

"Girl, you're going to have him eating out of the palm of your hand in this. Or eating something else."

She begins squealing when I detail the exchange we had

about our limits. I'd been embarrassed at first, but as we went through all the things I am comfortable with, which things I'm curious about trying out, and which things are a definite no for me, I appreciated his care and understanding. His attention to detail didn't go unnoticed as we discussed preferences for aftercare and what we were both wanting from this weekend. Megan snorts like a pig when I tell her the safe word I've picked. Only for her to say she will never be able to look at the fruit aisle the same way ever again. We both burst into fits of laughter. Dominic and I discussed protection and where we'd both recently been tested, we are both happy not to use condoms, especially as I have a coil in.Things really are ready to go. And as we say our goodbyes, I smile as the butterflies of excitement flurry through me.

Chapter Six

Willow

With my bag packed and loaded in the car, I double then triple check the house is all locked up and I have everything that I need. As I usually have two loud, rumbustious girls in the car with me, I notice, appreciate, and enjoy the solitude. The nerves are there, but right now they're just a light simmer.

By the time I arrive at the hotel an hour later, after listening to my playlist to make sure my head is in the right place, my stomach is rolling in knots.

My hands shake as the receptionist checks me in and although she is sweet and kind, I can't help but feel paranoid that she somehow knows what the whole evening ahead of me is going to contain.

"We hope the upgrade that was requested is to your satisfaction. Should you need anything, please feel free to call down," she says with a bright smile.

"Thank you."

I take the key card and follow the directions she gives to the room.

The second I enter, my jaw drops. The room, or better yet, the suite, is huge. On one side, there's a dining area with a welcome basket. While on the other is a door that leads to what I presume is the bathroom. But what takes centre stage is the huge four-poster king-size bed.

I slowly walk over and run my fingers across the ornate wood carvings and spindles on the bedposts as I try to settle my nerves.

Needing something to do, I lift my bag onto the chaise lounge positioned at the foot of the bed and begin unpacking my overnight bag.

Once I finish putting my toiletries in the bathroom, I debate whether to use the insanely large walk-in shower you could easily fit four people in. It has massage jets and so many buttons and dials that make it look like a cockpit. Or try the free-standing claw-foot bathtub that looks like a giant could easily lie in it. I check my watch and seeing I have plenty of time before Dominic arrives and I don't want to get my hair wet, the bath seems like the better option.

I drag myself out of the now-cooling water before my skin begins to prune. Then, I slather every inch of my body in lotion before I put on the silk robe I've brought with me.

After a quick FaceTime with the girls, I decided I'm going

to keep my makeup simple with some waterproof mascara, filling in my brows, and applying a red lip stain to finish the look. I'm keeping my coils loose, despite knowing I will likely have to tie them up later.

My phone is connected to the wireless speaker system when it loudly pings the message tone.

> Arrival is looking good for just after 6.
> Daddy can't wait to get his hands on his
> good girl.

My nipples feel like they're piercing the silk wrapped around me as his words seep through to my bones.

I want to come back with some funny or sexy reply, but right now my mind is completely blank.

This is really happening.

He'll be here in just under an hour.

Shit.

Okay, Willow. Take a deep breath. You're fine. You've got this.

After giving myself a little pep talk, I take a deep, steadying breath and pull myself together.

Given that I've made this lingerie myself, I know how to get in and out of it quickly. So, within fifteen minutes, I'm all strapped in and tie off my wrap dress with a happy but nervous flourish. Realising I still have half an hour left, I start pacing the room, my stockinged feet sinking into the soft fluffy carpet. I grab my phone and call Megan one last time.

"I'm sweating," I say, panting lightly.

"He hasn't arrived yet, has he?" she checks.

"No, but I can't keep still. This feels like it's been building up for forever and now the time is finally here, I'm shitting myself. What if—"

"Stop," she snaps. "I will not listen to you start doubting or talking negatively about yourself. If you've changed your mind and don't want to go ahead with it, that's fine. I'll stay on the phone with you whilst you pack back up and get in the car. I'll stay on the phone with you all the way home if I have to. But if you're questioning if you're good enough for him or thinking bad things about your body, I will hang up right now."

There's no arguing with her, and deep down, I know she's making sense.

"Yes. I know you're right." I take another deep breath. "He's gonna be here in about half an hour and the nerves are just kicking in."

"That's fine. I get it. Damn, even I'd be bouncing around with excited nerves if I was about to have a wild night with Daddy Dom."

Laughter bubbles through me and I feel myself relax.

"So, let's go through the checklist. Lingerie?"

"On."

"Dress?"

"On."

"Hair?"

"Fluffed."

"Makeup?"

"Done."

"Lotion?"

"Applied."

"Perfume?"

"Sprayed."

"Toys?"

"Uh?"

My eyes glance over at the bag sitting on the vanity. In the end, I decided to grab two of my vibrators, the wireless love egg, a butt plug, cuffs, and a blindfold. I sent her a picture of them as I packed at home, and she joked that I should add that picture to my dating profile.

"They're still in the bag," I mumble shyly.

"Well, get them out. Quit being shy. You are a strong, sexy woman who's going after what she wants. Take them out and just watch his face when he sees them."

I do as she says and as my hands go over the different textures, my muscles relax and tingles of anticipation run through me.

"Done."

"Now I want you to grab your purse, the room key, get your heels on, and make your way to the bar. Have a drink and get ready to enjoy yourself. Alright?"

"Yes," I say with more confidence.

We say our goodbyes and I promise to keep her updated on how everything is going.

There's soft jazz music playing in the background of the bar and I can feel the warmth of the fireplace a couple of feet away from the table I am sitting at. I'm just about to take another sip of Prosecco when I feel the energy around me shift.

Looking up, my gaze falls on the hot guy towering over me, whose pictures I've become so familiar with.

"Good evening, Willow. It's a pleasure to finally meet you."

Chapter Seven

Willow

My mouth is momentarily dry, and I don't quite know how I manage to stop my jaw from gaping open. As my eyes blink slowly, I realise I still haven't said a single word.

"It's great to finally meet you too, Dominic." My voice is slightly breathless, and I watch as his nostrils flare before he bends down and gives me a soft kiss on the cheek.

I'm hit with the masculine and earthy scent of his cologne. It isn't overpowering, but it has a strength to it that makes my mouth water.

Dominic settles in the seat beside me. His long legs encased in black fitted jeans and his muscular arms strain against his pale blue shirt, which has the top buttons undone, exposing a black t-shirt underneath.

A waiter makes his way over, so we order a bottle of Prosecco and make small talk until he returns with the bottle and fresh glasses.

Dominic waits for him to leave before he turns in his seat, fills his glass, and raises it.

"Here's to hopefully a wonderful night, fulfilling both of our fantasies."

The deep timbre of his voice sends a wave of lust straight to my pussy. As I shift slightly in my seat and our eyes remain locked, the sexual tension is palpable.

I lean forward, suddenly filled with confidence, and tap my glass with his as I say in a hushed tone, "Cheers to a wonderful night, Daddy."

His eyes widen and I could swear I hear a slight growl.

I'm surprised at how at ease I feel as we talk. We continued chatting about all the things we have in common, as well as the fact that he lived down the road from the secondary school I went to. His brother even dated a girl who'd been a few years below me. It's almost surreal that we had likely crossed paths and never known.

I was also fascinated as he talked about his job as a TV producer and I love that I made him laugh when I questioned why he'd chosen to be behind the camera, instead of in front of it, given his good looks.

Just listening to him speak, I can hear that he's well spoken, highly educated, upper-class. Yet he doesn't appear to be uptight or stuffy. No, on the contrary. He has this easy-going air to him. He's funny. Attentive. And a good listener. How is this guy single? I really hope there isn't going to be some scary or absurd surprise I find out about him.

Dominic's telling me about his avid interest in Judo,

which he took up about two years ago, and I can't help but chuckle.

"What's so funny?" he asks, smiling.

"Well, you know how I said my dad is into sports?"

"Yes."

"He's a former Judo champion and has multiple schools and gyms he's opened all across London."

"You're kidding me!"

"Nope."

"He doesn't happen to run Apex Fighting in Wandsworth, does he?" he questions curiously.

My eyes bulge and I have to bite my lip to stop myself from laughing hysterically as I nod.

"But he hardly teaches anymore, given his age. He only does drop-in sessions occasionally."

This time I do laugh as he suddenly looks relieved that it will be unlikely for him to ever have a class with my dad. I can understand any guy's apprehension of coming face to face with the father of the woman he's sleeping with or dating, whilst essentially grappling or wrestling with them.

I didn't realise my dress had ridden up to see the tops of my stockings until I follow his line of sight. His large hand drifts slowly up to the hem, running his fingers gently along the exposed lace. That slight touch makes me gasp. Then, to my surprise, he tugs the hem of my dress down, covering me up again, his hand lingering on my thigh. The move feels possessive and dominating and I absolutely love it.

Dominic's eyes are glued to my mouth, and it feels like we

are in our own little bubble. That is, until someone bumps into our table.

Suddenly, I become aware of how busy the bar area is. I remember overhearing earlier that there is a wedding here and I guess the guests are converging in the bar.

I rest my hand on his firm bicep and lean forward to whisper in his ear.

"I think it's time we head to the room, Daddy."

He turns his head, eyes drilling into mine as he asks, "Are you sure you want this?"

I don't even hesitate. "Yes."

Excitement surges inside me as I think he is going to kiss me. Instead, he grabs a leather duffle bag that I hadn't noticed him carrying when he arrived, stands, and motions for me to lead the way. He keeps his hand pressed to my lower back as we make our way through the crowd 'til we arrive at the door to the suite.

His large body cocoons me like a shield as I swipe the key card and we make our way inside.

The second the door closes behind us, Dominic drops his bag and spins me around, his hand fisting my hair, causing me to strain my neck as I look up.

"I need to kiss you right now." The way he is looking at my mouth is as if he is starving, and I am his first meal.

"Are you going to be my good girl and let me kiss you?"

He tugs my hair with more force and I moan my agreement. Panting. Waiting. He's watching me with a raised brow. And I realise he wants me to say the words.

"Yes, Daddy."

And he pulls me closer, capturing my mouth. His kiss is everything I have wanted. It isn't tentative or exploratory. It is possessive. Hungry. He is devouring me as his tongue twists and caresses mine. Then he bites down on my lip, the shot of pain making me moan louder. His hard cock presses against my belly as he pushes me against the door and pins my hands above my head. I whimper as he breaks our kiss and begins to trail kisses along my jaw and down my neck.

"Mmh, you are so sexy. Your mouth was made for me. I can't wait to lick, bite, and taste every inch of your body. But first, be a good girl and get on your knees."

Chapter Eight

Willow

Dominic releases my wrists, and, without hesitation, I sink down as instructed. My heart is beating so hard I'm sure he can hear it, my breath stuttering loudly in the quiet room.

"You look so beautiful on your knees. Ready and waiting for me. You're going to take everything I give you, baby, aren't you?"

"Yes."

He reaches out and grabs my chin. "Yes, what?"

"Yes, Daddy."

"That's my good girl. Now unfasten my belt."

My fingers shake slightly, though it isn't with fear, rather excitement. I make deft work opening it, but as I go to pull it through the loops of his trousers, his hand grabs mine.

"I said open it. I didn't say take it off."

I swallow down the whimper I am so desperate to let out at the sound of his commanding tone.

"May I touch you, Daddy?" I ask, seeing that he wants to control every moment of our time together, and I'm happy to submit.

"Yes. Open my jeans and take my cock out. Then I want you to beg for it. Tell me how much you want it. And if you convince me you're desperate for a taste, then I'll let you take it slowly into your mouth. All the way to the back of your throat. And I don't want you to stop until I say so. Do you understand?"

"Yes. I understand."

My body vibrates with anticipation. I open the button, the weight of his hard cock pushing the zipper down. Following his instructions, I reach in and take his cock out of his black briefs. It has been so long since I've been with a man that I gasp as my fingers struggle to close around his girth. His cock isn't monstrously long, but I know his girth is going to stretch me in the most delicious way.

"Please. Please let me taste your cock. My mouth is watering to taste you," I plead.

Looking up, I see him nod, granting me permission to finally have my fill.

My tongue follows the vein that runs from the base to the tip, lapping up the precum leaking from him. I close my mouth around the head and slowly take him deeper, and he lets out a primal growl that makes my pussy clench.

I continue working him in and out of my mouth, sucking him deep and slow. I want him to be as desperate and eager as I am. I may be on my knees for this man, submitting to him, but I am in control. I have the power. I am choosing this. I am giving it absolutely everything I have.

With each thrust, he goes deeper. So deep it becomes a struggle to swallow, so my spit begins to dribble out the sides of my lips. My jaw strains to stay wide enough to take him. Suppressing the need to gag, my eyes begin to water, each pulse turning me on more and more.

Grabbing my hair, he holds me in place, fucking my mouth and filling my throat. Breathing through my nose, I try to resist my body's natural reaction to panic. His mumbled words of praise making me want more.

Dominic's moans grow louder, echoing across the large suite. The sound of his enjoyment causing a rush of arousal to soak my panties, but instead of continuing to use me, his stern voice cuts through the room. "Enough."

He slips his saliva-covered cock from between my now swollen lips and staggers back slightly. "Mmh, you're just perfect, aren't you?" The words are so soft and quiet, I wonder if he meant to say them out loud. My skin hums under his praise.

With strong hands, he pulls me up to his chest before he crashes his mouth to mine.

I thought his kiss before was hungry, but it was nothing compared to this. He continues ravaging my mouth while walking me towards the bed.

The back of my legs hit the bed frame, both of our hands roaming and exploring each other's bodies. My palms glide across his firm muscular chest, whilst his grip kneads my hips before making their way over my belly, to my breasts.

My nipples peak to painfully hard points as he continues to squeeze and rub them. He swallows down my whimper as his hands leave my breasts and he bites down on my lip while one hand pulls my hair back, and the other grips around my throat.

"Your body was made for me. Your skin tastes like the sweetest dessert. These big, lush tits will be covered in my bites and marks, letting anyone else that sees them know they belong to me. I knew you were beautiful when I first saw your picture, but those photos are nothing compared to the sexy goddess in front of me."

He continues to hold my throat firmly, possessively, like a collar. And with every word he utters, I relax further into his hold, my mind floating in bliss under his praise.

"Now, undress for me. Take that dress off."

I'd chosen the wrap dress as I knew it would be easy and quick to remove. I bite down on the inside of my cheek as his eyes darken further when I let the dress fall to the floor. Feeling turned on and sexy, I straighten my spine as I stand before him in heels, stockings, the black and red lace basque, and matching thong.

"You naughty, naughty girl." His fingers trace along the edge of the lace cups and he leans down to bite along my collarbone. "Now be a good girl and get on the bed."

I climb onto the large bed, the sheets feeling cool against my flushed skin. Dominic's cock is still out and I'm desperate for more. Yet as I lean forward, he pushes me back and runs his hands up my legs until he reaches my panties, which he pulls down.

Running his fingers over the drenched material, a wry smile curls his lips. "You're my dirty little slut, aren't you? Your pussy getting so wet just from sucking my cock. Show me. Show me how wet your lips are. Open yourself up for me."

I reach down and spread myself open for him. My body allows my mind to be free. Not thinking about how I look, being completely vulnerable and exposed. Normally I'd be a bag of nerves and filled with insecurities and apprehension. Especially as Dominic is essentially a stranger. But instead, I feel freed by his compliments and praises about my body.

As he stands between my legs, he starts undressing, exposing more of his lean, lithe body, making my pussy clench.

"Play with yourself. Show me you deserve my cock deep inside you. Let me see if you're ready."

I'm utterly lost to the moment as my fingers brush against my clit. Moaning as my fingers get wet from my juices, sliding over and over.

My eyes spring open when his large hands spread my legs open wider and he moves to kneel on the bed between them. Ever so slowly, he bends down and licks languidly through my folds until he reaches my clit. Making firm circles with his tongue, he closes his mouth around my swollen bud and sucks.

A scream rips out of me, causing my back to bow, yet his big, strong hands pin me firmly in place. I buck and grind against his mouth as my whole body begins to tingle. I'm racing towards oblivion and just as I feel like I'm about to come, he stops. I want to scream and cry in frustration. His hand possessively cups my pussy as he looks up at me from between my legs and smirks.

"I didn't give you permission to come yet. I told you, this pussy and all your orgasms belong to me."

Chapter Nine

Willow

With an agonising slowness, he eases two of his thick fingers inside me.

Jesus

If this is how I'm reacting to just two fingers, how the hell am I gonna be by the time he sinks his thick cock inside me?

He thrusts his fingers in and out. Then his calloused tips find the soft spot inside me that has me moaning God knows what. His other hand presses down on my belly and it's like my body has been connected to a live wire. The loud, wet sounds should be embarrassing, but I'm not coherent enough to let it affect me. Just as I'm about to come, he stops. *Again.*

When he pulls his fingers out, I'm on the verge of bursting into tears, my body so desperate for release. My legs are shaking with frustration and I'm barely aware of him lifting them, bending me in half.

Holding me in place with one hand, his other grips his cock and slaps it down on my clit once, twice. Making me shudder as feelings of overwhelming desire ricochet through me. Just as I think he's going to do it a third time, I feel a pressure and in one long, hard thrust, he slams into me. My body arches as pleasure burns through me. My orgasm so close I can almost taste it. I have never felt so full.

Thank God I'm already dripping, as my pussy is struggling to adjust to his thickness.

"Fuck, your pussy is tight." He throws his head back as the muscles and veins in his neck swell, telling me he's as close to the edge as I am.

"Please, Daddy, fuck me. Please."

I don't care that I'm begging like a desperate bitch in heat. I'm strung so tight I feel like I'm about to snap.

As he pulls back, I can feel every inch of him drag along my insides, making me tingle even more with feverish pleasure. He finally gives into my begging, fucking me relentlessly. Each time he slams into me, he grinds against my clit to rub with his pubic bone, the feeling so exquisite, so electrifying I feel like I'm soaring.

Our bodies shine with a thin layer of sweat as he continues his brutal, unyielding pace. He rains kisses down my jaw, along my neck, and across my breasts. Using his teeth, he pulls down the lace of my corset, freeing my breasts before laving his tongue over one nipple then the other, laving and biting them, sending me into a frenzy of molten waves of pleasure.

When I feel the sharp sting of his teeth on my nipple, I scream out in pleasure.

It's been so long since I've had sex, even longer since I've had good sex. I can't ever remember it feeling this good. It's like he's been given the blueprint to my body and knows each and every spot to hit.

"Please, Daddy. Please let me come. *Please.*"

He bites down harder on my nipple before releasing it. Then with a leg over each shoulder, he grabs my throat, pinning me in place while he rubs firm and fast circles over my clit.

"That's it. Take what I'm giving you, baby. I can feel you clamping down on my cock. Your pussy is so wet I can feel you dripping. You're my good little slut, aren't you? Taking everything Daddy is giving you."

As I go to scream, he tightens his grip on my throat, limiting my ability to suck in any air.

"Now be my good little slut and come for me."

I can feel him swell even more as my pussy begins to spasm around his cock. Euphoric pleasure radiates through my entire body as I'm finally allowed to come. He removes his hand from my throat to grip my chin.

The second the command tumbles from his lips, the floodgates open as my body finally tumbles into a heart-stopping abyss. Wave after wave of rippling pleasure crash through me. Every atom of my body exploding, like the moment of the big bang.

"Look at me," Dom orders.

When I open my eyes, he continues to fuck me through my orgasm. My release feels never ending until I don't know where he ends and I begin.

Leaning forward, he pulls my chin. "Open."

I open my mouth and stick my tongue out. He spits, and I swallow it down, feeling grateful and thankful, just as he comes in a deep guttural growl, the hot heat of his cum painting the walls of my pussy.

As his thrusts slow, my body feels weightless with pleasure prickling through me. I wince slightly when he finally pulls out of me and gently eases my legs back onto the bed. I can feel our combined release spilling out of my pussy and onto the bed.

As we're both panting, trying to catch our breath, he surprises me as he lies back on top of me, his arms caging me in. This time when he kisses me, it's soft and tender and makes me melt further into the bed. We continue kissing, the previous wildness that consumed us both now being washed over with surprising gentleness. Dominic pulls back slightly. The way his eyes roam over my face and he smiles down at me makes me feel precious.

It's such a contrast to how he was just fucking me. But I love it either way.

"Why don't I call for some room service while you freshen up?" he murmurs against my lips. "I'll order another bottle of Prosecco and some food because you're going to need your strength. That was just the starter, Willow." He chuckles, his cock already hardening between us.

Chapter Ten

Willow

Relaxing at the dining table, we are about halfway through our second bottle of Prosecco. I laughed when I saw the food he'd ordered. Pizza, fruit, bread, chocolate, cheese, crackers, and cold cuts of Spanish and Italian smoked hams. I wasn't super hungry, as I was still pumped with excitement and adrenaline, but as I've been grazing on the fruit and crackers, I've watched in amusement as Dominic makes light work of the rest of the food.

I can't believe how at ease I feel just being in his company. It has been such a long time since a man has made me laugh and relax so easily. Another great thing is that he only decided to put his briefs back on, with me only wearing the robe I grabbed from the bathroom. And I haven't even bothered trying to hide the way I continuously keep checking him out.

He's muscular, but not bulky. His arms and legs are defined, but not like the jacked-up bodybuilders you see at most gyms. No, you could see he was naturally athletic and given the passion he shows whenever he talks about Judo or the Rowing Team he's still on, taking care of his body is something he seems to incorporate unpretentiously as opposed to for his vanity.

"You see, one thing I've always believed in is to be honest with who you are as a person. And it's usually the people closest to you that either benefit or are most affected by that. That can be things like giving a brutally honest opinion or standing your ground or even taking yourself out of difficult situations. Be that with family, friends, or an ex"

"Would you say you have any exes that would define that as one of your character flaws or pros?" I ask.

He turns his Prosecco glass in his hand.

"Well, say for example, my last ex... we were together for a really long time. All our friends were basically saying that we were the next ones they felt were going to be getting married and having kids. But after a while, things just weren't the same. She changed. I changed. And as time went on, I realised we both wanted different things. There's nothing wrong with that. Once things had changed, neither one of us could somehow manage to get back to the place we once were. Then we essentially were like roommates and friends that weren't sleeping together but still wanted the best for one another."

I nod along listening, intrigued by hearing things from a man's perspective.

"Anyway, after a while, I just felt like it was unfair for both of us. So, we had a chat, decided to end things, and wished each other well for the future much to my friends' shock.

They'd pegged us as being the first ones to settle down, but instead, several of my mates are either already engaged or planning on it, having kids or talking about trying, and I'm now the one that's out in the world, enjoying myself and seeing where life takes me," he says with a relaxed laugh and smile. "Enough talk about my past, I want to know about your family."

I reach for my glass and have another sip of Prosecco.

"So, Willow, you've told me how both your parents are from Trinidad. I've heard it's a beautiful island although I've never been before. Do you get to go over there a lot?"

"Not as much as I'd like to. When I was younger, we'd go every four or so years, and in between those trips, we had family come over here to visit. But as I got older, I've gone less and less."

I didn't want to delve into the massive way my life has changed. Holidays aren't relaxing anymore when dealing with two kids alone. Also, despite putting on my dating profile that I have children, it's something Dominic and I haven't talked about. And given how steamy most of our messages and interactions have pretty much from the beginning, chatting about my kids hasn't exactly been something I want to push, so I never brought it up. I guess in my head I just thought he wasn't ready to talk about it yet. Plus, given the fact that he's three years younger, and we live hours away from each other, it's not like either of us are looking for more than a fun time this weekend.

Focusing back on the present, I'm eager to know more about his work.

"What made you want to get into television?" I ask.

Laughing, he leans back in his seat, resting his hands behind his head. The position causes his biceps to bulge. Squeezing my thighs together, I attempt to alleviate the pulsing in my clit but the way he smirks makes me think he's completely aware of the effect he has on me.

"Well, I didn't want to get into television originally. It was never something I even thought about. Growing up, my family always wanted me to get into politics or law, but that never interested me. Then I went on to study business and ethics at university, but by the time I started looking for jobs, I knew that wasn't the environment I wanted to be in. One day, as a bit of a joke, I applied for a job as a TV producer's assistant, got it, loved the environment, and have been working my way up ever since. I can't imagine doing anything else now. There's always something new going on and I love the pressure and hard work, but most of all, I love creating something. Watching as it goes from an idea, to production, to program."

His passion is evident, and I admire that he's pursued something *he* wanted. As opposed to giving in to familial pressure.

"And what made you get into custom lingerie and sex toys?" His voice has a husky purr to it and I don't miss the way his gaze goes from the table that has the toys on it, then up my body before it lingers on my mouth and finally settles on my eyes.

The way he's looking at me feels like a predator watching his prey. My blood begins to hum in my veins. I'm struggling to stay focused on the question he asked as my body ignites with hunger for him. I take a tentative sip of my drink before answering.

"I only started during COVID. I saw a gap in the market and did something to fill it. Then, when I hit one year, I did a poll in my newsletter and asked customers if there was anything they wished I also sold, and the most common answer was toys. Especially things inspired by shifter romances. Initially, I didn't think I could do it, but once I found a company to make a collection of moulds, and I worked out how to make them, I realised it's much easier than you'd expect."

"Mmh. And which one is your best seller?"

"Either the wolf, which is knotted, or the Kraken that has the ridges and suction tentacles."

"And which is your favourite?"

My body heats as his intense gaze continues to pierce right through me.

"The love egg and plug."

His fists clench and he lets out a deep growl before slowly rising from his seat.

"Do you know how sexy you are? I can see how hard your nipples have got. I've watched the way you've been shifting in your seat, trying to ease the ache in your sweet, tight pussy. Sitting there telling me your favourite toys are an egg and a butt plug. Both of which you could be wearing anywhere, and no one would know. My baby's a dirty, dirty girl, isn't she? Before, you made me think you were a good girl, but now I know just how dirty you like to be. So, I think it's time for you to show me."

He pulls me up, kissing me with aching fervour.

I wrap my arms around him as he deepens the kiss. This time it's me that bites down on his lip, sucking it, but I know he's not impressed by me taking over when he spanks me hard on my ass.

Chapter Eleven

Willow

Dominic grabs the cuffs from the table before guiding me to the post at the foot of the bed. Then, with quick hands, he secures my arms behind me, locking my wrists to the post. He then brings a footstool from the sofa area and places it between my spread legs, stopping me from closing them.

My heart begins to race in both excitement and anticipation as I watch him make his way back to the table of toys. His broad shoulders stop me from being able to see what he's grabbed, but as he turns to make his way back to me, smirking with a raised brow, he offers me a look that sends a shiver down my spine.

Closing my eyes, I take a steadying breath. Just as I am about to open them, his mouth ghosts over mine before kissing me and sliding a blindfold over my eyes, locking me in darkness.

Bound, spread, and blindfolded, I am at his mercy. All that

I can do is listen and wait. I attempt to gauge where he is and what he's doing, but I can't make anything out. Nervous anticipation begins to creep over me.

We previously agreed on a safe word: *pineapple.* Yet there isn't an ounce of me that feels scared or worried. Just knowing I can pause or stop what we're doing with a single word makes me feel more powerful than I could have imagined. But there's no need for it. I want whatever he's planning.

I gasp in shock as something cool trickles down my chest before soaking into my robe. His tongue follows the trail of what I now realise is the rest of the Prosecco between the valley between my breasts, before sucking my nipples through the silk. My body squirms as he repeats it again and again until I'm begging for him to do more.

"Mmm, yes. Daddy please. Please. I want more. Please give me more," I pant.

When his fingers trail through the folds of my already wet pussy, I let out a strangled cry and I'm rewarded by him rubbing my clit in agonisingly slow circles. Something cold and hard rubs along my pussy sending shivers through me and sweat beads at my temple. He drags it through my folds and it begins to warm from my own body heat, before he begins pushing it in and out.

Suddenly, the sensation of what I now realise is the jewelled metal butt plug, vanishes. My hips buck forward, chasing his touch. I don't even notice the buzzing sound of a toy when suddenly, his finger gathers and spreads my juices, until I can feel him at my ass. Slowly and gently, he eases one finger in my tight hole, pumping in and out.

Time begins to warp and I'm not sure how long he's been prepping me before he pushes something into my ass. His other hand trails up my thigh and he pushes two fingers into my pussy, stroking my inner walls before making a come here motion with them at the exact same time he suctions his mouth on my clit.

I scream out at the top of my lungs at the sudden, all-consuming, overwhelming sensations. There's too much happening all at once. My mind can't work out which feeling to focus on as ingles of pleasure ricochet from the top of my head to the tips of my toes.

My head falls back, hitting the bedpost as I try to get control of my senses. There's still a slight burn as the tight ring of muscle continues pulsating around the plug in my ass. The way Dominic continues to rub my g-spot has me feeling delirious. The onslaught of pleasure is so intense it's bordering on painful. And his mouth is relentless as he continues to lick, nip, and suck my clit. I feel like a rocket, ready to take off. And when my orgasm finally hits, it's so hard and intense my knees give way. Dominic's hands tightly grip my hips, keeping me steady. Once my body finally comes back down to earth everything around me slowly starts to come back into focus.

He's removed the blindfold, but I keep my eyes closed. Once the cuffs are gone, he starts rubbing my arms and begins nibbling on the lobe of my ear.

"You took that so well, Willow. You're my good girl, aren't you?"

I'm still trying to catch my breath, so the best I can do is nod in agreement. There's something so warming whenever he praises me. Being a parent, you're the one always giving praise, not receiving it. It isn't until this very moment I realise just how much it both means and affects me.

He continues kissing my jaw until he gets to my lips. As his tongue rolls and caresses against mine, I can taste myself on him. The rest of my body continues to relax in boneless pleasure, but my ass continues to pulsate against the plug that he still hasn't removed.

Deepening the kiss, my hands drag over his shoulders, and I scratch my nails down his back. His cock is pressing hard against my belly and despite having just come minutes ago, I want him again. Usually, I'm too sensitive after coming. Not being able to stand or even wanting to be touched again. Yet with him, I want more. Need more.

"Get on the bed," Dominic growls. "I need to fuck you hard. I want you on all fours, and I want to watch your juicy ass bounce on my cock." But he grabs my face before letting me move. "The plug stays in."

Chapter Twelve

Willow

The force of Dominic's initial thrust pushes the plug deeper inside of me. I'm on the knife's edge between pleasure and pain. Though my body is still languid and pliable, each ripple of power cascades through me as Dominic ruts into me. The sensation is animalistic. It's like a switch has been flipped and he's gone from giving to taking. From upholding to pillaging. The bed shakes with the force of every drive.

"You're taking me so well. My perfect little slut." His hands grip my hips so tightly I know he's going to leave bruises and the thought makes me smile. I want to remember every moment of this night. Reaching round, his fingers find my clit, causing my muscles to squeeze around both his cock and the plug. I'm so full and stretched I don't know if I am going to burst or if I can take anymore.

"Fuck, baby. You're squeezing me so tight."

He pushes down between my shoulder blades, causing me to arch my back, as my face presses into the mattress.

"Oh, God. You're so deep," I cry. His thick cock feels like it's piercing right through me. "Oh my god, Daddy, that feels so good." Every slam of his hips hits against the plug, reminding me it's nestled there.

Slowing down his pace, he bites down hard on my shoulder.

I try muffling my moans into the mattress, but Dominic grabs a fist full of my hair, pulling my neck back at an obscure angle.

"Don't hide from me. I want to hear every cry, every moan that leaves your lips. Do you understand?"

"Yes," I pant in reply.

He follows with a rain of slaps across my back, all the way down to my ass. I cant help but find it weird being slapped down my back, I've never had that before and I'm not sure if I like it, but don't want to think about it and just focus back on the sensation running through me. I'm building towards release once again, and I'm not sure if my body can handle it. My muscles squeeze down on him, and he must realise I am getting close as he pulls out and lays down, his head against the pillow before he pulls me on top of him.

My knees shake with a struggling effort to stay up, but Dominic doesn't seem to care or notice. He lines up his cock at my slick entrance before pulling me down onto him, the angle of his cock hitting so deep my eyes roll back in my head.

My thighs begin to scream in protest, the muscles so unfamiliar with being in these positions. Despite my internal pleas of not being able to take any more and my body fighting to keep up with his stamina, I don't want to call out my safe word, but I know I need to adjust before my whole body gives in.

Leaning forward, bracing my arms on either side of his head, I change tactics and instead of bouncing up and down on his cock, I begin rolling my hips, grinding down, back and forth.

We both moan in combined pleasure with this new position.

"Fuck, yes. Fuck, that feels so good, Willow. Yes, just like that."

Energy blossoms within me and determination to make him feel as good as he makes me, gives me further purpose.

My hard nipples are sensitive, rubbing against his firm chest as he pulls me closer. He continues kissing me hungrily. His muscles tense, and I can sense him building towards his release.

I pull back and climb off. His eyes sharpen on me with a brief look of annoyance as he tries to work out what I'm doing. But once he realises where I'm heading, his nostrils flare and a deep hum vibrates out of his chest.

Settling between his legs, I take his cock into my mouth. It's covered in my arousal and I can taste myself mixed with Dominic's precum. My cheeks hollow as I suck him harder and deeper. This time it's him moaning out incoherently.

I don't let up as I roll and tug gently on his balls. The other reaches down, massaging his taint while I keep my eyes locked on him as he falls apart, his head thrashing from side to side.

He swells in my mouth before he lets out a roar of pleasure, followed by the first spurt of cum. He continues flooding my mouth and I have to swallow a few times to take it all. Dominic holds down my head so he can cum down my throat, jerking a little each time as I swallow. Once his cock begins to soften and slip from my mouth, I look up. Then I panic.

Dominic's not moving—not even his chest.

I scramble to my feet and begin shaking him. Finally, he takes a gasping breath, and I watch as his chest heaves, moving in and out in what looks like a normal rhythm.

"Jesus... fucking... Christ," he says, each word on individual breaths. "You sucked the soul right out of me."

I turn my head to hide my smile, but I still have adrenaline spiking through me from the earlier panic that he passed out, or worse. If it would happen to someone, I know it would bloody be my luck. The first guy I sleep with in years ends up passing out or needing A&E.

"Do you want some water?" I ask, finally starting to relax when I notice all the colour return to his face.

"Yes, please, baby. But I don't think I can move just yet."

Biting my lip, I climb off the bed and make my way over to the dining table, which still has a bottle of water and glasses left out. I pour one for him and one for me and make my way back to the bed. He still hasn't moved and now I can't help but giggle that he's still in the same position. He literally hasn't moved a single muscle.

Standing beside him, I offer him the glass.

"I can't move. I'm going to need you to give it to me," he says with a smile.

I don't want to pour it into his mouth, as I'm sure it will end up spilling over and onto the bed. So, I drink a large mouthful but don't swallow. Climbing up to straddle him, I nudge his arm that's covering his face to move it. Leaning down, I brush my lips across his and slowly feed him the water.

His eyes are still closed, and a huge dose of triumph runs through me that I've managed to get this man to this state.

Chapter Thirteen

Willow

It takes about twenty minutes until he finally has the energy to use his legs and swing them off the bed. It's so funny I have to hold my tummy as I continue to laugh.

"Hey, it's not funny. I'm pretty sure I passed out for a second there. That's never happened to me before."

He turns and cages me in his arms and rains kisses along my cheeks. We're both laughing now.

I feel so light and at ease, but suppress the sigh that wants to escape.

We both need to shower and even though it's more than big enough for both of us to fit in, I've never shared a shower with anyone before and I don't want this to be the first time. It's not because I don't trust Dominic. I've already given up my body to him in so many ways this evening. I think it's more because for me, showering with someone is such an emotionally intimate thing for two people to do. To me, it's intertwined with feelings of nurturing, cleansing, something almost spiritual. So, as Dominic showers, I brush my teeth, then go back out to the suite to clean up the toys and stack the empty plates together. Tidying away the mess is too ingrained in me. I don't know how people can go to sleep with stuff just scattered around. The thought makes me shiver.

I finish straightening everything up by the time he re-emerges with a towel wrapped around his waist.

"Shower's all your beautiful." He gives me a playful slap on the ass as he walks past.

"Thank you... Daddy," I say with a giggle.

I grab the silk slip I plan on sleeping in before heading into the shower.

The bathroom is steamed up where he's left the water running. Making sure my hair is up and out of the way, I quickly step under the hot water. Washing suds from the shower gel away, I take my time tracing the tender spots on my neck I know will come up in bruises. The thought has me smiling and wondering how I'm going to be able to get away with wearing scarves and turtlenecks for at least the next week.

My limbs feel heavy and tired as I shut off the water and dry off. Rooting around my toiletry bag I realise my cream isn't here.

Damn, where is my moisturiser? I must have lift with in my bag on the dresser.

I put my slip on and head back out to the bedroom.

When I enter the room, Dominic has turned the main

lights off, leaving just the bedside lamps on. The music is still playing softly in the background and he's still in his towel with his back leaning against the headboard. His eyes are closed, so I'm not sure if he's fallen asleep. I pad over to my bag quietly and grab my coconut oil.

I've just finished lathering my arms and legs when the sound of his voice startles me.

"I could watch you doing that for hours."

My head snaps to the side.

"Jesus you scared me. I thought you were asleep," I whisper breathlessly.

I can still see the lust in his eyes, but this time they also hold something else. Something more. I have to stop myself from getting carried away with how much I enjoy the way he's looking at me. I can't fall down this rabbit hole.

"Why don't you lie on your front, and I'll rub some on your back and shoulders?" I offer.

"You'll give me a massage? You really are too perfect for me."

Biting my lip, I shake my head and climb onto the bed. As he rolls over, removing his towel, I can't help but marvel at his tight, sculpted ass.

As I work through the knots in his back and shoulders, he asks me about my childhood and hobbies. We both laugh at how I love cooking, yet he can just about manage to do a tray of chicken with vegetables in the oven.

"Why do you look so shocked Willow?"

"I just, I don't understand how you don't get bored. Surely after a while everything is just bland. No spice? No seasoning or dishes from around the world?" I ask incredulously.

"Well, I don't get bored. I'm just not a great cook. But when I am feeling adventurous I do sometimes visit the Greek food stalls next to my office on my lunch breaks."

He keeps his hand on my leg and I'm not sure if he realises his thumb is mirroring the circular movements my hands are doing. I work my way down his back, his ass, his thick thighs, and calves. By the time I'm done, we are both covered in oil and could use another shower, yet neither of us makes an effort to move.

We're both lying on our backs in comfortable silence when his hand reaches over and grabs my hip, pulling me to him so we're face to face.

"This evening has been better than I ever could have imagined. I'm not gonna lie, there was a part of me that was worried I was going to turn up and you'd end up being some guy called Steve who's been catfishing me the whole time."

I laugh into his chest at that image.

"I couldn't agree with you more. I've really enjoyed myself tonight," I say looking deep into his eyes which look back at me with such honesty. Showing a gentleness that melts me, he cups my face and pulls me into the softest kiss. There isn't anything dominating or submissive between us. It's soft and sensual. This feels more raw and intimate than anything else we've done tonight. By the time he slides inside me again, we are still wrapped in each other's arms. Continuing to rock into me softly, he breaks the kiss and his eyes pierce right through mine.

"You're so beautiful." His voice is just above a whisper.

Emotion begins to bubble through me. I wasn't expecting him to have this side. I wasn't prepared for how cherished he's making me feel. This is just supposed to be an evening of fun, dirty fantasies, yet this man is showing me kindness and care I haven't experienced in years.

"I also wanna say, I'm surprised how easy it's been talking with you. You're a good listener. You've made me feel so at ease. I don't remember the last time I felt so comfortable opening up. That's dangerous. You seem to have some secret powers."

"Oh, stop it," I say breathlessly as he continues working his cock slowly in and out of me.

"I'm being serious. That's why it also pisses me off with the harassing and racist stuff you said you've received from other men on the dating apps."

I turn my head in embarrassment. I don't know why I brought that up earlier. I think I feel similar to how Dominic does. I find it easy opening up to him. But maybe I should start filtering what things I say, as I don't want to come across as vulnerable or some sort of damsel in distress.

"Hey, look at me." Dominic's voice is stern as he takes my chin between his fingers and turns my head so I'm looking into his eyes. "I mean it. I don't say things for the sake of it."

I capture his mouth, hoping he feels the gratitude in my kiss. We stay locked with one another, his cock buried deep inside my pussy as both come with silent cries. I have to close my eyes; the moment is too overwhelming. He kisses my shoulder before he rolls onto his back. Mustering up the last of my energy, I detangle myself from the bed sheets before getting up and making my way to the bathroom to quickly clean up.

Once I'm back in bed, he turns the lights out, pulls me into his arms with my back against his chest, and I melt into him as he kisses my neck.

"Good night, Willow," he whispers.

"Good night, Dominic," I murmur back.

Within a couple of minutes, his heavy breath against my shoulder tells me he's fast asleep, yet I feel wide awake with a million thoughts twisting around inside my head.

Chapter Fourteen

Willow

As hard as I try to relax and fall asleep, I just can't. My body is deliciously sore, but that isn't what is bothering me. No, it's something else.

I've always been one to over analyse and dissect each minute detail. A part of me still can't quite believe this night has happened. That I've gone ahead, put myself out there, and tried something new. Something different. Most people my age have already been there and done all this in their twenties, whereas I was settling down and starting a family.

Despite my relationship with my ex having ended in complete and utter shambles, and him never stepping up to the plate as a dad, I still wouldn't change anything as I have my girls and they're my whole world. But the older they get, the less they want to do with Mummy; the more they grow and become independent, the more I can't deny that I'm feeling lonely.

Tonight only solidifies I don't want to carry on like this. I want to get a part of myself back that has been gone for so long. I want to share things with someone again. Whether it's a meal, grown-up discussions, my body, or even just one another's company.

I'm not looking or expecting that from Dominic. Besides the age difference which I know many people wouldn't think three years is much, but it is when comparing at which stages we are in our lives. There is also the obvious issue that we live hours away from each other. On top of that, I know it's stupid and fruitless to even be thinking along these lines with the first guy I've hooked up with after finally jumping back into the dating game. Yet I can't deny the emotion that were triggered during the last time we had sex. *That's* what's keeping me awake right now.

Throughout the whole evening, I've blushed and preened and constantly melted every time he told me I'm beautiful or sexy.

I don't want to admit that I really am beginning to like him a lot more than I know I should. I wasn't expecting him to be so funny. So easygoing. So easy to talk to. I expected him to have an almost cold distance to him. It also didn't go unnoticed that as the night went on, he was acting less like a Dom and more like Dominic. As these thoughts race through my head, my body finally gives in to exhaustion, and I drift off into a restless sleep.

At some point during the night, I wake to the feeling of hands rubbing over my body. Momentarily disoriented, I don't know what is going on, but as I break through the fog of sleep, I remember where I am and who I'm with. My eyes open, adjusting to the darkness of the room. The only light is coming from a small crack around the bathroom door.

"I need you, Willow. Right now," he growls against my pebbled nipple before sucking it hard.

Both my mind and body are now wide awake as he moves down my body and licks me from ass to clit. He doesn't continue for long before he covers my body in his, lines himself up, and slides deep inside me in one long stroke.

Despite how many times we've already had sex, it still takes me a moment to adjust to his thick girth.

His thrusts are short and hard. Each pump deeper than the last, causing my breasts to bounce. As he closes his hand around my throat, his moans grow louder. Grinding his hips down on my clit as he sends me over the edge. Covering my mouth with one hand to muffle the sound, his other leaves my throat and pinches my nipple hard. My back arches and my hips lift and roll almost like I'm chasing to stay connected. My fingers feel stiff as they cling to the sheets. He releases the hand that was covering my mouth and it joins his other one and pinches my other nipple. Not only is he pinching them, he's pulling them, giving me that bite of pain I now seem to crave.

He brings his arms under my back and grips my shoulders, essentially caging me in. His teeth clamp down on my throat as he continues driving deep into me. The angle is so deep the tip of his cock hits my cervix. As his pelvis rubs against my clit with everything thrust, I cum again in a silent cry. His cock swells before his hot cum paints my inner walls.

No words are spoken after we manage to catch our breaths. The room is still dark and smelling of sex. After several minutes, our breathing is back to normal and once again, he pulls me into his arms, nuzzling my neck, inhaling deeply. And finally, together, we both fall back to sleep.

Chapter Fifteen

Willow

A painful crick in my neck wakes me. And as my hands move, I notice just how sore my body is. Flipping the pillow, I sigh as my cheek rests on the cool fabric. After several minutes of my body fighting to fall back asleep, my bladder has other ideas. The room is still dark, but rays of light shine through the gap of the thick, heavy curtains. Reaching over to the bedside table, I check the time on my phone and bite back a moan when I see it's only just gone seven in the morning.

Turning slowly, I break into a smile at the sight before me. Dominic is turned facing me, his arms crossed, a slight frown to his brow, lightly snoring. *Who sleeps with their arms crossed like that?* He looks like he's impatiently waiting for someone to answer him.

My bladder is now screaming for me to get up and pee, and it takes every ounce of strength to get out of bed and tiptoe over to the bathroom with how sore and tired my body is from all the delicious sex last night.

Turning the tap on in the sink to drown out the sound as I pee, I wince as I sit on the toilet. My ass feels tender and sore and I'm not looking forward to the drive back home. I wish I'd listened to Megan's suggestion and brought a cushion with me.

After cleaning up, washing my face, and brushing my teeth, I quietly head back out. Dominic is still fast asleep as I gingerly climb back into bed. I take a mental note of every part of my body that aches. I'm going to need weeks to recover from this. I don't know how people do this every weekend. Hell, I'm sure some even do this multiple times a week.

I lay there, staring at the dust flecks that glitter in the air. Daydreaming and reminiscing about everything that's happened in the last fifteen hours. More than that—everything that's happened since I first matched with Dominic. After about an hour, I find myself feeling slightly bored and restless.

At home I'm pretty much out of bed the second I wake up, with a million and one things to do. I'm not used to just lying here. Given that I hardly ever watch television, I decide to see if there's anything interesting on.

Making sure to keep the volume down, I flick through the channels, finally deciding on a cooking show.

I'm so engrossed in following what the chef is doing that I don't notice the snoring beside me has stopped. It's only when

I get the feeling of being watched, do I turn and see Dominic's eyes on me, a soft smile on his lips.

"Good morning." His voice has a deep, husky purr that sounds so sexy. Not sure how things are meant to be this morning, I try to keep things light and playful.

"Good morning. How long have you been laying there watching me like a peeping Tom?" I quip, keeping a smile on my face. His deep laugh literally makes the bed vibrate.

"Since he started prepping the fish," he said with a shudder.

Shaking my head, I laugh through my embarrassment as that happened about fifteen minutes ago.

As we fall into silence, I'm not sure how to approach this uncharted territory. What's the usual protocol when you wake up next to someone you met in person for the first time about twelve hours prior? He continues watching me like a hawk and I have to bite down on my lip under his intense stare.

He groans into the pillow. "Don't do that."

"Do what?" I ask.

"Bite your lip." I feel my cheeks warm. Then he stretches and climbs out of bed. I don't miss the tight grip he has on his hard cock, and he catches me staring at his naked body as he turns before opening the bathroom door.

"I'm gonna quickly shower, then we'll order some room service for breakfast. I'm not planning on letting you out of the bed until it's time for us to pack up and leave."

The cheeky wink he shoots me before closing the door has me giggling like a silly schoolgirl, and I feel myself relax again. I didn't realise how worried I was that things would be weird or off between us this morning. But given how relaxed he is and the way he's been looking at me, there's nothing for me to worry about.

My tummy begins to rumble so I grab the menu from the coffee table and start the hard task of deciding what I want for breakfast.

Chapter Sixteen

Willow

Dominic comes out of the bathroom in only a pair of fresh boxer briefs. Looking up, I find him once again staring at me with a fond expression before he shakes his head, smiling. The action makes him look younger than his age. It's almost goofy. The look makes me smile shyly.

"Do you know what you'd like for breakfast?" he asks. "I'm starving,"

"I'm stuck between the waffles with fruit or the pancakes with bacon. Both sound delicious, but I can't pick one. So why don't you pick for me?"

He's still looking over at the menu as I speak, then he sends a knowing smirk and a nod my way before heading to the phone.

"Yes, good morning. I'd like to order some breakfast. Yes. Can we get a pot of tea and coffee, the waffles with fruit, the eggs benedict, a bowl of granola with Greek yoghurt and honey, some toast with butter, two sausages. Oh, and the portion of pancakes with extra bacon on the side. Yes. That'll be great. Thanks."

He hangs up and smiles as my jaw drops wide open.

"Why did you order so much? And I told you to pick one of the two." Even though he's paying, I hate the idea of wasting food. It's something that's been ingrained in me since I was a kid.

"I told you I'm starving. And anything you don't want, I'll have."

"Where exactly are you planning on putting it?" I ask as my eyes roam his body.

"I'm going to need my strength to keep going for the next few hours. I haven't forgotten about the fact you made me blackout last night. It's only fair that I return the favour."

With determined strides, he prowls towards me and climbs onto the bed, nestling himself between my legs.

This morning his kisses are playful, at ease. I feel like he's showing yet another side to himself. It's like I've had a night with three different men rolled into one. First, there's his Dom side, then he surprised me with tenderness, and now he's like a playful puppy. He grinds his erection against my pussy, continuously teasing but never taking it further. I don't know how long we've been making out, but the sound of loud knocking interrupts us. "Room Service."

I climb under the covers as Dominic attempts to hide his erection in the band of his boxers with no success whatsoever. The tip of his cock is peeking out as clear as day and he's still going to answer the damn door. I see him look through the peephole before opening the door, angling himself partially behind it. A trolley is rolled in but the man doesn't step into the suite.

I manage to finish the pancakes and bacon and grab a few pieces of fruit, but then throw in the towel. I suggested we eat at the table, but he was having none of it and set up a mini buffet across the king-size bed.

I pour myself another cup of coffee and sit back, watching him devour the rest of the food. Even just watching him eat is making me sleepy. There's no way he isn't going to want to have a nap after all of that.

"If you could buy somewhere abroad, where would you pick and why?" I ask. We changed the channel, now watching one of those holiday property shows.

"Growing up, we went over to France a lot, and there are some beautiful places, especially in the south. But then we also did Italy a few times when I was a teen and there's nothing more beautiful than the Mediterranean coast, so possibly Genoa or Sardinia. What about you?"

"I love Italy too, but I think I'd pick one of the quieter Greek Islands. If I'd bought somewhere abroad, the main purpose would be for relaxation and getting away. I'd want peace and quiet, to be able to go to a beach or head to a market if I want. On the other hand, I'd love somewhere that had winter sun. I'd love to be able to go away, get out of the cold, dark, rainy British December, and just jet off to a tropical paradise. New Year's on a hot beach with a cocktail sounds much more appealing than a freezing cold pub," I say with a smile. I always wanted to see in the New Year on a warm beach. Just another dream of mine I've shelved.

"Sounds perfect. I'd want somewhere that has a large pool in the back, so when I eventually have kids, they can wear themselves out playing in it all day."

"As long as they don't have the danger nap in the late afternoon," I reply, laughing into my coffee.

"Do you think you'll want kids?"

I almost choke.

"I already have two," I respond, smiling lightly in confusion.

His head snaps in my direction and I'm taken aback at the almost angry expression that sweeps across his face. It's only there momentarily before he seems to compose himself again, but I can still feel a shift in the atmosphere in the room; as if the temperature has dropped several degrees.

"I'm confused. I thought you knew. It says it on my profile."

"No, I didn't notice that. Or maybe it slipped my mind."

He gives me a quick smile, but it's tight and doesn't reach his eyes. A shiver runs up my spine at how his eyes hold a look of betrayal in them. And it makes no sense. I haven't lied about anything. From the beginning of us talking to one another, it was clear that things had a strong sexual under-tone. Almost straight off the bat, we discussed our sexual fantasies, our conversations only ever sexy and playful. Neither of us ever delved deeper. This whole night had been planned and arranged for both of us to simply give in to our sexual desires. There was never even the mention of it going beyond this. Yes, we did talk a lot between sex, and yes, I did enjoy the way he made me feel at ease and how we laughed and talked. But not once did I ever let myself believe that it would ever be anything more. I'm being realistic. I was safeguarding myself by not wanting or letting myself fall any deeper. It makes no sense and is illogical for me to even plant any kind of seed of hope for anything more. I'm beginning to feel uncomfortable, and I don't want what has been, up until now, a perfect experience to be tainted.

"Is that a problem, Dominic?" Even I can hear the hesitancy in my voice.

He moves the plate that is in front of him to the side and reaches out, brushing his thumb over my cheek.

"No, no, of course not. It just took me a little by surprise."

I stare straight into his eyes and feel a sense of relief wash over me as he looks completely sincere.

"You are so much more than I had hoped you would be. As you've said, this is about us fulfilling our fantasies. And you are my very fantasy."

He pulls me into a deep and desperate kiss. His hands hold my head tightly as his lips and tongue devour my mouth. This is now something I recognise and feel comfortable with. He once again takes control of everything. Not simply like he's wanting it. But it's as if he needs it.

There is no finesse. No softness. It isn't tender. It's heady. Desperate. All-consuming. He has a wildness to his touch. One I know I am both beginning to crave and will go on to miss. Dominic has a way of making me feel insatiable by unlocking parts of me I have kept hidden away for years.

With every touch, every kiss, every moan, and groan, he has my confidence soaring higher and higher. It wasn't that I required a man to tell me I am worthy, beautiful, or wanted. No, he is making me feel that within myself. As that thought settles within me, I give him everything back. I kiss him, showing my gratitude, my appreciation, my thanks, and so much more.

Chapter Seventeen

Willow

Dominic grabs the whole duvet and rips it off the bed, with the empty plates and cutlery still entangled within, and pins me down with my arms above my head. The feral look in his eyes stokes desire inside me. He's like a wild animal that's finally been let out of its cage, and I am the prey he's going to play with before devouring me whole. His touch is continuous, as though if his hands aren't on me, I'll evaporate in a cloud of smoke.

My skin burns with need for him. I'm just as desperate as he is. Deep down, I know this is going to be our last time together, and I don't want to waste a single second. I want to give everything I have to him. I will take anything and everything he gives me and treasure it. I twist and writhe, bucking my hips up to his, needing more. Yet he pins me harder. His grip painfully hard but the sensation only pushes me into a submissive headspace.

"You are mine. Mine to play with. Mine to enjoy. Mine to

devour." His voice is so commanding it makes my nipples peak painfully hard. "Do not move your hands from above your head. If you move them at all, I will punish you. Do you understand, Willow?"

"Yes. I promise I won't move them," I pant breathlessly.

His hands trail down my legs before pushing them wide apart. His nails scoring my thighs have me hissing out and it takes every inch of willpower not to move my arms. I'm shaking with how desperately I want to reach down and hold on to his head or shoulders. Even though I'm not being restrained, I feel like a prisoner. He kisses and bites down all along my inner thighs. Sucking my skin into his mouth. Working his way down until finally, he reaches my pussy. I scream out as he latches onto my clit, relentlessly sucking and nipping.

"Please, please, let me touch you. Please, I need to move my arms. I can't hold on like this. Please, please, I'm begging you." I don't care how desperately I plead.

"I said no," he growls.

And instead of easing up, he goes harder, pumping two fingers in and out, curling up inside, rubbing against my g-spot.

Tears run down my cheeks as my clit tingles with sensation. Every inch of my skin feels like a live wire. I can't even decipher which feeling, which sensation is most palpable. The pleasure is so intense it's verging on painful. I don't realise I have moved my arms until his hands grip my wrists tightly and he pulls me up so I'm sitting.

"What did I say would happen if you moved your arms? I

gave you an order and you disobeyed me," Dominic says sternly.

My head spins and my body prickles with a pins and needles sensation. He flips me onto my stomach, smacking me hard on the ass over and over and over again. My already tender skin screaming out from the onslaught.

By the time he finally lines himself up and slams deep inside me, I am a complete mess. My throat is raw from moaning and screaming. Tears cascade down my face. He pulls my hips up so I am on my knees and grabs my hair, causing me to arch my back.

"Scream all you want. I'm not going to stop. You will take everything I give you because you're my good girl, aren't you?"

"Yes," I shout.

He picks up the pace even more, fucking me so hard the bed is shaking. Each thrust causing it to bang against the wall. My walls tense around his cock as I get closer and he must feel it too, because he slows down, making me cry out, desperate to come.

His grip on my hair is so tight I worry he might rip some out as he pulls me back to his chest, still sliding in and out of me. He tugs my head to the side, biting down on the soft tissue before sucking hard, and I know he's leaving a dark mark. In a place where someone could possibly see. With people guessing and working out that I got it by being owned. Marked. Owned. Realising how much I would love that, how it taps into my deeper kinks, that thought pushes me over the edge and I reach my peak as my orgasm spasms through me. My body shaking and shivering as the onslaught takes over.

Once I manage to get my breath back, he pushes my head down into the mattress. Holding my hips up higher, he brings his foot up flat on the bed, giving him better leverage.

He thrusts so hard it makes my teeth rattle, holding onto my shoulders, leaving me completely immobile, at his mercy. My body is solely for him to use.

He's breathing hard, like an angry bull, chasing his release. He's fucking me hard with ruthless determination. Like he's wanting to end this on the ultimate crescendo.

When he finally comes, the moan he lets out sounds almost demonic. His grip slowly starts to loosen as he pumps the last of himself deep within me. Then he collapses onto me, pushing me deeper into the mattress. His chest is soaked with sweat, and it combines with my heated and flushed skin in the most delicious way.

I wince as he pushes himself off me. I can tell my body is going to be feeling the effects for a while. My back is going to be sore for days, and my shoulders already feel like they are beginning to bruise. I slowly roll to the side and watch as he downs a glass of water before filling it up again and then handing it to me.

My mind is still scattered as I try to regain my senses. I wince again as I lean over and place the empty glass on the bedside table.

Looking up, I find Dominic watching me, then he gives me a slight nod. I got to ask him what that even means. "Wha—"

Dominic cuts me off. "I'm going to quickly jump in the shower, then I'll clear the plates and stuff up."

He doesn't give me a chance to respond before he turns and makes his way to the bathroom. Leaving me feeling really confused and overwhelmed.

Chapter Eighteen

Willow

The hot water is like a soothing balm as it cascades over me. If I could, I'd stay here forever. It doesn't take a genius to work out something is up with Dominic. When he came out of the bathroom, the smile he gave me didn't reach his eyes. I still feel too raw and vulnerable right now to even let my mind start delving into what that meant. It takes me a while to get cleaned up, as my arms feel like lead pillars. By the time I finally emerge from the bathroom, I'm beginning to feel a little more human. Dominic is sitting on the chaise at the foot of the bed, his phone in hand, still just in his boxers.

He clears his throat, then finally looks up at me. "Something has come up with work, so I've got to shoot off now and hope there isn't too much traffic. I called reception and settled the bill. The late check out has already been paid for, so you don't need to rush. You can take your time, relax a bit before you head home." His voice curt but he softens it was a sad, almost apologetic smile.

I swallow down the ball of hurt inside me. The way he's looking at me is as if I am a stranger. *What have I done wrong? Have I been too much? Not enough? Not good enough? Was I something of interest in the blanket of an evening, but the following light of day, found lacking? Have I made him feel uncomfortable?* Embarrassment and shame wash over me, causing my arms break out in goosebumps, feeling vulnerable still only in my towel. I paste on a smile before grabbing my robe and quickly putting it on.

He falls back into silence, and I busy myself by checking the messages on my phone as he gets dressed and packs his things. Now and then I catch him looking at me from the corner of my eye, but as soon as he sees me looking, he turns away. I'm finding it harder and harder to ignore the emotions rising to the surface, and I don't want him to see that the change in his demeanour is seriously affecting me.

I climb back into bed and focus on the TV in front of me. I just need to get through this. Part of me is hoping he'll realise he's behaving like an ass and just be an adult, but as the minutes pass and he still doesn't say anything, it isn't anger I'm feeling. Instead, I feel waves of shame and hurt crashing through me. The turmoil almost dizzying me with confusion. He's actively ignoring me.

The post-orgasmic glow I had is now dull. The tingles that buzzed excitedly are now turning into sore spots. I already feel physically exhausted after having such broken sleep, but now it feels like a weighted emotional blanket has been thrown over me and it's suffocating.

I hate that I am feeling like this. I wasn't expecting declarations of affection or even interest beyond this weekend, but I hadn't prepared for the feeling of being disposed of; used goods that need to be sent to the rubbish heap.

My heart rate begins to spike as I can feel the triggering emotions and demons of rejection from my past, bubbling to the surface.

I hate that the positive feelings are slowly being stripped away and replaced by negative ones. Or is this just how it goes? Is this the usual MO in these kinds of situations? Once again, I am aware of how out of my depth I am in this game.

Breaking my train of thought, I watch as Dominic puts his bag by the door before he walks over to me. "You're so beautiful. Perfect. Just what I want."

Between each word, he kisses me and it's as if he's tapped into my head, soothing the worries that have taken over.

He holds my face in his hands and his eyes bore into mine. He doesn't say anything just holds my gaze. Then leans down and kisses me with such tenderness, it's beautiful. I squeeze my eyes tightly shut, the feeling too overwhelming. When he finally breaks the kiss, he leans his forehead against mine, then kisses each eyelid, the tip of my nose, and finally my mouth again.

I hear him swallow before clearing his throat. "I'm so sorry I've got to go. But like I said, relax. And I'll text you." His tone somber.

I nod in response as he walks to the door and picks up his

bag again. My fingers twisting the duvet and I force a smile onto my face as I know this is the end of a great adventure. The feeling is bittersweet.

Wanting to show him I am okay and thankful, I look up, smiling genuinely this time. He drops his bag and strides towards me, kissing me hard. It takes my breath away and eases the tension that has built. He breaks the kiss before coming back two more times, which has me giggling once more.

"Get home safely," I say as he finally opens the door. He turns and gives me his real smile which I have grown to enjoy.

"I'll text you."

Then he's gone, and at the sound of the door closing, I fall back into the bed.

Chapter Nineteen

Willow

To say I am feeling overwhelmed would be a complete and utter understatement. Pain and aches are taking over every muscle. My joints have me groaning like an old lady. I need to use support to pull myself up or sit down. And emotionally, I can't work out which way is up.

I feel proud that I've put myself out there. Not only that, but I did it with someone who had shown similar kinks and fantasies as my own and hadn't shamed me for the things I desired. I'd effectively had my first one-night-stand, and I did that with a man who was younger than me.

I overcame the fears and insecurities about my body and allowed myself to give in to what I wanted, be present, and enjoy the moment. I let him see me. All of me. For the first time since having kids, since being with my ex-husband, I let a man look at me sexually and see the real, raw, unfiltered version of myself.

Last night was everything I'd hoped for and I enjoyed myself more than I thought I would. Even though I'd noticed that Dominic behaved less and less like a Dom as the night went on, and seemed to be more Dominic less *Daddy*. But I didn't mind it. I still enjoyed it. I'm still basking in the moments of praise, appreciation, and care he'd shown me. He learned quickly which things my body responded to the strongest and by the time we finished round four, it was as if he'd known me intimately for months, not hours. Maybe that's why I wasn't even allowing myself to open the Pandora's box of this morning.

Deep down, though, I couldn't kid myself that there hadn't been a clear shift after I told him I have children. A wall had gone up that hadn't been there before. I just didn't understand why. We hadn't implied or even hinted that anything would continue or happen again beyond this weekend. So, what difference would me having children make?

I presumed he'd noticed the box that stated I had children on the dating website, especially given how many of the other hobbies and interests I'd put on there that he'd remembered.

Maybe I am just looking for a negative that isn't there. Or possibly feeling bittersweet that I had the perfect evening and now was bummed it was over.

Giving myself a mental slap, I focus on the positives as I finish the last of my packing. I still have about half an hour before I need to return the key to reception, so I grab my phone and gently sit down on the sofa to call Megan. I know she'll be eager to hear how the night had gone.

"Well, well, well, look who it is. If it isn't Daddy's little girl," she purred.

I spent the next twenty minutes giving her a detailed, yet condensed, summary of all that happened.

"Girl, I know you're holding back on the nitty-gritty details. But I'm coming over for dinner on Tuesday, so I'll bring a bottle of wine and once the girls go to bed, I want every dark and dirty detail. Don't hold anything back."

I don't even bother to make a point about the fact that she's invited herself round for dinner. She knows she's always welcome anyway. I look at that time and realise I need to get going.

"Shit, Meg, I've got to drop the key back in ten minutes. And I'm moving at a snail's pace."

"Okay, okay. Wait, hold on. Before you go, you didn't tell me how things ended. Are you gonna see him again?"

I don't want to delve into everything right now because I need to get going and I still don't feel I understand quite how it ended.

"I already told you. This was a one-time thing. We kissed, said goodbye, and he said he'd text me. Let's see if he does. Right, I'm not so convinced that he will. No biggie."

I swallow down my sigh, shaking my head and plaster a smile on my face. Even though she can't see me, I still don't want Megan to catch onto my mood yet. "Anyway, I've got to go. Love you and I'll message you when I'm back home and the girls are back."

"Alright, drive safe. Love you," Megan says before cutting the call.

Making sure I haven't missed anything, I do one final sweep of the suite before I tentatively make my way down to the reception, dreading how uncomfortable the drive back home is going to be.

Chapter Twenty

Willow

A drive that should have only taken me just over an hour ends up taking twice as long. Obviously, at a time when I want to be laying horizontally in my bed, in comfy sweats, with a water bottle, and ordering some food, I've instead been sat in gridlock traffic on the motorway. Then I had a tractor in front of me going so slow I thought I'd fall asleep behind it.

I only managed to get back shortly before my brother dropped the girls off, and even though I love them and appreciate their enthusiasm for telling me every detail of their trip in a minute-by-minute account, I am utterly exhausted. My body is finally starting to shut down.

I've managed to convince Ayana and Mya that we should do a Disney movie day and order pizza. So, we spend the next few hours watching all the classics as I doze on and off on the sofa.

For once, the girls are as tired as I am and don't put up a

fuss as we get ready for bed and I put out their school uniforms for tomorrow.

Assuming I would pass out the minute my head hit the pillow, I instead find myself replaying all that has gone down.

My body is like a patchwork of evidence. Each sore, tender spot sets off a memory I languish in.

Despite the aches and pains, tingles of excitement shot through me as I grin with happiness at how much I enjoyed myself. I wish there was a way I could bottle up the moments of euphoric bliss and spray myself with it whenever I have a hard day or life just gets too much.

Megan sent me a bunch of memes and GIFs of women walking funny or people covered in bruises and bandages and I've now got to the point where it hurts to laugh, my ribs feeling unbelievably tender. Luckily, I've stocked up on painkillers and I know I'm going to be popping them like Tic Tacs over the next few days.

My phone pings with a message, and it takes me a minute to be able to roll over and grab it off the bedside table.

> I just wanted to say I'm really proud of you. You went after something, put yourself out there, and probably have the bruises to show for it. Has Daddy messaged asking if you got back, okay? Let me know what's for dinner on Tuesday so I make sure to bring the right wine. Speak to you tomorrow xx.

My eyes grow heavy reading over Megan's message, yet my pulse picks up when she mentions Dominic. Part of me is surprised I hadn't heard anything from him, considering how diligently he'd been messaging me before we met, but at the same time, I know now that we've had our night, things are not going to be the same.

I am shocked by the sudden well of emotions I have. Tears sting the back of my eyes, and I can't make sense of the feelings taking over me.

I'm not due my period, nor am I hungover, but those are the closest things I can relate to how I am feeling. *Why do I feel like I am about to burst into tears? Yes, I'm sore and tired, but I'm not unhappy.*

Finally, I let the tears fall, despite not understanding why. I cry until I soak my pillows. I've been sleeping alone in a bed for years. Yet right now, it feels unbelievably empty. I pull the duvet up higher as coldness washes over me but it doesn't matter how tightly I wrap myself up, the cold is coming from within.

When the tears eventually stop, I take several deep, steadying breaths and force myself to focus on the positives. On the moments of joy, happiness, and fun. I make an effort to recognise this as having been a stepping stone on my journey of finding myself and making sure I can see and appreciate that I *am* brave. I have my own business. I *am* strong and independent. If I want something, I *can* go for it.

I experienced a night of fantasies with a guy that I never would have guessed would have sought me out. I recognise that it's okay to put myself out there, and this was the first step. There isn't any need for me to feel sad or insecure. The voices in my head saying I'm not good enough or that I am too ugly and too fat and will never have a guy want me, or that I will never achieve anything; they can shut up. They're the voices of my past. The voice of my ex has taken up enough space, and it's time for him to no longer hold any power over me. They have no place in my future. My life is about me and my girls. I want them to see that despite things being hard and tough at times, I am a strong woman. One they can look up to. One they can be proud of and gain strength from. But I don't just want that for them, I also want that for myself. That one day I'll be at a place where my default mode won't be to self-criticise. No more what ifs or if onlys. I may be submissive in the bedroom, but I'm not in my life. My submission is earned. My time, energy, and attention will be earned. And only those deserving will get it.

It's those thoughts I let myself bathe in as I drift off to sleep. Yet in my dreams, I keep finding myself being watched by a pair of familiar, deep, and assessing hazel eyes.

Chapter Twenty-One

Willow

*T*hree months later

"Cheers. I'm so proud of you, Willow. I can't believe your designs are going to be available to the masses," Megan says, joy dripping from her words.

I join in with her toast and take a large sip of the champagne.

I still can't believe it myself. I never could have imagined that one of my orders was for an influencer and she made a video tagging me and my shop that ended up going viral. This then got the attention of someone at one of the most popular adult toy shops in the UK. Next thing I know, I'm going to London for a meeting and being offered a contract to collaborate with them. They realised how popular romance books have become and how big the market is. The one caveat I had was that I would only agree to four toys and four outfits, and they had to be completely different to the ones I sold in my shop. After some back and forth, I finally signed on the dotted line.

The money was obviously a huge incentive, but it's more than that. I felt I had really achieved something. Even though it would be my shop's name that goes with the collaboration, *I* knew it was me. I had done this.

"Cheers."

"Don't look right now, but there's a guy sitting at the bar checking you out," Megan whispers.

I roll my eyes at her as tonight I have no interest in looking for a man. Tonight is about celebrating me.

"Oh, come on, just look," she pleads.

Reluctantly, I do as she asks and slowly let my eyes drift in that direction.

"Are you kidding me Megan! He looks like fucking Santa. He's got to be at least sixty."

She howls like a hyena, causing the people at the tables around us to look over.

"You've experienced a daddy, so I thought the next step would be a granddaddy," she teases.

Even though I laugh along with her, there's still a pang in my chest. After our weekend of fun and fantasies, I never heard from Dominic again. It didn't take me long to realise he ghosted me. At first, I felt confused, then upset, then angry. It wasn't that I held out hope for anything, but surely it was simple human decency to check on someone after a night like we shared.

In the days that followed, Megan and I dissected the whole thing. I wanted to see if there had been something I had done wrong. At my low moments, I couldn't help the insecure thoughts creeping in and started questioning if I'd taken things too far, been too needy, too desperate... Luckily, it didn't take me too long to realise that I'd misread Dominic. He clearly wasn't a true Dom. That was evident in his lack of aftercare that morning. I mean, at a time when he was meant to be looking after me, he ran, never to be seen or heard from again. To make things worse, I'd also spoken to him about my nerves about having a sub drop when we'd talked about aftercare. I'd read up on them and the thought of feeling rubbish terrified me. He promised to take extra care with my aftercare.

The night Megan came over and I told her every detail, I couldn't believe how many things had gone over my head. I'd clearly been swept away in the moment and not seen the red flags that he was waving. The more I broke things down to her, the angrier she'd become. She joked that he was simply a man-child, who had bland taste in food, as he didn't enjoy or appreciate spice and flavours beyond salt and pepper, and wouldn't know honesty or decency if it hit him in the face. She also said she hoped he'd capsize the next time he goes rowing.

I loved and appreciated her support and the way she consistently shot down any attempts I made at blaming myself. But I also knew there was an element of responsibility I needed to take. In hindsight, the inconsistency in his behaviour was as clear as day. Throughout that night, I had very much stayed in my lane, in the role I wanted to be in. I'd given in to making it a night of fulfilling fantasies and he'd been the one with the intense stares, lingering looks, tender moments. That had all come from him. Yes, I might have got carried away and let his praise and kind words comfort me, but name me a woman that wouldn't. I never hinted, even playfully, about seeing him again or a future, even just in a sexual capacity together. He's the one who erected a wall of hurt and frustration after he found out I had children. None of that was on me.

Despite things not having ended in the best way, I refuse to write the whole thing off as a negative. I stuck to my guns and make a real effort at putting myself out there. I met a guy I was attracted to, we arranged a night for us to fulfil our fantasies. I enjoyed myself. The sex was great. I still give myself the occasional pat on the back that I'd got him to reach such pleasurable heights he blacked out. But the biggest lesson I learnt was I need to only focus on me and what I want.

In the weeks after, I found myself responding and interacting on the dating apps with a different approach. I also joined a couple of kink apps and those only proved how far away from a real Dom Dominic had been. Maybe it had been his first time and he'd just not been honest with me. There wouldn't have been anything wrong with it being his first proper time as a Dom. But if that was the case, he should have told me that. That was his responsibility. Not mine.

"Tonight isn't about daddies or granddaddies. Tonight is

about celebrating. I couldn't have done this without your help and support. I never thought something like this would happen to me. So, I've decided this year I'm gonna make it the year I keep doing what I want. Try out and explore all the things I've stopped myself from doing. And I've just decided something I'm going to do. Something I've wanted to do for ages," I say excitedly.

"Oh, tell me. Is it skydiving? Or learning how to ride a motorbike? I've seen the collection of biker romances you have on your bookshelf."

I laugh at her ridiculous suggestions.

"No. I'm not turning into a daredevil. But what I've wanted to do for years but haven't been able to do because of the girls, is go on a luxury holiday. I'm going to book a beach villa, either in the Caribbean or possibly Mexico, by myself."

"That sounds fucking perfect. When are you going to book it?"

"Well, you know the girls are with their dad for four days after Christmas. I'm sure if I ask my parents, they'll have them for the week after. So, I think that would be the best time. Winter sun, seeing in the New Year at the beach."

"If I wasn't going away myself, I'd ask if I could sneak into your suitcase. I'm going to be so jealous in my snow gear whilst you're drinking cocktails on a sunny beach." She groans before laughing.

She was right. And I couldn't wait.

Chapter Twenty-Two

Willow

Six months later

My shoulder aches as I deposit the heavy wicker bag that is full to the brim with trinkets and ornaments I found at the market that will make perfect gifts for the girls and the rest of my family.

It's my fourth day here in Anguilla and I finally decided to venture out of the villa to go to the market. I set an alarm for the first time as apparently the best time to go is first thing in the morning to beat the crowds and the heat.

Now back at my room, I peel off the white linen dress that is stuck to my skin and make my way to the large walk-in shower, sighing with relief as the cool water hits my back.

I originally planned on renting a private villa for the ten

days I'm on this magical island, but after extensive research, and a dose of paranoia after watching a true crime documentary, I found a complex that has individual units; on the beach but secure in private, gated grounds.

There are three restaurants and a spa in the main building, and guests can hire carts to the private golf course should they wish to. They have an app I downloaded to order room service or food and drink at the beach or pool, as well as booking in spa treatments, taxis, water sports, and day trips. There really isn't any need to leave the resort, yet I found myself eager to explore.

After my morning trip, I plan to spend the rest of the day at the private beach and will order lunch from the sun lounger. I charged my Kindle before I left and wasn't planning on moving beyond the swipe of a page.

After my shower, I change into my bikini and throw on a cover-up, then grab my phone so I can quickly FaceTime the girls.

"Mum, look, Nanna and Grandpa are letting me brush Bailey," Mya squeals.

My parents decided to adopt the cutest little cockapoo a few weeks ago. Their neighbour a couple of doors down had a stroke and wasn't able to look after it anymore. Even though Dad had been reluctant at first, my mum had managed to win him over.

Growing up, my brother and I always begged and pleaded for a pet, but as both Mum and Dad worked full time, they always said no.

The girls have done the same with me and even though I

work from home and would be around, I have enough on my plate. So, now that my parents have a dog, it's kind of ideal as the girls get to play and dote and have their fun whenever we visit and I don't need to add more responsibility to my over-flowing plate.

I watch in amusement as Bailey runs off with Mya chasing after him as Ayana takes the phone, filling me in on their plans for the rest of the week. I quickly catch up with Mum and she tells me she's already started looking into coming here herself after I sent her countless pictures of the stunning views and sunsets. We finish catching up and I promise to call again tomorrow.

Sun cream on, I grab my tote bag, making sure I have everything I need before I head out to the relaxation that awaits me.

After a swim, I must have fallen asleep because wake up to the sounds of waves and a soft breeze brushing across my skin. Readjusting myself on the lounger, I get comfortable before continuing the book I started earlier. It's a Mafia poly-why-choose and I'm loving every second of it.

I've also gone on several dates in the last few months, and hooked up with two guys I'd met on the kink app. The first guy was just for one night. The second had been a Dom named Ethan who has his own architecture company. We went on several dates but he was offered a contract in Spain, so we'd decided to call it quits.

Yes, I was gutted as he brought me pleasure beyond my wildest dreams, but I am grateful for the memories and fun I had with him.

I grab my phone and use the complex's app to order some lunch.

It must be around half an hour later when I hear something being placed on the small table behind me. Turning, I squint as the sun shines brightly in my eyes.

"Thank you," I say as I pull myself up and am about to grab my purse to give the waiter a tip when my skin breaks out in goosebumps at the sound of a voice I haven't heard in ten months but recognise instantly.

"Always such impeccable manners. Such a good, good girl."

Enticing Choices

Chapter 1

Willow

"What are you doing here?" I can't hold back the breathless tone of my voice. My skin is covered in goosebumps, my heart beating so erratically I'm sure it's going to rip out of my chest. I turn, staring into familiar hazel eyes I never thought I'd see again.

"It's a pleasure to see you too, Willow," Dominic says with a smirk to his lips. *How is this happening right now?*

My body is frozen in place, but my eyes track him as he slowly walks around me, like a predator circling its prey. This makes no sense. *Why is he here? How did he know I would be here? Am I fucking asleep? Is this is some fucked up dream and any minute now I'm going to wake up drooling and crusty-eyed?*

I don't realise I'm pinching my arm until his eyes land there and his mouth breaks out into a devious grin.

"Ah, that brings back memories of being the one to mark your skin."

I try to swallow, but my mouth is so dry. "Are you really here? What is going on?"

He laughs loudly, but it isn't cruel; it's jovial, as if I've told him the funniest joke. I don't know why, but somehow that puts me at ease.

I focus on his open shirt, showing off his bare chest, tanned and glistening with perspiration, my eyes dropping to his blue swimming shorts.

He takes a seat on the lounger across from me and leans back on his arms. The movement makes my eyes glance down at his muscular chest and abs and I see the evidence of his clear erection as it strains against the fabric.

I quickly raise my eyes to his face and the lift of his lips shows that he has caught me in my perusal. I feel like a child caught with my hand in the biscuit tin.

Taking several deep, steadying breaths to clear my head of my wayward thoughts, I ask, "Dominic, can you explain to me how you're here? Like right here, right now, on this beach, which is a *private* beach." I'm surprised at how sure and unnerved my voice sounds. Inside, I still feel like I'm in the damn twilight zone.

"I'm here for work," is all he says, as if we are at some landmark in London and just happen to walk past one another. He sure as hell needs to give me more than that.

"This still isn't making any sense to me."

He makes himself more comfortable, and this time, it's me that catches him eyeing my chest, then down to my waist before he focuses on my face again.

"Trust me, I was just as surprised this morning when I

saw you. I've dreamt about bumping into you several times in the last couple of months, so I had to pinch myself to make sure this wasn't just another dream."

"What do you mean, this morning?"

"The show I'm working on is filming here on the island. We're actually done with filming. There are just a few location shots that we still need. We've been on location for almost two weeks and we fly back the day after tomorrow. Anyway, this morning, me and a couple of the crew were out at the market grabbing some breakfast when I spotted you, but by the time I got over to where you were, you were gone. I thought I dreamt the whole thing. Like, seriously, what would be the odds? Then, I just decided to take a walk on the beach. That's when I saw you again. I'd recognise your body anywhere. So, when I saw one of the waiters making his way over, I decided to intercept him and give you a little surprise."

I still don't understand how casually he's saying every-thing. As if this is the most normal thing. We're both thou-sands of miles away from home. Neither one of us could have known the other would be here.

I swear, I always think these meet-cutes are crazy when I see them in a movie or read them in a book. Like, these things *never* happen in real life. Yet right here, right now, it's happening to *me*.

My brain is still trying to make sense of it all when I realise he's bypassed the other elephant in the room—the fact that he ghosted me after our time together. He must notice something on my face as his body language changes. The muscles in his face soften and his eyes lose the joking tease they had in them. Instead, they are filled with regret and something else I can't quite place.

"I still can't believe you're here. This is insane. And besides that, I'm surprised you even want to see me." This time, I don't even try to hide the hurt and frustration that seeps into my voice. His slight flinch shouldn't make me as happy as it does.

"I deserve that." He runs his hand through his hair. "I'm sorry, Willow. I don't know what else to say, besides that. There's so much I want to tell you, so many excuses I practiced for if I ever got the chance to see you again. But you deserve better than those stupid and childish explanations."

He goes to speak again, but the sound of a phone ringing interrupts him. Dominic grabs it out of his pocket, swearing under his breath. "I need to quickly take this."

I nod in response, my mind still a jumble from the last few minutes. I listen half-hardy to the one-sided conversation.

"Yes... No, I told them all the notices had already been sorted and filed away. Matthew, all of this was already done beforehand. I don't see why they're deciding to make an issue about it now... Okay, yeah, I'll be back in a couple of minutes. I'll call them and sort this shit out." He hangs up, shaking his head, before looking up at me.

"Sorry, I really need to go and sort this out, but you deserve an explanation. And I want to apologise properly. I didn't think I would ever get the chance. Will you please join me for dinner? I promise I'll explain it all. Then, if you never want to speak to me again, I'll fully understand," he says, looking remorseful and desperate.

I open my mouth to respond, but no words come out. A big part of me wants to say *no, fuck you* as, despite it being months ago, there's still a part of me that never let go of that hurt. That feeling of rejection.

"Please, Willow." The sincerity in his voice is one I've never heard before, or expected to hear. Given the fact I do actually want to know why, and the craziness of him being here, I know my answer.

"Yes, I'll join you for dinner."

His whole face lights up and he smiles as if I've given him a winning lottery ticket.

"Thank you." He stands, leans forward, and kisses me on the cheek. The smell of his cologne like a feeling of déjà vu, making my breath catch.

"Do you still have the same number?" he asks.

"Yes."

"Do you want to eat here or go out?" His phone begins to ring again, but he makes no move to answer it.

"One of the restaurants on the complex will be fine." This isn't going to be a date; this will be a way for me to finally get closure.

He nods as though expecting that to be my answer. "Ok. How does eight sound? And I'll meet you in the main lobby?"

"Yeah, that's fine." His phone begins ringing again. "You should get going."

He looks at me again, and once more I am transported back to that moment in the hotel room before he left, the look of indecision being the only thing I could see on his face.

"Go, it's fine. I'll see you this evening."

With a swift nod, he moves to walk away before he looks back over his shoulder.

"This evening, Willow. Thank you."

Watching as he disappears towards the complex, I reach for the drink he left and down it in one long gulp, the cool liquid doing nothing to steady my fast-beating heart.

Did that really happen?

This is utterly insane. I must look like a madwoman as I begin laughing at the absurdity of this.

There's no denying that he's a very good looking guy. That was never an issue. I doubt there are many red-blooded women who wouldn't want to sleep with him. But there's no way in hell I'm going to do anything with him. He's a chapter in my past. A pit stop on my journey. I don't want or need to go backwards. No, I intend to keep moving forwards.

On top of that, there are still too many unanswered questions, too much confusion, frustration, and hurt. I'm still unhappy with how he treated me, not just the fact he ghosted me, but also during that last time we had sex and his lack of aftercare.

Nope. Nothing is going to happen between us again. But I *will* get answers. I deserve them.

Laying back, I watch the waves rolling in and out, the motion soothing, calming, relaxing me completely. After a while, I reach for my phone to check the time and notice it's coming up to four o'clock.

I pack all my things back up and make my way back to my villa. Sighing in relief as the cool air-con hits my skin, I quickly throw my bag next to the bed and call the one person I know will be more shocked than me.

"Well, well, well, if it isn't my jet-setting bestie. How's the holiday going?"

"Megan, you're never going to believe who I just bumped in to."

Chapter 2

Willow

"You've got to be fucking kidding me. Willow, is this some sort of weird joke? Because you do realise this is the most insane shit. This doesn't happen in real life. Trust it to bloody well happen to you," my friend exclaimed.

"How on earth do you think *I* feel?"

"Are you actually going to meet him? If I were you, I'd stand him up. Then if I saw him again, I'd drown him in the bloody ocean or feed him to the sharks or stingrays or whatever."

Laughter bubbles out of me at her words. Once again, proving how much of an amazing friend she is. "Yes, I'm going to meet him. As I've already told you three times," I mutter, rolling my eyes. It's already taken me fifteen minutes to calm her down.

"I know. I just still can't wrap my head around the whole

thing. Like seriously, I never expected you to see him again, let alone when you're off on your celebratory holiday."

I put the phone on speaker, as my ears can't handle the volume her voice is reaching.

"What do you think his excuse is going to be? Like, what on earth could the man possibly think is a good enough reason? Unless he tells you he was abducted by aliens or is actually an MI5 agent and was sent away on a top-secret mission that meant he couldn't communicate or the whole country would be in danger, I don't really see any excuse that would be acceptable."

I laugh at her ridiculous reasoning. "The thing is, I don't think I'm even interested in there being anything acceptable. I'm sure he'll come up with something that he thinks justifies his actions, but I know I'll be able to read from his facial expressions just how much truth there is to them."

Grabbing the phone, I take it with me as I turn the water on for the bath.

"But if you don't need a real answer then why meet him? You don't still have a thing for him, do you?"

"No." The speed of my response isn't out of denial. I'm one hundred per cent certain that I'm not going to even entertain the thought. "I'm not going to lie. The guy is still hot. I think he's even better looking now than he was then, but I don't trust him."

"Wait, then don't go for dinner with him. Are you insane?"

"No." I laugh. "It's not that I think he would do something

to me. I don't trust him enough to let him in again. The biggest thing I've learnt, not just from that night with him, but the more I delve into the Dom/sub world, is how important trust is. How he was with my body on that last occasion breached something. But the fault doesn't just lie with him. That's also on me. I should have said my safe word. But I guess I was just in denial. And afterwards I was just as annoyed at myself for not trusting my gut. Not trusting my instincts. That's what I don't trust. Dominic has this charm about him that makes it so easy to fall into an imaginary world with ease, but now I can see that this is the issue. It's imaginary. Not real. I don't want to be stupid and let my hormones overrule my head."

"That's my girl. Look at you, being a sensible adult, whilst slipping in twice that you still would want to bone him."

"Jesus, Meg, how old are you?"

Her hyena cackle echoes over the bathroom tiles. "I'm joking, I'm joking. You know, if it was down to me, I'd just punch him in the dick, but I understand and respect that you know what you're doing. Plus, I do agree that whatever you guys talk about, you're in control. You'll know if whatever he says gives you closure. Or if you two have sat down and talked, maybe that in itself will be closure enough."

I hum in agreement.

"Imagine if that was a thing that everyone had to do? Like, any time there's a bad breakup with no real reasoning or miscommunication or ghosting, imagine if by law you'd have to meet up with that person. I'd probably be in prison if I was forced to meet up with my exes," Megan declares.

We both burst into uncontrollable laughter.

I say my goodbyes and promise to let her know how the evening goes.

The bath is just what I needed. The oils they have here are some of the most delicious scents I've ever smelt, and I need to make a note to see if there's any way I can bring some back home with me.

I keep my towel wrapped around me as, despite the sun having gone done and a light breeze still sweeping through, the humidity is insane today.

I grab a drink from the fridge and take it and my phone with me onto the terrace. Earlier, my mum sent some videos of the girls and, given everything that's transpired, I haven't watched them yet. I still have over an hour to kill, so now is the best time.

My heart squeezes watching the girls playing and having fun. It's crazy because when I am with them each and every day, I often yearn for these moments of solitude, yet right now I feel like I'm missing a limb. Along with that, there's the incessant guilt I feel whenever I'm away from them. Whenever I do anything for myself, I always doubt if it's okay. Always questioning if it makes me a bad mum. But deep down I know the more relaxed and mentally balanced I am, the better mother it makes me. There's no question about it. When times are hard and I feel like I'm at rock bottom, I know it affects the girls just as much.

It's funny because all of this really only started with that night with Dominic. I can honestly see and appreciate how big of a turning point it had been for me. Not just the fact that I finally put myself out there, or how it cemented that I'm seeking a Dom/sub dynamic in my partners. It was also the time I realised I need to focus on myself. Needing to find and make ways for my own happiness. There's no one else around to do that for me, so I need to do it myself, and I am happy with that realisation.

I feel as if I've finally been set free. Free from the voices of my ex. Free from the continuous self-doubt, self-loathing, and all the negative things I berate myself with on an all too regular basis.

With those thoughts, I finish watching the final clips before heading inside to decide what to wear. I know this isn't a night of rekindling, so there's no way I'm going to be putting a full face of makeup on—not that I've brought much away with me.

I lather up in cocoa butter, making sure my skin is as moisturised as it can be, given how much time I've spent in the sun today.

I decide on a white milkmaid linen dress I bought and still haven't worn. The material is light enough for the heat, yet the design's simple enough for a casual vibe.

I put my braids in a half up half down style and slip on my tan leather sandals.

Grabbing my bag, I throw in my lip balm, phone, room key, and remember to grab one of the citronella wristbands as

I don't want to spend the night getting bitten to death by mosquitos.

I take one last glance in the mirror, happy with how my skin contrasts against the white of the dress.

Chapter 3

Willow

As I walk to reception, I think about how much I'd have laughed if anyone had told me this morning I would be making my way to dinner with Dominic.

Part of me is expecting to feel tingles of nervousness, but that isn't the case. I think it's simply the fact that because I feel so sure about what I want from this evening—from Dominic—that there is no room for anything else.

I'm just about to walk up the steps when my phone pings with a message.

> I'm at the reception. I've booked a table.
> They said it's ready whenever we are.

It still baffles me that he had kept my number, given that he ghosted me.

Standing a few metres in front of me, in chinos and a loose, baby blue linen shirt, Dominic catches the eye of several women that walk by. I can't help but smile, which is what I'm doing at the exact moment he turns and spots me.

His smile mirrors mine, though I'm sure he doesn't realise that the only reason why I'm smiling is because of the effect he has on other women. He takes a couple of steps towards me before leaning in and kissing me on the cheek. I capture the scent of his unique cologne. I'm not sure what it is, but I've never smelt anything quite like it. Like déjà vu I remember the smell of this cologne from that night at the hotel. But unlike then, now it does nothing for me. Doesn't excite or stimulate me, only cementing my feelings that what I once felt is long gone.

"You look stunning, Willow." I can feel the path of his eyes as he leisurely scans me from head to toe.

"You don't look too bad yourself," I joke before he gestures for me to lead the way towards the restaurant.

He places his palm on the base of my spine, the pressure so light you'd hardly notice it was there. Where previously the gesture excited me, now I feel nothing.

We settle at a table out on the patio. After the waiter takes our orders and brings our drinks, we make general small talk before he asks me how things are going in my life. I fill him in on how well the business is doing and how I needed to hire staff to keep up with the growing demand.

"That's fantastic. I know it probably sounds stupid and presumptuous, but I'm really proud of you. You keep showing just how amazing of a woman you are."

Although his sentiments may be a tad extreme, I appreciate the sincerity I see in his eyes. Despite our easy conversation, there's still the obvious elephant in the room that neither of us has yet to address, but I can tell by the way he shifts in his seat he's a little nervous. So instead of asking him what I'm desperate to know, I decide to save that for later and instead find out how he got to be here.

"So, tell me more about how you've gone from meetings in your London office with the need to only make rare appearances on set, to being with cast and crew on location in Anguilla?"

His eyebrows raise slightly as I speak. "You remembered?" The surprise in his tone is evident.

"Yes, of course. It's not every day you meet a TV executive." I laugh before taking a sip of my wine.

His eyes darken slightly, and I can tell he's thinking about more than just the memory of him telling me about his work.

"Well, when I first pitched this show, despite there being immediate interest, one of the biggest issues we faced was budget. It wouldn't likely cover the expenses expected to go with shooting somewhere like this. The biggest cost on these locations is usually the insurance and the cost of hiring where we film. But I managed to help out with that. A friend of mine owns a villa here and after some discussion, he agreed to let us film here for free, as long as the name of his property was put into the script. He also wanted to make sure there was someone here during filming who would be able to monitor things, as he wouldn't be here. So that's when I offered."

I have to laugh at the way he makes it almost sound like a

chore. "You say that as if you're being forced to sit in a dark and dingey studio in Birmingham."

Dominic gives a slight tilt of his head in agreement.

"So, are the cast and crew also staying at the complex?"

"No, the crew is in the hotel next door, but the cast is here as the villas give them more privacy. And when I was making my own arrangements, I managed to book one of the last bungalows here."

His eyes bore into mine and I know what the implications are to him giving me that piece of information. It's his way of letting me know we were both here, both free, both close to one another. Yet despite the fact it would be just so easy for both of us to give in to the mutual attraction, I'm still as adamant as ever not to.

Not because I was scared or even worried that I would suddenly feel something for him again. But I have too much respect for myself to go back to something that left me hurt and doubting myself in ways I now know I shouldn't have. No, that ship has long sailed, and I have both grown as a person and a sub.

So instead of reacting to his hint, I settle into safer territory, asking him to tell me all about the different shows he's put together in the last several months.

I don't miss how his face drops slightly as he realises I'm not entertaining his suggestion, but he gives me a soft smile and proceeds to fill me in on all that he's done as we sit and enjoy our food together.

Chapter 4

Willow

I am surprised how enjoyable and comfortable our meal has been. There is even a part of me that believes that maybe the two of us can have a chance at a good friendship after this.

We both laughed at how he ended up doing one of my father's Judo classes and hadn't known whether to mention that he knew me or not. I was glad he hadn't, as that could have been an awkward conversation.

By the time we finished dessert, I felt content and comfortable enough to ask him what I'd been dying to know.

"So, we've pretty much covered all things except for the obvious. I just want you to know, I'm not annoyed or bitter, but I would like the truth, please. Why did you ghost me?"

He squeezes his eyes shut as if he is preparing himself to answer before he runs his hands over his face. I know this isn't going to be comfortable for him, but that is on him. The least he can do is tell me the truth.

"I've thought countless times about how I would explain what happened. There were so many silly and pointless excuses I thought would be okay or justifiable. But every time I practised saying them, they just sounded so hollow and immature."

He leans back in his chair, looking out at the darkening ocean for a minute before continuing. "When we first matched, I was obviously very attracted to your pictures. And then as the days went on, I couldn't believe how well of a match we seemed with our sexual interests. Given how good that spark seemed to be, I was eager to meet up and see if that translated in real life. Going into that night, I was set on hopefully having a wonderful night with a woman who seemed to tick every box for me. And you did. It was the perfect night. One I've thought back on several times. What I hadn't expected was for us to get on so well between the great fuck sessions. I felt able to relax and just enjoy myself in a way that made it seem like we'd known each other for a long time."

Everything he says is true, but I know there is more to come.

"To be honest, I hadn't felt such an instant, strong connection with someone, ever. And no, before you say it, it wasn't just sex. I don't think I've laughed that much in years. Not even my closest friends see me as content and at ease as I'd been that night. It was as if you wove some sort of spell over me. You put me at ease to the point I was opening up way more than I had thought I would." Dominic turns and looks at me head on. "The sex was fucking fantastic. When I think back, I realised how much I opened up, but in that same thought, I also realised I hadn't asked much about you," he says remorsefully as he rubs the back of his neck.

"Anyway, by the next morning, I felt pretty overwhelmed at how much I liked you. And I was trying to wrap my head around how I could approach making that more than just a one-time thing. So, as I was trying to come up with a plan in my head, that's when you said that you had children. I really hadn't expected that. Not that there was anything wrong with it, it's just the revelation really threw me."

Dominic looked at me almost pleadingly, as though he was desperate for me to understand where he was coming from. Yet, nothing he said justified his behaviour.

"If I'd have known beforehand, or if I hadn't been so stupid and noticed it on your page that you had kids, I think I would have steeled myself to not even think—not even contemplate—that it was more than a onetime thing. Again, I wasn't angry that you have kids. I guess a part of me was hurt."

I didn't even try to hide the shock on my face at that statement. "Excuse me? I'm confused. What were you hurt about?"

"When you told me you had kids, I took it as you saying you weren't looking for anything serious. And I guess my pride took a hit as I was drifting towards thoughts and feelings of more than a one-night-stand and in my mind, it felt like through you telling me, you didn't. You see, I've never been with someone who has kids and it felt like stepping into uncertain territory. I don't know if you remember me telling you, but my parents' divorce was really bad, and it fucked me up more than I realised. I think it tainted my outlook on parenting and child dynamics. So, I reacted like a child. I was hurt, frustrated that I'd met a seemingly perfect woman and she wasn't as into me as I was into her." He drops his head for a second before looking up at me with an expression on his face I can't read.

"I'm sorry," he continues. "My behaviour and detachment were a way of protecting myself. It wasn't anything you deserved and I hate myself more than you can imagine when I think back on how I acted. Even during those final moments together, I could feel myself ruining things, yet I couldn't seem to stop myself. I really am sorry, Willow. I hope you know how much I wish I could go back and undo my actions."

My mind is still processing his words. My head currently feels like a pinball machine, with feelings bouncing all over the place. I guess there are some elements of truth to what he's saying. I had suspected that he hadn't realised I had children, despite it being on my profile. I still don't think it's a justified reason for the way he behaved. However, I do think he's someone that likes things his own way, has usually got what he wants, and probably—usually—knows all that's going on. Yet with me, I guess I was a bit of a curve ball for him. And the fact that tonight I've seen him being nervous and showing a more vulnerable side, I do believe he's sorry. I can forgive him. Yes, he did behave like an idiot, but we all make mistakes. It won't help me to hold a grudge, so I'm happy to accept his apology.

"Dominic, I appreciate your apology and I believe you

mean it. That you're sincere. We're human. We make mistakes and I'd be the first to tell you, I've reacted strongly or irrationally in certain moments, so we can move past that. But why did you ghost me? Especially if you realised how you had acted wasn't right?"

I appreciate the way he focuses on me when I speak, and I don't miss the way he moves like he's about to reach for my hand, then pulls back to grab his glass instead.

"So, for the first two days, I'm not gonna lie. I was still hurt. The more I thought about how I behaved that morning, the angrier I got with myself. I guess because it was sinking in how much I liked you. Then, when I finally started thinking rationally, it was two days later, and I felt like shit that I hadn't messaged you. Even just to check that you got home safely. Then, by the time three days had passed, I knew it was too late. I've gone to call and text several times, but you deserved better. It wasn't your fault I couldn't get a grip on my emotions. And then, with how much time had passed, I knew that you deserved more than a simple call or a message. I couldn't send flowers as I didn't know where you lived. I was too ashamed to just randomly get in contact again, so I vowed that if I ever saw you again, it would mean fate was giving me the chance to apologise. And lo and behold, here we are."

Chapter 5

Willow

I can see the tension around his eyes as he tries lifting the mood, and though I do appreciate the apology, I still feel like it is more of an excuse than a true reason. I've also been contemplating if I should ask whether it had been his first time being a Dom. I've thought about it so often, and after my experience with Ethan, it's abundantly clear that Dominic may think of himself as a Dom and may have gained more experience, but he was not one that night with me. I'm sure Megan would be screaming at me to ask him, but to be honest, I'm not sure it really matters anymore.

As I let those thoughts sink in, a sense of contentment washes over me as though a weight has been lifted—one I hadn't realised I was carrying around—and a truly happy smile took over my face.

Dominic is still looking at me, obviously unsure why I'm smiling, but he returns with his own.

This chapter finally feels put to rest and maybe Dominic

has a similar feeling. Maybe he needed to get this off his chest and being able to do so in person allows us to move on with no hard feelings.

We both order another drink and are back to the level of comfortability we shared that night at the hotel.

"So, Dominic, I know this is technically a work trip for you, but I'm sure you've been able to slip away at times and enjoy some of the amazing things this island has to offer. Tell me, what have been your favourites? Or is there anything in particular you would recommend?" I ask.

"I wish I could give you a list of amazing things, but to be honest, I've spent more time inside than I would have liked. We did go on a drive around the island as the director wanted to see if there were any particular locations that would work well as backdrop or pull away shots, and as you know, I've gone to the market. We've all gone out to dinner every night, but besides that, sadly there hasn't been much else in the way of sightseeing. But if you're free, maybe we could spend the day together tomorrow, seeing all that this place has to offer?" His face lit up like a child on Christmas morning.

Despite the fact I was still physically attracted to him— seriously, with the way that man looks, tell me who wouldn't. The way he checked me out multiple times through dinner, which made it clear that the sexual attraction was mutual, add on the craziness of us both being here, I still don't think it is a good idea to spend too much time together.

Although he is leaving on New Year's Day to head to their next filming location and we could have easily just spent a day flirting and possibly even spending the night together, I didn't want to make this trip about him. I didn't want to go back to the past. My body may think it's a good idea, but my mind knows too much has happened. I may be able to forgive him for his coldness, his detachment, even the way he checked out emotionally and left without seeing if I was okay; not offering after care, then ghosting me, but I can't *forget* those things. I won't forget how I felt in the days after. The way I cried, worrying that there had been something wrong with me. Doubting myself. Questioning if I was good enough, if there was something wrong with me, with my body, with who I was. No. I can't and won't do that to myself again. So, I come up with the only lie I can think of that will spare me, whilst not coming across as rude.

"I'm sorry, but I can't. I've got a whole day of spa treatments booked tomorrow. I wanted to indulge in one last pamper session before starting the New Year." I feel bad as I watch his face fall. I don't want to hurt him. That isn't who I am. "But if you'd like, when I finish them, we can go for a walk along the beach?"

I try to add in as much enthusiasm as I can. And when he responds with a nod and a smile, I feel a little less guilty.

Chapter 6

Willow

I decide to actually book in some treatments and end up having a facial, a full body scrub, and then a hot stone massage. My skin feels as soft as a baby's and my body bonelessly relaxed. It was exactly what I needed.

After the spa, I laid out on the bed and had a lengthy catch up with Megan, filling her in on how dinner went, giving her a word-by-word run down on everything Dominic said.

To my surprise, she believed what he told me, telling me it kind of made sense and we both agreed it had been good for me and a great way to finally put this chapter to rest.

The weather today is even more stifling than it has been so far. I decide to go for a quick swim to help cool down, then turn up the air-con before taking a nap.

I am awoken by my phone ringing loudly. Momentarily disorientated, it takes a couple of seconds to clear the fog of sleep and answer.

"I hope I haven't interrupted you. But I've found this cool

little stall along the beach that sells cocktails, fruit, even some sort of dessert thing. Though I'm not sure I want to try the one that looks like a jelly with bits in it." Dominic's laugh booms through the phone, and I sit up, running my hand over my face to wake up properly.

"Hmmm, now that does sound intriguing. Let me quickly get changed and I'll come meet you there. Which direction do I need to go?" I ask, a little surprised that he's calling me but also somewhat intrigued, especially at the thought of exploring more of this island.

"Head to the left side of the private beach, through the security gate, and towards the pier where they do the water activities. You can't miss it."

"I'll be about fifteen minutes. Is that okay?"

"Yeah, that's fine. Take your time."

The hut is impossible to miss, as is Dominic in dark green shorts and a white linen shirt he's left open.

We order rum punch and opt for the mixed fruit platter which Dominic offers to hold, while both of us grab pieces as we stroll along the beach.

The breeze is divine, and we both slip into a relaxed comfortability as we chat about anything and everything. I find out more about what Dominic has been up to the last couple of months, and I'm truly fascinated when he says he's taking more of an interest in venturing towards producing and financing as well as his normal job.

We first walk away from the complex, before making our way back towards the private beach almost an hour later, the sun beginning to make its descent.

"So, we decided to combine our wrap party with a New Year's Eve celebration tomorrow. I was wondering if you had any plans. Would you like to join us?"

This time, I don't need to make up a lie or an excuse. I've already purchased a ticket to the party the hotel is throwing; a banquet meets New Year's Eve party.

"Thank you for the offer, but I've already made plans."

"I understand. How about when we're both back in the UK and you're next in London, we grab a coffee or bite to eat?" Dominic asks with a slight sigh as his brows lift somewhat hesitantly.

Part of me is apprehensive as I'm not sure if this is a step backwards, but I have a feeling that Dominic has the making of a decent friend.

"Yeah, sure. The next time I'm in London, if I'm free, I'll message you and we can meet up."

"Well, Willow, I can honestly say it has been the best surprise seeing you here. Again, I'm so, so sorry. It means a lot that you have given me the chance to apologise. Make sure you message me, yeah? Although I know the scenery or grey London skies won't be as beautiful as the crystal blue waters here."

I laugh along with him before giving him a kiss on the cheek, saying my goodbyes, and heading to my room.

Chapter 7

Willow

It's New Year's Eve and I genuinely couldn't be happier. Going into a new year on a luxurious tropical island, celebrating all that I have done and achieved throughout the year whilst excitedly thinking and planning all I have lined up in the upcoming one has always seemed like a pipe dream. Yet here I am. For the first time in I don't know how long, I am proud of myself. Proud that my hard work, the endless, gruelling hours, emotional ups and downs, the uphill struggle of being a single mother, it's all paying off. I am finally at a stage where I feel confident in my own skin. That my daughters can proudly look up to me, not just as a mother, but also as a woman. Seeing that, despite life with its endless hurdles and diversions causing you to want to give up, if you push through it and persevere, then it really is possible to achieve your dreams.

I'd FaceTimed Mya and Ayana earlier and they'd been so excited that my parents were letting them stay up 'til midnight. I always love the joy kids have when they are allowed to stay up. It reminds me of the times my brother and I would fight sleep to stay awake.

Ayana and Mya took turns telling me how my dad had got some fireworks and they were setting them off in the garden after the countdown and then I quickly caught up with my parents, wishing them a Happy New Year before promising to call tomorrow.

Megan sent me a video of her celebrating the countdown in front of the stunning snow-covered mountains.

"Hey babe, wishing you a Happy New Year, although part of me feels like I shouldn't, given how you left me hanging with the end of that video. Firstly, who are those gorgeous specimens you were kissing? And secondly, please tell me it was more than just a kiss. I expect every dirty and delicious detail. Can't wait to see you and thank you for all your love and endless support you give me and the girls"

Knowing the party this evening will likely go long into the early hours, I have a quick swim in the private pool, then take a nap, making sure to set an alarm so I have enough time to shower and get ready.

Chapter 8

Willow

I decided to go all out for tonight. My hair was in a half up, half down style and I twisted my braids on the side and put in a couple of flowers I found on my walk this morning after breakfast.

My skin has a glow to it from the last couple of days in the sun, so I don't bother with any foundation. I moisturise, fill my brows, add a rose gold eyeshadow, and manage a perfect cat eye flick of eyeliner to my outer corners. I finish it off with a double layer of mascara and a tint to my cheeks and lips.

My outfit is a turquoise dress with spaghetti cross straps over my back. I love that the built-in bra gives me both a lift and secures my boobs in place. I opted to go with tanned leather gladiator-style sandals with a matching clutch.

Feeling great, I snap a quick picture before making my way to the party. This holiday has been a dream of mine for so long and this party was going to be the icing on top, with all the exciting things the hotel has promised will be happening.

I am planning on starting the year as I mean to go on. With hope, happiness, and joy.

The whole evening has been amazing.

When I arrive at the party, there are around fifty of us there and I love how easily we all chat and mingle as they bring round non-stop platters of barbecued meats and fish, salads, breads, and vegetables, plus endless cocktails and champagne.

The live band playing upbeat music, adding to the party atmosphere, while fire eaters and dancers perform for us. Torches light up the beach and the large flames flicker and wave in the light breeze. As the clock hits midnight, the most stunning firework display lights up the sky as we all cheer and clap.

I'm not one to be regularly on social media, but there is no way I can stop myself from filming the breathtaking scene before panning back to myself. I look directly into the camera, wanting to capture the joy on my face.

"From me here in paradise, I want to wish you all a Happy New Year."

I blame the cocktails for the little kiss I blow to the camera at the end. I don't want to filter or edit anything, so I simply upload it and am surprised by the fast likes and comments that start coming through. Given the time difference, I thought all my friends would already be fast asleep.

Putting my phone away, I turn my attention back to the party, dancing, drinking, and enjoying myself until I'm tired, sweaty, and my body decides it's time to call it a night.

. . .

I manage to get back to the villa without falling, although I wouldn't say I am walking in very straight lines. Locking the door behind me, I let out a huff of annoyance that the light in the bedroom is on. I could have sworn I turned it off. Luckily, all the windows were closed, so I don't have a swarm of insects flying around.

I grab a bottle of water from the fridge, leaving it on the bedside table before heading to the bathroom to get undressed, wash my face, and brush my teeth.

By the time I climb into bed, it's almost 2 a.m. Just as I go to put my phone on charge, a message comes through.

> Willow, wishing you a Happy New Year. That view you put up on Instagram is breathtaking, and I don't just mean the fireworks. I'm glad to see you taking a well-deserved break and fulfilling one of your dreams. Sending warmest wishes from a not-so-warm Barcelona. Thinking of you, Ethan xxx.

Well, I hadn't been expecting that. It wasn't as if things had ended badly between us. And to be honest, if he hadn't needed to go to Spain for work for six months, there's a good chance we'd still be seeing each other. We could have carried on and done extreme long distance, but where we'd only been seeing each other for three months, it felt like too big of a step too early on. So instead, I decided to end it and just leave things open to see how we feel and where we both are when he returns.

My mind flickers back to the last time Ethan and I were together. Instantly, my body lights up at the memories of what he did to me. Laying naked under the soft, cool sheets, my fingers traced my collarbone, before making their way down my chest, my belly to my already wet pussy.

My back arches as my fingers rub over my clit. Going faster, feeling myself getting closer to release. I'm not sure if it's the alcohol running through my veins or the memories Ethan's message evoked, but in minutes my body seizes, then explodes, sending tingles down my arms and legs as I come in a breathy moan.

Once I finally have my breath back, I drink half the bottle of water before pulling up the sheets under my arms and taking a smiley yet sleepy selfie and sending it to Ethan along with a message.

Wishing you a Happy New Year (PS: also thinking of you) 💋 XX

Chapter 9

Willow

It was the first of January, and I've never enjoyed a New Year's Day more than I am right now, sitting on the terrace of the restaurant in a bikini and white crochet cover up.

Like several of my fellow patrons, my head is a little fragile from last night, but I'm hoping lunch will help lift, or at least ease, my hangover.

I bite back a smile as I think of the probable thousands, if not millions, of people that have started their new year tired and hungover. And despite me feeling the same way, it doesn't feel quite so bad recovering in this tropical paradise.

In desperate need to rehydrate, I practically down my fresh orange juice the second the waiter brings it, along with a bottle of water and a coffee. He takes my food order and just after he leaves, my phone goes off with a message.

> Happy New Year. I'm just about to check
> out, then will be heading to the airport. I was
> wondering if you were around so I could
> quickly say goodbye?

I feel a pang of guilt that I've completely forgotten about Dominic. Which is insane, given I still couldn't believe the odds of us both being here at the same time. I quickly type back a response.

> And a Happy New Year to you too. I've just
> ordered lunch. I'm on the terrace of the
> main restaurant. Why don't you pop by on
> your way out?

His reply was instantaneous.

> Perfect, I'll see you shortly.

Sipping my coffee as I look out at the beautiful view before me, I'm once again so glad that I came on this trip. It isn't just the joy of being on a luxury holiday. It is also the little things, like not stressing about what to make for dinner or getting through the never-ending pile of laundry. Even just being able to enjoy my coffee without the need to rush off somewhere made me realise I need to make it a priority when I get back home.

Movement in my peripheral vision breaks me from my thoughts. Turning my head, I watch as Dominic makes his way through the restaurant. Despite knowing that I won't be repeating history with him, my eyes scan his muscular frame. I can still appreciate the very attractive man he is.

"Just as beautiful as ever." The deep baritone of his voice vibrates all around. I gesture for him to take the seat opposite me, but he shakes his head.

"Trust me, if I had the time I would love to sit and have breakfast, but I'm going to be picked up any minute.

"I still can't believe my luck of bumping into you here. And for you not only giving me the time of day, but allowing me to apologise." His smile is soft as his eyes look into mine.

"Trust me. Bumping into you here wasn't on my bingo card," I say with a genuine beam.

He glances at his watch and lets out an audible sigh. "As much as I would love nothing more than to sit with you here and enjoy some lunch and a fantastic view, sadly, the taxi will be here any minute. However, I am looking forward to seeing you again when you're next in London."

I stand as he moves to my side, his hand resting on my upper arm. His touch, which used to give me sparks of lust that would seep through me, no longer affects me. There is nothing there. Only closure and feelings of contentment as we say our goodbyes. Going forward, I knew that the chapter between myself and Dominic is now closed. And hopefully, the new one would be one of friendship.

Chapter 10

Ethan

"I thought you said you wanted me to bring you back some of those handmade red necklaces. That's what you said last week, Sophie." I exhale with a chuckle. I love my daughter, but she jumps from one thing to the next.

"Dad, I said I wanted that as a backup if you couldn't find any evil eye jewellery. When we last came to visit you in Barcelona, I remember loads of the stalls had them, but I just wasn't into it back then."

She's talking as if that was years ago as opposed to the half term only three weeks ago.

"Anyway, those are what I would like, Dad. You know that book Nan got me for Christmas about the emotions of animals?"

"Yes, what about it?"

"Well, there's a section in it about how certain animals can sense and feel particular auras and vibes. Horses are known to sense things like a change in the weather, people's attitudes, and some even believe they can detect evil spirits."

I don't know how I manage not to roll my eyes as I watch her face morph from annoyance over the wrong jewellery to utter enthusiasm.

"And, given how important it is that I not only learn every possible thing I can about them, but now that I'm also helping out at the stables, I want to make sure that when I'm there, I'm bringing good, calm, and positive energy to them. Making sure to ward off all the negative vibes I can."

As always, looking at my daughter through the computer screen pulls at my heart. I miss my kids so damn much. Despite them only staying with me a few days a week, this trip really hit hard with how much I miss them. I call or Face-Time them every day, even when I'm back home, but these last three months have felt torturous. I've made sure to fly back every couple of weeks to see them, and they both came out for the half term, but I still feel awful for not being close to them.

"Alright, Sophie, I'll make sure to get the right ones. I called Lucas before his football training, so I'm now up to scratch on all that. I'm going to go and grab something to eat. I'm starving. But I'll call you again tomorrow, okay?"

"Yeah, Dad, I know. Love you. Bye."

"Love you too, sweetie."

Closing my laptop, I grab my phone and wallet before making my way out. I don't even bother debating where to head for dinner, as I've seemingly got into a routine since being out here.

After a ten-minute walk, I make my way to a table in the corner of this little gem of a restaurant. It's a small, family-owned business and I've been in here so many times they don't even bother asking me what I'll order. They usually just send me out whatever today's special is, which suits me just fine.

Taking a large sip of Mahou the waiter brought as I took my seat, I flick through my phone, seeing which meetings I have tomorrow, then scroll Instagram. I'm just about to exit it when a story from Willow pops up.

It's of a stunning sunset with the caption: *This may be paradise, but I can't wait to give my two little treasures the biggest squeeze. #threemoredays.*

I press the like button, then go to my photos and click on the one she sent me on New Year's. She looks absolutely stunning. So damn sexy and her smile has got to be one of the brightest and most seductive things I've ever seen.

It's funny because we'd only been together a handful of weeks before we both decided to cool things off due to me having to come here for work. But there's just something about her. Even back then, it felt like she was the one that got away. We first met on a kink dating app, and I first noticed her delicious figure that was encased in a black latex dress. But when I looked through her pictures, it were her eyes that enraptured me.

I've been with many subs over the years and have had relationships that allowed me to be the Dom I am, yet I've never seen the look of strength with simultaneous vulnerable submission as I did in her eyes. It was the first time I understood the saying that the eyes are the window to the soul.

The more we talked and got to know one another, the stronger the pull became. If we'd being seeing each other longer, I would have seriously considered turning this job down. But since things were still so new and neither of us were sure what we wanted, it felt like it would have put too much pressure on both of us if I'd stayed. But after I watched that video she uploaded on New Year's, it was like a light shining through a dense fog. Suddenly, things looked a little clearer. It's only been a couple of days, but we've been massaging non-stop. Just that has made me feel lighter, given me some sort of drive back. Even Lucas mentioned I seemed different—happier even—when I spoke to him earlier.

I thought this was going to be a straightforward six-month job, where I would just keep my head down, get on with my work, make some connections, then head back home to my normal routine: gym, seeing my kids, maybe catching up with a friend or two. But instead, it's made me look at what's missing in my life. I'm forty-six, divorced, with two kids. I'm in good shape, my business is doing better than ever. There's no need for me to feel like things should stay stagnant. One thing's for sure, if I have the chance and Willow is interested, I definitely want to pick up where we left off. Now more than ever.

Willow

I wipe the sweat off my forehead as I put away the final pile of ironing that's been sitting on the chair in the corner of my room for more days than I'd like to admit. Now this—the endless housework and chores—is definitely something I didn't miss when I was away.

I can't believe it's been a month since I got back. It's weird because before I left, I was so desperate to get away and time seemed to be going at a snail's pace. Then when I was there, the days seemed to just fly by.

I'm so glad I took the leap and went on that trip. It truly did wonders for me and I got the chance to reset. Not just my body, but my mind also had a reset. There wasn't a single occasion when I was out there that I let an intrusive or insecure thought take over. The trip also did wonders at giving me more of a drive and push with my business. Even though I didn't have a holiday fling or get any kind of action, I think just being able to feel rested, rejuvenated, and happy boosted something within me.

Work is currently doing so well, I've got to the point where I sometimes have to turn down certain offers, collaborations, and orders that are just too big.

Before, I would have grabbed any chance, any opportunity thrown my way, even if it meant working myself to the ground. But now I realise just how important it is not to take on too much. Despite how tempting certain offers look, if it means I'm burning the candle at both ends, it simply isn't worth it. Not for me. Not for my girls.

Obviously, I can't forget the utterly unexpected surprise of bumping into Dominic while I was away, which still boggles my mind. The odds of that happening are insane. But I won't deny how good it felt to finally get the closure I needed with him. I guess the cherry on top would be reconnecting with Ethan. That message on New Year's seems to have been a turning point for the both of us.

We've been messaging nonstop. He's been filling me in on how things are going on his project in Barcelona and how much he misses his kids. He's mentioned a couple of times that he's eager to meet up when he's back. As always, he takes such an interest in how I am. When I fill him in on how good things are going, I can't deny the butterflies in my tummy as he says how proud he is of me and my achievements. Even though I know I don't need or seek his validation, the earnestness and understanding in his words and recognition of just how hard I've worked truly means so much to me.

I love the way he asks how the girls are doing, and I'm

always amazed at just how much he remembers about the crazy and chaotic stories I tell him about them.

I don't think I ever realised how big an impact it has on me, speaking to a guy—a guy I like and have a past with—about my kids. I don't know if it's simply because he has kids as well, therefore he's likely to understand things better. But to be honest, I think it's just who Ethan is. He's a man of respect, integrity, and his words and promises aren't empty. He truly means what he says.

About two weeks back, he told me he was coming back to the UK for a long weekend to see his kids and asked if I'd like to see him. Despite the fact I really want to, I know how much he's missing his children, and I don't want to take away a single moment he could otherwise have spent with them. So instead, I made him a deal that the next time he's over for longer, we'll meet up and have a proper catch up together.

We were FaceTiming when he asked, and I remember the soft kindness in his eyes as I said it, making my whole body feel warm and fuzzy. Neither of us has outright said what exactly is between us, nor what we are working towards. I think in part, that's because he's still got a couple of months left on his job in Barcelona, yet at the same time, not even the ever-pessimistic side of me can deny how good and happy I've felt since reconnecting. He seems to have really worked out what I need and when I need it. It's as from how I phrase a message he can tell if I need a distraction, or if I'm too busy to talk, or when I'm interested in getting to know him, he regales me with stories and sends me pictures and videos of trips he's been on. The longer it's gone on, the more I've come to realise this isn't just how he is when he's a Dom. That attentiveness and caring side are part of his DNA.

Breathing out a sigh, I make my way downstairs, checking my watch and seeing I still have time for a quick coffee before getting ready to leave for the school pick up, when my phone rings.

My lips stretch into a smile as I look down at the screen.

"You really must have a sixth sense. I was just thinking about you."

Chapter 12

Ethan

"Is that so? And what exactly were you thinking about?" I say with a grin. The sound of her light laugh feels like a balm to my skin. Over the years, I've been lucky enough to have been with several very beautiful women, but there is just something about Willow that completely outshines all the rest.

Not only is she stunning, with a body like a goddess, but she has the most beautiful soul. The endless love and devotion she has for her girls, the long, arduous, and hard work she puts into her business, and the endless compassion she has for others, really make her even more stunning than she already is.

"Well, I was thinking about how attentive and caring you are. In more ways than one."

I can hear the grin in her tone, and my cock throbs as it presses against my trousers. This is what she is capable of doing to me. We might be thousands of miles apart and aren't even discussing anything explicit, yet it's as though we both know where her mind is going. We can both feel the magnetic pull between us.

"I could easily say the same about you, Willow. So how are you doing? Were you able to send out that interesting order you were telling me about?"

I didn't have to see her to know she was rolling her eyes at me as she laughed. When we'd first met, and she'd told me about her business, I was intrigued. And watching how much it has grown and how she has bloomed has filled me with immense pride.

I've had a look at her website on several occasions and I'm always hit with a wave of intrigue and curiosity with just how she comes up with these creations. Especially when she describes or shows me some of the custom-made orders. I've always been an open minded man, but even I have had to take several double-takes at some of the items, which Willow seems to find very amusing.

"Yes, I sent that out, and I won't lie. I'm glad that one is out of the way. I have never had an order with such precise and specific modifications. When they sent the order through, it felt like I was back at school reading a chemistry answer." This time I laugh, as I can only imagine what that must have looked like. I could honestly listen to her talk about absolutely anything for hours.

"Anyway, enough about me. How are you? Is it starting to warm up there yet?"

As always, she brushes herself aside, focusing on someone else. In this case, me. Normally I'd say something, but with the news I am eager to tell her, I don't mind letting it slide, just this once.

"Well, I've got some good news and some bad news," I tell her excitedly.

"Hm, okay, hit me with the bad news first."

"Remember how I said I was going to be able to come back to London for a week next month, and we were looking to catch up then?"

"Yes, is everything okay?" Willow asks, somewhat hesitant, the sound of worry clear in her voice.

I want to drag this out a little, but hearing the trepidation and the sombre tone in her voice makes me feel bad.

"I'm not going to be able to come for a week."

"Oh. Okay. I understand." Her pitch is low, the tone subdued.

Now I feel like even more of an asshole, so my words come out in a rush. "I won't be able to come for a week, as I'll be coming back for good." The only thing I can hear is the loud beating of my pulse. "Willow, are you still there?"

"Yes. Yes, of course. I... just. Wow, that's such good news, Ethan," Willow says rushed and breathless.

Slowly my pulse begins to steady as I hear the excitement in her voice.

"I'm so very happy, Ethan. And I'm sure your kids must be over the moon?"

Once again, it doesn't go unnoticed how she doesn't ever just think about herself. And the fact that she's also thinking about my kids means more to me than she could ever know.

"Yeah, I called them earlier. Sophie was squealing, and I

even managed to get an enthusiastic response from Lucas, which was more than I expected."

Having a teenage son who is basically the carbon copy of yourself feels like God is playing the biggest trick.

Willow's laugh brings my thoughts back to the present. "So, does that mean you're almost finished? How were you able to cut down the timeline so much?"

"Let's just say a few good things fell into place and a couple of manoeuvres and a few longer days, but it's all on track now."

With how I've got to know Willow now, there is no way I will tell her that I actually hired more workers, offering their pay to come out of my own contract and have been working 18-hour days for the past three weeks. No, I can't tell her that because then she will ask why, and I don't think telling her over the phone that the reason for all this urgency is because of her. Because I want to get back and give us a real chance.

"That is fantastic." And I know she means it. "So, when will you be back then?" The breathy tone to her voice makes my cock twitch, but the joyousness that comes through seeps straight to my heart.

"I'll be back in just over three weeks, so technically the timeline of when I was hoping to see you will still be the same, but this time I won't be flying back here after. I appreciated that you wanted me to spend as much time with my kids the last time I visited, but now things are different, and I won't lie to you. I'm very eager to see you again." His voice dips to a low gravely octave, a tone I remember well from when he's turned on.

There is no need for me to beat around the bush. We are both adults, both at stages in our lives where games no longer interest us. And even though we haven't outright said what we are doing, there is no denying that whatever is going on between us, it's strong, palpable, and not something to pass up.

"Of course, I want to see you as soon as you're back. Would you like to stick to the original date I was going to come up to London or would you prefer me to see if I can get my mum to re-arrange it?"

"No, let's stick with when we had planned. Is there anything in particular you'd like to do? Anywhere you fancy going?"

"Why don't you just surprise me?" Her voice hums with a seductive purr, and I blow out a silent and deep breath, controlling the desire that once again begins to burn through my veins.

"Alright. I'll make sure it's something you enjoy." I didn't miss the sharp intake of breath and I knew she could hear the difference in my tone of voice. The last time she heard it was the last time we were in bed together. "Now I'll let you get on, and I'll speak to you later."

There was a moment of silence, then in what I can only describe as words from heaven as she responds.

"Yes, Sir."

Chapter 13

Willow

"Dinner's ready," I shout up to Ayana and Mya as I place their plates on the table. It sounds like a herd of elephants crashing down the stairs. You'd think with how many hours of ballet they do a week, they'd have more grace and be lighter-footed. But no.

Rolling my eyes and enjoying the few minutes of calm that's only there because the girls' mouths are currently full of my homemade lasagne, I take a large sip of wine and take a deep, relaxing breath.

I never thought I'd get to the stage where I would be wishing I had fewer orders. I know I shouldn't be complaining, but sometimes I'd just like to have a little reprieve. Similar to how kids have school holidays, I could do with a half term or a couple weeks off here and there. No, that would be a great working initiative. But alas, even with me hiring a PA, who has allowed me to off load so much of the menial paperwork and admin duties, I'm still absolutely exhausted each and every night. Being a single mum, with no help from their father—the only help I get is from my parents —running my business, staying on top of housework, the cooking, the cleaning, the uniforms, school trips, dance classes – the list is never ending.

Whoever said we all have the same twenty-four hours in a day, clearing isn't someone that has to do every single thing themselves!

"What's for dessert?" Mya chimes in, breaking me from my thoughts.

"There's ice cream, or you each still have a doughnut left." I stand, taking both their empty plates and placing them in the sink.

"Can we have both?" Ayana asks in the sweetest voice she can muster.

"Yeah, please, Mum? Please, please, please," Mya begs.

"Please, please, please," both girls now singing in a chant.

"Alright, but only if you promise to tidy your rooms and lay out your uniforms before bed.

There is a moment's pause before they begrudgingly answer.

"Yeah, okay."

"Alright, I'll do it."

I laugh and roll my eyes at the cheek of those two. Yet despite how much the two of them send me stir crazy and make me feel like a referee more than a gleeful, doting mother, I wouldn't change them for anything in the world. Well, maybe I'd get them to argue a little less.

"It feels like forever since we've both had enough free time to meet up for a coffee," Megan grumbles before taking a sip of her cappuccino.

I glare back at her, especially considering most weeks, she will pop round to mine once or twice for coffee or invite herself for dinner.

"You do realise you're the person I see most often after Mya and Ayana?" I tease, shaking my head as she sticks out her tongue like a silly child.

"You know what I mean. It's not quite the same if I'm round yours having coffee as it is when we go out."

"Yeah, I don't have a menu for you to choose from." Looking over, I see that Megan isn't as amused as I am. But deep down, I know she's right. With how close we are, she's truly part of the family, so when she comes round, half the time I'm still busy doing other things, whether it be housework, responding to emails, or dealing with the girls.

"I know, I know, you're right. So how about I promise to try and do it that once a week we either go for coffee or lunch or even just a walk, and I can give you my undivided attention?"

"Now that's what I like to hear." She holds her cup up in a mock toast and I chuckle at the foam moustache that's now covering her upper lip.

Despite the fact that we speak every day, and I'm pretty sure she has already told me all of this, she spends the next twenty minutes filling me in on the three different guys she's currently dating. I can just about manage dealing with one, so I really don't know how she manages three. When I say as much to her, she explains that until she decides she wants to settle down and actually get into a relationship, she doesn't see why she should limit herself. Well, actually she said she doesn't see why she should only settle for one dick.

On more than one occasion, I've been tempted to get the things she says printed on t-shirts for her, which I know she'll wear with pride.

"So, have you spoken to Ethan since yesterday?"

"No, he tried to call earlier but I was on the phone with some suppliers. Other than our usual 'good morning' messages, there's nothing new to report since I filled you in yesterday," I tell her.

"I'm telling you, the two of you are in a relationship."

"No, we're not," I scoff, though I can feel my cheeks begin to heat because, despite how much I try to downplay her words, it does feel like way.

"Oh, shut up. I've listened to you go on and on about how neither one of you has put a label on things. Which I get. And understand. But let's be real. We both know when you go and see him, that is very likely going to be one of the first topics of conversation the two of you have."

Shaking my head and not wanting to admit she's right, I stand and tell her I'm going to the toilet and ask her to order another coffee for me.

As I make my way towards the back of the cafe, the loud sound of a phone ringing makes me jump. I never understand why people have them ring so loudly, especially in a quiet place.

As I pass the men's toilets, I'm hit by a wave of nostalgia, as the strong scent of men's aftershave hits my nose. It's a unique scent. And I feel like in the back of my mind I've smelt it somewhere before. I'm usually good at placing them, but I know this is a custom scent. Luckily, the lady's toilet is free, and all thoughts of that mystery smell leave my mind like a puff of smoke.

Chapter 14

Willow

Stretching out my neck, I groan in pleasure at the resounding crack of my spine and then I send the final email I've been writing to my PA.

I glance at the time and, as much as I would love nothing more than to make myself a coffee and put my feet up for a bit, my body is in desperate need of a shower.

Having stayed in the shower for much longer than I intended, all thanks to the mini concert I gave, I lather my pruney skin in moisturiser, humming out an encore when my phone goes off with a message.

> Afternoon. How's your day been? I hope you've made sure to find some time for yourself to relax a little xx

Just like it always does when I hear from him, my whole face lights up when I read the message from Ethan. The way he shows his care and concern for me makes me feel all warm and fuzzy inside. I've gone for so many years sitting back and accepting the bare minimum from men, yet now with Ethan, I can see myself needing it. Missing it if it wasn't there. Still smiling, I tuck the towel around me and sit on the edge of the bed to respond to him.

> My day has been good. Well, not good, but productive. I cleaned the house, then got some paperwork done. I wouldn't say I've had time to relax, I've literally just stepped out of the shower. How's your day been?

Not even ten seconds pass when my phone then rings. Looking down, I see it's Ethan FaceTiming me. I can't help but bite my lip as I accept the call.

"Well, this is a pleasant surprise," Ethan purrs.

I hold the phone further away from me than usual so he can get a look at my whole body, loving how his pupils dilate as he takes in the sight of me on my bed in only a towel.

The growl that spills from his lips goes straight to my pussy, causing my breath to catch and my nipples to pebble.

"I have never wished to have the power to teleport as much as I do right now. You look like a goddamn angel, sent straight from heaven, ready for me to ravish."

His words seep deep into the marrow of my bones. My skin suddenly feels too hot, my pulse racing with such yearning for this man. Despite how long it's been since we were physically together, he still has my body under his spell.

Our time apart and the growth I have gone through, makes me want him more than ever.

"Ethan," I moan breathlessly.

Ethan is sitting back against the headboard of his bed, the muscles on his bare chest distracting my focus. He has a look in his eyes that I can remember as clear as if it was yesterday. Gone is the sweet, kind man who reminds me to look after myself and in his place is a Dom. *My* Dom. And despite me having wanted to wait until he's back to do anything sexual, now my body is demanding I let him take control for a while.

Loosening the knot in my towel, I let it fall to the bed, baring my naked body to him. Like I'm in a trance, I watch his Adam's apple bob as he swallows, his eyes solely focused on me.

"Now, are you going to be a good girl for me?" The sound of his low rich voice like dark velvety chocolate.

"Yes, Sir."

"Good. Now, do you have a lamp on your bedside table?"

I nod, looking at the vintage gold and white lamp next to my bed.

"Words, Willow. You know how important they are."

"Yes, Sir, I have a lamp."

"Good, now I want you to place your phone there, making sure I can see you, then I want you to spread your legs wide open for me, making sure I can see everything. But your eyes? Your eyes must stay focused on mine. Do you understand?"

"Yes, Sir, I understand."

I follow his instructions, feeling pleasantly surprised that not a single worry or insecurity fills my mind. Seeing the way

Ethan is looking at me makes me feel powerful, like a goddess. Not a single part of me wants to hide away, nor do I attempt to suck in my stomach or push my arms together to make my boobs stay front and centre.

A warm, proud smile briefly tugs at the corner of his mouth, almost as though he knows the exact thoughts running through my mind. But all too soon that smile is gone as his eyes scan down my body to the wet, glistening arousal of my pussy.

"What I wouldn't give to run my tongue along your thighs and through your pussy, collecting every drop of your sweet nectar before sucking on your ripe and swollen clit."

My eyes begin to roll back at his words, but I remember his instructions and snap them back to focus on his. Once again, I am rewarded with a nod and a satisfied smile that makes my core clench.

"Now, would you like to use a toy or just follow my commands?"

"You. I just want you."

We both pause, as if we're letting the weight of that statement settle between us.

"Alright. Now, I want you to trail your fingers along your throat, imagining it's my tongue. Then I want you to play with your nipples before bringing those fingers all the way down to your pussy. Then I want you to slide two fingers in, and show me just how wet you are."

I do exactly as instructed, making sure not to deviate from the path he told me to follow. I gasp as I pinch my nipples that are already so hard they feel like they could cut through glass, causing my back to arch in writhing pleasure. My eyes locked on Ethan, who stays as still as a marble statue. Luckily, no one else is home, so I don't need to be quiet.

By the time my fingers slide into my pussy, I am a panting mess. I feel and there's a slight burn from the stretch of using two fingers, and I don't miss the way his mouth opens in a silent sigh when I start pumping my fingers in and out, making sure I tease him with the wet sounds of my pussy. I push my fingers as deep as I can, my walls twitching and tightening for more before I pull them out, showing them to Ethan. Both of us focus on at my glistening digits that are dripping with my arousal.

"That's my good, good girl. Now I want you to cover your lips in it, but don't suck on them." I do as I'm told, tasting myself as I hum out my arousal.

His instructions continue, my body vibrating with need. "Put your fingers back inside yourself. Do you think you can add another? I want to see how well your pussy could take my thick cock."

I groan at the thought of him inside me.

"Willow?" His voice snaps my focus back to him.

"Yes, Sir?" I mumble as I push my two fingers inside me and then add a third, my wet walls stretching easily to take it.

"Fuck yourself with them, but you are not allowed to come. Do you understand?"

My eyes struggle to stay focused as pleasure coils through me.

The noise of my arousal fills the room as my breaths become shallow and fast, my orgasm so close I can almost touch it. My breasts heave and my nipples are so hard they're almost painful.

My mouth is dry, my eyes pleading for permission to come.

After what feels like an eternity, my body shaking with need, his voice reverberates.

"Come." His command detonates my pleasure, obliterating my body into a million pieces, as wave after wave hits me. Sweat trickles down my spine, my heart hammers and I have to press my hand to my mouth to stop me from screaming out his name as aftershocks continue to cascade through me.

Breathless, I bask in a satiated daze as I realise that Ethan is still fully dressed, his cock tenting his jeans. Despite my arms feeling like jelly, I push myself up.

"But what about you? You haven't come."

The smile he gives me feels like a warm hug on a cold winter's day. Wrapping around me, making me feel safe and secure.

"This wasn't for me, Willow. This was for you to relax."

"But don't you want to come?" I ask, confused and slightly dazed.

"Of course I do. But I wanted to give you this."

"Thank you, Sir." This time it's me smiling and I don't even care if I look like a goofy fool right now.

"Ten days, Willow."

"What's in ten days?" My mind is still a little slow right now and my brain is scrambling to work out what he's talking about.

"In ten days, I will be seeing you. Touching you. Kissing you. Fucking you. In ten days, I will be able to mark you with my mouth, my hands, my cock, and with my cum."

That is so sexy. I love the way the sound of him talking about marking me makes me feel. It turns me on. Makes me feel special and unbelievably wanted and desired.

I bite down hard on my lip, and despite having just had a truly mind-blowing orgasm, I'm instantly turned on again. Never in my life have I wanted time to fly as much as I do right now. Because ten days feels like an eternity.

Chapter 15

Ethan

The oven is preheated and ready to go, the wine and Prosecco are chilling, and the rest of the food is prepped, marinated, and ready for me to finish later. Making my way out of the bathroom, I run my hands through my hair and then secure my watch, noting that Willow should be here any minute. Excitement courses through me at the thought of seeing her in the flesh.

As I'm giving my bedroom one last look over, I hear the chime of my front door.

Taking the stairs two at a time, I rush downstairs, not even attempting to deny my eagerness to see her after all this time.

The second I open the door, I am momentarily rendered speechless. Willow stands before me in a grey form-fitted maxi dress, with a chunky cardigan that's fallen slightly from one shoulder, revealing her smooth skin that has my mouth watering and my teeth clenching with the urgent need to mark her.

"Hi." The soft breathiness in her tone goes straight to my cock.

"I'm so glad you're here," I tell her honestly. I can't begin to guess how many times I've imagined this moment.

I take her weekend bag and step aside, letting her in. She steps through the door and I close it behind her, immediately cupping her cheek. The second my palm touches her soft skin, a jolt of lightning shoots through me alongside a sense of calm, like I'm finally home.

I slowly lean forward and kiss her, showing Willow everything I can't put into words.

It starts off tender and soft, then evolves into something stronger, more possessive, all-consuming.

I have to force myself to stop. I have a whole evening planned and I'm not going to rush this.

Gently biting down on her pillow-soft bottom lip before releasing it, my blood hums in excitement as I watch her dazed eyes come back into focus.

"There's going to be more than enough time for more of this. It's time to get you relaxed and settled."

I made the decision that what I wanted from this night, this weekend, wasn't just sex. Wasn't just going to be exploring, enjoying and reconnection with Willow's body. No, I wanted more than that. I wanted to spend the time treating her. Offering her body endless pleasure and desire and her mind with relaxation. I get so much satisfaction from taking care of her.

When we first met, Willow opened up about her past relationships, which gave me an insight into the things she has gone through. I knew building trust with her was as important as getting to know her body and, having been away for so long, I want to make sure that trust is there still.

This isn't just about escapism. We both have experienced too much in life to label it as such. No, this is who we are. Both different people, different characters, different people. Yet together, we fit perfectly.

Leaving her bag at the bottom of the stairs, I guide her down the hall into my favourite room of the house: my open plan kitchen with floor-to-ceiling glass walls. The island sits in the middle below the steel beams that are the only thing breaking up the glass panes of the skylight ceiling.

"Take a seat." I pull out one of the bar stools for her before making my way over to the wine fridge.

"Would you like a glass of wine or Prosecco or something else?"

"Prosecco would be lovely. Ethan, this room is amazing. I love the mix of old and new. This is probably a stupid question, but did you design the entire house yourself?"

I open the bottle and pour us each a glass before handing her one.

"I did. I didn't want to take away the character and roots of the place. It was built in the 1800s, but I wanted to be able to bring in modern technologies and make it both ecologically helpful, and of course, wanting it to feel like a family home at the same time. When I bought it, I gutted it to its foundation, then basically started from the ground up. But we did manage to keep several of the original features."

I've always been proud of my home, but watching the way Willow looks around in amazement, it's as though I'm looking at it all again through fresh eyes, and I can't deny the warm and fuzzy feeling that's seeping through me.

Taking the chair next to her, I sit with my legs on either side of hers. Lifting my glass, I look into her eyes as I toast us.

"Here's to reconnecting and to great times ahead."

"And to you, Ethan. To you being back, and all that's to come."

My eyes can't help but focus in on the way she bites her lip, holding back her beautiful smile. Lifting my hand, I gently pull her lip free before leaning forward and speaking just above a whisper. "The only person biting your lip will be me."

Her mouth opens in a slight gasp, but I kiss her quickly yet firmly before pulling back and taking a sip of my drink.

We spend the next couple of minutes talking, with Willow asking how my kids are and how it feels to be back. Just like before, there is no unease; it's never uncomfortable. And it's not just because we have been talking daily since New Year's. From the moment we first met, I have felt comfortable talking with her.

We finish our drinks, then I take her hand and give her a tour of the house. Making sure to stop and touch or kiss her in every single room. I want her body yearning and desperate by the time I finally consume her.

As Willow steps out on the Juliet balcony in my bedroom, I tell her I'll be back in a second and quickly jog downstairs and grab her bag, bringing it upstairs, and place it next to my bed. Then I head into my ensuite and run the bath, making sure to add the bath oils I brought back especially for her.

Making my way to her, I place an arm on either side of her, caging her in against the railing.

"Now the plan for this evening is as follows. There is a bath running for you and I want you to relax and soak whilst I finish making dinner. I want your mind and your body as loose and relaxed as possible. Then once you're done, you can change into whatever you're comfortable in, whether that's a shirt of mine or anything you've packed, and you'll make your way downstairs where I will feed you. After dinner, I will have my dessert. Off of your body. And once I've eaten my fill, that's when I'll be eating you and the real fun begins."

By the time I'm finished talking, her pupils are blown wide, her mouth open slightly and there's a blush creeping up her cheeks. Before my eyes, I watch as she transforms into the submissive I have missed more than I thought possible, before responding breathlessly.

"Yes, Sir."

Chapter 16

Willow

Leaning my head back against the lip of the tub, I watch the swirls of steam rise from my arms as I lean back. Every muscle in my body feels like jelly. I think the last time I felt this relaxed was when I was lying on the beach in paradise. But that was different. Relaxing on holiday and relaxing at home are never comparable. At home, if you are lucky enough to get a moment's peace, something as simple as enjoying a cuppa in silence, or having a rare lie in can feel unbelievably relaxing. Something so mundane can really stand out and be little moments of heaven as you just survive your day.

Yet right here, right now, I feel so calm, so at ease. It's like someone has rolled a full body massage, mini getaway, and the weight of the world off my shoulders all in one. And all I'm doing is sitting in a bath. But that's the thing. It's not just as simple as me sitting here. It's the thought, effort, and care that's gone behind every single thing Ethan has planned.

From the moment I walked in the door, he's demonstrated just why I liked him so much before. He doesn't do things without reason. Every action, every gesture is thought out.

When I first saw him today, my initial reaction was to jump him like a spider monkey. Despite us having FaceTimed several times in the last couple of weeks, I'd forgotten just how drawn I am to him. He has this presence, this aura about him that completely sucks me in.

I don't think I realised just how much I missed Ethan. Never in a million years did I truly think we would get the chance to pick up where we left things. And even though we left things on good terms, I guess a part of me just always thought that he had fun, been a good match, but things just weren't destined to be. Yet now, as I'm in his bathtub, in his gorgeous home, being pampered and treated like a queen, there honestly isn't anywhere else in the world I would rather be.

Finally deciding I've had enough time soaking, as I can feel my fingers beginning to get wrinkly and pruney, I climb out of the tub and wrap the warm soft towel he left out for me around my still-wet body and make my way into his room.

Opening up my bag, I grab my moisturiser and lather my skin. The oil Ethan put in the bath had the most delicious orange citrus scent to it, and with coconut-scented body cream I packed, my skin now smells like a tropical cocktail.

As I didn't know what he had planned for us for the weekend, I packed a mix of everything. Pulling out the different garments, I negate the dresses, and the jeans and t-shirt combo I packed. Instead, I grab the silk and lace teddy with matching robe. As my fingers trail along the buttery soft material, I know Ethan will be happy with my choice.

With the sun beginning to set, the room is awash with warm light, and I make my way over to the window to close the shutters so I have complete privacy to get changed. Ethan's bedroom takes up the whole top floor, with the Juliet balcony and ensuite overlooking his back garden, and large bay-style windows looking out to the street. So, I only need to close these ones.

Just as I'm shutting them, I look down at the parked cars lining the road and notice how my car is the oldest one parked there. And what's crazy is that is not even that old. My trusted Nissan Qashqai stands out like a sore thumb against the sleek saloons, convertibles, and 4x4s parked alongside.

I always knew Ethan was financially comfortable. He works hard and has built up his company from a small one-man show to being the large success it is now. But now seeing his home, the area he lives in, all makes me respect just how understated about his wealth he is.

I've never been someone that into flashy things, designer clothes, or that belief that money buys you class and God knows what. And knowing that Ethan has reached the levels he has through hard work, with not an ounce of nepotism, only makes me like him more.

Brushing those thoughts aside, I close the shutters and get changed.

Securing myself in the teddy, I walk over to the large mirror on the wall, looking at my reflection and see my eyes are so bright they are practically sparkling. The contrast between my skin and the tangerine hue of the teddy couldn't look any better. And as I adorn the matching vintage-style robe, I feel like I'm one of the old Hollywood actresses. I take the clip out of my hair and fluff my coils until they settle in place.

Taking one last look in the mirror, I smile as unbridled excitement rushes through me.

As I make my way down the stairs, I'm hit with the most delicious smells coming from the kitchen and my tummy begins to rumble.

There is soft jazz music playing from speakers somewhere, and it perfectly accompanies the sounds of the sizzling food and the soft clatter of Ethan cooking. Leaning against the doorjamb, I watch on.

He must sense my stare as he slowly turns, scanning me from head to toe, and when his eyes finally find mine, he speaks.

"Jesus fucking Christ, you look incredible." The deep timbre of his voice vibrating across the room.

Chapter 17

Willow

Dinner was phenomenal. I also like the fact that he set it up so we are sat on the large island next to one another. And whenever Ethan wasn't using his hands to eat or drink, he would be rubbing along my leg with soft sensual touches. But even that didn't manage to distract me from the amazing food he cooked. Ethan made a rack of lamb with parsley and pine nut crust that was absolutely to die for. I don't think I've ever had anyone, let alone a man, cook a meal like this for me. We also shared a bottle of 2007 Catena Zapata Malbec that a former client sent him as a thank you.

I've never been a wine snob, but this has to be one of the best I've ever tried.

Our conversation turns to my trip and how I spent New Year.

"Well, for me, I think that was the best New Year's I've had in a long time."

I look up and see a depth of honesty in his gaze that takes my breath away. Licking my lips, I turn slightly to face him better.

"And why is that, Ethan?"

Slowly, he places the glass of wine that was in my hand down onto the counter, while the other softly trails up my arm and rests around my throat. The action brings excited goosebumps to my skin as my eyelids close slightly and my heart begins beating like a wild animal.

"Because as I watched that video of you, it felt like I found a missing puzzle piece. I came to the conclusion that my life, which I thought was ordered and complete was, in fact, dull and subdued. It was missing light, missing excitement, missing someone. And that someone is you. I'd let work get in the way previously, but when I saw you in that video, I knew it was a sign for me to grab what I wanted, what I needed, and make it mine. Make you mine."

I know he can feel the lightning-fast beat of my pulse under his fingers as my heart reacts to those beautiful words. I don't know if it's age or just the things both of us have been through in our lives, but we don't need to discuss what this is between us. We both know. We can both feel it. It's too strong, too palpable to deny.

I don't have the words to express how much I want this. Want him. So instead, I let my body lean into his hand holding my throat, showing him my submission, my trust. I know he can see me not only giving in and agreeing to this evening but also to more. To us. To whatever the future holds.

· · ·

I try to help tidy away after dinner, but Ethan insists I sit and relax. That's when I remember what he had said about dessert and my nipples harden and my clit begins to tingle.

And as my eyes glance up, I find him watching me. With the slight lift to the corner of his mouth, it's as if he can read my thoughts.

Despite being six foot four with a large muscular build, Ethan has grace in the way he moves. An assuredness. There's no hesitation, no wasting energy on something unnecessary. Everything he does has a purpose.

Watching, he takes out a tray from the cupboard then walks to the fridge where he takes out some strawberries and whipped cream. Shivers of feverish anticipation ricochet through my body as he goes to a warming drawer next to the oven and takes out a bowl of melted chocolate and honey. Lust and hungry eagerness thrum through me. And it's not due to the food, it's because I can't wait to see what he is going to do with it all.

"Now, Willow, I want you to grab a bottle of champagne from the cooler and make your way upstairs to my bedroom. I would like you to take off your robe, but leave that teddy on as you look fucking exquisite in it. Then kneel next to the bed and wait for me to give you your next instructions." His tone is firm but not cold.

My skin is burning and as I look over, I catch his cock tenting his trousers. The veins in his forearms stand out as he holds the tray with the strawberries, cream, honey, and chocolate. When I reach his face, I watch as he raises a brow and runs his tongue along the edge of his teeth. Seeing just how much he wants me, the effort he has gone to, and the excitement of him taking ownership of my body once again, has me so turned on I can't help the light squeal that bursts from my lips as I excitedly make my way upstairs, and hear the slow, steady footsteps of Ethan at my heels.

Chapter 18

Ethan

Taking a deep breath, I make sure to calm myself and my desire. I have to make sure everything is right for her. I can't let myself be overcome and controlled by how much I want to sink my cock so deep into her pussy.

I've always known Willow deserves the best. She deserves to let go and just feel. It's so important to me that I give her a night she won't forget.

I make my way to my room with the tray in hand and proudly smile as I see that she has followed my instructions.

"That's a good girl. Now get on the bed and stretch open your arms and legs. I want to have complete access to all of you," I demand.

Placing the tray onto the coffee table in the corner, I grab the chocolate, honey, and whipped cream and place it on the bedside table where she left the bottle of champagne.

I make quick work of opening the bottle and look over to

see that I have her undivided attention. I have to bite the inside of my cheek to suppress a moan as Willow presses her thighs together, seemingly unaware she's even doing it. It takes everything in me not to trace my fingers along her thighs and find what I know to be nirvana.

As if she can read my thoughts, she lets her thighs fall open, letting me see a small damp spot on her teddy that has obviously got caught between her thighs and soaked with her arousal.

This time I can't suppress the rumbling growl that vibrates through my chest, knowing she's already so wet for me.

Grabbing first the honey, I dip my finger in, then walk over to the bed, standing over her, and drip the sweet sticky nectar along her shin before repeating the motion on the other side. Her gasp is loud and seems to even take her by surprise. I watch as her body tenses as she awaits what I do next.

Taking the melted chocolate, I again dip my finger in, the sweet coco smell permeating the room. This time I trail my finger from her wrist, up to her shoulder, watching the goose-bumps that appear in the wake of where I've left a trail of chocolaty goodness.

"Oh... oh," Willow moans.

Making sure my finger is coated, I write the word MINE across her chest. Leaning down, I pull the thin lace cups her breasts are encased in with my teeth, finding her nipples piqued into tight points. My cock is so hard it's straining against my briefs and I can feel my precum leaking. I know if

I looked, the head would be an angry purple colour with how turned on I am right now.

I cover them in the melted chocolate, noticing how her nipples are the same colour, blending together seamlessly. Looking down at her, I have never been more desperate to devour anything as much as I want to feast on Willow.

Next, I take the whipped cream and strawberries and place them between her legs resting on the bed. I take my time unbuttoning my shirt and discarding my jeans, leaving me in only my boxer briefs. Making her wait. Wanting and needing her to be as desperate as I can get her.

"Please, Ethan. Please. Please. Please touch me, please kiss me. I need you. *Please*." Willow pleads desperately.

"Aw, my needy, needy girl. Do you want my hands? Do you want to feel my fingers pinching your nipples or rubbing your clit? Or is it my mouth you want on your body? Licking and tasting every inch of you? Or is my girl just desperate for my cock? Wanting to be filled and stretched as I sink into your hot wet pussy?"

My engorged head that's poking out the top of my briefs is dripping with precum. I hiss as the cool air hits it, but make no move to adjust myself, needing to keep my focus on Willow, but also because I want her to see how desperate I am for her.

I luxuriate in the sight of her spread before me. Her chest rises and falls faster and faster with each passing second. Her hands claw at the sheets in desperation. And hearing her whimper as her body continues writhing in front of me is a sound I would gladly listen to every day. Getting on the bed, I make myself comfortable between her legs. Given the width of my shoulders, Willow opens her legs up wider for me. Seeing her pussy spread wide open for me has my mouth watering. It takes everything within me to stay focused and controlled, not giving into the temptation of teasing my tongue along her entrance or sinking my throbbing cock deep inside her.

"Never have I seen a sight as truly stunning as this. Now remember what I said. It's time for me to have my dessert, and once I'm done, then it'll be time for yours."

"Yes, Sir, I remember." Her breathy submission only makes my cock leak more.

I lower my head, breathing in the scent of her arousal mixing with the food I've covered her in. It's taking every ounce of effort not to bury my face in her pussy. I drag my tongue up first one leg, then the other. Her thighs tense as she shivers. Once I've cleared away all the honey, I sit back onto my knees, grab a strawberry, and bite into the sweet, juicy fruit. Then, grabbing another, I look at Willow with a devilish smile.

"Now, this one I want you to hold between your teeth, but you're not allowed to bite it. I will be needing it soon. And I mean it. I don't want you biting it. You've got to be a good girl for me and do exactly as I say."

Taking it in my mouth, I push it between her open, waiting lips. As she holds it there, my tongue trails along her pillow-soft lips, licking up the droplets of juice.

I slowly and teasingly lick up the chocolate, letting my

tongue spell out the word that means so much but feels so right.

I turn my attention to her nipples, sucking them into my mouth before releasing them with a light pop.

"Oh.. mmh, yes," Willow moans barely audibly around the strawberry. Her muscles tense and tighten as she struggles to stay still, a moan slipping out around the strawberry she's still holding in her mouth.

Licking all the chocolate off her chest and nipples, I position myself between her legs and lift them.

"Look at you. Your pussy is dripping for me. My dirty, dirty girl,"

My face right in front of her pussy, her legs resting on my shoulders.

Grabbing the whipped cream that's still cold, I completely cover her pussy in it, making sure not an inch is left uncovered. First, she screams as the cold cream touches her then the sounds of her murmured begging washes over me like a symphony in my ears.

"You're my desperate girl, aren't you?" I tease, then, grabbing a berry, I scoop up the cream that's right by her hole and eat it all. The flavour of the sweet berry, mixed with the velvety cream and the sweet tangy taste of her juices, burst in my mouth, making me moan in satisfaction.

Leaning down, I move my mouth to her pussy and eat it like a man on death row devouring his last meal. Her thighs lock around my head as she pants and writhes in pleasure. Knowing that she's getting closer, I ease up and lick away the last remnants of cream. Then I lean up and take the one from her mouth, running my tongue along her lips, letting her get a taste of just how delicious she is. My ultimate dessert.

With the berry in my mouth, I press it to her clit and along her folds and to her pussy, the juices of the fruit now filling my mouth.

Using my tongue, I push the strawberry against her clit and begin sucking hard. Her moans explode and reverberate around my room.

Her back arches and bows off the bed, her cries so loud I know that if anyone else was in the house, they'd hear. I graze down on the berry and her clit simultaneously. Willow comes in a flood of ecstasy, covering most of my face with her arousal so it dripping down my beard and covers the bed.

My cock throbs to the point of pain, and while she recovers, I discard my boxers.

Kneeling between her spread thighs, I smear the precum over the head of my cock and down my shaft, my balls pulling with need as I stare down at her swollen pussy.

"Willow, do you remember your safe word?"

Chapter 19

Willow

My mind is struggling to form a coherent thought. Every inch of my skin feels electrified as I come down from the wave of orgasmic aftershocks.

Ethan's voice seems like it's somehow in the distance, yet I know he's right there, just in front of me.

Shaking my head slightly to gain some semblance of clarity, I attempt to blink away the fog that's engulfing every pore on my body.

This time, I hear Ethan's voice more clearly.

"Willow, do you remember your safe word?"

"Yes, Sir," I answer breathlessly.

Ethan is watching me with an intensity so all-consuming that my mind, body, and soul feel as if they are about to erupt.

The orange and red glow from the setting sun set beams off his body, shining a spotlight on the intricate tattoos along his upper arms and chest.

His cock stands hard and erect and my mouth waters as my eyes follow the throbbing vein that runs from base to crown. The mushroom head, leaking precum, is so engorged it's taken on a reddish-purple hue, while his large hand slowly strokes up and down his length, teasing me because I'm desperate to touch him.

Laying over me, he rests his hand around my throat and kisses me with such passion that I lose myself to the moment.

My hands roam over his chest and up his shoulders until I bury my fingers in his hair. He lets me take control for a while, moving his head where I want him while my mouth explores him, but I know it won't last long.

The sting of him taking my bottom lip between his teeth and gently nips tells me my Dom is back. He pins my hands above my head with one hand, and with the other, lines himself up by my entrance. I'm so desperate for him to fill me, to sink deep inside my pussy that's tingling with desperate need that I lift my hips, bucking up, trying to get him inside me.

Looking down at me with eyes that seem to pierce deep into my soul, Ethan holds himself completely still.

"You've been a very good girl, Willow. You know your safe word. It's time I truly made you mine. And I'm going to that right fucking now."

The primitativness of his words has me burning with want and desire.

Without missing a beat, he pushes the head of his cock inside me; the stretch making me cry out, not sure if I need him to wait while I get used to him or if I need him to fill me completely. Before I can decide, he slams himself into the hilt, taking my breath away.

His thick cock edges my G-spot as he begins fucking me, any pain instantly forgotten as pleasure pulses through me with every thrust.

Every buck of his hips is controlled, dominating, possessive, raw, and my body cries out for more. My pussy clamps down on his cock, pulling him deeper, milking his pleasure from him as hard as he demands mine.

Ethan shifts and sits back on his haunches, pulling me with him until I'm sat on his lap, his cock so deep I can barely breathe.

He wraps a thick strong arm around my back, his other hand once again around my throat, not fully choking but just tight enough to partially restrict my airflow. He has complete control over me and my body, and I absolutely love it. He takes my mouth in a bruising kiss, swallowing down every moan as he fucks me.

I feel truly consumed by this man. His punishing rhythm never stutters and as the grip of his fingers tightens, taking more of my breath away, my walls tighten around his cock as my orgasm builds.

A tidal wave hits me as my body bursts with pleasure and I'm almost blindsided as I come. Ethan doesn't let up, fucking me through my orgasm and straight into another. My body turns to jelly as my release drips from me, covering his cock and balls.

"I.. want... two... more... out... of... you... before... I... come. Do... you... understand?" he demands with a strained voice. I shake my head as I can't take anymore. I don't think my body can handle it. I don't even have strength to speak. Ethan flips me over, positioning me on my hands and knees like I weigh nothing. He wastes no time thrusting back inside me, groaning loudly as if my pussy is his favourite place to be.

Pulling my hair, he fucks me from behind as I bury my face in the sheets, unable to hold myself up. He picks up his pace, his thrusts getting shorter and faster, hitting my G-spot again and again until I can't focus on anything else but the pleasure he's giving me.

I scream as my next orgasm hits me and he bites down on the soft pocket of flesh by my shoulder. Black dots cloud my vision as I get lightheaded from coming again so soon after the last one.

My body begins to shake as Ethan's moans grow louder.

As his fingers connect with my clit, I'm on the precipice of using my safe word. I can't take another. I've got nothing left. But I don't. His cock swells inside me and despite the foggy haze, it pushes me to the edge again, my core tightens. He pinches my clit, tears springing from my eyes as painful pleasure rushes me. The moan he releases is the most primal sound I've ever heard, giving me goosebumps as the sensation of his cum spilling inside me almost makes me orgasm again.

His hips slow as he pumps the last drops of his release inside me before bringing us both to the bed, never letting me go.

Finally, after several minutes or seconds, I have no idea, his cock slips out of me as does our combined cum that trickles down my ass and puddles beneath me. Slowly, we both manage to get our breath back. I can feel his smile as he gently kisses my back, causing me to shiver with how sensitive I still am.

"You did very well, Willow. I'm so proud of you. That's my good girl," Ethan says before kissing my forehead, making me feel cherished.

"We're going to shower, then I'm going to give you a massage. Do you think you can stand, or would you like me to carry you?"

"No, I can walk. Just give me a minute."

The smile Ethan gives me warms me to my core. I don't even try to hide the blatant way I check out his arse as he walks to the ensuite while I think to myself, *how did I get so lucky?*

Chapter 20

Willow

I somehow manage to muster the strength to get up and join Ethan in the shower. He covers my body in a similar citrus shower gel, making sure not to miss an inch of skin. The steam from the bathroom and the fact that my bones still feel like jelly, make me feel like I'm floating on a cloud.

Once we're showered and dry, Ethan lays me on the bed and begins massaging me. And as he loosens and releases each knot, I find myself melting further into the mattress.

I'm not sure how long he massages me for, but when I'm on my back, I tenderly stroke his cheek.

"I was wondering earlier; how did I get so lucky?"

Ethan leans into my touch. The gesture is so simple, yet at the same time, it's one of the most vulnerable moments we've had.

"I could easily say the same about you, Willow. I know we've hinted and talked in roundabout ways about us reconnecting, and I knew even before you turned up this evening that I don't just want one night. One weekend. I want more. I know it's not going to be easy or straightforward, but I can honestly say that there isn't a thing you could say that would make me doubt that I want this."

I'm at a loss for what to say. Not because I'm conflicted or don't feel the same—because I do. Yes, I feel the same. Yes, I want this. Yes, I also think this is worth it.

Wrapping my arms and legs around him, unable to get enough, it's as if I want to fuse our bodies as one. We continue to kiss and embrace, and for the second time this evening, Ethan fucks me with everything he has. Yet this time it isn't hard and fast. It's slow, sensual, yet still controlled. It's not wild, fast fucking. His strokes are slow and deep yet still hard. His fingers are firm and determined as they caress my breasts and pinch my nipples. Or the way his thumb firmly presses against my clit. He's still dominating my body. Showing that even within this dynamic, it doesn't always have to be hard, brutal, or aggressive. He's showing that even slow and control he still has complete power over my body. Over my mind. Just like the words he wrote on my chest earlier with the melted chocolate, he is mine. Just as I am his. And as we come together, he swallows my moans as he kisses me.

I'm momentarily lost in a cloud of confusion as I drift from deep sleep to consciousness. I let out a moan, and it takes me a second to realise that the pleasure I was having in my dream was, in fact, not a dream. It's real and happening right now.

Ethan's tongue licks along my folds and then circles my clit. I don't know how long he has been eating my pussy, but in no time, I feel myself building up to an orgasm so fast I'm rendered speechless. Only once I manage to catch my breath and come to my senses, do I try to move, planning on returning the favour. But Ethan gently pushes me back down, and his light chuckle vibrates deep from his chest.

"If I let you start now, we will never get out of bed. And I need to feed you. Especially as we missed breakfast."

Looking over at the clock on his bedside table, I see it's already 10:40 a.m. and my eyes widen in surprise as I don't remember the last time I slept in this long.

"I'm going to quickly jump in the shower, then I'm taking you out for breakfast. There is a little place not far from here that serves the best brunch."

Chapter 21

Dominic

I barely acknowledge the waitress as she puts my coffee down in front of me. She's been overly attentive since the moment I walked in. Maybe it's because I have my baseball cap pulled down low and she is trying to see if she can recognise me. Or perhaps she thinks my intense stare is for her.

Who the fuck knows?

She continues to linger, although doesn't say anything. I shift myself so I can look past her, and it's only then that she gets the hint.

Finally.

My eyes now fall upon the woman who has consumed my every thought for almost a year. The woman I didn't realise how damn special she would prove to be.

I know I fucked up back then. But this time? This time I won't let Willow slip through my fingers.

I'll do whatever it takes.

Heady Desires

Chapter 1

Willow

"Oh, shit." I jump back just in time to avoid the splatter from the jar of pesto that somehow slipped off the shelf and smashed into tiny pieces around me. Luckily, a member of staff is already making their way over with a mop.

"I'm sorry. I have no idea how that happened. Let me help you clean that up." I go to crouch next to her, but she puts out a hand, stopping me.

"No, no, it's fine. And I know it wasn't your fault. I saw it happened, so you won't be charged."

"Thanks. That was weird. It's like a ghost or something knocked it off." I laugh, but it's slightly hollow and I can't help but notice as goosebumps that skate across my arms.

She laughs. "Nah, I doubt it's a ghost. More likely someone didn't put it back on the shelf properly. It only takes a nudge or a knock to make it fall."

I scan my trousers, checking that there is no sauce on

them, then carefully steer my trolley away, making sure to avoid any broken glass.

Despite that silly accident, I don't care what anyone says, there is something calming and almost relaxing about doing the food shop without your kids. Not being bombarded with endless requests of *"Mummy, can I have this?"*

Doing it alone means I can stick to my list, with my headphones in, listening to my podcast in peace. I might even treat myself to a coffee at the drive-through next door.

Luckily, the rest of my food shop is uneventful. And I even remember to pick up a card and present for the girl's school friend who's invited them to her birthday party this weekend. Now, all in all, I'd say that was quite a successful trip.

Oh fuck. Why did I say that?

The second I step out of the shop, I'm pelted with heavy rain. I have to play dodgems with my shopping trolley as I run to my car while the heavens decide to open, soaking me completely by the time I have the bags in the boot.

Once I'm safely inside the car, I don't even need to look in the mirror to know that I look like a drowned rat.

The drive back home takes longer as everyone struggles with the downpour. Typical bloody British summer. The wind felt so cold I even had to turn the heating on in the damn car.

Why is it that every time I think things are going smoothly, am I quickly put back in my place and reminded that nothing, and I mean nothing, can go without a hitch? There is always bloody something.

Pulling up at my house, my eyes scan the distance between my car and the front door, then up at the incessant downpour.

Nope, there's no way for me to get this shopping in without getting soaked again.

With a huff, I turn off the ignition and grab my handbag before managing to get all my bags loaded into both arms. *Who needs the gym when you've got daily housework and powerlifting bags through heavy rain?* Luckily, I manage to get inside without slipping or falling over.

Once all the food is packed away, I check the time and thank fuck that there's still enough time for me to have a quick bath before the school run. Even the thought of soaking in the hot water gives me a full-body shiver.

Feeling the need to give myself even just the smallest ounce of self care, I add not just oil, but also a bath bomb to the water. Then I waste no time stripping out of my wet clothes and throwing them into the laundry basket before eagerly getting into the steaming water.

I've always enjoyed super-hot baths, and this one is pretty much as hot as my skin can handle.

I go to reach over and grab my shower cap but remember that my hair is dripping wet already. I know I won't have time to properly wash and deep condition it, so a quick co-wash will just have to do for now.

As my body finally begins to warm up and my arms and

legs luxuriate in the heat of the water, I finally breathe out a contented sigh.

Despite attempting to relax, my mind can't help running through the list of things I need to do this week. Mentally, I tick through the orders I've sent out and the ones I still need to do. I have two Zoom meetings, parents' evening for both girls, which luckily I get to do in one sitting, with them having the same teacher.

I also need to give Megan a call and have a catch up. She's been so busy with work I feel like I haven't seen her in ages. And then my mind drifts onto the man who has seemingly burrowed his way into my little bubble and into my dreams.

Ethan.

Chapter 2

Willow

Morning baby. How did you sleep? And I
know you said you've got a busy day today,
but remember to take a break for yourself.
Give me a call whenever you're free xx

Waking up to messages like this every morning always brings the biggest smile to my face. There is no better feeling than waking up and knowing you're on someone's mind.

It still amazes me that my life has settled into this blissful new norm. My business, though at times tiring and too busy, continues to thrive. My girls keep my heart full and my to-do list busy. And now I also have Ethan. Several months ago, I never could have imagined he would have come back into my life, and now we're in a relationship. Who would have thought posting that video on New Year's Eve would have been the beginning of us reconnecting?

It still amuses me that we've kind of done things in reverse. When we first met last year, it was in a casual Dom/sub dynamic, with no strings attached. Then, when he got offered the job in Spain, it seemed like it was fate's way of telling us things had run their course.

However, now I couldn't imagine being without him.

During that weekend I spent with Ethan at his house three months ago, we decided to give us a real shot. Explore if our connection would work beyond just a casual situation. And so far, things have only got better.

I mean, it's still difficult due to distance. It's not like we can just pop over for a quick coffee or go for a walk. And on top of the distance, we both have kids and busy, demanding jobs. However, we do put in the effort and try to meet up every other week.

Obviously, with things still being new, I haven't introduced him to the girls yet. It's not that I'm ashamed or even apprehensive. I think it's more to do with the fact that I have never introduced them to anyone I've dated before, obviously, as this is the first time since they were born that I've even been on the dating scene. I always said I wouldn't do that until things became more serious and Ethan has respected that.

Maybe if we lived closer it may have sped things up, but until now, it felt too soon for them all to meet. However, when I was on the phone to him last week, I blurted out that I wanted to introduce him to the girls. He asked several times if

I was sure. I think the old me would have overthought it, doubted myself, and berated myself for the cock-brained idea, but this isn't a fling or a bit of fun. I don't want to hide the reason for my smile and happiness from the girls.

Now, even though we don't get to see each other all the time, we make sure to call each other several times a day. Ethan always makes the effort to let me know he is thinking about me. That I am on his mind. There are no games, no second guessing. He has always made it clear how he feels. And speak of the devil. My phone rings, breaking me from my thoughts.

"Were your ears burning, or have you become telepathic? Because I was just thinking about you."

"Oh, really now? And what were you thinking about, baby?" Ethan asks.

It doesn't matter how many times he calls me that, it still makes my tummy flutter every time.

"I was just thinking about how you always manage to make me feel special, remembered and important.".

"That's because you are, Willow. And I will continue to every single day. So tell me, how's your day been?"

"It's been alright. Pretty much non-stop phone calls to suppliers, a Zoom meeting with the warehouse manager, and I've lost count the amount of emails I've replied to."

"And have you been a good girl and remembered what I said? And taken breaks for yourself?" I ask.

"Yes, I have. I made myself a nice lunch and even sat in the garden as I enjoyed my coffee. I didn't even take my phone with me. Just sat in the sun and relaxed."

"That's what I like to hear. You need to make sure you keep it up. Can't have you working yourself too hard. You need to make sure you keep a good balance." I mean it. it really is something she needs to keep working on.

"I am. It still feels weird as I have to actively stop myself from not doing something from the never-ending list of things to do, but I am getting better at just taking time for breathers throughout the day. I've also noticed I'm starting to sleep better as well. So that's probably the biggest improvement."

"That's exactly why you need to keep it up. See, you're already benefitting from it. And like I said, after a while, you'll get used to it and it'll become second nature. Alright now, I need to go but I'll give you a call when I finish before I head to the gym. Oh, and Willow, look out for a little delivery that'll be arriving soon. It's nothing big but will help with some more relaxing later. Speak to you later, baby."

"Aw Ethan, you shouldn't have. You're always spoiling me." I can hear the smile in her voice.

"That's because you deserve it. No complaining allowed. Besides, I know you'll enjoy this one."

"Thank you. Speak to you later, babe."

I don't remember the last time I felt so cherished, protected, or cared for. Ethan doesn't need to be standing in front of me to care of me. For the first time, there is someone watching out for me. He has me and my wellbeing at the centre of his focus, and I seriously underestimated just how special that makes me feel.

Chapter 3

Willow

Feeling warm, relaxed, and rejuvenated, I climb out of the bath, wrapping my still-dripping body in a towel before I head to my bedroom to change into some warm clothes.

Considering it's early summer, it's utterly laughable that I'm in warm comfy joggers and a crew sweatshirt.

Wrapping my hair in a bun, I head downstairs and heat myself a bowl of last night's pasta. Grabbing a glass of water, I take a seat at the dining table and just as I'm about to take my first bite, the doorbell rings. I sigh in frustration at the interruption.

Opening the door, a delivery man stands, holding a heavy-looking box.

"Delivery for a Willow Anderson."

"Uh, okay, thank you." The confusion is evident in my voice.

I sign for it and am slightly taken aback by the weight of the box.

I'm a little confused as I haven't ordered anything, but I can't help the buzz of excitement running through me.

Carrying it through to the kitchen, I take a knife from the drawer. Placing it on the table, I make quick work of slicing through the tape.

Opening it up, I find it's full of books. A smile spreads across my face as I realise someone has treated me to books from my Amazon Wishlist. I do a little happy dance before taking the books out gently, reading through the titles, not even remembering putting some of them on the list.

Taking a seat, I scan the blurb on the back of each one and notice a bit of a theme. Yes, most of them are taboo, spicy, or just downright one-handed reads, but these are basically all Dom/sub books. With a couple having obvious *Daddy* references in them.

Looking back into the box, I check for the note, but it's empty.

How odd.

But then saying that, I know they are most likely from Ethan, wanting to give me a nice surprise. Once again, I'm touched by how sweet and often he does things for me. So many kind and unexpected gestures. Whether it's bouquets of flowers or exotic plants being delivered or opening up my Kindle and seeing new books there. Just the other week, it was a case of my favourite wine. And not only does he spoil me, but he's also ordered things for me to enjoy with the girls. From board games to fancy craft kits to a Polaroid camera with extra film and a beautifully handcrafted vintage-style photo album we will be able to fill.

Remembering my bowl of pasta, I quickly wolf it down before grabbing my new books and adding them to my ever-growing bookcase as I try to work out which one I should pick to start reading tonight. *Oh boy, this is going to be a hard choice.* I wonder if maybe I can get a little suggestive help from a special someone.

I make myself a coffee before grabbing my phone to call Ethan and thank him for the lovely surprise.

As I bring up his number, I can't help biting my lip as I think of ways I can show him just how thankful and appreciative I am, and every idea is hot and delicious. And not just for him.

Chapter 4

Willow

My knee bounces slightly with excitement as I call Ethan.

"Mmm, and how is my favourite woman doing?" he purrs through the phone.

"I'm not too bad. Are you busy?"

"Not right this second, but I do have a meeting I need to leave for in about fifteen minutes. Oh, and there is something I actually was going to call you about."

"Do go on." My interest is now very much piqued.

"Well, as you know, I'm excited to see you in a couple of days. I've even ordered a few new toys for us to enjoy. It may even include a few things that you might have mentioned that you haven't tried before."

I suppress a groan before listening to him continue. "But besides all the exciting fun I know we will be having, I wanted to just check if you're still okay with the plans for Sunday?"

Ethan is coming over on Saturday and the girls will be

staying the night with my parents. Then on Sunday, they'll drop them back, and to save them driving all the way, I thought it best to meet halfway, which is only about forty-five minutes from my house. There's a family pub that does amazing Sunday roasts, and the plan was for me to introduce Ethan to the girls.

Ethan was the one who suggested we meet somewhere neutral, as he didn't want the girls feeling like he was imposing on their home. To be honest, I hadn't even thought about that and just proves, once again, how considerate and caring he is.

"Yes, Ethan. I'm more than okay with the plans for Sunday. And do you want to hear something funny?"

"Always."

"Well, you know how I told you I'd brought it up during dinner, as I wanted to make sure they were fully listening and giving me their attention?"

"Yes, I remember you saying you didn't want them on their devices in case you couldn't differentiate whether their response was to the games they were playing or to what you were saying," he says with a chuckle.

"Yeah, well, obviously I was keen to have them be serious for a moment and even though I wasn't anxious about talking about it, I was dubious of how they would respond, given it's never something I have brought up before."

"Okay." I can hear the slight hesitation as he elongates the word, probably wondering where I'm going with this.

"Well, when I did finally tell them that I've been seeing someone and I felt it was time for the three of you to meet, even I was surprised at just how excited the girls were. They've obviously heard me talk about you and were always happy and excited when they got your gifts, but I'd never clarified *who* you are to me. So, it turns out that they realised I had a boyfriend quite some time ago. They went on to tease me, saying they started suspecting something when I'd get a big smile on my face when my phone beeped with a message."

His laugh warms me and sets off my own.

"I guess I didn't hide things as well as I thought I had."

"No, I guess you didn't. And I'm guessing they weren't angry that you hadn't mentioned anything yet?"

"Oh, on the contrary. Turns out they'd made two little bets amongst themselves. The first being, who could get me to admit it first, with the loser having to do the winner's chores for a week. So many of their random questions and conversations the last couple of weeks now make a hell of a lot more sense."

"Now, that is very clever of them. And I love what they chose as their winnings. So, what was the other bet?"

I groan in embarrassment and I'm suddenly glad that I'm not FaceTiming him as I know for a fact, despite my complexion, my cheeks are burning bright red right now.

"So again, I guess my subtlety wasn't as good as I had imagined. Apparently, I bring up your name more times than I realised. They were in hysterics when they told me their second bet was to see how many times I would bring up your name in one day. Ayana bet it would be between five and ten, and Mya bet more than ten times."

My voice is muffled as I bury my head into the pillow in

embarrassment. Yet, even despite how utterly embarrassing it is that the girls have done this, hearing his sexy and happy laugh manages to ease the sting slightly.

"And who guessed correctly?" The playful excitement in his voice is palpable.

"Ayana," she laughs.

"Is it bad that part of me was really hoping that Mya would win this one?" This time it's me that barks with laughter.

"Oh, don't you worry. By the mischievous looks on their faces, I'm sure they have more bets like this lined up in the future. Anyway, I know you said you have to leave for a meeting, so I'll leave you in peace, but before you go—"

My phone beeps with another incoming call. Looking down, I see it's the girl's school.

"Shit."

"What's wrong? Is everything okay?" The worry in his voice melts my insides.

"It's the school calling. I've got to take this. But I just wanted to quickly say thank you for the books. I'll speak to you later. Bye, babe."

Chapter 5

Ethan

Work felt like a complete drag today. I know everyone has up and down days, but what the hell? First, it was a missing delivery, then the fire alarm accidentally going off in the office. The meeting I had earlier was a shit-show as the translator hadn't shown and with no one in the office being able to speak Portuguese and Google translate being as reliable and helpful as a paper umbrella in a rainstorm, we needed to reschedule. Which really isn't ideal, given the time constraints and that the client now wants to go with a whole list of different materials that hadn't been agreed in the original contract.

Luckily, I was able to let off some steam and frustration at the gym. My friends always laugh at me and call me Mr Predictable, simply because I like routine and structure. Guess that's why I love my job and have my days mapped out. The only days that differ are when I've got my kids. On those days, I make sure I'm working from home so I can pick them up from school. If they have a club, event, or appointment, I take them there, then we all head back home. While I make dinner, they either do homework or recently they've both enjoyed helping me cook. And I didn't realise just how special those moments have become.

Obviously, I wish I could see them every day, but the system their mother and I have in place works well for everyone.

The gym is only a fifteen-minute drive from my house, and with how hard I pushed myself, my body is in desperate need of fuel right now. For once, there's no traffic and I suppress the groan as I grab my gym bag from the boot of the car, make my way into the house, and head straight to the fridge to get a start on dinner.

With the leftover rice from yesterday, I decided to make a stir-fry as it's easy and quick.

Ten minutes later, with dinner ready, I grab a bottle of water from the fridge and take a seat on one of the bar stools by the kitchen island, scarfing down my food. Finally with my stomach full, I call Lucas.

"Hey, Dad."

"Hiya, Lucas. How's your day been?"

"Eh, alright. We've got a new physics teacher, and she's insane. Imagine if someone made a hybrid of Margaret Thatcher meets Ursula, the sea witch. That's her."

I can't stop laughing at his analogy.

"Plus, she smells like burnt sesame seeds."

"What?" I splutter, still laughing.

"I'm telling you, Dad, it's like a nightmare mixed with

torture. Plus, Jason, who's in my class, sits at the front and said her breath smells like cat food. Like doesn't she brush her teeth?"

I can't stop laughing as I imagine his face pulling in utter disgust, likely followed by a shudder.

"Lucas, stop. Please stop."

"Dad, you know physics has been one of the subjects I've struggled with. How am I expected to learn and concentrate now?"

Managing to get myself back under control, I take a quick sip of water.

"Lucas, listen, you're doing well. Unless your work has suddenly taken a plunge since your last report, you're gonna be fine, kid. And if you really feel worried, let me know and we can arrange some tutor sessions."

"Could I pick the tutor this time? And can I pick someone hot?" the cheeky little shit responds.

"Watch it, kid."

"I know, Dad. I'm just joking. And no, I won't need a tutor. It's not that bad."

"Good. Glad to hear it. Now I'm picking you guys up from school tomorrow and I'm gonna do a food shop in the morning. I messaged Sophie earlier, asking if there's anything in particular she wants to eat. The only request was to have Pho on one night and that you can pick the rest. So, what do you fancy?"

"Hmm. Can we order pizza when the football's on?"

"Yeah, can do."

"Oh, and can you do your lamb chops? You haven't done them in ages."

"Yeah, of course."

We talk for another ten minutes and then I ask him to remind Sophie to message me when she's back from her volunteering at the stable.

"Alright, love you and I'll see you tomorrow."

"Love you, Dad."

I'm finishing off my second bowl of dinner when my phone pings with a message.

It's a picture of Willow in the bath. Or rather her legs, a book in one hand and a glass of wine in the other. Instantly, my cock begins to thicken as my eyes trail over the luscious curves of her legs. I rub my hand over my mouth, picturing the feel of my calloused hands running over her buttery soft skin and thinking of Willow gasping in excitement.

That reminds me of how she excitedly thanked me for some books earlier. It confused me, as I'd ordered her a couple last week, but they went straight to her Kindle. She must have only just noticed them now. Either way, none of that matters, as my cock is now painfully straining in my pants. I type out my reply to the picture she sent.

Are the girls asleep?

No, not yet. They're watching TV in their room. Why?

Okay, so no phone or video calling, but let's see if Willow will behave for me.

I pull my straining cock out of my boxers and shuffle in my seat while I push my joggers down my thighs. Spitting into my palm, I start to slowly stroke my cock.

> I had planned to get you to do something else, but we'll go with Plan B. I was going to get you to lay down on your bed naked and follow my instructions as you played with yourself, then I'd have told you to get one of your toys that you told me you have in your nightstand. But you can't.

I spit down onto my cock, getting it as wet as possible and keep stroking myself as I picture Willow's mind running away with possible ideas.

> So instead, you just get to imagine. Imagine the feel of your pussy being stretched by the large dildo. Imagine first my teeth biting down on your hard nipples before I clamp them. Are you picturing it, Willow?

Yes, Sir.

Good girl.

> I want you to imagine the feel of your nipples in the clamps, your pussy being filled, and then imagine the feel of my tongue as it works its way to your ass.

Are you touching yourself picturing it?

Yes, Sir.

Stop. I haven't given you permission. I haven't said you're allowed to touch yourself.

Oh God, Sir please. Please let me.

No. Your not allowed to. I'm the only one allowed to touch. Like now with the way my hard cock is fucking my fist.

Are you behaving yourself?

Yes, Sir.

The whole time I've been typing, my hand continues to stroke my hard cock. The head continuously leaking pre-cum. My heart is racing, just knowing the effect my words are having on Willow as she reads it, sets off tingles at the base of my spine.

As I can't see or speak to you tonight, I want you to prove to me what a good girl you can be. So instead of you playing with yourself, I want you to picture it. Picturing all the ways I'll be devouring your body. Making you come over and over again. How the next time I get my hands on your body, I will push you to your limits. And you will thank me and enjoy every second of it.

My grip gets tighter as my strokes get faster, and I know it won't be long before I cum all over myself.

> I want you to imagine you're on your knees
> for me, with your mouth waiting and open.
> Spit trickling down your chin and dripping
> onto your chest. Picturing me pushing my
> cock deep into your mouth, having you
> swallow me down. Fucking your throat. Only
> being allowed to breathe when I pull your
> head back, before fucking your face again.
> Being my own personal fuck toy. Tears
> streaming down your cheeks as you fight
> the need to gag. And I don't stop until your
> pretty little mouth makes me cum and
> swallow down every last drop. Then I'll
> reward you by burying my face in your wet,
> desperate, needy pussy.

The groan I let out echoes across my kitchen as I cum all over my hand and cock. With a slightly shaky hand, I take a picture and send it to her before reaching for some kitchen roll to clean myself up.

> Now you'll be my good girl and won't touch
> yourself until I see you, won't you?

> What? But that's four days away!

A mischievous smile spread across my face as I type my response.

> I know.

Chapter 6

Willow

I've been nonstop today. My parents have already left with the girls and I've blitzed the house from top to bottom, had a shower, washed and dried my hair, moisturised every inch of my body, and laid out my outfit on the bed. Yet at the same time, there's a part of me that feels like I have missed something. As someone who loves lists and plans, you'd think I'd be less scatter-brained.

Knowing there is no point worrying, I connect my phone to the speaker, put on my classic nineties R&B playlist, and make my way over to my vanity to start getting ready for Ethan's arrival.

Given that we don't get to spend as much time together as we would like, on the occasions that we do, we tend to stay in bed for hours. Now, I'm not complaining, as I could happily spend endless days in bed with that man, but I want to do something a little special tonight. Especially given how many surprises Ethan has planned for me.

Even though where I live—I guess you could call it a small town—isn't exactly in the middle of nowhere, we still have a few fancy places that we can go to. There's a golf club nearby that has a Michelin-star restaurant attached to it. The waiting list is usually months in advance, but Megan knows the manager and has spun her magic and sorted me out a table, for which I am so damn grateful. I can't help but laugh as I think back on how Megan sent a list of things I could give and cook for her to express my gratitude.

I know for sure that tonight is going to be amazing. Not only am I getting to spend some much needed quality time with Ethan, but I can't wait to get dressed up and enjoy a fancy meal without needing to do any washing up. And as we are getting a taxi there, it means that we can both enjoy a drink.

My skin tingles as I think about the evening ahead. I have been edging myself for four days. *Four days!* Never in my life have I wanted to test my limits like this. It's the longest I've gone without finding some sort of release. Even though at times it has made me cranky and unbelievably frustrated, I know it will be worth it in the end. I want to show Ethan just how good I have been, watching his face fill with pride and respect that I have followed his instructions. My pussy throbs at the thought of just how amazing the rewards for my good behaviour will be.

After applying some lip balm, I grab my hair pick and start fluffing out my coils when my phone rings. Grabbing it from the bed, I smile as I see it's Ethan. I quickly answer and put him on speaker so I can finish doing my hair.

"Hiya, how's the drive going?"

"It's been pretty good, baby."

I get a shiver of excitement every single time he calls me that. You think I'd be used to it as he's been doing it since we officially got together, but there's just something about the nickname that makes me feel warm and fuzzy inside.

"The sat-nav says I should be there in around ten minutes."

The deep timbre of his voice is one of the many things I find unbelievably sexy about this man. And with how primed and eager my body is after days of edging, it's going to take everything in me to not simply combust when he arrives.

I try to contain my arousal. "That's perfect. I'm just finishing getting ready, and the taxi I booked won't be here for another forty minutes. So, we've got time for a quick drink before we go."

"Brilliant. Can't wait to see you."

Hearing the smile in his voice only makes mine spread further.

Willow

Now I will never be the kind of woman that says you should dress for a man. I have never done it and I don't think I ever will. However, I will credit Ethan for giving me the extra boost and confidence in myself. Confidence that was already on the way up but he just added to it. Something about the way his eyes roam up and down my body, the way I can see him undressing me in his mind whilst we FaceTime makes me want to dress the way I want. Embrace colours and patterns that complement my skin tone instead of my usual all-black outfits.

So, for tonight, I decided to go with a silk coral slip dress. The built in, hidden corset smooths and secures my belly, whilst still allowing me to not only breathe but also sit and eat comfortably.

I've gone with a teal lace strapless half-bust bra with matching lace thong. Keeping my jewellery simple, I've gone with a set of pearl stud earrings my parents got me for my thirtieth birthday, and my gold bracelet with A and M pendants on them. To complete the outfit, I'm wearing the only stilettos I find comfortable and luckily for me, they are gold and go with pretty much anything.

Giving myself one last look in the mirror, even I can admit that I look hot tonight. I'm glad I pinned the front sections of my coils out of my face as I want Ethan to see the sensual glow that's emanating from me.

Taking a deep, steadying breath, my hands skim down my dress before I make my way down the stairs just as the doorbell rings. I'm always so excited to see him that I have to give myself a second and close my eyes to calm myself before I open the door.

I watch as he takes in all of me. If the way his eyes are devouring me is any sign of what's to come, then I know this evening will be one I won't forget.

As I open my mouth to greet him and tell him to come inside, his hand cups my cheek and he guides me to him, literally taking my breath away in an all-consuming kiss. My hands slide against the solid muscle of his chest, feeling the vibrations of his growl as his other hand grips my ass.

Eventually he ends the kiss before resting his forehead on mine.

"Hey, baby."

"Hello to you too," I answer breathlessly. "Come in."

Closing the door behind him, Ethan follows me into the kitchen as I take the bottle of rosé from the cooler and pour us each a glass.

"Cheers. Here's to a great night"

"Here's to a perfect night with my perfect girl."

I intentionally bite my lip as we lock eyes and clink our glasses. That's when, in the corner of my eye, I notice that I left out a basket of dirty washing. Fuck, I thought I'd cleared everything away. Wanting to distract him before he notices, I steer us out of the kitchen and give him a quick tour of the house.

Not so long ago, the thought of having a man in my home would have sent me into a spiral, but instead, I feel proud as I show Ethan around, pointing out pictures of me and the girls. I laugh as he recognises my bathroom from some of our more fun FaceTimes.

Opening my bedroom door, I lead him in but make sure to stay close to the door as I know that if I get within one meter of a bed with Ethan, there will be no chance of us making our reservation. And the way that he's looking at me with his sexy smirk, it's as though he can read my mind.

Making our way back downstairs, I spot his overnight bag next to the sofa.

"Why don't you put your bag upstairs whilst I quickly clear up the kitchen?"

I wait until I see his legs disappear up the top of the stairs and quickly grab the basket and hide it in the utility closet.

Damn, I'm starting to feel sweaty now. Grabbing a take-away flyer from the kitchen drawer, I fan my face. The air instantly cooling my heated face. Putting the flyer back, I'm just about to call out to him when I hear his footsteps coming down the stairs.

Handing him his glass, I lean back against the counter facing him and he lifts his glass so we can toast again.

I motion for him to sit at the table but Ethan puts my drink down beside me. He then lifts me, making me squeal in shock as he places me on the counter.

Placing his palms on my thighs, making room for himself as he stands between my legs, and hands me back my drink.

"Now. That's perfect."

His large, calloused hands continue their leisurely journey up and down my thighs, sending a tremble of excited anticipation through me.

"So, how's your day been, baby?"

It takes a second for my brain and mouth to catch up with one another as the tips of his fingers get higher and higher, skimming along the edge of my lace panties. The sexual tension is so thick I can't seem to form a proper sentence.

"I... ugh... I... it's been... fine," I stutter breathlessly.

When I begin to squirm, Ethan firmly grips my chin and makes me look into his eyes.

"We'll be leaving shortly, and I can't wait to see every man look at you with lust and at me with envy. And every woman wishing she was as beautiful and sexy as the goddess that you are. When they see the pride in my eyes, they will respect that I know my place and know just how lucky I am to be by your side. We will enjoy a delicious dinner, and get to spend some quality time together. I will be a true gentleman." His voice turns gravely. "Until we get back here. The second we return, you will follow the instructions I will give to you shortly. There won't be any time for questions or second-guessing.

Yes, you are a goddess, but even you know just how much power you hold whilst you're on your knees for me."

My whole body ignites in a frenzy of feverish exhilaration. My skin tingles both from his actions and his words.

"Now, Willow, have you been good and behaving yourself? Have you touched yourself since I told you that you weren't allowed?"

"Yes I have been good. And no, Sir, I haven't touched myself." My voice is barely recognisable, even to myself.

"When we get back, the second we come through the door, I want you to lock it. Then I want you to stand at the bottom of the stairs, take off your dress, and make your way to your bedroom. You will lie on the bed and put the blindfold on that I've left out for you." He gently grazing his finger over my clit through my panties.

"You will wait, with your arms and legs spread wide. At no point are you allowed to reach for your blindfold or try to take it off. Do you understand?"

"Yes, Sir," I answer eagerly.

"I've missed my baby girl and I plan on showing her how much. All. Night. Long. But I will only do that if she behaves."

Dinner is going to be the longest two hours of my life.

Chapter 8

Willow

The food has been absolutely amazing and the wine pairings that went with each dish were truly phenomenal. But it hasn't just been the mouth-watering food that's been amazing. From the second we arrived, the atmosphere felt magical. The soft music in the background, the lighting, the décor, all of it has clearly been chosen for the purpose of giving you a romantic yet debonair ambiance. The staff have been unbelievably attentive. But not just them; Ethan has demonstrated in every way possible that I am his sole focus.

Our discussions have flowed from childhood to hobbies to travels to embarrassing stories from our teenage years. We never have difficulty talking or communicating, yet tonight I feel almost awed. Both of us have opened up to one another on a level neither of us has done before.

There isn't a single thing I could want or ask for to make

this evening any more perfect. My feelings for Ethan only continue to grow stronger and blossom.

Just before our digestifs arrive, Ethan leans forward, brings my hand to his lips, and softly kisses each knuckle, then my palm.

"I want you to go to the bathroom and I want you to only use your index."

His lips gently brush against said finger before nipping it lightly with his teeth, then he leans forward and whispers in my ear.

"I want you to use this finger and slip it into your pussy. Getting it nice and wet. Then I want you to rub your clit. But you're only allowed to do ten circles. Then you need to slip it back inside your hot, wet pussy before doing ten more circles. I want you to repeat that one last time. But you are not allowed to come. You're also not allowed to wash your hands. I want you to come straight back here. Will you be a good girl, and do as I say?"

My mouth feels extremely dry, my breath coming in fast pants as my pussy throbs with desperate need. But somehow, I manage to look him straight in the eyes as I respond.

"Yes, Sir. I will do everything you ask."

My nipples feel so hard it's almost bordering on pain, my legs so shaky they resemble that of a newborn calf. Yet somehow, I get to my feet and slowly make my way to the bathroom. Despite having the desperate urge to turn around, I know I don't need to as I can feel Ethan's eyes following my every step. And it's with that feeling, that knowledge and excitement of what's to come that my steps turn to excited strides as I make my way across the room.

Chapter 9

Willow

Thank goodness no one else has come into the bathroom. Despite my best efforts, I haven't been able to stay quiet. Moan after moan, gasp after gasp, my body is engulfed with unbridled lust.

My hand is so tense it has begun to twitch and shake.

Despite that no one else is in here, there is something so sexy and naughty about him asking me to do this. I am so close to the edge, it would be so easy for me to come right now. I could do it and not tell him. But I won't. I want to follow his instructions. My finger is wet and glistening with my arousal and I don't even want to wash it off. I want him to see how turned on I am. How good I'm being. Knowing I will be rewarded.

Ethan watches me like a hawk as I make my way back to our table, his eyes filled with fire. There is a hunger to them that I know I will happily drown in.

Using my left hand, the one I didn't use on myself in the

bathroom, I pick up my martini glass the waiter must have brought while I was *busy* and turn my attention to Ethan. My brows furrow slightly in confusion as he places his hand, palm side up, on the table.

My eyes bounce between his hand and his face, and I watch as he raises a brow. It is then that I realise what he wants me to do.

I place my right hand in his, rolling my lips together to prevent my moan from escaping as he brings my fingers to his mouth and kisses my knuckle.

To anyone around us, it would simply look like a romantic gesture, but what they can't see is the moment he licks along my finger, devouring the evidence of what I did in the bathroom.

His pupils darken to almost all black as he tastes the sweet and tart juices of my arousal that coat my finger.

His low growl vibrates from his full lips. The feeling so base, such undiluted carnal desire that I almost drop the glass I'm somehow still holding in my other hand.

Suddenly I'm too hot. My skin too sensitive. Perspiration settles on the nape of my neck. My nipples are so hard that I'm sure they could cut glass and my pussy palpitates with desperate need. I wouldn't be surprised if I have a wet patch when I stand. I don't care about finishing our drinks. I don't care about the ambiance and people around us anymore. I just want to get back. I need to feel Ethan's hands possess my body.

The corner of his eyes crinkles slightly as they narrow in focus.

I know without a doubt he's aware of every thought racing through my mind. My teeth bite down on my lower lip as my eyes widen, silently pleading and begging him. Wishing he will just put me out of my misery and let us leave. Instead, he kisses the tip of my finger, then my palm before resting it in his hand on the top and taking a sip of his cocktail. I want to scream out loud in anguished frustration.

I know he won't give in. He's making me wait and there's a huge part of me that is desperate to scream out that I've waited long enough.

However, I know this is all part of the build-up. The anticipation of what's to come. And the only thing that makes it manageable for me to breathe right now, for me to not spontaneously combust, is that I trust him. I trust that it will all be worth it. I trust he will nurture my body in a way that I won't be able to think straight anymore. That he will guide me down a river of euphoric pleasure. I trust him and I know it will be worth it. So, I manage to subdue my frustration as we finish off our cocktails.

I'm not sure how long we stay there until he finally gives me what I want. "Alright, Willow, I think it's time for us to leave."

Ethan stands and makes his way around the table to pull my chair out for me. I look over, expecting to see a waiter flag us down to pay the bill.

"I sorted it while you were in the bathroom." Despite being impressed that he once again seems to have been able to read my mind, I still bristle slightly at the unfamiliar feeling of having someone take care of me; paying the bill and treating me.

Ethan's lips on my bare shoulder break me out of my thoughts as I stand and take his hand. As we pass the maître d', I hear him tell Ethan that the taxi is waiting outside.

The cool breeze feels heavenly on my overheated skin, and I allow myself to settle in the knowledge that it won't be long now until I finally get what I want.

Ethan opens the door for me, allowing me to get in first. And I can't help but smile as he takes his seat and pulls me closer, possessively draping his arm over my shoulder.

As the driver pulls away, he leans in, his lips against the shell of my ear.

"I cannot wait to trace every inch of your body with my tongue when we get back. The taste of your pussy was the best thing I've had so far tonight."

Chapter 10

Ethan

From the moment my gaze fell on Willow when she opened her front door earlier this evening, I've felt like I've been in a trance.

She has truly bewitched me. With her breathtakingly stunning face. Her body, which would make renaissance painters weep, have the devil sell his very own soul. Any man that is lucky enough to be near her, would be as hard as steel.

That luxurious body that's encased in her reddish-orange dress. The colours look like the most beautiful sunset I could sit and watch for hours.

Her skin glows like she's somehow been dipped in a vat of diamonds.

But it's not just the masterpiece on the outside.

There is an aura, a presence to her that some might find blinding, but for me, I'm like a moth to a flame, lured in.

Usually, I'm a man who can easily stay in control, but from the second she appeared from behind that door, words failed me. Manners were gone. All sense of propriety vanished. I needed her. Needed to touch and taste the goddess before me. I don't know how I held back as long as I did.

When I gave her instructions to go to the bathroom, my eyes followed her every step, taking in the sultry sway of her hips and the bounce of her hair that cascaded down her back like a waterfall. I remembered the animalistic pleasure that surged through me when the taste of her arousal coated my tongue and flooded my tastebuds, making my mouth water. It wasn't just the enjoyment of how good Willow tasted. What made it even better was how she followed my instructions. Without hesitation. Trusting me, giving herself to me, and submitting to me in a public place.

It's a heady feeling being given that trust and authority, and I know there are many out there that would exploit it and get carried away. Now is more important than ever to stay focused, stay in control, and respect and cherish the submission Willow is gifting me.

If I were a lesser man, I'd simply strip her down and fuck her hard and fast on her couch as it's the closest surface right now, but I am being patient.

I've spent years being in control, mastering not to listen to my cock, but instead listen to my head. However, Willow is the first person to have me teetering on the edge.

Back in her house, Willow places her small bag on the side table, her eyes never breaking contact with mine. Her face is awash with lust, the apples of her cheeks have a red hue to them, her eyes molten with fire, her tongue running along her lips, tracing the path I will soon be following with my own mouth. Having a woman as truly remarkable as Willow giving herself to me in this way is more than anything I could ever ask for. I've been allowing myself to sink into my second skin as a Dom. As Willow's Dom. Revelling in it all evening. Knowing it's not just about the amazing sex. It is so much more than just that.

I catalogue her every move as she begins to undress. She begins by pulling the shawl that was wrapped around her arms, and I watch as it falls to her feet. Then she reaches around, I'm guessing to a zipper or button and her dress begins to give way. Her movements are slow and sensual; this isn't like a striptease. Instead, it's like she's a flower, each item of clothing like a petal opening up, revealing the beautiful bud of her at the centre. Not a single word has been spoken. Nothing needs to be said. I can tell every thought and emotion simply from looking at her face. The only sounds I can hear are her rapid breathing and the solid tempo of my heart beating in my ears. The silence isn't one of awkwardness. Instead, it seems to heighten the fire that's burning between us.

Now it is my turn to take a deep breath when I see what she has been wearing underneath her dress as it pools at her feet.

Her large ample breasts are encased in a green bra. The colour against her skin makes me think of beautiful forests sitting below a mountain's peak. The small glimmers of perspiration, dewy drops that lead down a path my tongue is desperate to follow.

As my eyes work their way down to her soft hips, the tips

of my fingers tingle in anticipation of me running my hands over her skin. Knowing that, by tomorrow, there will be evidence of me having enjoyed every part of her body marring her flesh.

Her pussy is hidden behind the smallest lace thong that I know I could easily rip apart with just the flick of my fingers. I can clearly see the dark, wet patch of her arousal. I feel momentarily lightheaded as I realise I haven't taken a breath.

Ever so slowly, Willow turns slightly and bends down, taking off first one heel, then the other. The light thuds as they hit the wooden floor bringing me back into focus. She takes one last look back at me before taking one step at a time upstairs.

I wait until she is almost all the way up before following her. My breathing shallows as I straighten my spine, becoming the predator and she the prey. There is nothing that could stop me from hunting her down and consuming her whole.

Chapter 11

Ethan

The sight before me is one I will have imprinted on my brain forever. Willow laid out on her back, her arms and legs spread out wide. Just like I instructed, she's secured the blindfold.

Looking over to the side, I smile as I know she'll have spotted the toys I left on the dresser. I move to her bedside drawer and groan with pleasure when I see her own array of toys nestled in there. I remember her telling me that she keeps a sample of her custom orders and the knotted blue dildo—complete with suction tentacles and the bear mouthed, tongue licking vibrator—are the two I eagerly add for us tonight.

"Between your toys and those that I've brought with me, I think we are in for a very enjoyable evening." The sound of my voice seems to surprise her as she gasps and jolts, but being the good girl that she is, she makes the conscious effort to stay completely still.

Starting at her right ankle, I softly trace the tips of my fingers up her shins, slowly circling her knee before tentatively making my way up her thigh. Keeping my touch soft and delicate, I trace the contours of her hips.

Spreading out my fingers, I guide them across her stomach, watching as it caves in on the intake of a gasp. As my fingers trace up her ribcage and along her chest, Willow opens her mouth in a silent moan, forming a perfect circle that has my cock hard, imagining how good it's going to feel when I feed it down her throat.

I continue making my way up the right side of her body. Reaching her collarbone, my fingers skate along the delicate skin along her neck and I feel the rapid beat of her pulse in her neck.

Making sure not to break contact with her skin, I reach over and grab the spreader bar from the dresser. I make my way back down her body, but make sure my fingers coast along skin I haven't touched yet. Wanting to fulfil my promise to touch every single inch of her body.

Once I get down to her foot, I place the bar between her legs and secure one ankle, then the other. I mirror my touch, up along the left side of her body and by the time I have reached her face, her breathing now comes in needy pants.

I place a knee on the bed, allowing me to get closer to her. Leaning down, I brush my lips against hers, swallowing her gasp in a passionate kiss, letting her know just how much I want her. How much I desire every part of her. Bringing the kiss to an end, I take her bottom lip between my teeth and bite down. A pleading, desperate moan escapes her. Taking my time, I reach beneath her and unhook the clasps of her strapless bra, tossing it on the floor.

Grabbing the nipple clamps from the side table, my tongue finds her breasts, softly licking and sucking the strained peaks. Following the soft and gentle caress of my mouth, I counter that as I attach first one clamp, then the other, that are connected by a chain, on her nipples. The bite of the clamp's teeth eliciting a loud, sharp moan from Willow. Her body bucks, and she attempts and fails at closing her legs, the spreader bar keeping her legs wide open for me.

I make quick work of ripping off her thong. The thin lace silk joining her bra beside the bed. Then I grab the flogger and feather from the dresser.

"Do you remember your safe word, Willow?"

She nods, but that's not enough.

"Willow, I need your words," I demand.

"Yes, Sir. I remember my safe word."

I start by making light circles along her thigh with the feather and follow it with the biting crack of the flogger. My hand tingles and my cock twitches. I love watching the way her body jerks the moment she feels that bite of pain. Willow screams out and I watch as her hands grip the sheets, her hips grinding and writhing, like her pussy is searching, seeking out my cock to fill it. Her pussy glistens as it's dripping wet. The muscles in her thighs tense as her moans grow louder.

"Please... Sir... please." Her pleading is so garbled I don't think she even knows what she's begging for. I continue playing with her, alternating between soft and hard touches. Mixing it up, never letting her know which one is coming next. I know the anticipation will drive her mind as wild as her body. And for me, the power and control heighten my own arousal. Having her on the precipice like that makes me feel like I'm on top of the world.

I work my mouth along her neck and collarbone. Kissing, biting, and sucking my way along her skin. Simultaneously, my hands roam across the swells of her full large breasts. My fingers skate along the chain attached to both nipple clamps, and I gently tug. Her whimpers now flood the room, and I don't let up my ministrations. Continuing to pull on the chain, kiss, and bite all along her chest. Sucking and marking her beautiful, soft skin. It doesn't take long before my ears are filled with the resounding cries of Willow coming. The sight before me is so fucking sexy it's transcending.

Her stomach caves in as her body shakes and shudders with aftershocks from her orgasm. My cock is so hard I feel like I'm about to explode. Listening to her cries, watching as her eyes squeeze shut, seeing the sweat bead along her chest and temples. Never before have I felt so powerful, so in control, like a God overseeing her body. And I haven't even touched her pussy yet.

The tips of my fingers tingle with desperate need to touch her. Knowing how good her wet pussy is going to feel wrapped around my cock, has it leaking. My hand works its way up to her throat before my fingers wrap around her delicate neck. Collaring her. I tighten my grip to the point where breathing is more difficult. Showing my power. Casting my possessive ownership.

Reluctantly releasing her as I can't hold back any longer, I waste no time stripping out of my clothes and giving my cock an eager stroke, collecting the pre-cum that's leaking from the head.

"Open your mouth." I command, kneeling next to her heard. "I want it open nice and wide so I can slide my hard cock into it, all the way down your throat. And if you're lucky, I might just let you catch a breath."

I lean over her and she opens her mouth. The feeling of her warm, wet tongue is so good I have to momentarily lock my knees.

"Oh, yes. Just like that. Mmmm." My hands fist the sheets beside her as I'm bent over and the vibrations of her humming adds even more pleasure.

"Willow, your mouth feels so fucking good… yes..that's it. Swallow me down." I increase the tempo of my hips thrusting as I continue fucking her mouth.

"I want my cock dripping with your spit. Get it nice and wet… yes just like that." I fuck her mouth, pushing deeper with each thrust. She begins to gag as I hit the back of her throat, but I don't ease up. I keep going. Looking down, I watch as her eyes water, her mouth drooling as her mouth stretches around my cock, gagging as I move in and out.

Chapter 12

Ethan

Needing to have my own taste, my fingers part her pussy lips, exposing her clit that shimmers like the rarest pearl. Leaning down, I wrap my lips around it and suck on it like a succulent berry. Beneath me, Willow bucks, the bar keeping her legs pinned wide.

We continue devouring each other, and I add two fingers, pumping them in and out of her pussy, making sure to curl them so I stroke her G-spot.

Willow lets out an inaudible growl around my cock and the walls of her pussy tighten and clamp down as I increase both my pace and the pressure of my tongue and fingers. I pull out of her mouth as I fuck her with my fingers, pumping in and out of her as I go to town on her clit.

"Yes. Yes. Yes, Sir. Oh, God. Yes. I'm going to come. Please. Yes. Oh. Oh. God. Yes." Willow screams at the top of her lungs before my fingers and face are covered in her juices. I lap up every last drop. And although I initially wanted to use those two toys of hers before I fucked her for the first time tonight, I simply cannot wait. I need to be inside her.

Willow is a panting mess; curls stuck to her temples with sweat, her breasts heaving, and her nipples swollen under the clamps. She's never looked more beautiful. But there's something missing.

Standing up, I reach down, take off the blindfold and as her eyes slowly adjust, the missing piece is finally in place.

Lifting up her legs so the bar sits behind my head, I basically bend her in half as the spreader-bar still prevents her from moving. I settle myself between her legs, rubbing the head of my cock along her clit, making her shake and whimper before burying myself deep inside her pussy in one thrust. She's so wet, she takes me easily, her fingers digging into my shoulders as she cries out my name.

"Sir, yes, oh yes, God that feels so good," she pants.

Each drive is hard and deep. Her tight inner walls lock me in. Pulling me in deeper. My lips find hers as I increase the rhythm, beads of sweat rolling down my shoulder blades and spine as tingles begin to build at the base of my spine.

Pulling back, I lift her legs and place a pillow under her ass, allowing me to go deeper. Sinking back into her heat, I increase my pace, feeling myself racing towards rapture.

"Fuck, baby. You feel so damn good. Nothing feels better than the way your pussy grips my cock."

"Oh, Sir. Please. I can't take anymore. It's too much. I... I..." Willow moans in a breathless jumble. Her nails clawing against my arms, and I love the thought of her marking me.

With one hand beside her head to hold me up, I reach

down with the other as I tug on the chain. The muscles in my shoulder are burning, yet I don't stop. I continue fucking her, feeling every pulse and squeeze. Her whole body is vibrating and she tumbles over the edge once again, making me cum so hard I see black dots behind my eyes.

"Fuck," I say breathlessly. I take a second to get my breathing back under control before detangling Willow's legs from behind my head and freeing her ankles from the spreader bar.

"Uh. Oh, God," Willow cries as I take off the nipple clamps.

I gently roll her onto her side, placing the pillow beside her, and begin massaging her calves and thighs, before working my way up her back. I spend the next twenty minutes massaging, kissing, and caressing her, making her as relaxed and nurtured as possible.

"You're such a good girl," I say between kisses. "How are you doing, baby?"

"Mmmm. I'm good. But I don't think I want to move."

I laugh as she stretches out on the bed.

"Alright, I'm gonna quickly jump in the shower. But the second I get back, I've got a surprise for you."

Willow's eyes are suddenly alert and filled with excitement. "A surprise? How about you give me it first, then shower?"

The sound of my laugh barrels across the room and I can't help the warmth that seeps through me as I know how big of a thing it is for her to not just show excitement for a gift, but the vulnerability in her expressing that.

Wanting to keep the smile on her face, I reach for my weekend bag and grab the box out of the inner pocket. Sitting beside her on the bed, I hand her it and watch as she looks at it nervously.

Sitting up, she gives me a soft kiss, then slowly opens the box and gasps when she sees what's inside.

It's a collar. Thin and delicate, it is subtle enough for her to wear every day. Anyone who notices it will think it's just a pretty necklace, but Willow and I know its bigger meaning.

"Ethan, it's beautiful. Thank you so, so much." Her eyes glisten with unshed tears.

I can see from the softness of her features just how much it means to her. I smile as she grabs the back of my head and kisses me with such fervour that by the time we stop, my cock is hard again.

Taking it out of the box, I secure it around her neck and kiss it in place. Looking up at Willow, I grin when I see her eyes alight with pleasure and eagerness.

"Thank you for this, Ethan."

"You're more than welcome."

"I promise to wear it with pride. Now how about I show you just how thankful I am?"

I follow her line of sight before she jumps up off the bed and grabs the bear-mouthed tongue vibrator and the tentacle dildo.

Sitting back against the headboard, Willow straddles my thighs and hands me the toys.

The shower can wait. I think it's time I get first hand experience of just how good her creations are.

Chapter 13

Willow

The gentle, reassuring weight of Ethan's arm wrapped around me brings me out of my deep sleep. I take in a deep, steadying breath and luxuriate in the warm embrace.

Despite wanting to stay like this for hours, my bladder has other ideas. I manage to detangle myself from his embrace without waking him and quietly make my way out of the bedroom to the hall bathroom instead of the small en suite, as I don't want to disturb him as I pee and brush my teeth.

After freshening up, I grab a robe from the back of the bathroom door and debate whether to get back into bed. But I decide against it, making my way downstairs to get a start on breakfast instead and smiling to myself at the thought of bringing him breakfast in bed. God, Megan would slap me round the back of my head if she saw the giddy state I'm in.

Busying myself in the kitchen, I lay out all the ingredients for me to make some waffles with Nutella, coffee, and fruit.

Turning the Alexa on, I get some Motown Classics going in the background.

I get into the swing and rhythm of my happy place, which is cooking and caring for those that mean a lot to me. And it is as clear as the sky is blue that Ethan is becoming a very special, important part of my life

Never in my life have I ever felt so wanted. So comfortable to bare myself. To fully surrender. To embrace my body and share it wholeheartedly. Not once doubting or questioning how I look or if my body is one that Ethan wants. One he desires. I don't need to question anything because his actions prove just how he feels about me. His actions, the way his eyes hungrily take me in, and the attentive care he gives me grounds and reassures me more than any words and platitudes ever could.

Finishing up our breakfast, I'm just about to put the plates on a tray when I hear Ethan's footsteps making their way down the stairs.

I refrain from letting out a groan at the sight of the sexy man standing before me. Dressed in only a pair of tight boxer briefs and nothing else, my eyes map his strong, solid chest. The intricate tattoos that wrap around his arms depict a forest with wild and mythical animals roaming through it. It spreads over onto his chest and what looks like a glass treehouse. The whole scene goes all the way around to his back. I finish my perusal by the time he joins me.

"Morning, baby," he says, grabbing my hips and pulling me to him before capturing my lips in a hot, needy kiss.

The rough and sexy timbre of his voice this morning is

doing nothing to subdue the desire I have for him that's already beginning to simmer. Well, it could be his voice or the teasing way that he's running his fingers sensuously along the edges of my robe.

"Good morning to you too. I was going to bring this upstairs so you could have breakfast in bed."

There is something sweet and innocent in the look in Ethan's eyes as he takes my face in his hands, pulling me in for another kiss, and letting me taste the minty freshness on his tongue as it caresses mine. Unlike the previous kiss, this one feels deeper, somehow more emotionally charged. As our kiss ends, I open my eyes as Ethan rests his forehead against mine.

"Thank you for making me breakfast, baby. That's very sweet of you. And I'm touched that you wanted to bring me it in bed. I don't think I've had anyone do that since I was a kid."

My heart warms at the sweet vulnerability in him right now.

Wanting to keep in the spirit of giving, I take his hand and lead him to the couch, grabbing his coffee and plate and hand them to him.

Despite that I made Ethan twice as many waffles as I did for myself, he still manages to finish his and his bowl of fruit before I finish mine. Once we're done, I take our plates to the kitchen, loading them straight into the dishwasher before making us each another cup of coffee and joining him back on the couch.

We spend the next hour talking, laughing, and enjoying each other's company.

My fingers stroke along the tattoos on his arms, tracing the patterns and various swirls and shades. That's when I realise, I've never asked if they have any meaning or if he simply chose them because he liked them.

Ethan explains each one, his muscles tensing and rippling as he moves, which only makes me want to straddle him.

My eyes must give me away, as the next thing I know, we are kissing, his large hands gripping and kneading my curves. But before Ethan can do anything else, I drop down onto my knees, settling between his thighs. I ease down his briefs and his long, thick cock springs free, making my mouth water.

I work his cock in and out of my mouth. Sucking the head, I can taste his precum, the sweet and salty essence of Ethan explodes over my tastebuds. Teasing his slit first, I flatten my tongue along the shaft, making it nice and wet. Working my way back up, I use my hand to stroke him, helping me as I work him deeper and deeper. It's only with the use of both my mouth and my hand that I can work his entire cock. He's just too big. With my other hand, I begin to roll and tug on his balls.

Hearing him groan and watching as his hips buck and his thighs tighten in pleasure makes me feel so powerful. Ethan threads his fingers in my hair like he's using my mouth as his own personal fuck toy. I give everything I have to this blowjob, wanting to continue to show him how much I want him. How grateful I am to him.

Seemingly unable to take anymore, Ethan grabs my arms then lifts me onto him, seating me straight onto his cock and I moan as I feel myself stretch to adjust to his size before he begins to fuck me with no mercy.

Matching his pace, I ride and grind down on him. Pushing my robe off my shoulders, Ethan's mouth latches onto my nipple and the extra stimulation sets off my orgasm, causing us both come with breathless cries.

Ethan's mouth finds my ear as our combined arousal drips from me, despite him still being semi-hard inside me.

"Now that was the perfect start to the day. I could easily enjoy that every morning. Come on, let's jump in the shower and get ready. Because if we don't, I can't guarantee I won't drag you back into bed."

And despite how good that sounds, I know we need to get ready, as Ethan will be meeting the girls for the first time.

Chapter 14

Ethan

I wish every morning could be like this one. And although I'd have loved to have woken up with Willow in my arms, the fact that she got up to make me breakfast in bed was so sweet.

Having her wanting to treat me and take care of me only goes to show how phenomenal she is. How she looks after those around her. Then following that up with the way she got down on her knees and took my cock in her mouth. She was like a Hoover, sucking me deep. It felt so good that I had to get her to stop, as I knew I wouldn't last much longer and I was desperate to feel the warm, tight grip of her pussy.

I was expecting Willow to be super nervous this morning, but she was so calm, collected, and even excited. As a parent myself, I know how big of a deal someone meeting your kids is. Knowing all the things Willow has explained about her past and her previous relationships, I'm not going to take for granted just how significant this is.

We discussed that, although it technically would be easier for us to drive in separate cars, she wanted us to go in one. I couldn't help but tease her, asking if she just didn't want to spend time apart from me. But Willow, being the quick and smart woman that she is, managed to humble me by saying that Ayana really loves fast cars and would love to be driven in one, so we should just take mine.

The drive up to the pub is comfortable. Willow has taken control of the music, and again, I am reminded of how many of our interests align.

Tina Turner's "Proud Mary" comes to an end as we pull up in the car park. I haven't even had a chance to turn the engine off when out of the corner of my eyes I can see a whirlwind of curls and limbs jumping out of a car and running over towards us. Looking over at Willow, I see her face break in a beaming smile along with an eye roll. It doesn't take a genius to work out that the bundles of smiling excitement are Ayana and Mya.

Following in their wake are who I'm going to presume are Willow's parents. I remember her telling me that her father was a former Judo champion and, from the way that he holds himself, his stature and gait are one of resolve and discipline.

Walking around the car, I open Willow's door and help her out. I don't miss the head-to-toe scan her dad gives me, followed by the slight nod of approval at my gesture. Next to him is his wife, Willow's mother. She and Willow look alike. They have the same skin tone, the same smile, and identical eyes. Although Willow has her father's nose and face shape.

Willow embraces her daughters, then, holding their hands, turns and faces me.

"Ethan, I know I have told you a lot about my daughters, and I would like to pre-emptively apologise for whatever embarrassing things that are about to come out of their mouths. Well, here goes nothing. Ethan, this is Ayana, and this is Mya."

"Ayana and Mya, this is Ethan."

"It's lovely to meet you both," I say as I take turns shaking their outstretched hands.

I respect the protective, assessing once-over they give me. After all, they are understandably protective of their mother.

I'm then introduced to her parents, who, although are assessing me and closely watching both mine and Willow's interactions, are also watching how I am towards the girls.

We ask them to join us for lunch, but they decline, needing to head back, but promising to join us next time. They also invited me to join Willow and the girls for a barbeque at their house. I don't miss the unexpected look on Willow's face at their invitation.

"I would enjoy that very much. Thank you."

After saying our goodbyes to her parents, I follow Willow, Mya, and Ayana inside and the girls waste no time in peppering me with a million questions from how old I am to if I have kids. I told them about Lucas and Sophie, showing them pictures and making them laugh as I shared some stories.

"I don't get it. Your kids look much older than us, but you

don't look super old. Except for the white bits in your hair. Are you sure they are yours?"

"Ayana," Willow exclaims.

I look over at Mya, who's giggling into her glass of apple juice.

"Don't be rude. You know better than that." Willow's tone is firm but quiet. A lethal combination.

"But Mum, I mean it as a good thing." Ayana beams.

I know I shouldn't laugh, especially as I can tell by Willow's stern facial expression she really isn't impressed, but wanting to keep the mood light and relaxed, I make a show of touching my temples where I have the most grey coming through.

"Do you really think these make me look old?" I jest.

The girls look at each other, seemingly having a tele-pathic-twin conversation, while under the table, I reach for Willow's knee and give it a reassuring squeeze.

"Okay, you don't look that old," Ayana and Mya both note, then giggle.

"Phew. Well, thank God for that. I'll just have to focus on the bit where you said I don't look that old. And yes, Lucas and Sophie are mine. And maybe one day you both could meet them?"

As soon as the words are out of my mouth, I realise it maybe wasn't the best suggestion for me to make before discussing it with Willow, but when I see her warm smile and nod, I take a deep and relieved breath.

The rest of lunch goes without a hitch. Mya and Ayana don't let up on their questions, but I make sure to answer them honestly. When they're finished with me, I sit back and watch the way they enjoy pushing Willow's buttons. As a parent, I can relate to Willow's frustration at times, but as a partner, seeing the way she manages the girls, navigates both their characters and opinions, and very much giving them both respect as individuals while also drawing that clear line that she's their mother, has been fascinating to watch.

All in all, lunch has gone really well, and both girls try to get me to drive beyond the speed limit on the way back. But, despite all their enthusiastic attempts, I don't drive at full speed, I do however accelerate quickly a couple of times which makes then giggle, but I always make sure to keep everyone safe and back in one piece.

Arriving back at their house, both girls tell me that I have their seal of approval, even with the flecks of grey in my hair. And I don't hold back the smile that takes over my face, as I know just how big of a deal it is.

Walking them to the front door, both girls give me a high five as Willow unlocks the door and lets them run in as they wave their goodbyes over their shoulders.

"Thank you for a great evening last night, and for lunch today. And you survived meeting the girls and my parents."

Laughing, I wrap my arms around her. "I am the one that's thankful. It has been the perfect weekend. And the girls really are a testament to you."

"You mean they don't have a filter and get excited over the silliest of things?" Willow asks, looking up at me with a cheeky grin.

"Well, maybe those points also, but I mean they are kind, intelligent, tenacious, beautiful, and strong young ladies."

Willow buries her face in my chest, hiding the blush on her cheeks. Taking her face in my hands, I lean down and tentatively kiss her. The feeling of her lips on mine is something I will never tire of. As our kiss deepens, I have to remind myself to keep things PG as we're on her doorstep and are quickly reminded of that fact, as we get interrupted by the sounds of the girls singing.

"Mummy and Ethan sitting in a tree, k-i-s-s-i-n-g."

My lips stretch into a smile as our kiss comes to an end. I give her one last peck before saying my goodbyes. As I get into the car, I wave to Willow and watch as she waves back, and her fingers rub along her collar with a smile.

And as I drive off, pure contentedness washes over me.

Chapter 15

Willow

My house feels like a sauna. I've got the stove and oven on, with dinner cooking. The washing machine is currently doing the third load of the day. With this stupid British weather and the endless downpours, I've got the previous two loads drying on airers and I've just finished ironing a pile of uniforms and bedding.

Shutting the iron off, I'm just about to put the board away when the Alexa speaker starts blaring out *The Weekend*. The sudden noise makes me jump and I'm damn lucky I didn't have the iron in my hands, as I'd have badly burnt myself.

"Ayana, Mya, stop messing around. I told you both to cut it out. It's not funny," I shout up at the girls. Sometimes, I hate stupid technology. I don't know how they've managed to rig it to go off without them in the room, but I'm really not in the mood or impressed.

"Alexa, off," I shout at the stupid speaker, and the instant silence feels great.

Washing my hands, I plate up dinner and set the table.

"Girls, dinner's ready."

The girls make their way downstairs, sounding like a mariachi band is making its way through my house.

"Mum, Mya's chicken pieces look bigger than mine. That's not fair," Ayana whines.

"They are the same sizes. Just eat your food and stop complaining."

Looking over, I raise a brow at Ayana as I hear her mutter under her breath.

"What was that?"

Eating now seems more important than answering my question as Ayana focuses all her attention on the plate in front of her.

We manage to eat in silence for a few minutes before Mya starts singing at the top of her lungs.

"Mya, enough. We're eating dinner. And that reminds me. The two of you better not set off the Alexa again. Do you know how close I was to hurting myself with how much it scared me?"

Looking over at both of them, they both are scowling and rolling their eyes. Only adding to my already fraying nerves and frustration.

"Mum, we already told you. We didn't do it. You must have. Or maybe you put it on and then forgot," Mya says with an air of condescension.

The girls are acting up and I know why. Their dad was

meant to have them this weekend, but surprise, surprise, he cancelled. Not only did he cancel, but he couldn't even be bothered to tell them himself. No. He left that to me. So ever since I broke the news to them, they've both been stroppy, argumentative, and completely acting up.

This is what's so hard. It's not their fault and I can understand their annoyance. The only thing they can rely on from their dad is him letting them down. And as always, I'm the proverbial punching bag. I'm left to deal with the disappointment and I have to somehow pick up the pieces.

I hate even thinking this, but it would be so much easier if he left their lives for good. There is no structure, no regularity, no gesture or clear actions of his that show they are in any way a priority in his life.

I don't manage to lift spirits during dinner, but we do somehow get through it without too much animosity or any more arguments.

"Put your bowls in the sink. Then go and have a quick shower, brush your teeth, get your pj's on and if you both manage to finish that in the next twenty minutes, you can watch TV for half an hour," I say as I clean up the dining table.

I feel really drained as I finish clearing up the kitchen, load up the dishwasher, and hang up the final load of washing.

The girls are now in bed. I've had a hot shower that I was hoping would ease some of the tension in my shoulders, but instead, it feels like I've just burnt my skin.

I've just finished moisturising my face when my phone

begins to ring on the bedside table. Making my way over, I crack a smile for the first time this evening when I see it's Ethan calling.

"Hey, baby, how are you doing?"

"I'm okay." The melancholy is evident in my voice.

"Tell me. Tell me what's bothering you."

I take a breath and climb into bed to get comfortable.

"Tonight was just tough. You know how I told you earlier that the girls' dad had cancelled?"

"Yeah." The annoyance in Ethan's voice is crystal clear.

"Well, not only did he cancel, but he said he didn't have time to tell them, so I had to. I'm sure you can imagine how that went down."

He gasped. "I'm sorry. I know it's not my place to say anything, but that is such a pathetic, spineless thing to do."

Not wanting to spiral myself into a worse mood, I change topic. "Anyway, enough about that. Tell me, how has the rest of your day?"

There is a momentary silence and I can imagine Ethan warring with himself, wanting me to talk and open up about the things troubling me, while also respecting and understanding my need to talk about something else.

We spend the next twenty minutes talking about his day. He tells me he's had to deal with what he suspects to be a disgruntled former employee, who's been review-bombing his company all over the internet. This just makes me so angry, as I know how hard Ethan has worked to build up his company.

"Well, how would you like to hear some good news?" he asks.

"Please. Yes, tell me something good."

"You're beautiful."

"Ha." I laugh at his cheesy attempt at good news.

"Well, you are. But we already know that."

"I hope you've got better news than that."

"Don't dismiss my point, but yes, the other news is good too. You know the hotel complex I designed in Barcelona?"

"Yeah."

"Well, they are having their grand opening in a month and have invited me over. I would love it if you could join me."

"Oh, wow. I can't believe it's all already finished and ready. How long would we be gone for?"

"It would be four days in total and that includes the travel days."

My mind does a quick scan, trying to remember if there's anything important happening around then, but nothing is sticking out to me.

"I would love to go with you. I'll have to ask my parents if they can have the girls, which I don't think will be a problem, so it should all be fine."

"Perfect."

Unsurprisingly, my mood is now lifted, and I smile with excitement, thinking about a nice little break with Ethan in the Catalan sun. We continue talking for a little while until it's clear I'm struggling to stay awake.

"Night, baby. Sleep well."

"Good night."

With that, I fall into a deep sleep with a big smile on my face.

Chapter 16

Willow

These past two weeks have been completely draining. Not so much mentally. Well, at least no more than usual, but damn, has each day been relentless.

The girls have had a dance show, with three productions being put on. Obviously watching them perform makes me unbelievably proud. The first night it was just me watching. The second, my brother came, and for the final show, my parents came to see them. I was originally planning on inviting Ethan but I knew he had his kids on those days, and with it being school nights, plus the distance, I knew it wouldn't have been possible.

Then, on top of the shows, I have had roofers sorting out a leak in the attic. And let's just say they have not been quiet. Moreover, I have been inundated with orders. I know it's a good thing and something I couldn't be prouder of, but I won't lie. Between making the orders, dealing with the accounts, and—despite having a PA—I still have numerous things I need to do and accomplish each and every day. But I still feel overwhelmed, like I'm in over my head on most days. Doubting myself in every way.

It's great that things are going so well on the business side of things, but it's been truly draining. Now, if I had a nanny, a cleaner, and a chef to help me out with all the other things I need to do each day, then maybe I wouldn't be so tired. And even though I could really do with a nap, there was no way I was going to turn down Megan's offer of a coffee and a catch up.

I don't know how she always accomplishes it, but Meg always seems to find the rarest little gems or pop-ups or hole-in-the-wall locals. Just like the one I'm meeting her in now.

The waitress came over to take my order, but I said I'd wait until my friend arrived. I'm just about to grab my phone to check the time when the telltale sounds of heels clicking on the stone floor make me look up.

"Well, well, well. I must be seeing things as it appears to be my best friend standing in front of me. And she's actually on time." I tease.

"Oh, shut it, you. I'll have you know my time management has got a hell of a lot better recently."

She gives me a kiss on the cheek before taking the seat across from me and the eager waitress from earlier returns and takes our orders.

By the time our coffees arrive, Megan has given me the rundown on everything happening with her at the moment and I fill her in on how the girls are doing.

"Man, I was so gutted I had to go to that stupid HR team building trip and miss their shows."

"Don't worry, their dance teacher already sent out an email with the upcoming things they are putting on this term. I'll be sure to drag you to one of them."

"Hey, it won't be you dragging me in. More like dragging me out. Especially if there's some stuck-up Karen sitting next to me, gushing over her precious Princess Fiona, who only got the lead role due to Father's large donation. It sure as hell isn't because of her two left feet or the way she waddles like a damn duck when she walks."

"Don't remind me." I laugh, holding my head in my hands as I remember the exact thing happening last year.

"So, I've waited patiently enough. Tell me. How are things going with Ethan?"

Taking a large sip of coffee, I smile at Megan's excitement.

"Honestly Meg, it's really going great. I don't know how he does it. Every time I think that there isn't any way possible, he can impress me more. He does."

"How so?"

"Well, you know how I told you how Ethan reacted to finding out Asshole wasn't having the girls?"

"Yeah. He definitely got some extra brownie points from me. It's good. You know how I feel about Asshole, and your family hates him just as much as we do. But I think it's good having Ethan react in the same way. Not just because he's your partner, but also a parent himself. And I think having that male and paternal opinion, supporting you and being there is going to be exactly what you need."

Nodding along, I take another sip of coffee.

"I know. I agree with you and that's why it meant so much to me when he got the girls a surprise."

Megan's eyes light up in excitement. "Tell me, tell me, what did he do?"

"He sent two large boxes. One for each of them. And inside were four smaller ones. Each individually wrapped. One box for each day that they were meant to be with their dad. Each day they opened the designated boxes and there were colouring books, pens, pencils, books, jewellery making kits, arts and crafts, board games, notebooks, stickers, and children's cookbooks."

I have to laugh at Megan's mouth that's gaping open.

"Babe. That man. I swear even I can feel a tingling in my ovaries. See, this is what I'm talking about. I'd have picked maybe a bunch of toys, thrown in a couple of bags of sweets and chocolates... but he picked things for them to do. Things that are creative to keep them and their minds busy. Wow, Willow. This guy really is something else. And I mean that in the best way."

"I know." If this were a cartoon, I'd have hearts in my eyes and birds flying around me like some sort of Disney Princess.

"Willow?" Megan's voice breaks me out of my silly daydream.

"Yes?"

"Are you falling in love with Ethan?"

There's a tenderness in her eyes and I know that she understands how big a question that is. I already knew I had strong feelings for him that continue to grow stronger each day. The way he makes sure to follow up on every promise. There are never empty words. He always delivers. And in both smaller actions as well as bigger ones, he proves time and time again that I am one of his priorities. That my girls play an important part to him simply because they are the most important things in my life. And though it may have seemed like a small gesture to some people, for me, giving the girls those treat packages only cemented just how I feel about him.

"Yes. Yes, I am falling in love with him," I admit. "But I'm not ready to tell him yet. Not because I think it's too soon, or because I doubt what we have. I just want to wait for the right moment. The right time."

I'm surprised at how good it feels saying that out loud. It's as if deep down I've known for a while.

Meg and I clink coffee cups in celebration, and she shows me some places she recommends Ethan and I visit whilst in Barcelona.

"Do you want another coffee?" Megan asks.

"Yeah. But make mine a decaf, please. I need to go and pee quickly. Oh, do you fancy sharing a slice of carrot cake? It looks delicious."

"Ugh, yes to the carrot cake, no to the sharing. I'll order two. You go pee."

Weaving my way around the tables, I make my way to the bathroom. Just as I'm passing the men's room, I accidentally bump into someone. The guy has a baseball cap pulled down low but doesn't stop or turn. He simply says, "Sorry" in a gruff, croaky voice, before vanishing around the corner.

Weird.

I don't know why, but a shiver runs down my spine. Luckily, the pressing issue of my bladder distracts me and I brush it off.

Once I finish in the bathroom and get back to the table, I'm just about to tell Megan about the weird guy, when I spot two plates with large slices of carrot cake on them. Laughing at their size as I sit down.

"Did you ask for extra large slices or something?"

"Maybe." The devilish grin on her face only makes me laugh even more.

Our coffees arrive and we both demolish our cake. Just as I finish, my phone goes off with an email notification.

"Oh my God," I screech.

"What is it? Has something happened?"

My eyes continue scanning down, reading the email.

"Willow?" Megan says sternly.

"It's not bad news. It's fantastic news." I push my phone over so Megan can read it as well. My heart is racing, while my hands and underarms begin to sweat.

I watch on as she reads, seeing the joy and excitement spread across her face as she reads an email from one of the biggest lingerie and sex toy companies, wanting to meet and do either a larger collaboration or discuss the possibility with me being the main collaborator to the X-rated range.

By the time Megan finishes reading, we both are squealing with excitement.

"I knew it. That's my girl. I told you that you are unstoppable. And I think this is definitely a sign that you're going to need to hire some more staff."

"Oh, I definitely agree with you on that."

Megan, being the tenacious woman that she is, grabs a notebook and pen from her bag and starts making lists of things I need and the possible positions I need to fill. And just like that, all feelings of tiredness and exhaustion are out the window as excitement for the future runs through me.

Chapter 17

Willow

I was expecting to be filled with nerves, doubt, worry, and apprehension. Yet as I'm sitting on the train, waiting to pull into London Victoria Station, I feel strong. Assured.

I know the hard work I've put in, and for the first time, I feel deserving of the opportunity that's hopefully coming my way with this meeting I'm on my way to.

We've already had a preliminary Zoom call with one of the creative heads and someone from their marketing department. Now I'm meeting with the managing director and buyers.

After the train, I jump on the tube, and again am reminded why I chose to move out of the city. I get the appeal, but for me, the hustle and bustle, the tinned can squeeze, and the incessant urgency seemingly running through everyone is just too much.

But luckily I'm heading straight home after.

I manage to get to their offices with ten minutes to spare. Grabbing my phone to put on silent, I see messages from Megan, both my parents, and Ethan all wishing me good luck. There is absolutely nothing that can wipe the smile off my face right now.

"They are ready for you now. If you take the last lift on the right, up to the twentieth floor, the receptionist there will show you to the conference room." The receptionist hands me a lanyard, then points in the right direction.

The meeting couldn't have gone any better if I'd dreamt it up myself. Making my way out of the building, I turn my phone back on and see a message from Megan asking me to call her as soon as I'm finished. Smiling, I pull up her number and the call button.

"How did it go? What did they say? Will you be on billboards? Tell me everything," she says breathlessly.

I laugh at her excitement and also at her somewhat ridiculous notion.

"Firstly, I never have been and never will be on a damn billboard. And I can't see all of society suddenly accepting and being okay with a five-metre poster of an octopus-inspired dildo."

A man walking beside me suddenly gasps, reminding me I need to keep my voice down.

"Willow, anyone that isn't interested in seeing something like that is stupid."

"Well, I can tell you that no, I won't be on a billboard, but yes, I am doing a collaboration. And not only that, but they have also asked me to partner up with them to do a limited, special edition Christmas hamper. That proposal is for me to not only work with them but twelve indie authors for the twelve days of Christmas and each day will be themed on a different book. I will design an item of lingerie or outfit and create a befitting toy. There'll be a copy of the book and they will be adding in some other goodies too" I tell her, as excitement buzzes through me.

"Shut the front door. That's fucking brilliant. And whoever came up with that idea is a bloody genius." I have to pull the phone away from my ear with how loud she is shouting and it makes me happy that she's just as thrilled as I am.

"I know. And I think they've realised it's a great marketing idea, doing collabs with smaller businesses, because even though we don't have quite the reach the bigger ones have, our customers are very loyal. Plus, in reality, their outgoing in these collabs will be much less working with smaller companies like mine, than they would with the big celebs and influencers."

"Oh, I'm so proud of you. Did you ever think, way back when you started this, that you'd be going to meetings and negotiating deals like this?"

"Ha, no. Never." I honestly never thought things would get to this point. I really cant quite believe it.

"Well, I did. I always knew you were destined for great and amazing things."

"Aw, aren't you a sweetie pie?"

"I mean it, Willow. For years, I have watched you graft and work tirelessly. Always going above and beyond. Doing everything you can to give the girls the world. You have always put yourself last, and not just with Ayana and Mya. Also with the rest of your family, with me, and with your relationships. You have got to this point because of *you*. Because of your hard work. Your dedication. I've always known just how talented you are, but finally, the world is going to see it too. And I am so, so proud of you."

"Babe, you're making me cry." I can't help the tears welling in my eyes at her kind and sweet words. "Thank you. You know I couldn't have done all this without your support. The way you always support and cheer me on."

Now it's Megan's turn to cry. "Alright. Enough with the tears. Even though these are happy tears, we are past them. It's time to fucking celebrate. So, what's the plan?"

I laugh at her ability to have me crying and laughing in the span of two minutes.

"Well, I'm going to grab a bite to eat, then head to the station. My train is due to leave just before two o'clock. The girls have after school club and then I'm thinking maybe ordering us in a takeaway."

"Make sure you grab a bottle of bubbly to celebrate. I'm coming to see you on Saturday, and I won't be leaving until we get through at least four bottles."

"Four?"

"Yes, four. I was going to say twelve to go with the whole twelve days of Christmas theme, and I know I'm pretty good at handling my drink, but I think that's too much, even for us."

I cannot contain my laughter. "Yes, twelve is way too much."

My cheeks are getting sore from how much I'm smiling. I finish my chatting with Megan, thinking about where I should grab a bite to eat, and go to message Ethan to let him know how today went when someone bumps into me.

Chapter 18

Willow

I cannot believe my fucking eyes. No way. This can't be real.

"Dominic?" I say, stunned at the man standing before me.

"Willow. What are you doing in my neck of the woods? Also sorry for bumping into you." A smiles beams across his face.

It takes me a second to form the words to respond. What are the odds? Of all the millions of people currently in London, what are the odds of me bumping into this man? Here? Today?

"Um, I, uh, I had a meeting. Needed to come into town for it."

Dominic is smiling at me with joy and wonderment. That's when I realise there's another guy standing next to him. waiting a little awkwardly. Dominic follows my line of sight and quickly makes introductions.

"Willow, this is Greg. We work together. We just went out to get a bite to eat. Greg, this is Willow."

I don't miss the way Dominic bites his lip after saying my name, nor do I miss the way his eyes squint as Greg shakes my hand.

"It's a pleasure to meet you Greg."

"Likewise."

"So, how long are you in town for?" There is a slight hopefulness to Dominic's tone that hits me with a pang of regret.

Just as I'm about to respond, Greg quickly cuts in.

"I'm gonna head back to work. I've got a shit tonne to get through before the end of the day. Was lovely meeting you, Willow."

"I'll see you later," Dominic says.

"Goodbye," I add, somewhat awkwardly.

My mind still can't compute that I'm standing here with Dominic. What is it with this man popping up in the most unexpected of places?

"So, how long are you here for? Do you have any plans?"

"No, no plans besides the meeting, but I'm heading straight back home. I was actually on my way to grab a coffee and some food for the train."

There's something almost comical in the sad puppy dog eyes Dominic is giving me. "Oh, that's a shame. What if I quickly join you for a coffee?"

I look down at my phone, checking the time.

"Please, Willow. What are the chances of us bumping into one another? And for the second time. Though I did prefer the settings of the beach, rather than these grey skies."

I chuckle in agreement.

"Come on. Just a quick coffee. If this isn't a sign for a quick catch up before you leave again, I don't know what is. Plus, there's this great little deli down the road that makes the best cappuccinos and the most delicious sandwiches outside of Italy."

Knowing I will still easily have enough time before my train, I agree. Dominic's smile is beaming as he leads the way.

I take my first sip of my coffee and realise he was right. This really is good coffee and it's going to take every effort for me to eat my sandwich with some decorum on the train as it looks so damn good. My tummy is already rumbling in excitement. I spend the first ten minutes filling him in on what has brought me to the city and how the meeting went.

"Wow, Willow, that's fantastic. You must be so excited. Should I get your autograph now before you become too famous to be mingling with the likes of us peasants?"

"Oh, stop it." I shake my head at the absurdity. "Don't be silly. You're making it sound like I won an Oscar or am lifting the winning trophy at the Grand Prix."

Part of me thought this could be awkward, possibly even a little uncomfortable, but it's fine. Nice even.

"It takes a lot of work and a strong woman. Clearly two traits of yours. Ones that you excel at."

"Thank you. That really is very kind of you." And I mean it.

"So, Dominic, how about you? How's your work going?

Last time I saw you, your job made you endure sunsets, tropical islands, crystal blue waters, and idyllic beaches."

His laugh is light and relaxed, and I take genuine interest when he tells me things are good. He's doing more work. Several of his projects have been picked up and optioned. A couple of projects have taken him abroad, which was fun. And from his cheeky smirk, I can only imagine were filled with moments of debauchery. He also goes on and talks about a dancing competition show they wrapped in Ireland.

"See, I bet you didn't think you're the only one sitting through dance shows and performances. So yeah, so far this year it's been a good mix. A couple of the shows will begin to air in the summer, with the rest out across November and December."

We continue to chat as we finish off our coffee. The more we do, the more I realise there's something different about him; a maturity that wasn't there before. Yes, he still has little moments of that young bachelor mindset, but overall, he seems to have grown.

Noticing the time, I realise I've got to go.

"It was really nice bumping into you. I'm glad we caught up."

"Me too. It was lovely seeing you again. We'll have to do it again sometime."

With a smile, I nod in agreement and hug him goodbye. I wouldn't have expected it, but I'm glad I bumped into him. I appreciate he didn't make any advances or any silly, uncomfortable sexual innuendoes like last time. And he didn't make a point about me being in London and not reaching out to him.

As my body sways gently to the rocking of the train, I can't help but feel a little gutted that I hadn't thought ahead of time to try and meet Ethan, given I was coming up to London. But I guess where I knew it was only going to be a really quick trip, I knew I'd only be frustrated at only getting a passing visit with him. Between my flying visit, which was in central London and him having back-to-back meetings at his office on the other side of Greater London, and not finishing until five, it just wasn't possible to fit in. He had offered to try and move some meetings around, but I didn't let him. Especially as I wasn't staying for long.

I did manage to speak to him between his meetings and fill him in on how everything went. The pride and joy in his voice brought a tear to my eyes. He told me there'd be a special delivery arriving for me later on.

There are only two more stops before mine, so I spend the last bit of peace and quiet scrolling through Instagram. As I'm scrolling through the feed, my mind suddenly snags on something. I'm looking at a picture I uploaded of the girls at their performance. In the captions I wrote, *'The hours of practise, rehearsals, and watching multiple performances are all worth it when your girls smash it and shine like the diamonds that they are #proudmum #dancemum.'*

When Dominic said I wasn't the only one having sat and watched dance shows, how had he known? This picture is on my personal account and we're not friends on there. I don't remember telling him. We've not spoken since New Year's but I must have mentioned it today. Silly me. I must be getting old or losing my mind. Laughing to myself, I shake off the thoughts of my clearly fraying memory and take a picture of the grey, rainy backdrop out of the window, sending it to Ethan, along with a text.

> I've had enough of this rain. Barcelona can't come soon enough. Sun, sea, sex, and most importantly, spending quality time with you xxx

Searing Need

Chapter 1

Willow

The past few weeks have been pure bliss. After Ethan met Ayana and Mya, and I didn't need to keep things secret anymore, the girls have become just as enamoured with him as I am. There have been many times that he has called or FaceTimed and I've ended up being the one speaking to him for the shortest time as the girls bombarded him with detailed rundowns of their day. And when Ethan has come over to stay for the night or weekend, they have loved not just the gifts he regularly brings but also the enthusiastic discussions at the dinner table, or watching a movie together.

Two weeks ago, I met Ethan's children and honestly was more nervous than I'd been with Ethan meeting my girls. I'm not sure if it's because Lucas and Sophie are older, so their opinions and potential judgements would be different, more intense, or if it was because of how much I cared about

Ethan. But luckily for me, my worries and anxiety were unnecessary.

Lucas is the spitting image of his father. I expected a typical surly teenager who would be glued to his phone, clearly having no interest in meeting his dad's girlfriend. Instead, he is a polite and understanding young man and has a passion and talent for football, which Ethan boasts about proudly.

His daughter, Sophie, is like the Energizer bunny. Beautiful, smart, and tenacious. She reminds me a lot of my girls.

It's clear that Ethan and his ex-wife have both raised two wonderful children. And given that his ex remarried several years ago, there doesn't seem to be any animosity. My heart nearly burst when it was time for me to leave and Sophie gave me a huge hug, whispering into my ear, "I don't remember my dad being this happy in a really long time. Thank you."

I'd felt both honoured and touched by her words. Gone was the worry and fear that they wouldn't like me or perceive me to be some sort of evil villain in their story. As a daughter, I understood she wouldn't have said that if she hadn't meant it. As a parent and partner, I appreciated that through the blessing and acceptance we got from our children, we really have been able to take our relationship to a new level.

People say that once you stop looking for happiness or love or good things to happen, then they will. I used to think it was just a load of bull and it would drive me crazy because surely, if you don't put yourself out there, then how on earth are you going to meet someone?

You do need to allow yourself the possibility of meeting someone. And I did that. I put myself out there. I met Ethan and now we have been able to blend our lives, our families, and I can't wait to see what the future holds for us.

Chapter 2

Willow

Sometimes I swear it feels like my house is a laundrette. I'm washing at least one load a day, yet there never seems to be a dent in the endlessly overflowing washing basket. Just as I'm putting on the next load, the sound of the doorbell breaks me from my thoughts. Then a second later I hear the door open, which would usually send sheer panic through me. But I know who is coming even before I hear the distinct, loud, melodic voice of my best friend.

"Yoohoo, it's me. Where my bestie at?" Megan bellows.

"I'm in the kitchen," I shout back.

The telltale clicks of high heel shoes echo down my hallway. I see a very happy-looking Megan who has a large, heavy-looking box in her hands. Making my way over, I kiss her cheek and am a little confused as she hands me the box.

"Ooh, what's this? Did you bring me a surprise?" I ask.

"Nope. It was on your doorstep when I arrived."

My brows furrow. I didn't hear the doorbell go, but then I did have the music on loudly. Taking the box, I put it on the counter and start up the coffee machine.

"I'm glad you have today off," I tell her. "I'm in desperate need of your help. You'd think someone as organised as me would have already packed everything for Barcelona. But instead, I'm leaving the day after tomorrow, and every time I look at my wardrobe, I can't work out what to pack."

"That's what best friends are for."

I add a splash of hazelnut syrup to both our cups before topping them up with coffee and milk and taking a seat at the table opposite Megan. I'm just about to take a sip when I feel her eyes on me.

"What?" I ask, confused when I look up to find her expectant expression.

"It always amazes me how slow and unexcited you are about things. I've been here for almost five minutes, and you still haven't opened the box. What is wrong with you? Or do you know what's inside and you're just trying to keep it from me? Girl, you know I'm going to make you open it right now."

I laugh at Megan's childish excitement.

"I just forgot. I have no idea what it is. I haven't ordered anything. And besides, why would I have presumed it was a surprise from you if I already knew what was inside? Make it make sense."

I stand and grab a pair of scissors to cut through the tape. Megan rushes over, bending over the counter with her head practically inside the damn box.

"You gonna give me a chance to have a look?"

Smiling, she stands as she rolls her eyes and takes her seat again. Opening it, I pull out the tissue paper and throw the foam-packing peanuts on the side.

Looking inside, I can't help feeling confused. It's from a company that also sells sex toys, but these aren't just dildos and vibrators. Some of these things are a bit darker, the kind of toys you'd enjoy if you were into the heavier side of BDSM. I take everything out and place it on the counter. As I do, I notice a piece of paper at the bottom of the box.

A special gift, to show you how dark your desires truly are.

That's it? No name. Nothing. This is so confusing. I haven't ordered anything. However, since I started doing collaborations, I have been receiving more promotional packages and PR boxes.

Megan is squealing like a kid in a candy shop. Picking up and closely inspecting each item.

"What's this?" she asks.

"That's a Wartenberg Wheel."

"Ooh, and how about this?"

"Hmm, looks like an electro-leather paddle."

As my eyes skim over the items, my pulse begins to spike in both unease and foreboding.

"And what about these?" Even I can hear a slight edge of apprehension in Megan's voice.

"That's a pussy pump, clover nipple clamps, and adjustable screws or something."

A full-on shiver rattles down my spine when I look at the puppy hood Megan is holding up between her fingers. On the hood, there is a tag. As I look closer, I see it has the company's logo on it.

"They must have seen one of the campaigns or social media posts and sent me a PR box."

Megan's eyes squint slightly at my explanation, but it's the only logical thing that makes sense.

Grabbing my phone, I Google them. I've never heard of them before, but as I'm browsing their page, I see they sell most of their products on Etsy. Knowing and understanding how difficult it is to run a small business, I make a mental note to reach out to thank them for the PR box when I get back from my trip. Yes, this is much darker than what I'm into, but that isn't their fault. How are they to know?

Prying all the items away from Megan, I pack them back into the box. Ignoring another shiver running down my spine. "I don't get it. Like, I know I'm into certain things that some might consider darker, but it's really nothing. Especially when you compare it to this. I... I just don't get it. This seems like a really out there thing to put into a PR box."

This is so weird.

Pushing those thoughts aside, I grab my coffee and join Megan at the breakfast bar. We spend the next thirty minutes talking about my upcoming trip, then we head upstairs, and she helps me pick out all the outfits and even works out the accessories I need for Barcelona.

My mum will be coming over and staying at my house with the girls, as it's mid-week and they still have school. And we are flying out from Heathrow, which it's nearer and easier for me to stay with Ethan beforehand. He's rearranged the dates Lucas and Sophie are with him and they've requested that we go out for dinner before he drops them back to their mum. And it's with those happy and exciting thoughts that I forget about pinwheels and extreme clamps and instead think of delicious meals, sunsets on the beach, and amazing memories to be made.

Chapter 3

Willow

I don't care what anyone else says, there is a huge difference when travelling with a partner. The last time I'd flown was on my solo getaway, but before that, it was always with the girls. I haven't flown with just a partner since before I was pregnant. I've forgotten how enjoyable it is. How fun it is people watching, relaxing in the lounge, nibbling on snacks, and sipping champagne. And of course, the biggest and best difference is the gorgeous man who's by my side. We've practically been joined at the hip since I arrived at his.

One thing I love about Ethan is his constant craving for physical touch. I think the only time his hands haven't been on some part of me was as we went through airport security. It makes me feel so nurtured and cared for by how attentive and protective he's being. My protector from fellow travellers, making sure I have everything I need, all the while being utterly oblivious to the envious looks I've got from other women who have watched how amazingly he treats me.

"Tell me what's put a smile on your face so I can try to either do it or buy it for you every day," Ethan murmurs as he lifts my hand to his lips, kissing my knuckles softly.

Seriously, can this man get any better?

Leaning forward in the plush lounge bucket seat in the business class lounge, I look Ethan in the eye and run my tongue along my lips.

"I was thinking about you. Thinking about how amazing you've been, and how, even though our trip has only just begun, I'm already loving every second of it," I say before giving him a deep kiss, hoping to show just how happy I am and how much he means to me.

"Mmmm," he hums against my lips.

Before we can kiss again, our flight is called and I sigh with disappointment, not wanting to move.

"Don't worry, baby. There will be enough time and opportunities for me to make sure you have an amazing time this trip."

Taking my hand in his, Ethan holds it tightly, intertwining our fingers as we head to our boarding gate. We board the plane and take our business class seats Ethan surprised me with.

The cool air on the aircraft gave me shivers and, in no time at all, Ethan requested a blanket from the air stewardess and put it over the both of us. Instead of holding my hand under the blanket, he began stroking my upper thigh over my dress. It wasn't just due to the blanket that my body began to warm, and I turned to look into the eyes of the man that has a hold of both my body and my heart. Leaning in, he gives me a kiss and the grip he has on my thigh tightens. Pulling back, he spears me with his gaze.

"When we get the hotel, I am going to eat your pussy until you're begging me to stop. I want my face to be covered in your juices. Then I'm going to slide my cock into your dripping wet pussy and fuck you until your eyes roll to the back of your head and your screams and moans come out in a mumbled mess." Leaning in his lips brush against the shell of my ear before he pulls back again.

"So you're going to need all the energy you can get. You might as well sit back and relax now as the second I have you alone, I won't stop until I have my fill and you're milking every last drop of cum out of my cock," he whispers.

My teeth bite down the inside of my cheek, I'm desperate to moan as I picture the scene he's described. My body shivers again, but this time it isn't from the cold, but from arousal. How the fuck am I going to get through the rest of this flight?

Making himself more comfortable, Ethan lifts the armrest between us, pulling me in close, and hands me my Kindle. Shaking my head to clear the erotic thoughts swirling through my mind, I take a deep breath and try to get control back of my body.

Sitting back with Ethan's arm around me, we relax and enjoy a comfortable and turbulence-free flight.

As both of us only have carry-on cases, we are able to get through passport control quickly, and with our fingers interlaced, Ethan guides me through the crowd to a man with a sign bearing Ethan's name. We make our introductions to the driver, who takes our bags, and follow him out of the terminal to the waiting car.

There really is no better feeling than being hit by that wall of heat when stepping out of the airport. Ethan must sense something as he brings us to a stop, putting his arms around me so my back is to his chest. Then, pushing my coils over my shoulder, he runs his nose along my neck before planting a soft and chaste kiss.

"Welcome to Barcelona, baby. Let this be the first of many trips and memories for us," he whispers and I can't help smiling at the idea of a future with him.

Turning in his arms, I look into the eyes of the man who has already given me so much joy and happiness in such a short time. Running my fingers along the nape of his neck, I push up on my tiptoes, brush my lips against his, and kiss him.

"Come on, I want to really get my hands on you, and I don't think the Mossos d'Esquarda will allow me to get away with doing what I've got planned for you and your delectable body in such a public place."

Chapter 4

Willow

oly shit balls. When the receptionist checked us in downstairs, Ethan was speaking in Spanish, so I didn't understand what they were saying. I did understand when Ethan took my hand and guided me to the lift, telling me, "Let's head up to the room."

But this isn't a simple hotel room, it's a sprawling suite. There is a huge lounge area big enough for more than fifteen people to sit and watch TV comfortably, and a large, open plan kitchen with a massive welcome basket filled with fruit, snacks, and drinks on the kitchen island.

Walking down the corridor, there's a stunning bedroom with a king-size bed and floor-to-ceiling windows offering a breathtaking view of the city. Across from the bedroom is a bathroom that is basically the same size as the bedroom, with a large walk-in shower, the biggest bathtub I have ever seen, and even has a vanity unit with lights, all ready to be used.

Making my way back towards the lounge, I see that Ethan

has left our bags next to the couch and is watching me with a smile.

This suite is stunning, and I feel giddy with excitement as I make my way over to the balcony, opening the doors. The temperature is already in the warm mid-twenties. With the balcony facing the beach, I luxuriate in the warm, gentle breeze as it coasts across my skin.

Closing my eyes and leaning my head back, I take a deep breath, basking in the feeling of the sun on my face and the salty sea air filling my lungs. Ethan's strong arms wrap around my waist; the thick, sturdy bands of muscle, like the ultimate security blanket. I don't remember ever feeling the same level of peace as I do in this moment. Being in this beautiful city, with this phenomenal man, is something I know I will cherish for a very long time.

Despite the breeze and the thin linen of my maxi dress, goosebumps prickle my back. Not from being cold, but from feeling turned on as Ethan begins kissing his way down my spine. His large, firm hands sensually run over the curve of my hip, slowly working their way up across my stomach.

He moves upwards, the tips of his fingers teasing along the band of my bra. My breath comes in a pant as his fingers skate across my nipples. The thin lace of my bra does nothing to hide my peaked, sensitive nipples. Excruciatingly slowly, Ethan rolls them between his thumb and index finger, his tongue laving and licking just beneath my ear. His touch so soft, so delicate it's bordering on torture.

His teeth gently graze along the delicate flesh at the nape of my neck, still rolling my nipples between his fingers. My head lolls back against his chest as my breathing becomes more erratic. My hips grind and press against his hard cock. The feeling of his thick solid length pressing against my ass, knowing I am the reason for this reaction, only makes me press against him harder. My pussy drips in my panties with how turned on I am. Needing more. Wanting more. Desperately seeking a harder touch. Ethan knows exactly what he's doing and is fully aware of the effects he is having on my body.

"Please, Ethan. Please. I want more. I need you to touch me harder. Please," I implore breathlessly. I know how desperate and needy I sound right now, and there isn't a single part of me that cares. "Please. Please," I moan.

"Mmmm." The vibration of his deep groan vibrates through me, only adding to my desire.

Ethan continues his onslaught, his fingers pinching down hard on my nipples as he simultaneously bites my neck. The sudden shot of pain after his soft touch has me crying out.

"Uh, uh, Willow. I want you to behave. You're not allowed to make a sound. You need to be quiet. If you make any noise, I will punish you." He nips my my ear lobe just hard enough to remind let his words sink in. "But if you're good, if you behave and stay silent, then I will reward you. Can you do that for me? Can you be my good girl?"

My mind is awash with contradictory thoughts. Obviously, I want to be his good girl, doing as he asks and being rewarded for my efforts. But the other part of me knows I will struggle. I'm so turned on that it's going to be next to impossible for me not to make a sound. And there's a part of me that wants to see how he would punish me.

My body is on fire, and the thought of Ethan disciplining me almost makes me shout, "Make me." But then my mind drifts to the possibility that his punishment might be to *not* touch me. Make me wait, never knowing if or when I might get a single ounce of pleasure. That thought feels like utter hell. Cementing my decision, I know I will be his good girl.

"I asked you a question, Willow," Ethan growls.

"Yes. Yes, Sir. Yes, I will behave and stay quiet," I say breathlessly.

"Mmmm, that's my good girl," he purrs. "I want you to go over to the sun lounger, take off your dress and underwear. Once you have taken it all off, I want you to lie back on the lounger and spread your legs wide open for me."

Chapter 5

Willow

My mouth feels dry as I listen to Ethan's instructions. It's only after he mentions it do I glance over and spot two sun loungers that are nestled in a small alcove on the side of the balcony. Luckily, the balcony walls are a dark grey stone, so I know no one will be able to see me. Still, I can't help but glance over at the buildings that are further away.

Even though some are at quite a distance, there are a couple that are the same height, if not taller than the hotel. If anyone in any of those buildings were to look over or use the zoom of a camera or a pair of binoculars, they would definitely be able to see me. And I can't help the thrill of excitement that runs through me at the thought of someone watching us.

The old me would have been filled with worry, apprehension, and insecurity, but not a single bit of fear or trepidation is running through me. Only excitement. Anticipation. Unbridled lust and desire to follow and obey Ethan's instructions. And it's with that I roll my shoulders and walk over to the lounger.

Grabbing the soft linen of my dress by my knees, I slowly pull it up, then lift it over my head before letting it fall next to me. Never breaking eye contact with him, I reach around and unclasp my bra, slowly pulling the straps down, before freeing my breasts and letting it fall on top of the dress. Lastly, I slide my thumbs into the waistband of my thong and drag it down my legs before stepping out of it.

Tingles of excited eagerness ricochet through me as I lay down on the sunbed, resting one leg on each arm of it, spreading me wide open. I'm so wet that the gentle breeze touches my exposed clit. The sudden feeling so strong and intense it's as if a vibrator is being held against it. And I feel a rush of excitement and nerves as I'm being spread open like a butterfly. Staring into Ethan's hooded eyes, the aching tension between us is palpable. My blood runs like molten lava through my veins.

He unhurriedly reaches behind his neck and pulls off his shirt. My eyes greedily take in the wide, thick muscles across his chest that have a light smattering of hair across them and his thick and prominent shoulders decorated with the intricate swirls and patterns of his tattoos. Following the trail of hair that leads down his defined stomach until it disappears in the band of his briefs. He opens the buttons on his trousers but doesn't make a move to take them off.

Moving closer, his steps measured but sure, he reminded me of a predator on the prowl. Coming to a stop at the bottom of the lounger, he drops down to his knees, his head aligning perfectly with my pussy.

He's so close I know he can see my lips glistening with arousal. Having his face so close, knowing what he's about to do, a burgeoning frenzy begins to build within me, and I go to moan but catch myself just in time.

"That's my good girl," Ethan praises. My mind elated at his praise and the knowledge that he is proud I'm following his instructions, but my body is screaming for more.

As my eyes flicker down, all I see is a look of pure satisfaction on his face before he dips his head and begins to lap up my arousal. His tongue plunges and swirls in and around my lips before using the tip to tease the tiny bud of my clit. A vortex of heady sensations bounces through me. My hands trail over my chest as I knead my breasts and pinch and pull at my straining my nipples.

Ethan continues eating my pussy with a wild, almost reckless abandon. Doing everything in my power to stay quiet, my jaw hurts from how hard I'm clenching my teeth. Every time even just the slightest hum or moan escapes, Ethan's fingers knead and dig deep into the fleshy part of my inner thighs.

He pushes two fingers inside me, and I almost lose it, my body arching from the intrusion. The only sounds are my loud breathing and the wet squelch of Ethan's fingers as they pump in and out of my pussy, curling them up in a come-hither gesture and his mouth suctions onto my clit. That combination has my body twisting and writhing as sweat begins to bead over my skin. Shockwaves of pleasure sizzle through me, having me desperate to scream out, but even more desperate to obey. The feeling is so good, the pleasure so exquisite, yet at the same time, I feel like I'm on the brink of madness, not being able to make a sound.

Increasing his efforts, my body hovers on the brink of detonation. And finally, just as I think I can't take anymore, can't stay silent as I know I'm about to come, my eyes shoot open.

As my gaze meets Ethan's, it's as if time stops. He gives me the slightest of nods and the dam breaks. The sounds I have been forcing down explode, flooding through me. I slap my hand over my mouth as my orgasm explodes in a mind-blowing eruption so intense I momentarily lose my sense of hearing.

I can't focus on anything. All I can do is feel. Completely and utterly lost to my senses. My arms and legs tremor. Spots dot my vision. My skin is so sensitive almost feels like it's burnt. That has to have been the most intense orgasm I have ever had in my life. I feel like I've died and transcended into heaven.

Ethan rises, scoops me up in his strong and solid arms, and carries me inside, closing the balcony door behind us. He carries me to the bed and lays me gently on top of the cool sheets.

Stepping back, his hard cock springing free as soon as he takes off his trousers and briefs. My eyes zone in on the thick throbbing vein that runs from the base to the crown leaking pre-cum. And despite the fact I'm still feeling the aftershocks of my orgasm, seeing his thick hard cock already has me desperate for more.

"You did so good. I'm so proud of you. Now it's time to give you your reward. And don't worry, you can scream as loud as you want this time."

Chapter 6

Ethan

Watching Willow put on her earrings makes me wonder if the famous Renaissance painters felt like this as they watched their muses. Jesus, when did I get so poetic? But it's true. Willow has brought something to my life I hadn't realised was missing and I can't help but smile at how happy I am to be here with her. I meant what I said to her yesterday. This may be the first trip I take her on, but it sure as hell won't be the last.

A younger me would have probably taken the piss out of myself, ribbing and teasing that I'm going in too hard. Too fast. He would have probably tried acting cool, not wanting to come off as interested, and wasted time playing stupid little games. How naïve and stupid I'd have been if I'd have done that. Luckily for me, I grew up. The older I get, the more I learn and understand how precious life is. How you only get one and should live it to the fullest. If you're lucky enough to meet someone special, you should hold on to them. I think when you're younger you see the end goal as *getting* the relationship, the partner, that's the result. When actually, that's just the start. Getting the girl isn't the prize. Keeping her, cherishing her, growing together, that's the ultimate prize.

And that's how I know that what I have with Willow is so special because that's what I want with her.

I continue to watch as she finishes getting ready. She's wearing a yellow dress that looks almost like liquid gold. The way it glides silkily over her delectable curves has my cock beginning to thicken. The top looks like a corset, her breasts look mouthwatering pushed together invitingly. And I keep seeing glimpses of her thigh through the slit in the skirt, knowing my hands will enjoy teasing her there throughout the evening. There's also a thick band that drapes across one shoulder, and as she leans forward, looking in the mirror, it allows me to see a slight mark that's darkened on her skin.

Sitting here watching her, my mind instantly goes back to last night and how my mouth left that mark on her neck.

After I'd eaten her pussy on the balcony, I wanted to reward her for her good behaviour. So, I carried her back to the bedroom and fucked her every way possible. Having her screaming and moaning so much I wasn't sure if she'd still have a voice for the rest of the trip.

Afterwards, we both took a nap, Willow never leaving my arms. Once we finally drug ourselves out of bed by late afternoon, we showered and decided to go for a walk around town, as I played tour guide, pointing out some of my favourite spots.

I had taken her to one of my favourite restaurants; a small hole-in-the-wall type of place only locals know about.

We were there for hours, having dish after dish of delicious food, and as the early evening turned late, a band started playing. The look of surprise on Willow's face when I stood and offered my hand to dance was priceless. The memory still makes me smile.

It took her no time to set the rhythm as her hips rolled and swayed to the sensuous beat. Every touch, every grind, every caress, and stolen kiss had me more and more desperate for her. It didn't take long for me to know I needed to get her out of there so I could have my way with her.

Quickly, I paid the bill. Despite wanting to get her back to the hotel, I simply couldn't wait. I needed to have her. Walking swiftly down a few cobbled streets, I found a deserted dead end dimly lit by the moonlight. Pulling Willow into the shadows, she came willingly, and I was glad to see it wasn't just me who was desperate.

We couldn't keep our hands off one another. There was no finesse as I pulled her dress up around her waist and freed my cock, slamming into her already wet pussy in one thrust as she muffled her cries in the crook of my neck when I sucked and bit down on the tender skin of hers. Marking her. Branding her as mine. The love bite still looks good from my current view.

We fucked hard and fast, her nails digging into my neck and back, creating marks that I am wearing like a badge of honour.

After I'd filled her with my cum, we got a cab back to the

hotel, but I still hadn't had my fill of her. So, I had her again but against the balcony door.

Even though I didn't fuck her as fast, I still fucked her hard, letting her see just how desperate I was for her. Hell, I'm still desperate for her right now.

As I drifted off to sleep last night with her body wrapped around mine, I knew in that moment there was no other woman for me. She is the one.

"Alright, I'm ready," Willow says, startling me from my memories as she takes one last look in the mirror before walking over to me. My cock is thick and throbbing now, which is becoming a regular occurrence whenever I'm in her presence. Just before she gets within arm's reach, there's a knock on the door. When I open it, I am greeted by the concierge as he hands me a large bouquet of red roses. Giving my thanks, I shut the door, noticing how Willow's eyes light up at the flowers in my hand.

"Ethan, they are beautiful," she says breathlessly.

They are. But they aren't from me. Who the fuck are they from? Why is someone other than me sending Willow flowers? That's not right. I really don't like it. I check to see if there's a card, but there isn't.

"You're right, they are beautiful. And as much as I'd like to take the credit, sadly, I can't. These aren't from me, baby."

I expected her to be annoyed, or maybe even a little disappointed that I hadn't got them for her, but she isn't. Instead, she bursts out laughing. Probably because of the scowl that's plastered across my face.

"It's probably from the event organisers," Willow says reassuringly.

I nod along distractedly but deep down, I don't believe it's from them. And I can't help but think back to the weird things Willow has mentioned recently, like that box of sex toys, and regularly receiving books that neither she nor I have ordered and can't work out where or who they're from. Well, she's then brushed off, dismissing them as nothing important. I'm just about to ask her if she thinks there could be a connection when she grabs something out of her bag with a grin that's full of trouble.

Placing the flowers on the counter, I pull her into my arms. She wraps hers around me and consumes me in a kiss. Her pillowy-soft lips against mine as her hands rub up and down my chest, have me growling for more.

I'm just about to suggest we skip the event when I feel her slip something into my pocket. Willow quickly breaks the kiss and makes her way to the door, grabbing her bag along the way. My cock is so hard it feels like it's about to rip through my pants. I'm just about to tell her off when my fingers grip what she slid into my pocket. Pulling it out, my eyes land on the lacy little thong I'd seen her put on earlier, before shooting up to hers as she giggles. My thumb rubs against the inner lining and can feel a damp spot. Now it's my turn to smile.

"Oh, you are in for so much trouble tonight," I say devilishly.

Let the tormenting begin.

Willow

Red carpet events have never been something I would consider the norm. Neither has it ever been something I aspire to do. Yet as the car pulls up and Ethan steps out, I can't help but feel a little awestruck.

There is an actual red carpet, as well as sponsorship backdrops, TV crews, and more paparazzi than I have ever seen in my life. Names are being shouted out at such a rapid speed, it feels like gunfire. A shiver runs down my back and it makes me pity artists and celebrities who have to do this all the time. There isn't a single thing about it that appeals to me.

Ethan's hand rubs my lower back assuredly as he guides me through the throng of people. The mere feel of him is a soothing presence. Not to mention the fact that he looks so damn sexy in a crisp, dark blue suit, the colour so deep and rich it sets off the faint salt and pepper in his hair. And I'm not the only one noticing how alluring he looks. Some women may feel insecure or uncomfortable having other people checking out their partner, undressing them with their eyes. Yet with the way Ethan looks at me, all it does is make me realise just how lucky I am. He is mine and I am his.

Most of the other guests around me are focusing on one another, mingling, socialising, networking, and the flowing drinks with a celebratory atmosphere. My eyes, however, continuously dart around, taking in the design and layout surrounding us as that's the only reason I'm here.

"Ethan, it's absolutely amazing. I love how you've mixed old and classical shapes. It's the perfect balance of old and new. I'm so proud of you." Turning in his arms, I go up on my tiptoes and kiss him briefly.

"Thank you, baby," he says against my lips.

When he first got hired to do this job, I think there was a part of me that was bitter about it. Like I resented the mere thought of the building. If only I knew then how things would be. How we would find our way back into each other's lives. That I would fall in love with him.

The evening has been amazing. They haven't confined everything to one room. No, they've spread it out across two floors. I love that they are showcasing some of the fantastic things they have to offer here. There are multiple bars set up, offering delicious cocktails from all around the world. Food stations offer delights from three different Michelin star chefs and a Michelin star pâtissier, offering samples of the food that will be available in the different kitchens. As much as it breaks my heart not having a third helping of the peach, cherry, and bloody orange tart, I think my dress will burst if I eat anymore.

On the upper floor, there is a band playing, with guests making use of the dancefloor. And after dancing with Ethan in that restaurant last night, knowing that there's another thing he's good at, another thing his body feels amazing against mine doing, I have swiftly taken up every offer he's made to do it again. The floor-to-ceiling windows wrap all the way around, giving us the most breathtaking three-hundred-and-sixty-degree views of Barcelona. And as the sun begins to set, the golden hour light only amplifies how magical tonight is. My cheeks hurt from how much I'm smiling.

Several people have come up to us, congratulating Ethan on his work. Most people would lap up the compliments, gushing about how hard they worked, and revelling in the praise, but Ethan praises everyone who worked with him instead. Tonight has only cemented something I already knew. Ethan doesn't do his job for the money, fame, or recognition. No, he does it because he loves it. I truly believe he would have as much pride in designing and creating a studio shed in someone's garden as he would a luxury hotel.

"How about we head outside for some fresh air?" Ethan suggests, leaning down to my ear so I can hear him over the music.

"Yeah, that sounds great." I can feel a light sheen of sweat forming on my back from both the dancing and the crowds. We make our way over to the terrace, getting stopped twice on the way by people who I think worked with Ethan.

"How is your Spanish so good? Could you speak it before you worked here?" I ask as we find a quieter, more secluded spot outside.

"I actually couldn't speak any before. We did a job a couple of years ago with a Spanish developer back in London, and at the time I was lucky as his English was really good, and any points he struggled with, his PA translated. It was actually through him I ended up getting contacted for this job. But when they offered it to me, and I knew I'd be out here for several months, I didn't want to risk any delays or have there being any major problems because I didn't speak the language. So, I signed up for an intense course and also down-loaded an app to help me. Plus, it's true what they say: there is no better way to learn than just being there. I guess I was just lucky I was able to pick it up alright."

"I'd say it's more than just alright. If I didn't know you, and hearing the way you speak with others, I'd say it sounds like you're bi-lingual."

"Oh, it's definitely not that good," Ethan says with a sweet grin.

"Well, I think it's just another example of how amazing you are. And I know I've said it a hundred times this evening already, but I'm really proud of you." Wrapping my arms around his neck, I push up on the balls of my feet and let my lips show just how glad I am to be here with him, celebrating his accomplishment.

"I'm so glad you're here with me this evening. There isn't anyone else I would want. And there are two things I want to tell you."

Chapter 8

Willow

There are moments in life where you know nothing will ever be the same again. And standing now with Ethan, I know this is one of them.

"Willow, last year as I was aimlessly scrolling through my phone. Little did I know that I would come across the most beautiful woman, and that I'd be a lucky son-of-a-bitch that this goddess would message me back."

I laugh softly, remembering when his profile first popped up.

"After getting to know one another online, I knew I couldn't blow it when we finally met in person. There is something about you that's truly unique. Sexually, you are my perfect submissive, yet at your core, you're a true nurturer. There were moments at the beginning when I wondered if you'd be able to relinquish control; really allow someone to dominate not just your body but also your mind. If I would be worthy of the job." His thumbs gently run along my cheeks and the corners of my mouth.

"We'd both agreed to keep things casual, but I think we knew those quickly became fruitless words. Did you know I was counting down the days until we'd be able to meet up again, until I had my hands and mouth on your sexy body? And just when I thought maybe, just maybe, we'd have a shot at turning what we had into a real relationship, I was offered the job here. Even though we parted amicably, I felt really torn those first few months. Questioning almost daily if I'd made a mistake. I also felt guilty as part of me was hoping you'd stay single, at least until I got back. But the other part of me just wanted you to be happy."

Shaking my head, I can't help but smile. I appreciate his honesty.

"Then on New Year's Eve, I remember waking up early as I couldn't sleep. And as you know, I'm not someone that goes on social media very much. But for some reason I was." The soft smile on his face is one of the sweetest I have ever seen on him. "Now I know why. It was fate. I believe we were destined to reconnect. And everything that has happened since only reiterates my feelings. I think I fell in love with you when we first were seeing each other. But that was just the surface." His thumb brushes along my lower lip. "These last few months, I have fallen deeper and deeper in love with you. Seeing the way you put everyone before you so selflessly. Watching and seeing how phenomenal of a mother you are. You are a warrior. A goddess. And I don't want another day to go by without you knowing just how madly in love with you I am."

Tears of pure joy and happiness gently fall down my cheeks and Ethan brushes them away before his lips find mine. This kiss feels more. Bigger. I could stay like this forever. But I want to tell him how I feel. That he isn't alone in these feelings. I look up into his beautiful eyes.

"Ethan, I love you too. I've known for a while. I think I've loved you for longer than I've admitted to myself. Last year, I honestly never thought I'd meet someone, let alone a kind, sexy, caring, and remarkable man like you. But for once, things aligned for me. I love you, Ethan. You make me so happy, and I want us to work out a way for us to spend more time together when we get back. I know it'll be difficult with the distance, our jobs, the kids but—"

Ethan cuts off my ramblings with an all-consuming kiss. His hands possessively and indulgently caress my body over my dress. All I can focus on is him. Not our surroundings. Not that we are still at the event. Just Ethan.

"Mmmm. Well, that's the other thing I wanted to talk to you about." I can hear the slight breathlessness in his voice. "I've spent a lot of time thinking about how we can make things work. Obviously, I don't want you to feel pressured or uncomfortable, but I've thought about it, and I do have an idea. I was thinking I keep my house in London. As on the days that I have my kids, I would stay there with them so as not to disrupt things. I could even arrange it so my meetings coincide with the days I'd already be in London. Then on the other days,

I could be with you at your place. If it's too soon or you think Ayana and Mya wouldn't want me there, I fully understand. They come first and we can just come up with another idea."

Once again, I am so touched at just how much he has both me and my girls at the forefront of his plans. I just can't believe I have found someone that cares so much about me and proves as such, just like in the way he is willing to split his life like this.

"I want to make this work. I want us to spend as much time together as we can. I want to help out and cook dinner and run you a hot bath after you've had a long day. Or help out with school runs or dance class pickups. I want to kiss you as you fall asleep in my arms and wake up with my hands and mouth all over your body. I don't want to disrupt you and your girls' lives. I don't want to do that to my children either. But I do want to find some way for it all to work. So, I feel, if everyone would be on board, it'd be the ideal situation. What do you think?"

There are no words. He has thought of everything. Bursting with joy and excitement, I bounce on the balls of my feet. My hands rub over his chest that's encased in the soft cotton of his shirt. "I think it's perfect. Obviously, I will need to talk to the girls and see what they say. It would be a significant change, but if they are happy and agree to it, then yes, I would love for us to move forward and do this."

Pulling his head down to mine, I crash my lips to his, pouring out every ounce of love, thanks and appreciation I have for this man. My body and mouth pressed against his tightly. I don't know where I stop, and Ethan begins. I feel on cloud nine right now and I don't know what I've done to be so lucky to have this man. To love him and be loved in return.

"I love you so much. And I can't wait to continue showing you just how much each and every single day. Now I think we've been here long enough. What do you say we get out of here and really celebrate? As even though we don't have any toys with us, I can be very creative with some of the things back in the suite."

Nodding along in agreement, I'm suddenly desperate to get out of here. Just as we go to leave, I stop at the sound of my name being called out.

"Willow. I thought it was you."

Shock racks through me as I turn in confusion and see Dominic standing before me with a warm smile and a tall, beautiful woman on his arm.

Willow

Have I somehow fallen and hit my head and this is one of those fucked up dreams where random people from your past appear out of the blue? Like seriously, this is insane. This is the third time I have bumped into Dominic in the last places I'd ever expect to.

Eyes wide, I'm frozen in shock. Truly unable to believe that he is here. A weird sense of unease slithers through me, but given that he has a woman on his arm who looks up lovingly at him, my apprehension begins to melt away. Stepping forward, Dominic kisses me on the cheek.

"Hi, I'm Dominic, an old friend of Willow's. Nice to meet you."

"Ethan," he responds with a curt nod.

Ethan shakes Dominic's outstretched hand, but does so with a guarded expression. I give his hand a reassuring squeeze, continuously rubbing his knuckles with my thumb.

"Scarlett, I'd like you to meet Willow. Willow, Scarlett."

I reach out to shake her hand and although she shakes it, anyone would think she's touching a piece of wet lettuce.

"It's nice to meet you, Willow," she says politely, yet the frostiness emanating from her towards me is clear.

"Likewise."

Ethan squeezes my hand, letting me know I'm not the only one noticing her behaviour. Scarlett is a beautiful woman. In her heels, she must be close to six feet. Her shiny blonde hair is perfectly styled—not a single strand out of place. She looks like a mix between a perfect English rose and a model with an air about her that screams aristocracy. Her slim frame is encased in a beautiful black knee-length silk dress.

She scans me from head to toe, before turning her attention to Ethan, where that cold frosty stare melts as she introduces herself to him.

"Dominic, I'll be honest. I never would have expected to bump into you here."

"I'm here for work. We've been working on a documentary, filming some of the most luxurious places in Europe. The top ten places to stay before you die essentially," he says with a chuckle and I find myself smiling awkwardly.

"Anyway, this place was meant to be featured, then we weren't sure if it was going to be completed in time for our production, but obviously, they managed it somehow. So, as they're having their grand opening, they invited us here to both stay a couple of nights and get some footage to use for the show."

Now the smile beaming off my face is genuine. "Well, you'll be able to add that you met the architect."

Dominic looks at me with an almost comically confused expression.

"You see, Ethan designed it. Isn't it fantastic?."

I stare at Dominic, expecting some sort of response, but instead, his expression is cold and somewhat hostile. Ethan notices it too. There is a frostiness between the two men that's beginning to feel pretty awkward. From Ethan, I think it's more of a possessive thing, although he hasn't given off any of the same vibes when I've been introduced to or spoken with other gentlemen this evening. It's Dominic's frostiness that makes no sense to me.

The last time I saw him, he was nothing more than friendly, so I don't get the reason for his demeanour. I never actually told Ethan about Dominic. At least not by name. I have opened up to him about the night I had with Dominic, but it was in relation to the Dom/sub elements and all that had transpired. And I remember how angry Ethan had got when I told him how badly the guy had reacted to finding out I had kids and the turn things took. But I never actually told Ethan the name of the man.

"So, how is your business going? When I saw you in London not that long ago, things seemed to be doing really well," Dominic asks, breaking me out of my thoughts. I also don't miss the emphasised point he made of bringing up that he saw me not too long ago. *What the fuck is his angle?* Ethan tenses slightly, but then relaxes as he begins to rub his hand down my back. At this point, I'm not sure if he's doing it for my comfort or his own. Either way, I'm glad. No one else's touch soothes me the way his does.

"It's going really well. I'm very lucky."

I then turn to Scarlett, who quickly tries to hide the look of confusion on her face.

"Are you also in the television business? Do you work with Dominic?" I ask. But before she has a chance to answer, Dominic puts his arm around her and pulls her closer.

"No, she doesn't. She's actually a family friend. We've known each other for years. And even went to the same university. Scarlett works in fashion. First as a buyer, but now she has her own website informing everyone of all the up-and-coming designers, reviewing fashion showers and much more."

Dominic proudly talks about her accomplishments, and for the first time since they arrived, I find myself begin to relax, leaning back into Ethan's chest. Maybe I misread the room. Maybe it was me who just felt uncomfortable with Dominic and Ethan meeting. And as I watch the way Dominic affectionately strokes Scarlett's shoulder, looking into her eyes longingly, a genuine smile spreads across my face. Scarlett is exactly the type of woman I'd picture Dominic with. Looks wise they make a perfect couple and with their backgrounds already intertwined, they really do make the perfect match.

With all feelings of unease now settled, I soundlessly sigh with optimism, ready to make a move back to the hotel with Ethan.

We say our goodbyes and it's much more relaxed than our greetings were.

My hand tightly grips onto Ethan's bicep as he guides us towards the lift. Once outside, it doesn't take long for him to flag down the driver and we are finally on our way back.

Nestled comfortably in the back with his arm around me, Ethan kisses my temple, then turns my head towards him.

"Was that the guy?" he asks, his eyes softening as they stare into mine. I don't need him to clarify what he means.

"Yes. But how did you know?"

"I'm good at reading people. I know what it looks like when a man's eyes land on something precious."

Laughing at the ridiculous comment, I shake my head. "Don't be silly. He's clearly happy with his partner."

Ethan grunts, but then leans in and kisses me. "Anyway, where were we before we got interrupted?"

Turning in my seat to face him better, I kiss his chin, then just below his ear. "I was telling you how much I love you. And you came up with the great idea that we should leave and get back to the room. You also mentioned something about your creativity due to lack of toys," I whisper.

Chapter 10

Willow

"Thank you for driving me back. I just wish you'd have been able to stay tonight instead of needing to drive back to London."

"I know, baby. Trust me, if I didn't have a meeting first thing in the morning, you know exactly where I'd be. I tried to move it, but there was just no luck."

"I know. And I wouldn't have wanted you to move things around. I think I've just got greedy these last couple of days, having you all to myself. Ignore me. Anyway, I need to make a move and pick the girls up from school. Make sure you drive safely and let me know when you get home."

"I will do. Say hi to them from me. And Willow..."

"Yes?"

"I love you."

"I love you too, Ethan," I reply with a smile. And just like that, my mood is once again lifted.

Ayana and Mya were so sweet after I picked them up. My mum told me that she had even managed to rope the girls into cleaning their rooms and she also cleaned the house for me, whilst I was away, so I wouldn't come home to any mess.

As soon as we got in the door, the girls rush to their rooms to check their beds as I told them I'd brought them back something. Leaving them to it, I finish cooking.

"Girls, dinner's ready," I shout up to them.

They've both been asking me a million questions about my trip, so I think now would be a great time to talk to them about Ethan.

"Ayana, Mya. I need to talk to you both about something important."

"Okay," Mya answers tentatively, as Ayana nods along.

"Don't worry, it's nothing bad, and no one is in trouble or anything. I guess it's actually the opposite. It's good news. Or it could be." My tummy flutters with nerves as I take a deep breath. "You know how Ethan and I are in a relationship?"

Both girls nod.

"Well, we care a lot about each other. We love each other. And because we love each other, we would like to be able to spend as much time together as we can." I take a quick sip of water before continuing. "How have you both felt when he's had a sleepover here?"

"It's fun. I like it," Ayana says.

"I like it too. Plus, he always makes you do your big smile that makes you look like a hamster," Mya adds.

My heart warms that they notice the effect Ethan has on me. Even if it's with a backhanded compliment.

"Good. I'm glad. So, like I said, we would love to spend more time together, but it's difficult because we don't live close. So, we've come up with an idea and I want to know what you both think of it."

I look both girls in the eyes, making sure I have their undivided attention.

"On the days Ethan has Lucas and Sophie, he would be with them at his house in London. But on the other days, he would stay here. But that would only happen if you two would be okay with that."

"So, he would move in with us?" Mya asks.

"Yeah. Well, partially. On the days he's not with his children, yes." My nerves are through the roof as Ayana and Mya look at each other before leaning in and whispering amongst themselves. I genuinely don't remember the last time I was this nervous. After what feels like an eternity, both girls face me. Their expressions are serious.

"We've thought about it. And we've decided," Ayana declares.

My stomach drops. I know they aren't going to agree to it. And the thing is, I understand. It's only been me and them since they were little. I'm not even sure they have any memories of their dad living with us. It's not wrong of them to not want change. And maybe one day in the future they might change their minds.

"Ethan can come and live with us. But only if sometimes we can go to his house and we want to meet Sophie and Lucas and to see the horses that you and Ethan told us Sophie looks after," Mya explains.

It takes a second for my mind to catch on to what she's said. And my breath hitches.

"Do you both mean it? Are you sure? I want to make sure you're a hundred per cent sure. You can be completely honest. I promise, I won't get angry or upset." I reassured them, meaning every single word.

My heart races as my eyes bounce between the two of them.

"Mum, we said he can come and live with us. We want him to. We like him. He's nice, gets us cool presents, and he remembers stuff. Like when we have something important at school, he remembers and then asks us how it went. And he listens. Even to Ayana and her super long stories."

"Hey, my stories aren't super long. They're just more important than yours," Ayana claps back.

"No, they're not."

"Yes, they are."

"Alright. So, you both mean it? And you promise to let me know if you change your minds or feel differently?"

"Yes, Mum," both girls say as they roll their eyes and laugh.

Getting up, I walk around the table and give them both the biggest squeeze. "Thank you. I love you two more than anything in the world."

"We love you too."

Chapter 11

Willow

Looking out of the window to the dark grey clouds and the pouring rain hammering against the glass, you'd never think we were in the last week of July. I don't know if it's because we've had nonstop rain for the past week, or because the weather in Barcelona was so amazing, but it feels like such a paradox.

It's been two weeks since we got back, and I guess the only silver lining is that I still have a glow and a tan from the Catalan sun. I can't help but smile at the memory and the reason why I have a lack of tan lines.

The day after the grand opening, Ethan had surprised me by hiring a boat for the day. We sailed down the coast before anchoring not too far from the shore, but still far enough that there was no one around us.

I think I unintentionally set Ethan a challenge after I told him I've never had sex on a boat before because he fucked me on every surface he could.

It didn't take long to realise that there was no point in keeping my bikini on. A point Ethan also stressed, stating it would eliminate tan lines and would allow easier access for him.

Once again, Ethan created the most perfect day. Sun, sex, sea, seclusion, and feelings of serenity. I would do anything to be back on that boat right now.

Groaning in frustration, I rise from my desk, stretching out my arms and back. Since dropping the girls off at school, I've been doing nonstop paperwork.

"Rachel," I say to my PA as I answer my ringing phone. "I was just thinking about you.

"Only good things, I hope?"

"Yeah, nothing to worry about. I'm just doing some paper-work. I swear to God every time I think I'm on top of every-thing, a new email comes through or something needs to be signed off, arranged, or proofed."

"Well, don't worry, I'm not calling with any more work for you. I just wanted to let you know that our last three posts have gone insanely viral. I've been monitoring the analytics and put together a spreadsheet so we can utilise that data and apply it to specific posts in the future. But I know we're having a meeting on Friday, so I can discuss it in more detail then."

"Yeah, let's do that."

I finish my call with Rachel and the sound of my stomach rumbling gives me the perfect excuse to finally take a break. As much as I know I should make myself something nice and fresh, I'm too fucking hungry to wait. So I grab a tin of tomato soup and, whilst that's heating up on the stove, I make a quick cheese toastie to have with it.

"Alexa, play Capital Extra Reloaded," I shout to the speaker.

Getting a bottle of water from the fridge, I take my soup and toastie to the kitchen island, glad there is no one around to watch the unladylike way I'm demolishing my lunch.

"For fuck's sake." Soup drips onto my top.

Trust me to be the idiot who thinks it's a good idea to eat tomato soup in a cream silk shirt. Yeah, this needs to be dry-cleaned.

Finishing up quickly, I put my plate, bowl, and glass in the dishwasher before I run upstairs to change.

With a fresh shirt on, I make my way downstairs, where I notice a letter lying on the mat. *Huh. That's weird.* The postie has already been today, as I had a letter I needed to sign for. And it's not like we get two deliveries a day.

Chapter 12

Willow

I rip open the envelope and I'm surprised to see that the letter is handwritten.

Dear Willow,

My, my, I'm sure you are feeling a little confused and sore right now. Is your head feeling a little fuzzy? Are you finding it difficult to remember last night? Is the last thing you remember lying on the sofa, watching TV perhaps? You probably don't even remember the feeling of a sharp scratch on your neck. Well, once you were fast asleep, I got you up the stairs and stripped you out of your clothes. With you being so pliant as you were unconscious, I didn't feel the need to tie your hands and legs. I put the inflatable ball gag I brought with me in your mouth. Pumping it as far as I could make it go.

You looked like the perfect sacrifice. Quietly waiting for me to play with you. Have my way with you.

You play the sweet and innocent role to perfection, but I know your dark side. Know that you crave the pain. The darkness. You're really just a desperate and needy whore. Offering up all of your holes, just waiting to be filled. So, I pushed your thick thighs apart, your pussy bare and open, ready for me to destroy. My fingers slid along your pussy and you're not wet. But that's only because you're unaware it's me touching your body.

Leaning down, I spat on your pussy. Getting my fingers nice and wet. And began pumping them in and out, faster and faster. This isn't a time for nice and soft. So, it was time to bring in a little bit of danger.

Grabbing my penknife from the back pocket of my jeans. I rubbed the handle along your clit, then slid the handle inside your pussy. Seeing the way the handle glistened with your juices had my cock painfully hard.

Unbuckling my belt, I took out my big, throbbing cock. Resting the knife against your throat, knowing how much it would turn you on. The danger. The risk. The thrill. Collecting the pre-cum from the tip, I smeared it across your face. You're such a dirty little slut I could probably piss on you, and you'd enjoy it.

Mark you in the most primal way. But I decided to save that for another time. Wasting no time, I fuck your pussy. My teeth sucking and biting your large nipples. I continue pumping in and out, watching the knife as it shakes against your throat. Wondering what will happen first. Me coming or the blade nicking your skin. That thought sends tingles down my spine, so I quickly pull out and cum all over your tits and stomach.

Giving myself a rest, I sit back watching you, my cum drying on your skin. It isn't too long before I'm hard again. This time, I take the gag out of your mouth and fuck your face. Using you like the worthless toy that you are. The tight feel of your throat making me moan out in pleasure.

Pulling my swollen cock out of your mouth, I move your legs up to your head, then push my cock through the tight ring of muscle in your ass. It feels like I've died and gone to heaven. Fucking your ass until I come deep inside you. Grabbing your nightie from the end of your bed, I slipped it over you. Wanting to leave one last mark, I slid my tongue over your lips and then spat on your face. There, my perfect little fuck toy. Then I fasten my trousers before leaving your house. And as I drove away, I thought of all the fun I'm going to have the next time I pay you a surprise little visit.

How did you enjoy my little fantasy, Willow? Did it turn you on? Make your nipples hard and your pussy *wet? I'm sure it did. Now I bet you wish this had really happened, don't you? Well, let's wait and see, maybe one day you might just be lucky enough.*

My hands are trembling. *What the fuck is this? Why would someone write this?* Focusing on the handwriting, I don't recognise it. I've never seen it before. It doesn't belong to anyone I know. This isn't just bizarre, this is fucked up. I know I have certain kinks, but this is so much darker than anything I would ever want. *Is this some sort of twisted joke?* This isn't sexy or entertaining; it's cold, dismissive and brutally dark. There is something so callous about the way the person describes what happens. This isn't like some sort of erotic love letter. This feels like someone's fucked up fantasy that they are trying to justify. Make it seem erotic and sexy, but that's the last thing I am feeling.

Beads of sweat collect on my brow and my stomach knots, making me feel sick. *Who the hell would think to send me this?*

With trembling fingers, I pick up the envelope, hoping to see if there's a return address or stamp indicating where it's come from. There's nothing on the back. Looking at the front, it hits me: this was hand-delivered.

Lasting Impression

Chapter 1

Willow

"Are you sure there isn't anything I can help with?" Lucas asks as he makes his way over to me while I continue clearing away plates from the table.

"No, it's fine. I've got this."

Looking over, my heart melts at the sweet sincerity of the teenage boy before me. Ethan's been splitting his time between his home and living with me now for almost two months. And it's been great. It's gone so much smoother than I could have ever hoped.

Next week is my birthday and Ethan has arranged a romantic weekend away for the two of us. So, as we're away for the actual day, I decided to do a family barbecue. I've met Ethan's kids a couple of times now, but we haven't had the chance for them to meet my girls until today. And to say Ayana and Mya have been ecstatic would be an understatement. Since the second Sophie stepped through the door, they have been glued to her side. They were also excited to meet Lucas, but I think since he's a boy and a teenager, there hasn't been quite the same level of excitement about him. Especially not when Sophie brought her iPad and has been showing my girls endless videos and pictures of the horses she works with at the stables. I think Sophie has become their new idol.

"Oh, there is one thing I meant to remember earlier, but it just completely slipped my mind," I say, turning to face Lucas with a smile. "My dad had asked me if you've ever been interested in martial arts?"

"Um, it's not something I've ever really considered. I've only ever been into football. But after you told me your dad used to compete, I did start looking it up, and it seems kinda cool," Lucas tells me with a clear spark of intrigue and enthusiasm.

"Well, I know how much he likes talking about training and competing, so I know he'd be more than happy to tell you all about it. Do you want me to call him over? I think he's probably chewed off your dad's ear enough already today." I laugh as both Lucas and I look over and see Ethan and my dad deep in conversation on the other side of the garden.

"No, it's fine. I'll go over to them. Thanks, Willow," Lucas says before making his way over to them. I balance the last of the plates and bowls in my hands and head into the kitchen where I find Megan talking to my mum.

"Where's George?" I ask. George is the guy Megan's currently dating. He's definitely not her usual type, which is overly confident, to the point of being arrogant. Also, usually very flashy and pretty superficial. Yet George is so nice. He brought me a huge bouquet of flowers and a bottle of champagne and seemed to slip in perfectly to our mad little mix.

"He's just on the phone. Remember how I told you that his brother's in the army?"

"Yeah, why? Has something bad happened?" I ask, somewhat worried.

"No, no, he's fine, but he's only allowed to call on certain days. So whenever he does, I always make sure to let George talk to him in peace."

"Aww, bless him. I don't know how his family handles that. I couldn't imagine having someone I love and care about being deployed. It's bloody terrifying."

I shake off the shiver that runs through me at the thought of my own brother being away in some war zone. Loading up the dishwasher it makes me wish my brother, his wife, and my nephew had been able to come today. But sadly, they've all got the sickness bug that's been going around.

"So, Megan, how are things going with you and George?" I snort a laugh at my mum's nosy question.

"Yeah, it's fine. It's good. I like him, I guess. He's a good guy. Things are good."

My mum and I look at one another with a knowing look. Megan more than just likes him. The repeated use of 'good' and the blasé way in which she responded is so much more telling than her actual words. I love her to death, but she is the worst when it comes to men. The ones that really like her, she's usually not as into, but when she likes them, she always downplays it to the guy, to the point where he ends up thinking she's not that into him and things fizzle out. And with how nice George is, I just hope she doesn't hide away her feelings and end this before getting the chance to see where things go.

"Anyway, enough about me. Willow, how do you feel today has gone? I know you were a little nervous with it being the first time my goddaughters meet Ethan's kids, but from what I've seen, it seems to have all gone smoothly."

"I wouldn't say I was nervous. It was more the fact that this was something new to all of us. The first time both our families get together as one. But I'm happy to say it's been amazing. I don't know if it's because we've come together for my birthday, or because it's here, but it's been so relaxing—no stress or bother from anyone else. Everything just feels so right," I say with a sigh of satisfaction. It takes me a second to notice the silence from my mum and Megan, and when I look up, they are both beaming at me with happiness.

My daughters managed to rope us all into the longest game of charades and we were all pleasantly surprised when Lucas and George paired up and were like the dynamic duo, beating every single one of us. Even my girls didn't moan at the fact that they lost. It really has been an amazing day.

"Mmmm, there you are. I feel like I've hardly got any alone time with you today," Ethan whispers in my ear as he wraps his arms around me. My tummy flutters at both his words and the warmth of his embrace.

"Aw, I'm sorry, babe. I just wanted to make sure everyone was settled and have everything they need."

"There's no need to apologise. I just always want more time with you. And you've done an amazing job today, baby. I feel guilty that there hasn't been more you've needed the rest of us to do."

"That's only because I'm fussy and wanted to make sure no one was left wanting. And besides, I was nice and delegated the actual grilling part of the barbecue to my dad. That was a big thing for me to do," I say, laughing.

"That's right, baby. And I now know where you inherited your grilling skills from. Your dad also managed to recruit Lucas into starting judo training. I don't remember the last time I saw Lucas so excited about anything other than football. He told me your dad was showing him photos of his medals and clips of competitions some of his guys have competed in. I'll bet you anything he will spend most of the drive back either talking more about it or looking stuff up."

I know which direction Ethan's mind is about to go. He's going to be bringing up his concern about me being in the house alone, something he's struggled with ever since I've received that letter. And as much as I appreciate his concern, it's really not necessary and I want to momentarily distract him.

I turn in Ethan's arms, push up on my tiptoes and give him a kiss. As always, the second his lips touch mine, I get warmer as my body temperature rises. Deepening our kiss, Ethan begins to slowly walk me backwards until the banisters presses almost painfully against my back.

Ethan swallows my gasp as his thumb swiftly sweeps across my nipple and his other hand grips my hip firmly.

Before my body even gets the chance to catch up with my mind and remember where we are, Ethan wraps his hand around my throat, breaks our kiss, and slowly pulls back.

"I know what you're doing, Willow. And even though I love your methods of distraction, it still doesn't take away my worry."

"I know. But I've told you, you really don't need to worry about me," I reassure Ethan.

Ever since I received that letter, he doesn't like me staying in the house alone. Both Ethan and Megan said I should have gone to the police with it, but I knew it was just a silly prank. No need for the police to get involved. Ethan really didn't like it. And I know he's been on edge whenever he's back in London at his house on the days he has his kids. But I just continue to reassure him that I'm okay, that it's not a big deal as it was just someone messing around. Hopefully, soon he will finally realise that there really is no need for him to worry.

"And besides, my parents are staying over tonight, so there's even less for you to be concerned about."

"I know. I know. I still just hate the fact that it happened in the first place."

We never found out who the letter was from. Megan said I should go to the police, but I said that was pointless, as I'm sure it was just a stupid prank from someone in town. Word had got out about my business and, let's just say a few people weren't too happy about it when they found out that I was running a sexy toy business. I still think it's ridiculous as it's not as if I'm advertising it all over the place. Anyway, I'd heard whispers on the school run of people being unhappy and, as in most small suburban villages, news about what I do spread like wildfire. I bet the letter was just a bunch of sad and silly teenage boys that thought it would be utterly hilarious to write a dirty letter and hand delivered it to me.

Ethan had asked if the letter could have been Dominic, but I laughed off the absurdity and told him that suggestion was impossible as I'd never told Dominic where I lived. There was no way it could be him right? So, the only plausible conclusion is that it was some silly local boy. That's why it's a non-issue for me. I haven't got any more letters so it's not something I think about. It's done. In the past.

"I promise, I'm fine, babe. We've had a great day and I'm so happy right now. I won't let anything burst my little bubble."

Chapter 2

Willow

Sometimes I really have to stop and pinch myself with how lucky I am with my life right now. Work keeps getting better and better. I've had to hire even more staff and with the help of Ethan, we found a warehouse that we run everything out of now. It's big enough to have an office where me, my PA, and office manager work. There's also space to house our stock, ready to be shipped out. There's also another section that we've made up for the two seamstresses who make our custom lingerie and outfits. The operation I used to run out of my shed is long gone.

On top of the warehouse, we have a factory where we produce our toys. That is the level things are at now.

I regularly take moments to just sit back and reflect on the fact that I started this as a hobby out of both boredom and frustration. Working first from my kitchen table, then out of my garden shed, to now working with a factory, having my own warehouse and members of staff. For the first time in my life I am in a very comfortable position financially.

We are leaving today for my birthday surprise from Ethan and he still hasn't given me any indication of where we are going. The only thing I do know is that it isn't abroad as he said I didn't need my passport.

I decided to treat myself to a mani-pedi before we leave and as I get into my car to drive back home, I quickly give Megan a call back as I couldn't answer while getting my nails done.

"Hey, hun."

"Hiya, what are you up to? I tried calling earlier."

"Sorry, was getting my nails done and couldn't answer."

"Oh, nice. Which colour did you go with?"

"I think it's called Ferrari Red."

"Oooh, that sounds very sexy," Megan says with a giggle.

"So, how's your day going?" I ask.

"Meh, it's fine, busy but not hectic, which at least is helping the day go by quickly. I can't chat for long. I just wanted to see how you're doing and if you've managed to get any more information out of Ethan regarding your birthday surprise?"

"No. And as much as a surprise is all cute and nice, I thought I'd be able to get at least some hint out of him. But no. He's stayed completely and utterly tight-lipped. Nothing. And trust me, I have tried all types of tactics. I even tried to get the girls to help me, but they refused. And check this, he's already promised them a special treat if they manage to keep the surprise and stop me from finding out anything," I say with an air of frustration. By the sound of Megan's hysterical cackling, it's clear that I'm the only one bummed that I haven't been able to find anything out.

"Damn, the guy really has all bases covered," Megan says, still laughing.

"Ha ha," I mock laugh. "Yes, it's downright hilarious. If you could see me now, you'd see me rolling my eyes at the irony of you. The woman who hates surprises, being tickled with joy at my frustration."

"Oh, come on, Willow. You can pretend how eager you are to find some clues, but we both know you love it. Don't try and deny it. You love that he's gone to great lengths to arrange something for you. Let's not get it twisted."

I smile, as I can't deny the truth to her words.

"And I'm gonna take your silence as you agreeing with me," she says gleefully.

"Alright, alright, maybe you're right."

"Ha, there's no maybe about it. I'm always right."

I cough to cover up my laugh at her silly arrogance. "Let's not go that far."

"Okay, as much as I'd love to keep chatting and giving endless examples of how I'm always right, I've gotta get back to work. So just drop the detective work and let the excitement take over. You know you will have a great time and make sure you call me as soon as you can to fill me in on all the exciting details."

"I know. I will. I promise."

"Love you and speak to you later, babe."

"Bye, hun."

I hang up and check the time on the dashboard. It's almost lunchtime. My parents are going to be picking the girls up from school and taking them to their house as next week is half term. It worked out perfectly that the girls would stay with them over the weekend, then Ethan and I would be picking them up on Tuesday on our way back home.

Speak of the devil. I press the 'Accept Call' button on the steering wheel.

"Hey, I was just thinking about you," I say with a light purr.

"Oh, were you now? Anything in particular you'd like to tell me about?"

A smile spreads across my face as I know I made it seem like I was thinking about something dirty or sexual. Following Megan's advice to embrace my excitement for my surprise, I decide to play along and see if Ethan's in a playful mood.

"You want to know what I was thinking about, do you?"

"Yes. I want to know exactly what is going through your mind, Willow."

I hum with excitement as the tone of his voice dips. "If I told you what's running through my mind, I wonder if it would turn you on. If it would make your big cock nice and hard. If the tip would start leaking with pre-cum. If your hands would twitch with the desire to touch me. I wonder if I told you, would your touch be soft, or would it be hard?" My heart begins to race and my stomach flutter as my own words begin to turn me on.

Ethan takes in a deep breath. "Willow, I've already asked

once. I won't do it again." His voice is stern and serious, only further fuelling the desire that's already running through me.

"Make me," I say breathlessly.

A few seconds of silence pass before Ethan's voice comes through the car's speaker again. "Ah, Willow. I see what you're doing. But you seem to have forgotten who's in charge. You've forgotten that for the next few days, each and every orgasm you have belongs to me. I get to decide when you're allowed to come, *if* you're allowed to come. I decide if you stay on your knees for hours, with your lips around an O-ring gag with your spit dripping down onto your tits, or if I give you a full body massage, teasing you mercilessly with my tongue, always stopping just before your body detonates. Your mind and your body are completely and utterly mine. And Willow, trust me, you will be punished for this little act of defiance later on. Don't you worry about that."

I can hear the smile in his voice. My mouth is as dry as a dessert. *Shit.* I wanted to get him all worked up and desperate, but instead, he has flipped it on me.

"Willow, did you hear what I said?"

Licking my lips, I begin to nod, then realise he can't see my response. Quickly clearing my throat and answer, "Yes, Sir. I heard you."

"Mmh. Good girl, that's what I like to hear. So, are you all finished and on your way back?"

I shake my head and try to focus on both the road and his question. It always amazes me how Ethan manages to get me into a wet quivering state one second, then talk about something simple and mundane the next.

"Yeah. I'm all done and just driving back now. Um, do you want me to make some lunch before we go?" I somehow manage to get my words out and focus fully on driving.

"No, babe. There's no need. We can grab something on the way."

"Alright. I should be back home in about ten minutes."

"See you soon."

"Love you."

"Love you too."

Chapter 3

Ethan

Willow's actual birthday isn't until tomorrow and I know she usually just celebrates it with Ayana and Mya, so when I first thought about her surprise, I did ask them if it was okay for me to take her away. They gave me permission, however, there was a catch. I was allowed to whisk her away but only if I told them what I was getting her. It's funny because I was actually going to be asking them an even more important question next. And when I told them that I had something special I wanted to ask and that I would fully understand and respect whatever their answer would be, I didn't even have the chance to sit down in front of them before Mya squealed in excitement. "Are you going to ask Mum to marry you?" I remember looking at them both, trying to gauge their reaction when I said yes.

It felt like the biggest weight was lifted from my shoulders when both girls jumped up and down, screaming with excitement. They then also asked if that meant Sophie and Lucas would become their brother and sister. When I told them that it would, both girls tackled me, giving me the biggest hug. The joy and hope that poured out of them meant more to me than they could ever know. It was the same when I told my kids what I was planning. Sophie burst into tears, soaking my top as she cried, saying how happy she was I'd found someone as nice and lovely as Willow. She also loved the fact that she wouldn't be the youngest girl in the family anymore. Lucas also took me by surprise as he gave me a big hug, saying he will have to put all his energy into learning judo, as now he won't just be chasing off boyfriends for one sister, but three.

I honestly can't explain just how touched I am by how excited all the kids are and how well our two families have already blended together. Now all that's left to do is make sure all the little surprises I have planned go smoothly and obviously the main surprise of my proposal goes just as planned.

I've already got my bag packed and loaded in the car. Mya and Ayana each made two sets of cards and banners. One set for Willow's birthday and the other, if and hopefully when, she says yes to marrying me.

I'm just going through the final checklist in my head when I hear Willow's car pull up into the drive. I quickly make my way to the door and open it before she even gets a chance to put the key into the lock.

My eyes scan the stunning woman standing before me that has captured my heart, body, and soul. I wrap my hand around her throat, pulling her into me and kiss her passionately. Her lips taste like vanilla and sin and it's an intoxicating combination I am truly addicted to. Even though she only left the house this morning, my body is desperate with desire for her. My cock begins to harden in my briefs and I pull Willow in even closer, making sure she feels just how much she turns me on. But knowing that I have her to myself for the next four days, I pull back and get myself back in control.

"Hey, baby," I murmur, our foreheads pressed together.

Willow's eyes open slowly, and I rub my thumb down her throat and along her collarbone before taking her hand in mine, leading her inside, and closing the door behind us.

"Heya. See, getting greeted like that is why you moving in was a great idea," she says breathlessly. I can see her nipples are taut through her top and after the little stunt she pulled on the phone in the car, I know that if I put my hands in her panties, my fingers would come away wet from her dripping pussy. I want her so desperate, a pleading frantic mess, that she won't know whether to moan in euphoria or burst into tears. It will happen, all in due course.

"So, I'm fully ready. My bag is all packed and in the car. Do you need me to help with anything?" I ask.

"No, babe, I think I'm fine. I packed my bag yesterday and the only thing I need to add is my toothbrush and phone charger. Other than that, I'm all set."

Willow walks over and gives me a quick kiss before making her way to the stairs.

"I'll double check the windows and the back door are all locked up whilst you go and grab your stuff. Then we can head off."

"Sounds good. I'm also gonna quickly go to the loo, especially as I have no idea how long we will be driving for," she says with a slight smirk. I raise my brow at her fruitless attempt for me to give any hint of where I'm taking her.

"Oh, and Willow, make sure you only use the bathroom. Remember, you aren't allowed to touch yourself in any way that'll stimulate you. Even if your nipples are eager to feel the bite of pain from being pinched, or if your clit is throbbing for even just the stroke of your fingers, you're not allowed. So, you be a good girl for me, okay?"

Her pupils are blown and I know if she wasn't thinking about doing something before, she is now. I'm very eager to see if she will follow my instructions. Despite the fact that both of us would clearly like to go upstairs and have a quick fuck, the strong undercurrents of more and delayed gratification fill the room.

Giving her a final nod I turn and make my way to the kitchen to check the doors are locked securely. I smile to myself when, after several seconds of silence, I hear Willow making her way up the stairs. And I can just picture a look of frustration on her face, not sure whether she should give in to what her body is screaming out for, or if she should be my good girl and behave.

I'm feeling pretty confident that she won't give in to temptation. Besides, I'll know the second she comes back if this evening will consist of more punishment than pleasure. Either way, I can't fucking wait.

Chapter 4

Ethan

Willow's face had been an absolute picture of elation when we pulled up to the Manor Hotel. The tree-lined half-mile driveway felt like something out of a Jane Austin novel. I'd thought long and hard about where I wanted to take her away for her birthday and the proposal. At first, I was thinking of whisking her away abroad, but then I thought back on how we first met. When we first hooked up, it had been meet-ups in nice hotels, and I knew she'd find it both funny and recognise the deeper meaning that I was taking her to a luxury hotel. But on this occasion, I'd be asking her the most important question. Binding us together forever.

We are staying in the presidential suite, and I was grateful to the receptionist that she hadn't given away any hint of the surprises I have planned. Opening the double doors to the room, I follow Willow in with our bags in one hand as her hand envelops my other.

"Ethan, this is stunning," she says, speaking softly, almost as if she's afraid to break a spell. I'm the one who's spellbound, watching her as her eyes sweep across the room, taking in the marbled floors that lead us into the lounge, the six-seater dining table, and the large lounge that overlooks the fireplace.

"I'm glad that you like it. Shall we have a look around before we get ready for your first surprise?"

"First?" she asks with wide eyes and unbridled excitement. I love seeing her like this. It's taken a while, but she's finally accepted the fact that when it comes to her, I enjoy treating her. Buying things, surprising either her or the girls with treats, just for my own pleasure. At the beginning, I knew it was difficult for her to accept things from me, and she explained it wasn't because she disliked the stuff I got her, but because she was so unused to being on the receiving end of getting spoilt. But now she's used to it, and even though she will still roll her eyes or raise a brow, stating I should save my money, she doesn't take away the excitement of the moment. Just like she is now.

"Yes, the first of several surprises, Willow. This is your birthday treat. You didn't think the only gift was going to be staying at the hotel, did you?" I ask in a teasing tone as I pull her body against mine.

Running my hand along the back of her neck, I look down into her eyes. Leaning down I brush my lips against hers. My tongue traces her pillow soft lips before she pushes up on her toes, obviously impatient at my slow exploration. I only take a few seconds before I tighten my grip on her hair, pulling her back a few centimetres as my teeth bite down on her lower lip. I feel the vibration of her moan against my teeth. My cock begins to thicken as I know she already turned on from being edged earlier. But like I said before, only good behaviour will be rewarded.

Smiling down at her, seeing her eyes unfocused and her breathing becoming more rapid, I take her hand in mine and guide her around the rest of the suite.

The terrace doors lead out to our own private heated pool that I know I will definitely be having some fun in with Willow later. There are two bedrooms in here, the master that has a huge king-size bed in the middle with a clawfoot bathtub that sits under the window overlooking the beautiful green rolling hills in the distance and the large ensuite has a shower that easily fit ten people. I stand behind her as I reach around and open the door to the second room. Inside there are two massage tables set up, ready for our couple's massage.

"Alright, let's get changed and I'll call down to reception and tell them we're ready. It's probably easiest to change into swim stuff as after the massage we can take a quick dip in the pool."

Willow bounces up and down in excitement, then wraps her arms around my waist and gives me a chaste kiss. "Thank you, Ethan. This is already an amazing birthday and we've only just arrived. Thank you, thank you."

"Oh, baby, it's only just begun."

"That has to have been one of the most relaxing massages I have ever had," Willow says as she swims over to where I'm resting in the water with my arms stretched out on the edge of the pool.

"I'm glad to hear it. Especially as you looked a little sceptical when the masseurs first walked in," I say with a chuckle.

"Hey, that's not true. I was just a little taken aback as the woman assigned to me looked like she could crush a person with her bare hands, and your guy looked like a henchman from a Bond film." I burst out laughing at her description. Mainly because she's right. Before booking them, I had looked up the staff photos and picked the two I felt would be least likely make either myself or Willow feel uncomfortable. Besides, there was no way I was going to have some young model looking guy be in the same room getting any wrong ideas whilst Willow moans out in pleasure as knots get eased out of her muscles.

"Well, you enjoyed it. That's all that matters. Plus, your skin is glowing."

"That's because the oil she used has seeped deep into my skin."

"Mmmm," I purr as I slowly walk over to her. "There is nothing better than you being covered in oil."

I wrap my hands firmly around her hips and pull her through the water until she's astride my thigh. There's no way she can't feel my hard, throbbing cock. I've been hard since the minute she took off her robe and got into the pool. Seeing the reflection of the water bouncing off her glistening skin, her coils clipped up off her face with a few strands fallen, she looks like the most beautiful, ethereal mermaid.

Willow's hands run up my arms and over my chest. I don't think she realises she's started slowly grinding against my thigh. Taking her mouth with my own, I swallow the soft moans that escape her. Allowing myself to give in to my own desires, I feel her luscious curves beneath my hands. I can feel my pulse begin to pick up and have to remind myself that I want to draw out this moment for as long as possible. Even though right now my body is screaming at me to take things further.

I start kissing down her neck and along her shoulder, enjoying her moans growing louder. Then, much to Willow's dismay, I take her hand and lead her to the steps and out of the pool.

"Come on, let's go have a shower and get nice and clean because I want you ready for what I have planned to do with your body before dinner."

Like the good girl that she is, Willow follows me into the shower. I make sure to rub and clean every inch of skin before telling her to come out in five minutes.

"And when you enter the room, I want you to secure your hands in the cuffs I've left out, resting them on your thighs as you kneel next to the bed with your head bowed where you'll wait for my next instructions. Do you understand?"

"Yes, Sir."

Chapter 5

Willow

I've managed to regulate my breathing and have stopped squeezing my hands together that are cuffed and resting on my thighs as I wait with anxious excitement for Ethan to enter the bedroom. My body feels like it's vibrating with how long he's been dragging out everything. Even though he has edged me for longer periods before, on those occasions, he wasn't physically with me. Having him by my side today, each and every intentional touch makes it all the more difficult.

Desire slithers through every bone in my body. My ears strain as I try to listen out for any sounds that tells me he's coming. Finally, after what feels like an eternity, I sense Ethan's presence behind me.

The hairs on the back of my neck stand up as the cool feel of leather glides against my overheated skin. I don't dare to turn or look around as I haven't been given permission. As Ethan moves to my side, I get a glance at the riding crop in his hand. My nipples tighten as he runs the leather tip along the slope of one breast, then the other. Keeping my gaze down, I fight to keep my gasp silent as he lifts the crop, and I await the bite of pain from it coming back down on my skin. Yet he does nothing. I wait and wait until I'm on the verge of screaming, then finally his voice wraps around me like a shroud.

"You're being a very good girl for me, Willow. Watching your body tense with anticipation, not knowing where I'm going to mark your skin. Yet you stayed still. Now, when we were at home, I'd told you not to touch yourself, and I know you didn't, so I will reward you. As your hands are cuffed and you need to stay on your knees, I'm going to place the crop by your pussy, and you're going to grind on it until you make yourself come. Once you have, you're to get onto the bed, on your knees, and bend over to wait. Can you do that for me?" My chest is rising and falling rapidly at his words. I was already so turned before that I know I will come in no time.

"Yes, Sir," I answer as I lift slightly onto my knees so he can place the crop between my thighs. Sitting back down, I begin to writhe and buck along the now warm leather crop. My pussy is so wet I know I'm soaking it. Shivers run down my spin as my moans grow louder. Fiery tingles ricochet from my clit. My thighs tense as I continue riding and grinding. Like an explosion, my orgasm detonates and has me crying out in pleasure. Sweat breaks out across my overheated skin, my breathing loud and laboured as I slowly try to get my senses back.

Remembering the instructions Ethan gave me, I muster

up the strength and do my best to keep my balance as I get up and climb onto the bed. I'm still trying to get my breath under control as I get into position.

"What a delicious sight. I wish you could see how beautiful you looked rubbing your pussy on the crop," he tells me, his voice deep with a husky timber in it.

The loud sound of the crack of the crop against my skin echoes across the room. I was not expecting it and shout out in surprise. The sharp sting, strong and burning, only lasts a few seconds before warmth runs through me. My body luxuriating in the pleasure and pain of it. I bury my face into the duvet to muffle the sound as Ethan's warm mouth licks and sucks on the area he just hit. He continues this all along the back of my thighs, each cheek and even my pussy. The sharp sting of the crop followed by the warm, soothing feel of Ethan's tongue and mouth turns my brain to mush at the overwhelming, conflicting sensations. Pain followed by soft, tender pleasure.

I don't know how long Ethan continues this onslaught before the head of his cock presses against my entrance and plunges his thick, hard erection deep into my pussy. I feel like my head's been underwater and I've finally been allowed up for air. *Finally.* Finally, he's giving me what I have been craving. I feel like I could explode again already with how desperate I have been.

"Yes, fuck, Willow. Your pussy is gushing. Fuck, you feel so good." My walls tighten from both his words and deep thrusts.

"Oh, yes. Your wet, hot pussy is squeezing my cock like a vice. I want you to come again, Willow. Now."

I don't even have time to respond before his fingers begin rubbing my clit. The position I'm in allows Ethan to fuck me so deep, along with the steady and continuous pressure against my clit, and I find myself falling over the edge once again as I climax. My orgasm feels like it's rolling over and over as his fingers leave my clit, then edge the rim of my ass before gently pushing through the tight ring of muscle.

My body squirms as I'm overwhelmed by the heady sensations fluttering through me. Ethan's moans grow louder as his cock swells more before he lets out a deep loud groan and cums deep inside my pussy. His thrusts slow before they finally ease. Gently, he takes his finger out of my ass, which makes my body shiver as tingling sensations still run through me. The feel of his lips as he kisses his way across my back brings me back down to earth. Ethan gently eases my knees down so I'm laying flat on my stomach before he releases my wrists from the cuffs.

"Mmmm, you did so good. Just perfect." Ethan murmurs between kisses along my shoulders. My eyelids feel as heavy as my limbs, and I don't even notice Ethan getting off the bed until I hear the sound of the tap running in the ensuite. I'm struggling to stay awake by the time I feel Ethan pull me into his chest as he strokes my hair and continues kissing my forehead and telling me how good I am and how much he loves me. And it is with those words, my body satiated and weightless, that I fall into a deep sleep.

Soft nudges against my shoulder wake me.

"Willow, Willow, baby, it's time to get up."

Opening my eyes, it takes them a moment to come into focus. It's then that I notice Ethan is up and dressed in trousers and a light blue shirt.

"Hey, baby," Ethan says brightly as I turn over onto my side and push myself up, sitting on the side of the bed.

"I wanted to let you sleep as long as possible, but I know you wouldn't want to miss our dinner reservation."

I clear my throat as I wake fully. "Thank you. That's fine. How long have I got?" My voice is still slightly croaky with sleep.

"Thirty minutes."

With a nod, I stretch and get out of bed. I give Ethan a swift kiss before putting my hair up in a high bun and have a quick shower. Due to the lack of time, and the fact that I appreciate that Ethan let me sleep, I make sure that I'm ready and dressed on time. We even have seven minutes to spare.

Hand in hand, we make our way downstairs to the restaurant. It's there that I find out there's an amazing Japanese chef who cooks in front of us and the diners have the choice to join in if they want. The wildest smile hasn't left my face, and I can't stop my knees bouncing with excitement.

"Oh, Ethan, today has been so amazing. Thank you so much," I say before leaning over and giving him a kiss.

"And there's still more to come on your birthday tomorrow."

Chapter 6

Willow

Dinner was to die for. Five other couples joined us and everyone really made the effort having a go at flipping and flambéing. The men caught bites of food the chef flipped with the blade of his knife, and they gave us a break down of the origins of each dish.

I don't remember the last time I felt this light, or laughed and smiled so much. As we walk through the door to our suite, I'm desperate for Ethan. I'm so grateful for all that he's done for me. I want to show him just how thankful I am. We haven't even made it to the sofas in the lounge when I run my hands up and down his pecs, luxuriating in the feel of the strong, solid muscle beneath my fingertips.

Crushing my lips against his, I pour everything into the kiss. How much I love him, how appreciative I am of every-thing he has already done, of how happy and excited I am that I get to spend my birthday with him tomorrow. Pushing my body into his, I attempt to get as close to him as possible. His hands grip my hips firmly, letting me feel his erection pressing into me. A frenzy overcomes both of us as we start ripping each other's clothes off. Moans, groans, and heavy breathing are the only sounds coming from either of us. That is, until the shrill sound of Ethan's phone cuts through the room.

Neither of us acknowledges it and we continue kissing, desperate to get the barrier of our clothing out of the way. Just then, his phone begins to ring again and this time I break the kiss. In a daze, I look up at Ethan. "You should answer that," I say breathlessly. Reluctantly, Ethan grabs the phone from his pocket and looks down at the screen with a confused look.

"Who is it?" I ask.

"My neighbour," he says before answering.

Ethan's whole body freezes as he listens to whoever is on the other end.

"Fuck," he shouts. "Are you being serious?" He still hasn't moved a muscle. "Is anyone hurt?" I try to gauge what the hell is going on, but it's so hard as I can only hear one side of the story.

"Yes... yeah... thank you. Yeah... I umm... I'm not close by, but I'll get there as quickly as possible."

I listen as he finishes his call, every horrific scenario running through my mind as I try to work out what's happening. My heart is pounding so hard it feels like it's going to beat right out of my chest. Complete and utter shock and sorrow wash over Ethan's face as he turns toward me.

"My house is on fire." I gasp and my hand covers my mouth. "He said all the neighbours have been evacuated as the firefighters continue battling the flames."

Ethan's face is ghostly white, and I wrap my arms around him. "Ethan, I'm so sorry. I'm so sorry."

After a few seconds, he slowly puts his arms around me, and I can feel the slight tremors running through him. Part of me is too scared to speak or move, I'm hoping this is just some sort of crazy dream. It breaks my heart to see him like this, and I feel so hopeless that I can't undo what is happening right now. But I know, in this moment, me being worried, fragile, and hopeless isn't going to help Ethan whatsoever. Right now, he needs me to be strong and supportive. That's what you do for the people you love.

"Hey, baby," I say softly, looking up at him. "Why don't you get started packing? I'm going to call down to reception and let them know that we need to check out and leave ASAP. I know you didn't really drink at dinner, but would you prefer me to drive?" I continue keeping my voice soft as I rub circles along his back.

He clears his throat before I hear him speak just above a whisper. "I'm so sorry, Willow. I'm sorry your weekend is being ruined."

"Shh, stop. Don't. Don't apologise. You've done nothing wrong. It isn't your fault. But we need to get going, okay?"

Ethan runs his thumb across my cheek. "Thank you. I love you so much."

"I love you too."

"Regarding driving, it's fine. I'll drive. I'd prefer to be

focusing on the road and the drive rather than sitting in the passenger seat thinking about everything." I nod and give him another kiss.

"As long as you're sure?"

"Yeah, I am."

"Okay, let's get going."

Chapter 7

Willow

Understandably, the drive back is a solemn, quiet one. The tension that permeates the car isn't one of anger or frustration, but dread and devastation. The only words spoken were Ethan apologising for the weekend ending like this and when he called his kids to let them know what has happened. Reassuring them we are both okay, he promises to call them in the morning once he knows the extent of the damage. This situation is just such a horrible, unfortunate tragedy.

A massive part of me is really dreading the sight we are going to see when we arrive. Just picturing flames engulfing the building sends shivers down my spine. Ethan spends most of the drive with one hand on the steering wheel and the other holding mine. Every time I look over and see the anguish on his face, it breaks my heart. I have never felt so helpless as I do right now.

By the time we arrive, it's just past one in the morning.

Police and fire trucks have blocked off access to the street. So Ethan parks the car down the road so we can then walk up. As we're getting out, he grabs a hoodie from the backseat for me to put on, which I'm grateful for as my body is chilled from the drop in temperature in the late-night air, but also from the horrible sight I know we are going to see.

As we walk towards the top of his road, we're stopped by the tape from the police cordon.

"Sir, I'm sorry, but you can't come down here," the officer tells us.

"It's my house that was on fire," Ethan states with a sad strain to his voice, grabbing his wallet to show the officer his driving license. The officer talks into his radio and after a few seconds, he lifts the tape and allows us to walk on.

There's a secondary cordon where the fire trucks are and as I look past them, I let out a loud gasp when I see what used to be Ethan's home.

The whole thing has been engulfed. The fire brigade has managed to put out all the flames, but even from here, there's still a sinister heat coming from the embers of the building. The air around us is thick with the stench of heavy smoke and all you can make out are the black, charred remains of the house's skeletal frame.

It's clear that not a single thing is salvageable from the wreck. Absolutely nothing. Looking at Ethan, I see his face is as pale as a ghost and there are tears in his eyes. Seeing that sets off the first of my own that begin to fall down my cheeks.

"Ethan. Ethan, I'm so sorry."

He pulls me into his chest, and I wrap my arms around

him, squeezing him as tightly as possible. Another police officer and a firefighter make their way over to us. We spend the next hour or so talking to neighbours, the police, and fire investigators. While he's currently talking to one of the officers, I grab my phone and call my mum.

"Hi, Mum. Sorry to wake you."

"That's okay. What's happened, Willow? Are you and Ethan alright?" she asks, her voice shaky.

"No. We were at the hotel when Ethan got a phone call saying his house was on fire. We've rushed back, but Mum, the whole thing is gone. It's destroyed."

We both get upset as I explain just how bad it is and eventually, when we say our goodbyes, she reassures me that she will watch the kids for as long as needed while we get everything sorted, even if it takes a couple of days.

"Get some rest, dear," Mum says before we hang up. That's when it occurs to me that we don't have anywhere to stay. Wanting to be helpful and at least sort something out, I look up the local hotels to see if any have any availability.

The first three are unhelpful, but the fourth one is a success. After explaining our situation, they kindly offer us a room that we can check into immediately. However, the only room they have available is one of their most expensive suites. I don't care how much I have to pay, I just want to get this sorted. So, I agree and give her my card details over the phone, securing the booking.

As I make my way over to Ethan, I notice the sky is slowly beginning to brighten and I know it won't be long before the sun begins to rise. Ethan wraps me in a big hug, then buries his face in my neck. When I look up at him, his face looks even more devastated than it had before. I think it's all starting to hit him. He looks so tired, so drained, and it's one of the saddest things I've ever seen.

"Baby, I know I've said it before, but I'm so sorry. I know this isn't any kind of consolation, but I've managed to book us a room at a hotel for tonight," I tell him.

"Oh, shit. Fuck. I should have thought about that. I should have called somewhere as we drove up. I should have sorted something. It's not good that you've had to stand around in the cold this long. Fuck, it's your birthday and I should have made sure you're warm and safe whilst I sort all this mess out. I'm sorry. I'm so sorry." The sorrow and despair in his voice is heartbreaking as he paces before me, running his hands frantically through his hair.

"Hey, hey look at me. None of this is your fault." Grabbing his face I make him focus on me and my words. I need him to understand. "You have so many things running through your head, on top of wrapping your head around all this," I say, waving my head towards the wreckage. "Ethan, we are a team. We are going to get through this together. I will do any and everything I can to help. Honestly, I'm glad there was something I could do to help. And over the next few days, I want you to lean on me, okay? You always do so much for me. For the girls. Now let me be there for you."

Chapter 8

Ethan

To say I'm feeling devastated right now would be a complete and utter understatement. I'd been trying to prepare myself for just how bad it was going to be on the drive up, but there was honestly nothing that could have prepared me for what I saw.

A part of me pictured there being damage to maybe one room, or possibly even just something ruining the outside structure. Never in my wildest dreams did I ever think I'd see the charred remains of what used to be my home.

I know the materialistic things like furniture and clothes can be replaced by the insurance, but what hurts most of all are the photos of the kids from when they were little. The pictures, drawings, notes—all the mementoes of them. Videos of their first steps, gifts they had made me when they were little. All those things I will never be able to replace.

I feel like I'm in some sort of trance, stuck in a nightmare I can't wake from. I also can't fucking believe this has happened on Willow's birthday. The whole damn thing ruined. Never did I think today would turn out like this. I thought I'd be spending it spoiling her, treating her, lavishing her with love, affection, and gifts. Then ending it by asking her to marry me. But instead, I'm trying to wrap my head around a way for me to salvage this mess and destruction that now is my house.

My head is throbbing as we check into the hotel that Willow managed to organise for us. I'm guessing she had explained some part of what was going on to the lady at reception as I notice her eyes wash over us with sympathy.

I'm not taking in the words she and Willow are exchanging. It's like I'm underwater and the sounds are muffled and distant. Then slowly, as if I'm emerging out of the watery depths, Willow takes my free hand that isn't holding our bags and leads me to the elevators. Her touch is like an anchor, holding me, keeping me secure.

I don't even take note of which floor we got off at or the number on the door. Every breath, every step is my body simply on autopilot. All I feel is numbness. Shock and the inability to comprehend it all. These are feelings I don't think I've ever felt. At least not to this level. All my life, rules, structure, and control have been the foundation of who I am. Even when things didn't work out, like my marriage, both of us knew why. When my children were born, I felt fear, not from them, but fear that there would be a time I wouldn't be there to protect them. When I set up my company, I knew and understood the potential financial risks at the beginning. But one thing that always grounded me was that as long as I knew and understood all factors, all the risks and elements, then it would all be fine. Yet right now, control and understanding are the last things I feel.

The warmth from Willow's hand brings me back out of my thoughts. With the softest and gentlest touch, she slowly starts unbuttoning my shirt. Once all the buttons are undone, she slides it down my arms, takes it off, and lays it on a chair beside her.

Next, she moves onto the buckle of my belt, then opens my trousers. Numbness still prickles through me as she gets down on her knees, taking off first one shoe and sock, then the other, allowing me to step out of my trousers before she stands up in-front of me. It's surreal the way in which our roles have basically reversed. And as that thought sinks in, do I recognise that this isn't the way things should be.

"I'm so sorry. I'm sorry that the surprises have been ruined. I'm sorry that I'm not being the way I should be. It should be me doing these things. I'm the one that's meant to be looking after you." My heart breaks for him and the fact that he is thinking about me, worrying about me and my surprises when he's got bigger things to worry about. This only goes to prove how amazing of a man he is and why I love him so much.

"Ethan, stop. I've said it before, and I will keep saying it until you fully understand. We look after each other. We are in this together. There are times when I will fall, and I know you will be there to catch me. In the same way I am here to catch you. None of this is your fault."

My eyes tingle with unshed tears as I close them and kiss

her softly. Her lips against mine feel like the first drops of rain after a month-long drought. Love and devotion wash over me like a tidal wave, grateful that, despite my own frustrations, I'm given unbridled care and support. I knew from the very first time I met Willow that she was special, but at a moment like this, after everything that has happened, I can really appreciate her love for me.

"I love you so much. I honestly don't know how I would be able to get through all this right now if it wasn't for you."

"Well, you don't need to think about there being a situation with me not being here. I know everything is hell right now. I understand that you're also annoyed and frustrated that because of the fire we're here now. But right now, all that matters to me is you're safe." I rub my hands up and down his arms in a slow and soothing rhythm. "All our kids are safe. And we're here together. We will get through the rest. Together."

There's steely determination to her words and I grab onto it in hopes I can try and use it as my own springboard for seeing a light at the end of the tunnel.

Wrapping my arms around her, I squeeze her close. I feel her yawn against my chest. She must be utterly exhausted. Neither of us has slept yet. Glancing at my watch, I see it's gone five in the morning. Knowing we both need to get some sleep, I finally muster up the energy to help Willow undress and slip her nightdress over her. Then we both brush our teeth and get into bed. Pulling her in close, I kiss just behind her ear.

"Happy birthday. I love you," I whisper.

"Thank you. I love you too."

She really must have been running on fumes as within minutes, her breathing evens out and she's drifted off to sleep.

I thought I would crash the second my head hit the pillow as I've been running on adrenalin for the last couple of hours. Instead, as I lay here in the dark with Willow in my arms, all that reverberates around inside my head are the words the police and firefighters said that I haven't told Willow about.

"This wasn't an accident or from an electrical fault. It was intentional. Cans of accelerant were found in almost every room." Someone did this. Either to destroy me or with the hopes of potentially killing me. And all I can think is that's exactly what I want to do to them when we find out who did this.

Chapter 9

Willow

The sound of the shower running wakes me. As my brain fully awakens, I notice that I'm in the exact same position I fell asleep in. I must have slept so deeply that I didn't move at all. Yet, even if I did manage to get into a deep sleep, I still feel absolutely exhausted.

Pulling myself up, I reach for my phone that's on the bedside table. Rubbing my eyes, it takes me a second to realise I have several missed calls and a flood of messages. I also see that it's just gone midday. We must have got about six or so hours of sleep, yet I feel like I could still do with another ten. For the first time in hours, I managed to smile as I read off some of the birthday messages I've been sent.

My brother sent a picture of my nephew with a paper in front of him where they used his footprints to make a heat shape with the words *'Happy Birthday, Aunty Willow'* written underneath. I also got messages from my PA and office manager, which is both surprising and sweet as I didn't realise that they knew it was my birthday.

I silently chuckle as my eyes skim over the beginning of my dad's text.

> Happy Birthday, Sugarplum. I hope you have a great day; the girls are fine. Your mum told me what happened and I'm so sorry. Tell Ethan to let me know if there's anything I can do. I love you with all my heart and I'm so proud of all that you continue to do and achieve. Love you xx

When I was younger, I was so obsessed with the Nutcracker that I remember making Dad rewind the VCR tape we had of it so many times, wanting to rewatch the dance of the sugarplum fairy. It's what made me get into dance. And although I enjoyed the nickname he gave me, as I got older, I didn't enjoy the moniker as much. And luckily for me, he now saves it for the privacy of my ears and eyes only.

Clicking on my mum's message, I see it's a video. My heart warms as the girls sing and dance, wishing me a happy birthday. Although I'm a little confused with the bit at the end when they talk about the banners and cards. They must have made something for me at Mum and Dad's that they'll show me when we pick them up.

When clicking on Megan's, I laugh out loud.

> Happy Birthday to my bestie. I'm sure
> you're feeling your age even more with all
> the things I can guess Ethan has been doing
> to your body. Remember a hot bath, a cold
> compress down there, and whenever you
> are sitting, put a pillow down first. Love you,
> girl. xx

Then I notice she sent another one an hour later.

> Woman, he really must have gone to town
> on you if you're still sleeping and haven't
> responded to my message.

I'm just about to reply when Ethan emerges from the bathroom and makes his way straight over and gives me the biggest, deepest kiss.

"Happy birthday, baby. I'm sorry that we aren't doing the things I had planned. I really wanted to make the day special for you. I'm sorry."

"Hey, we talked about this yesterday. No more apologies. I know this isn't how either of us expected or hoped today would go, but we're going to get through it." There's such a heaviness in his eyes that makes me just want to wrap him up and take all the pain and anguish away. "I know you were on the phone with the insurance company last night. Did they give you any indications of how or what the next steps are?" I ask.

He sits next to me on the bed, still in only his towel, and I watch as droplets of water from his wet hair slowly run down his back. Noticing how his broad shoulders tense up.

"I need to forward all the information and reports from

the police and fire department. I actually need to go and sign some paperwork at the station that I then can pass on to the insurance. Hopefully, after that, things will be a bit clearer and we know what to do next. It shouldn't take too long. I reckon an hour or so at the most."

"Do you want me to go with you?" He's still not facing me but continues to rub my leg over the duvet.

"No, baby, it's fine. It shouldn't take too long. I'll quickly head there now. Why don't you just sit back and relax whilst I'm gone, plus it'll give me time to work out something to do. See if there's some way I can try and make your birthday good. Do you want me to order you some room service before I go?" he asks as he gets up and makes his way over to our bags that are still in the corner.

"No, don't order anything. I still need to wake up some more. When you get back, we can go out and get some food."

He turns after grabbing some clothes from his bag. "That sounds good to me. Is there anything in particular you fancy having?"

"I'm not sure. I'm going to run the bath and have a soak."

I know his head is all over the place, as he doesn't even make a joke or innuendo about me being in the bath. If it were any other time, he would be saying something teasing or sexy. But right now, his thoughts are miles away. And my heart absolutely breaks for him.

Sitting back, I watch as he quickly gets dressed, every now and again looking over at me with a sad smile. As he dresses, I realise how lucky we are that we had had clean stuff with us for the weekend, and that more than half of his wardrobe is at my house. Because if it wasn't for that, then the only items he'd have left would be the clothes on his back. The thought makes my eyes sting with tears. I close my eyes so he doesn't see the sorrow in them. Then the bed dips with his weight and his hand gently cups my cheek.

"Hey, are you okay?"

Pasting on a smile so as to not give him any further worry, I squeeze my lids before opening them again.

"Yeah, I'm fine. I promise. I love you."

"I love you too. Do you want me to start the bath on my way out?"

"No, it's fine"

"Alright, I'll be as quick as I can," he tells me, then gives me another kiss before heading out the door.

Chapter 10

Willow

"Ah, there she is. Sleeping Beauty has finally awoken from her birthday slumber. About time. I don't think I've ever known you to sleep in this late. Damn, you guys really must have had a crazy night," Megan chuckles.

"You could say that," I say with a sad laugh.

"Hey, what's happened? Are you okay? Is everything alright?"

Taking a deep breath, I tell her what happened. From how great yesterday had been, arriving at the hotel, our massages, the dinner. Then how everything went wrong after we got back to the room and Ethan got the phone call. To the drive and the state of what used to be the house, and where we are now.

"I swear, when he first answered the phone, the way he froze, I thought someone had died. And as we were driving back, I think both of us thought the damage would have only been to one room or something, but when we saw it. Fuck, that's an image I will never get out of my head. I can still smell that horrid acrid burning stench."

Even just saying it now makes me feel sick.

"Fucking hell. Oh, babe, I'm so sorry."

"Megan, when I tell you there is nothing left, I mean it. I've never seen anything like it." I sob as I think of how the whole thing is just gone. All the memories and items he's accumulated over the years. All gone. Just like that.

"Man, I just can't believe this. This feels like a stupid question, but how's Ethan holding up?"

"I honestly don't know. Last night, well actually this morning when we got back here, it was like he wasn't even here. His body was, but that was it. I've never seen him like this. He's always so strong. But he was broken. In shock. It's just so fucked up."

"And I'm sure the fact that it's happened on your birthday out of all days is probably not helping the matter. Damn, that man loves you so much. I bet that's eating away at him as well."

"Yeah. But I don't care about my birthday. None of that matters. I just wish I could take this all away."

"I know you already know this, but let Ethan know that if there's anything I can do, any way in which I can help, just let me know, alright?"

"Thank you."

"And I'm sorry that this is all happening on your birthday."

"It's fine. My only worry is Ethan and how he's going to handle everything."

We chat for another couple of minutes before saying our goodbyes and I promise to keep updated on everything. Heading to the bathroom, I check the water and see the tub is filled. Just then, an idea pops into my head.

I quickly head back to the room and grab my iPad out of my bag. Going to the notes app, I set a reminder to message Lucas and Sophie later, asking them if there are any particular things that they remember being in the house. See if they have any photos of inside where we can start putting together a list and maybe between the three of us, we can see if we can try and replace some of those things. Or get any copies of anything. Maybe there are some things from when they were younger that their mother has that she maybe wouldn't mind the kids giving to Ethan. Just something we can do that's special for their dad. Feelings of hope and determination slowly seep through me. I will do everything I can so we can give him something that'll hopefully bring a smile to his face.

Just then, I get a text.

> I think I'll be finished here soon. They said it won't be safe to step into the property for at least forty-eight hours. I've spoken to my solicitor, and he's already sorting things out with the insurance company. I'll see you soon. Love you.

A shiver runs down my spine as I think back on the state of the house. One thing that occurred to me was given that all the houses on his road are detached, I guess you could say everyone was lucky. Lucky that the fire didn't spread to any of the other buildings. And also, lucky that the neighbours on both sides had been home and were able to call the fire brigade. With how bad the damage is, I can't even begin to imagine how big and intense the flames must have been. It's really lucky that nobody had been hurt.

Feeling overwhelmed and cold to my bones, I grab my iPad again, put some music on, turning the volume up not to full blast but enough so I can hear it in the bathroom, and chuck it next to my phone on the bed before stripping out of my nightdress and heading to the bathroom.

The steaming swirls rising from the water are a welcoming sight. The water is almost scalding, and I hiss out as I climb into the tub. It doesn't take long for my body to finally begin to feel warmer. Closing my eyes, I luxuriate as my muscles finally begin to loosen. And with each and every passing minute, I can feel all the tension gradually start to leave my body.

For the first time in about twelve hours, I begin to relax. The music playing in the distance is the perfect accompaniment to the warm water soothing my skin.

It's only when the water eventually begins to cool do I realise just how long I've laid here, not moving a muscle. I'm just about to turn the hot tap on again when I hear the room door open then close.

"That was quick," I call out. "I'm still in the bath. Sorry, I forgot to think about where we should eat. But to be honest, I'm not fussed where."

A few seconds pass, but there's no response. Maybe he's

on the phone or something. Deciding I might as well get out, I climb out of the tub then pull the plug, feeling a little light-headed as I wrap a towel around me.

The ongoing silence from Ethan is now beginning to worry me. Did he get more bad news after he messaged me? Oh, I really hope not. Maybe we should stay in and just be in each other's arms for the rest of the day.

"Babe, maybe we should just order in some food so we can just stay in bed for the rest of the day. What do you thi—"

My words fall away as the man standing before me isn't Ethan. No. It's Dominic. And the slow, sinister smile that spreads across his face is one of the scariest things I have ever seen. He might look put together with his hair perfectly styled and dressed like he's on his way to work, but that perfect façade on the outside only makes the dark, menacing look in his eyes all the more terrifying to me.

Chapter 11

Willow

"Wh-wh-what are you doing here?" I stutter. My chest hurts with how fast and hard my heart is beating and my knees feel weak, like they are about to give out.

"Now that's a bit of a silly question, isn't it, Willow? I'm here to come and pick you up, obviously." The calm and almost jovial tone to his voice doesn't match the menacing content of his words. My eyes watch him like a hawk, and it takes everything in me not to flinch when he raises his arm and checks his watch.

"We're on a bit of a tight schedule and we need to get going."

"Are you fucking insane? I'm not going anywhere with you. How on Earth did you even get in here?"

Instead of answering, he takes a step towards me, and I take one back. That's when I notice he has my iPad and phone in his hand. Before I take another breath, he throws them into the now half-empty bath and they sink. I slap my hand over my mouth to silence the whimpers that want to escape.

"There's no need for theatrics. Just think of this as the groundwork for our upcoming scene." He leers at me before taking another step forward. "We'll have all the time later for fun, but now it's time to go." His voice is cold, detached, and laced with such finality that it sends goosebumps over every inch of my body.

He lunges forward, grabbing my arm. I manage to pull it free and dart past him as he momentarily halts, clearly surprised by my reaction.

I run out the bathroom door, adrenalin pumping through my veins, but I only make it a few steps before he catches me, grabbing my arm, and pulling me back by my hair. He manages to pull my towel off as I lose my balance, and he pushes me down onto the bed, climbing on top of me. I hate how exposed I am. I don't have anything covering me.

The taste of bile begins to burn the back of my throat. Shrieking, I try to buck and push him off me, but he manages to get a tight grip on both my arms, holding them securely above my head as he smiles down at me.

"Now this sparks some of my favourite memories of our time together."

It's then that I feel his erection digging into my stomach. I scream at the top of my lungs, continuously trying to get him off of me, hoping either someone will hear my cries, or I manage to get away from him.

Panic courses through me as the more I fight to buck him off, the tighter his grip becomes.

"Stop," he shouts. But I don't stop. I keep trying. Keep fighting. "Think of Mya and Ayana."

Although he spoke the words softly, they feel like bullets hitting me. My body freezes as he says their names. I know for a fact that I never told him their names. Never. There is no way that he should or could know them. I can't move. I can't breathe. Panic is clawing at my vision.

He reaches back and retrieves his phone from his pocket with his free hand. After several seconds, he turns the screen so I can see it clearly. I gasp the second I realize what I'm seeing. It's a video of my mum with Ayana and Mya on either side of her. I recognise where they are instantly: the pond near my parents' house, feeding the ducks.

"I've got someone watching them right now. I know the girls are staying with your parents. Your mum has taken the girls out and your father is currently at the shops. I've got someone following him too. So, will you stop struggling now and listen to what's going to happen?"

My eyes are wide, tears running down, dripping onto the duvet under my head.

"Aww, I prefer seeing your eyes water when I'm pushing my big, hard cock down your pretty little throat. And don't worry, we'll get to that later. But I asked you a question. Are you going to stop struggling and listen to my instructions?"

The fact that he's gone to these lengths, has people watching my parents and daughters, I know he is completely insane. I thought I was scared before, but that was nothing on what I am feeling right now. Knowing I have no other choice, I nod.

"Ah, ah, I need to hear your words."

My lips and mouth are so dry, but I manage to get the words out. "Yes, I'll stop."

"Yes, what?"

Confused by what he means, I repeat myself.

"Yes, I'll stop. And listen."

"You forget the most important word. Say, 'Yes, *Daddy*, I'll stop and listen.'" The deep ominous growl to his voice sends shivers down my spine.

My stomach heaves at the thought of calling him that. But when I see the crazed look in his eyes, I know that I don't have a choice.

"Yes... Daddy. I'll stop and listen."

His face lights up with unhinged glee. "Good. I'm going to get off you and you're going to get dressed quickly. We're going to go downstairs together and leave in my car that's parked outside. If you try to make a sound or run, I will punish you. And we both know you love it when I punish you, but you won't enjoy this punishment as it'll involve you watching the people I have keeping an eye on your parents and daughters. Let's just say I've told them things will get a little creative, should you not do as I say. Keep your head down as we walk and don't even try to get anyone's attention downstairs. You're going to be my good girl and do everything I say, aren't you?"

I can't get the words out. I can't believe this is really happening. Surely, he can't really think he will get away with this? But when I think of who might be close to my girls, my mum, my dad, I know I have no choice. I have to do as he says. There's no way in hell I'm risking anything happening to them. All I can manage is a slight nod, which seems to be enough to please Dominic.

Finally, he lifts off me, making me wince as the blood rushes to my extremities, before throwing an oversized t-shirt and basketball shorts at me. I don't recognise them, so he must have brought them with him. My hands tremble as I quickly get dressed.

My clothes feel like a shield, giving me a momentary sense of relief that I'm no longer naked. I know it's not much, but at least I don't feel quite as vulnerable. My eyes quickly glance at the telephone in the room, but as I look further, I can see that the wire has been cut. Turning back, he stares me down with a raised brow. I quickly stuff my feet into the Converse he's thrown down next to me, and once they're on, I wrap my arms around myself. Feelings of terror shoot through me as I have no idea what he has planned and what's going to happen once we leave this room.

Chapter 12

Willow

Dominic takes my arm in a vice-like grip and pulls me towards the door. I want to scream out as his fingers dig into my arms painfully but with how insane he's behaving, I'm too scared of what he will do if I say anything. He opens the door, looks in both directions, then pulls me out after him. The door closes behind us with an ominous click, and not knowing what will happen next sends pains through my chest.

Walking down the corridor, I do everything I can to keep up with his pace. His stride is much larger than mine and twice I have to catch myself from tripping over my own feet.

We get to the lift, and I expect him to stop and press the button but he pulls my arm and leads us to the stairs instead. Once again, I struggle to keep up with him as he drags me down the stairs. The sounds of our pattering feet and my heavy breathing echo across the stone walls. My boobs hurt as he didn't give me a bra to put on and with how fast he is going, it's actually painful as we practically run down the stairs.

When we finally reach the bottom, I take a steadying breath and do my best to seem somewhat normal. I've kept my head down the whole time, but just before we pass the reception desk, I take a quick peek over. Dominic tightens his hold on my arm and leans to my ear. "Remember what I said. I told you to keep your head down, be my good girl, and keep walking." Although he said it in a whisper, I heard every single word loud and clear.

There was no way I am willing to do anything that could potentially put my family at risk. If I need to go with him right now just to guarantee they are safe, then so be it. My heart breaks as bile once again rises in my throat at the thought of someone watching them. Potentially harming them. How can this be happening? This can't be real. Did I fall asleep and I'm going to wake up still in the bath? But as the warm air hits my face as we step outside, Dominic's fingers grip my arm so tightly, and I know I will be left with bruises, I know this is all real. This isn't a nightmare I'm going to wake up from. It's a living nightmare that I'm walking through. The only hope I have right now is that Ethan will be arriving back soon. I know he will search the room looking for me. And once he notices my phone and iPad in the bath, he will know that something is wrong. *Right?* Then he will call the police. I'm sure there are cameras dotted all over the hotel. And when Ethan sees that it's Dominic taking me, I know he'll come and look for me. So right now, the only thing I can do is follow Dominic's instructions, stay quiet, and not do anything to aggravate him.

He doesn't ease his hold on my arm as he steers me through the car park. When we come to a stop, he opens the passenger door to a large black Range Rover with tinted windows. There's no extra step and due to my height, Dominic had to boost me up to get me in. The second the backs of my thighs touch the seat, he grabs the seatbelt and fastens it across me, locking me in. Still, I don't move. Dominic then reaches out and strokes my cheek. I flinch away but that only makes him grip my cheeks painfully.

"I've missed you," he says those words so normally, as if this were some sort of regular interaction. When in reality, it's anything but. "Did you miss your Daddy, Willow?"

I want to scream. I want to spit in his face. I want to head-butt him. I want to punch that stupid smirk off his face. I want to kick him in the fucking balls. I want him to feel every bit of pain and fear that I am feeling right now. I want to tell him how much of a fucking psychopath he is. That he should be put down like the disgusting piece of vermin he is. And if it was only me in danger, if I would be the only one who could potentially get hurt if I did all those things, then I would. But I can't. I can't risk anything happening to Ayana and Mya. I can't risk anyone laying a finger on my family. So, I have to swallow it. I can't let him win.

Dominic shuts me in and gets in on the driver's side. As he turns the ignition on, he smiles sweetly over at me. "Now, don't you get any silly ideas." He presses a button next to the steering wheel and I hear clicks of the doors locking around me. "Can't be having you trying to get out. I've got to make sure my girl is safe and arrives in one piece."

Chapter 13

Dominic

I don't understand why Willow's acting so scared. Jesus, surely she should be excited. I know she's had a keen interest in Primal and slave stuff. I gathered that from how much so enjoys reading dark romance books. And I haven't even taken things that far. Yet.

My cock is throbbing to the point of pain with how achingly hard I've been. Since the second she was beneath me, pinned to the bed, my pants have felt like they're about to burst.

The feel of her sexy, soft body under mine brought all those memories back as clear as day. It took everything in me not to bite down and suck on her large nipples as they bounced whilst she struggled. And she behaved like the good girl I knew she would and followed my instructions. So why is she acting so scared? She should be loving this. She's clearly got into her own head. I bet that stupid fucking Ethan guy has broken her. Crushed away all her great submissive traits.

That guy is the biggest fucking waste of space. He was never going to be man enough, a true Dom like me. He'd never be able to control Willow, her mind, her body, all of her the way that I know I can. I thought my work behind the scenes was going to make this nice and simple. But with how shocked, how scared and timid Willow is acting towards me, I realise just how much I still need to do. I need to undo all the senseless shit that fuck-bag Ethan has done.

We carry on driving for another twenty minutes or so and now the silence from Willow is really starting to grate on me. Taking the turn onto the motorway, I move into the middle lane and tap the cruise control button. Reaching over, I hold on to her thigh, her whole body tensing up immediately.

"You need to relax." I soften my tone to try and change my approach.

"Why are you doing this?" she finally asks.

I don't hear the same fear and worry in her voice as earlier. Letting the question roll through my head, I think about it and realise I want to be open and honest with her. I want—no, I need her to understand just how much she means to me. How much I want her, miss her, need her, love her. I think once she understands the lengths I have gone to in order to win her back, she will be pleased. She will be so moved and grateful. And I can't wait for all the ways she's going to demonstrate her gratitude towards me. Nodding to myself, I decide this is the best time to tell her everything.

"This isn't some last-minute, hare-brained plan. Not a day has gone by where I haven't thought about our night together. It was the best night of my life. For the first time, I was the real, genuine me. It's as if that night, you set me free. Freed me of my shackles and let me soar. Then when you'd told me you had kids, I was put back in a cage. I thought, up until that moment, you would be there. For me. For me to play with. To pet. To use. To enjoy. But suddenly you had this whole other life. With duties, responsibilities, and ties. When in reality, that night you bound yourself to me."

The more I'm letting out, the more weight feels like it's being lifted from my shoulders.

"But as you know, I was shocked. I didn't take the news well. I was angry. Hurt. Offended. I couldn't deal with it so I took it out on you. Then, after a couple of days, and once I'd cooled down, I understood I'd fucked up. And it was too late to just simply message you and get you back the normal way. So, I started planning. I knew if I found ways to insert myself into your life, show you that through my actions I could make it better, you'd appreciate it. You'd love it."

I adjust myself in my seat, glancing in the rearview mirror at the busy traffic before continuing.

"The first step was convincing them to shoot the TV show on location instead of an actual studio. I'd found out you were going there on holiday so it felt like the perfect opportunity, and I knew if I just turned up, seemingly taking a trip too, then you'd probably find it weird. But I knew you wouldn't question me being there with a bunch of actors and a full crew. I won't lie. It was really hard not being able to watch you all the time. Then I got worried you'd get lured in by some guy, so for your protection, one of the nights you went out for dinner, I went into your room and put in a camera. I did think you were going to invite me back after we went out on the island, but I could tell you were still hurt by my previous rejection. So, I needed to up the ante."

Licking my lips, I smile as I know she's going to be impressed with the next bit.

"I reached out to an old school friend of mine who's the head buyer at a certain adult sex toy shop that we both know. I was owed a favour, and they pushed for the collaboration with you. And look just how amazing you're doing. I also remembered your love of dark romance, so I ordered you those books I felt would be good for you to use as both research and that you could add to your collection. When you still hadn't reached out to me, I started to get worried. On the dark web, I managed to find someone that could hack into your phone, your social media, your home speaker, all of it. That's when I found out about Ethan, and as I'm sure you can imagine, I wasn't happy." Even just saying that assholes names pisses me off.

"I needed to find out who my competition was and needed to bring him down. I started with his company, getting them bad reviews, but that didn't do anything. Then I needed to check in on you and see that you were alright. So, I did. The locks at your house really aren't very secure."

I shake my head as I remember feeling frustrated at just how vulnerable she could have been to the wrong person.

"Anyway, I helped get you another collaboration, called in another favour. Funnily enough, you bumped into me on your way to the bathroom at the coffee shop just before you found out. I also sent you a box of goodies with the knowledge that eventually I would be using them on you. I convinced my company to film and feature that hotel in Barcelona. That trip had a couple of purposes. I wanted Ethan to see who he was going to lose you to, and I also wanted to make you a little jealous, having another woman on my arm. I sent you flowers that I knew you'd love and I even hand delivered you a special letter." Looking over I smile at her as I proudly point out all of the things I have done. For her.

"Afterward, I pictured you with your hands in your panties, rubbing your wet pussy as you read the words on the page.

Then one of the times I was listening in on your speaker, I heard a conversation between Ethan and your daughters that gave me great concern, causing me to bring my plan forward. This has now been going on for long enough. I had to get you back. That's why I set his house on fire." A smile breaks out across my face as I lightly tap my fingers along the steering wheel.

I feel like I've smoked a joint. I didn't realise how good it would feel to finally tell her everything I've done. Everything I've done for her. Looking over, I see tears silently running down her cheeks and her hand covering her mouth. She should be *grateful*. Happy and appreciative. But there's nothing. She hasn't said a word. Nothing, and that really infuriates me. Calming myself down, I reassure myself that she just needs a bit of time. She needs to let it all sink in. So I focus back on the road.

We drive for another forty-five minutes, before I take the exit that'll take us to one of my family's properties. Once we're inside and settled, I'll get her to message that idiot, tell him that she's done with him. She doesn't want a useless man like him, and that he's to leave her alone and never contact her again. I know I'll be able to make Willow see sense. I was stupid before. I panicked when she told me she had kids. But I've learnt my lesson. And given a little more time, I know Willow will come around. We are destined to be together. She can give me everything I need. I don't even mind that she has kids. Plus, they're already older, it won't be too many years until they leave the nest and I'll have her all to myself. I don't mind playing step-dad in the meantime. She'll come around. I know she will.

Chapter 14

Willow

We come to a stop outside what looks like a small manor house. My mind is reeling from the horrific monologue of his confession. I just can't believe it. I can't get over everything he has done. The extreme lengths he has gone to. The lies, the deceit, the manipulation. I feel sick to my stomach with the level of his stalking, the way he has violated my privacy. The chaos and destruction he has caused is incomprehensible.

Getting out of the car, Dominic walks around and opens my door, leaning in close to unfasten my seatbelt. He already made me feel horrible enough before, but now, after discovering everything he has done, I feel completely numb. I can't fathom why he has gone to these lengths. Nor do I understand what he plans to do. I don't get the things he thinks his actions are going to be able to achieve.

Grabbing my now bruised arm, he leads me into the house and straight up the spiralling staircase to what I'm guessing is the main bedroom. What the fuck is he going to do to me in here? Is he going to lock me in? Assault me? Worse? I want to fight. My instincts are telling me to fight him, but my head is telling me that will only make things worse. I can't stop shaking, which only makes him grip my arm tighter, pulling an uncontrolled whimper from my lips. The room is huge and fully furnished, but it has this horrible stale smell to it. Like it hasn't had any fresh air for months.

"I know this is all a lot to take in, but I have a really special birthday present for you," he says it so sweetly and softly that anyone would think he genuinely means it. That this was somehow normal. Kind. Thoughtful even. How can he not understand how fucked up this is? What part of his brain can rationalise any of his behaviour? Is he planning on keeping me here forever? Is he going to blackmail me into doing things for him? Will I have any choice? I can't risk anything happening to my girls or parents. My chest feels like it's caving in. I'm finding it harder to breathe. I just want to get out of here. I can't take it. I can't handle this. Sobs tear me as my whole body begins to shake, tears stream down my cheeks.

"Please... please... please don't do this. Please, stop. Please, just let me go. I don't want this. Please. I'm begging you. I won't tell anyone about this. Please, just let me go. Tell those people to leave my kids alone. Leave my parents. Just let me go and I won't tell a soul. Please ,Dominic." My voice hitches as I frantically beg. I'm desperate. I'm scared.

His face contorts further into anger, nostrils flaring, and eyes wild, glaring at me like a wild beast. "Don't you see you're only here because of your own actions, Willow? You made this happen. Are you really willing to risk your family, let them come to harm simply because you can't admit that you have caused all of this? Are you willing to be so selfish that you put yourself before your parents? Your daughters?" His tone is so cold and menacing.

How can he be saying this? I haven't done anything.

"I never asked for this."

"I'm going to give you some time to calm down. You're not thinking straight. I don't like seeing you all hysterical like this. So, I'm going to give you some time to pull yourself together. Once you are, you'll be ready for the next part of my plan to show you we are destined to be together." His smile shows he genuinely feels his words are true.

His strides to the door are sure and resolute, closing it behind him as he walks out. I hear the loud and ominous click of the lock. Running over to the door, my fists pound on the dark, heavy wood. I shake the handle, but it's no use. Despair races through me and my eyes sweep over the room. There's another open door that leads to a bathroom with a toilet and bathtub inside, but there are no windows in there.

I trip over my feet as I run over to the large windows that stretch across the other side of the room. Yanking the old handles so hard that I rip several of my fingernails. I try each one, but they won't budge. As I look closer, I see they have been nailed shut.

Fuck. Fuck. Fuck.

I'm trapped. I can't get out. I can feel myself begin to start hyperventilating. The walls feel as if they are begging to close in on me. Scrambling around, I try to find something I can throw at the glass to smash it, but there's nothing. The only things in the room are the large, heavy-looking furniture. A four-poster bed, a huge wardrobe, and a solid antique dresser. No chairs, no vases or boxes or chests I could use to help me get out.

What the fuck am I going to do? I need to get the hell out of here. I can't stay here. How long is he going to keep me locked up? What god-awful things is he going to do to me? Terror racks right through my bones. Who is this man? Did this madness always lurk beneath the surface? Was it hidden in the shadows that night at the hotel? Or did this morph and evolve over time? Surely, I should have noticed he's unhinged. Some sort of instinct should have kicked in. How could I have been so wrong? How far has he pushed himself into my life? Invaded it.

My stomach churns as I think about how often he's spied on me. Spied on my girls. Did he go into the house when they were there? Whilst they were sleeping? What if he went into their rooms? What if he touched them or hurt them in their sleep?

I scream. Out of fear, anger, frustration, and growing rage. How dare he?

Rushing to the bathroom I just manage to make it in time to empty the contents of my stomach into the toilet. My eyes burn as I keep heaving until eventually nothing more comes out. Using the back of my hand, I wipe my mouth clean, but the taste of bile still sticks to my tongue. Rolling myself into a ball, my head resting on the cold tiled floor next to the toilet and tears continue to flow as my mind goes to Ethan. What I would do to be in his safe arms and have him reassuring me that everything will be okay. Surely, he would have returned to the hotel by now. There is no way he wouldn't have noticed I was gone. I know he'll have seen the devices in the bath and called for help. I can't even work out how much time has passed. How long would it take for the police to get involved? How many hours have to go by before they check the security footage? Is there a way they would be able to track Dominic's car? See where it went? I can't work out if any of the things I've seen on TV actually happen in real life. Or are they just made up for entertainment? This just can't be happening. It can't. The sound of a loud knock startles me and, as Dominic begins to speak, I squeeze myself into an even tighter ball.

"I promise I will make it up to you, Willow. I've got a surprise for you. I've been taking cooking classes and have a special dinner I'll be making for you. I will make up for how I failed you after our special weekend. I won't fail this time."

Chapter 15

Willow

My knuckles have turned white with how tightly I am grasping my knees. Cold sweat trickles down my back, making me shiver. The muscles in my arms and legs ache as I can't stop shaking. I feel too weak and dizzy to try and lift myself off the cold floor. Every blink hurts. It's like there's a hot metal rod piercing through my skull. I feel broken. So broken.

For the first time in my life, I have no idea what to do. The things Dominic has done, the calculated, intrusive, and malicious actions he has taken play on an endless loop in my mind. I can't help thinking how much I have failed. Not just my family or Ethan, but I failed myself by not putting the pieces together. Not realising or recognising any of the signs. Why was I so stupid and ignorant to dismiss things that didn't make sense, such as the books, the toys, and especially the letter? If I had taken those seriously, if I had listened to both Ethan and Megan, perhaps we would have found out then that Dominic was behind it all. If I'd done that, then I wouldn't be here right now. None of this would be happening.

I should have listened to Ethan. He was right about Dominic. I remember laughing off his suggestion that Dominic still had feelings for me. Thinking that there was no way, after everything that happened, that he could somehow still have feelings for me.

For me, Dominic had only been a chapter. But it's clear now that, for him, I became the whole story. Yet there is no romance, this isn't a love story. This is horror. There is no happily ever after. There can't be. Not like this. I hate how much he has taken away from me. The feeling of safety in my own home. He's taken away my belief that I can and have protected my daughters. He's stolen any sense of pride and achievement I felt at my own success. I'd thought that it was due to my hard work that I've managed to take my work, my company to where it is, when in reality, it was due to him and his connections, pulling strings, and cashing in on favours owed.

Why? Why did he do that? Was it so I would feel less than? That I would be indebted to him. Was he expecting me to get down on my knees and thank him for all he has done? There isn't a single thing I want to give this monster. I just want to go home. I want my life back.

I must have passed out from emotional exhaustion and am suddenly awoken by a loud bang. Pulling myself onto my knees, I stand and cautiously make my way out of the bathroom. More banging and crashing comes from somewhere outside my room, and now it sounds like it's getting closer.

Rushing back to the bathroom, I quickly slam the door shut and attempt to lock it. Wanting an extra barrier between us. Even just to slow him down. But there's no key. I crouch down and hide behind the freestanding bath. My hands tremble as I cover my mouth, trying to stay silent. What is Dominic doing out there? Has he lost his mind even more than he already has? My fear reaches a new peak. He's going to kill me. He's realised his plan isn't going to work, and he's going to kill me.

Sobs break through as I realise I'm never going to see Ayana and Mya again. That I won't get to hold them, hug them, kiss them. I won't get the chance to watch them grow into the beautiful young women I know they will become. I won't get to see my parents, my brother, my nephew. I won't get the chance to live the life I'd hoped I would with Ethan by my side.

The loud noises get closer and closer, and I know any second now Dominic is going to come crashing through those doors and end my life. Suddenly, I hear shouting and I know that's not the sound of Dominic's voice. The person says four words loud and clear.

"Police. Police. Get down."

My heart stops. I then hear more shouting then the loud bang of a door being smashed open. I'm still hidden behind the bath, shaking in fear when the bathroom door swings open. Two armed officers stand there, checking the room, before one of them speaks. "All clear."

There is so much noise. So much going on. A tidal wave of overwhelming confusion washes over me. There's still so much shouting, so much talking, I can't differentiate one voice from another. It feels like I'm underwater. My mind is racing to process everything that's going on around me. It's like everything is happening all at once but, at the same time, in slow motion. Another officer, this time a female, notices me and makes her way over to me, gently helping me to my feet.

"It's okay. You're safe. It's okay. We're getting you out of here." Her voice is so soft and gentle, a complete paradox to how I am feeling right now. She goes to put her arm around me, but I flinch. The look in her eyes is filled with care and sympathy.

As she guides me out of the room, I take in more officers who are making their way through the house. My legs feel weak and unsteady as we make our way down the stairs.

"There's an ambulance outside, ready and waiting to check you over."

"Willow." Ethan's voice rings out, clear as day. My head shoots up and I spot him standing behind a group of officers who are keeping him back.

"Ethan," I croak. Fresh tears stream down my cheeks. The officers finally let him through, and I run straight into his open arms. He pulls me in, squeezing me tightly and I bury my face into his neck as relief pours over me and I break down.

"Shhh, shhh, I've got you. I've got you." His hands stroke my hair, the feeling so soothing, so reassuring. Kissing my head, he continues to rock me in his arms as I sob uncontrollably.

"It's over, Willow. I promise it's all over now. You're safe. I've got you." I don't know how long we stay like that before I finally get my breathing under control. I look up into the eyes of the man I love. The man I was so scared I'd never see again.

"Baby, it's all over. I've got you. I promise," he says like a vow. And I believe him.

The moment my lips touch his, it's like a current of electricity runs through me. As if life has been brought back. And finally, finally, I realise that it is really all over. The nightmare has ended.

Chapter 16

Ethan

My hands grip the steering wheel as I glance over at Willow as she sleeps in the passenger seat. We're finally on our way back home. I'm still trying to process everything that happened in the past twenty-four hours. I'm glad Willow is sleeping. She needs it.

After I finally got her back into my arms, we were taken in the ambulance to the hospital, as they wanted to run tests on her and keep an eye on her. I also wanted to make sure that she was okay. Or at least as okay as she could be. While we were waiting, the detectives came in and took Willow's statement. Sitting there listening as she methodically recounted every step of her ordeal was one of the hardest things I've ever experienced. Never in my life have I wanted to kill a man more. I felt so useless sitting there as she told them that she was convinced he was going to kill her, that she'd never see her girls or family again. I wished she didn't have to go through it all again, but understood the police needed all the information for their case.

Once they took her statement and the doctors gave her the all-clear I asked if she wanted to stay somewhere near by, or head home. With a sad, broken smile, she chose home. Earlier on, when she'd given her statement and explained that Dominic had people watching her parents and Ayana and Mya, the detectives arranged for the four of them to be taken to Willow's house, where officers would be stationed outside.

She hasn't moved a muscle since she fell asleep. Loosening my grip on the steering wheel, I think back on what happened this morning.

I was on my way back from the police station; they hadn't been able to give me much more information other than that they knew what happened at my house was arson. They were checking to see if there was any camera footage from any of the neighbours that may have caught the person behind it. Obviously, I wished they'd have had more information to give me, but I was at least glad that they had an active investigation underway.

As I pulled into the car park of the hotel, I made a resounding decision that despite everything currently going on, I was going to do everything in my power to salvage Willow's birthday. I cut the ignition and grabbed my phone out of the cradle to call my solicitor when I saw a man and a woman walking towards a black Range Rover on the other end of the car park. I didn't realise it was Willow, mainly because I presumed she would still be upstairs in the room, and also because the clothes weren't items I'd ever seen her wear, but when I saw the man close the passenger door and walk around the car, that's when I recognised that asshole, Dominic. He got into the driver's seat and took off. And that's when I realised the woman that had been walking beside him was Willow. What the fuck was he doing here? Something didn't feel right. I tried calling Willow's phone, but it went straight to answerphone. Not knowing what to do or what was going on, I turned on the ignition and started following them, hoping that there was a harmless and simple explanation. Maybe they bumped into each other and he's giving her a lift to a coffee shop or something. But even as I thought it, I know how ridiculous it sounds. There really can't be any reason for her to leave with him. Not today. Not after what had happened last night. Not by her own choice. Fuck. I really fucking hate this. After following them for around ten minutes with no sign of them stopping, any excuse of him giving her a lift or then grabbing a coffee or something went out the window. I know something bad is happening.

I decide to call the police. At first, they tried to make out that I was making things up, then that I was being dramatic. That, as Willow is an adult, and I hadn't seen any signs of harm to her, it could just be that she was leaving me. When I explained all the weird things that had happened, and how the previous night my house had been torched and that it was arson, they suddenly showed more interest.

By this point, we were on the motorway. I'd given them the car's plates, but they said it didn't match the vehicle I'd described. Finally, it felt like they were taking my worries seri-

ously. They informed me that officers were on their way, and I should stay on the line so they knew where we were, and under no circumstances should I try to intervene.

After coming off the motorway, Dominic pulled down the long drive. The police officers waited until he was out of sight, then cordoned off the top of the drive, blocking what I was hoping was the only way out. I was told to stay back as they were waiting for more units to arrive. It felt like time was at a standstill. I'd heard one of the officer's radio go off and they'd said he had a shotgun and firearm licence and shotguns were registered to this property. So armed response were on their way and were to be arriving shortly. Once they finally had the house surrounded, I watched as armed officers entered the building.

It felt like hours, but it was probably only a couple of minutes when I saw two officers exit the house with Dominic in handcuffs, before leading him off to a police car. But there was still no sign of Willow. I stepped out of my car and began pacing back and forth, every worst-case scenario running through my head. After another couple of minutes, they let me get closer, but still made me stand back behind the officers. The second my eyes landed on Willow, relief seeped through me. She looked so scared, so broken, so tired. Yet I had never seen someone as beautiful as her. And once I had her back in my arms, felt her skin beneath my fingers, her lips against my own, I felt complete again. I had her back. And there was no way I was ever going to let her go again.

. . .

Pulling the car to a stop outside Willow's house, I gently wake her. Wrapping my arm around her, I lead her through the door where her parents, Ayana, and Mya await. Both girls rush over to her, crying, hugging, and kissing her. Looking over at her parents, I see them both crying as well. After several minutes, the girls finally loosen their grip and Willow's parents both engulf her in a hug. The room is filled with sorrow, relief, elation and heartbreak. I can't imagine what must be going through Willow's mind right now. She must be so happy to be back. To be safe. To be around everyone she loves and who loves her. But watching as she continues to cry in her parents' arms nearly crushes me. I hate seeing her so broken. But if today proved anything, it's just how truly fragile life really is.

Ayana and Mya make their way over to me and give me a big hug. Wiping away their tears, I look them both in the eyes. "Mummy's back. She's safe. And I promise I won't let anything happen to her or *any* of you, okay?"

They both smile and nod before hugging me again. Then Mya taps my arm and pulls me closer. "Did you get to ask the question?" she whispers.

"No, not yet."

The girls look at each other, seemingly communicating with one another without words. Each girl taking one of my hands, lead me Willow and her parents.

"Mummy, Ethan has an important question he needs to ask, and we think he should ask it right now," Ayana declares.

Willow wipes her eyes before taking a seat on the sofa.

Although this wasn't how I had planned to do it, there was no way I was going to waste another moment. Life is too short.

"Willow, I had planned on doing this differently. But the plan had still been to do it today." Taking her hand in mine, I get down on one knee. Her eyes widen and I reach up and wipe away the tears that begin to run down her cheeks.

"You have been through so much. And I promise to be by your side as we navigate the future. I love you more than words can describe. I need you more than my next breath. I want to continue building a life together with you, with Ayana and Mya, and with Lucas and Sophie. I want us to work together as a team, navigating the hard times and celebrating the good ones. I cannot imagine a single day without you. I love you. I'm lucky that Ayana and Mya have already given me their blessing to ask you this." I have to pause to take a shaky inhale. "Willow, would you do me the greatest honour of marrying me and become my wife?"

Epilogue

8 *Months Later*

"It is my honour to now pronounce you husband and wife. You may kiss the bride." The words of the officiant are drowned out by the cheers and claps from those around us. Looking up, I see tears in Ethan's eyes as he smiles before kissing me.

The love I have for this man, for my husband, is beyond anything I could have ever hoped for. There is never a time when I have to work out or decipher what he thinks, what he feels, or how much he loves me. He makes it clear and shows me every single day.

The last couple of months have been some of the best and hardest of my life. Dominic's arrest and trial ended up becoming a media sensation, as I later learned just how well known his family is. They have connections with some of the wealthiest and most affluent families in England. When I found that out, I really worried that he'd somehow find a way to buy his way out. But with how public it became and the scrupulous interest from across social media, the tides turned in our favour and he essentially was made an example of. With the long list of crimes he committed against me, he faced up to twenty-five years in prison. He ended up taking a plea deal of fifteen years and there is a lifelong restraining order protecting me and my family when he does eventually get released.

I've been seeing a therapist for PTSD and working on healing all the damage he inflicted. And Ethan has been there, loving and supporting me every step of the way.

Ayana and Mya rush over, almost tripping up on the sand despite being barefoot. "Congratulations," they both squeal. Lucas and Sophie join next, both giving us a hug, and together as a family, we make our way back down the makeshift aisle on the beach.

Looking out over the sunset, Ethan's arms wrap around my waist. "Thank you for making me the happiest man in the world and becoming my wife. I love you with all my heart."

Turning, I look deep into the eyes of the man I know I couldn't live without. "And I love you with all of mine."

Acknowledgments

This series initially started out as a diary entry. The first novella was in essence a form of therapy. I'm going to let you in on a little secret. Some of the things that occurred in this series are based off of real-life events that happened. Now I won't tell you which things are real and which moments we created from my imagination (mainly because I know certain family members of mine will read this). You'll just have to enjoy guessing which parts really happened.

With that I would like to begin my thanks to Mr J.F. for being the man you are and allowed me to dig deep and write one of my most enjoyable works so far. Who'd have thought meeting you would have led to me writing a whole series of novellas!

I would also like to thank my amazing editor Sarah Baker @ Wordemporiumeditor – for helping me push myself out of my safety zone, giving me the best notes that varied from making me blush to having me in fits of laughter and keeping up with the chaotic workings of my brain. Thank you. I am so glad I found you, your work is so good, and I can't wait for us to work together again on my next few releases.

I would also like to thank my amazing proofreader Kerri from Dark Bear Media. The things you catch are profound, you really have an eagle eye and loved and appreciated the way you dug deeper and gave me so much more than just suggestions on punctuation. Again I am so happy that we will continue to be working together on my next books, and I can't wait!

Obviously I know I wouldn't be anywhere without the queen of book covers, my graphic designer, Samantha at Samantha Designs. I don't know how you always manage to take the random ramblings and descriptions I give you and you always manage to turn them into infinite times better versions than what I had pictured in my head. You're a truly amazing artist and also friend. Thank you and yes I am working to be pumping out as much books as possible so we can reach that weekly (*maybe more of a chance of monthly*) book release target.

I'd also like to thank my PA Natasha JPA for your hard work, listening to my breakdowns when I felt I couldn't do it and just tireless support.

Finally I'd like to thank my best friend Rowena. You were literally along for the whole journey of this. You were so integral that you needed to be put in the book itself! Thank you for always being there, for giving me a reality check when I need it, for letting me moan and cry and fall apart then putting me back together. I honestly wouldn't know what I'd do without you.

And thank you to YOU my readers. I know how endless TBR lists are, and it means the absolute world that you've read my work. I cannot wait for you to see what's coming soon.

About the Author

Natasha Allen is a contemporary romance author born and raised in London, now based in East Sussex.

Inspired by the works of Sylvia Day and Kennedy Ryan, she loves to write about diverse and interracial relationships.

When she's not crafting steamy love stories, Natasha can be found lost in a good book.

With a focus on diversity, Natasha strives to create inclusive and relatable love stories that reflect the world around us.

Keep an eye out for her upcoming releases, as she continues to enchant readers with her heartfelt tales of love and desire.

instagram.com/natashaallenauthor

Also by Natasha Allen

Decisions and Destiny Series

Beyond Expectations

Entangled Paths

Book 3 - Coming Soon

The Pursuit of Pleasure Series

The Perfect Stranger

Enticing Choices

Heady Desires

Searing Need

Lasting Impression